THE DARKNESS

ALSO BY L. A. BANKS
(IN READING ORDER)

Minion
The Awakening
The Hunted
The Bitten
The Forbidden
The Damned
The Forsaken
The Wicked
The Cursed

ANTHOLOGIES
Stroke of Midnight
Love at First Bite

THE DARKNESS

L. A. BANKS

ST. MARTIN'S GRIFFIN ✖ NEW YORK

THE DARKNESS. Copyright © 2008 by Leslie Esdaile Banks. Illustrations copyright © 2008 by Dabel Brothers Productions, LLC. All rights reserved. Printed in the United States of America. For information, address St. Martin's Press, 175 Fifth Avenue, New York, N.Y. 10010.

www.stmartins.com

Illustrations by Chase Conley

Library of Congress Cataloging-in-Publication Data

Banks, L. A.
   The darkness / L. A. Banks.—1st ed.
     p. cm.
   ISBN-13: 978-0-312-36874-6
   ISBN-10: 0-312-36874-7
  1. Vampires—Fiction. 2. Antichrist—Fiction. I. Title.

PS3602.A64 D37 2008
813'.6—dc22   2007045848

P1

Do not be afraid. I am the First and the Last. I am the Living One; I was dead, and behold I am alive and forever! And I hold the keys of death and Hades. Write, therefore, what you have seen, what is now and what will take place later.

This particular installation of the series is for anyone who believes that there is more out there than meets the naked eye . . . for people who intuitively know that this struggle of human existence, which has gone on since the very beginning of time, is not just a battle of physical and mental survival, but also involves the spirit. May love, peace, joy, Light, abundance, and a sense of the everlasting always reside in your spirit. As long as you have hope, you cannot be defeated.

ACKNOWLEDGMENTS

I will always have to give special recognition to the members of my Street Team, who have my back, keep the energy high, and keep joy and laughter a part of this whole experience. *Thank you* sooo much! I couldn't do it without you, gang! This time around, special thanks to Alicia, who went through a really rough period with me—always sending me uplifting reading material, pastoral words, and beautiful cards of hope just to keep my inner hope and inspiration burning bright. Bless you, lady. Then there's "The Mod Squad," LOL . . . Manie, Monique, and Colleen, with support from the rest of the St. Martin's dream team. Thank you all for "making it do what it do!" And Iola, who knows how special she is on so many levels that I cannot even begin to explain it. Last but never least is my sister, Liza, and my daughter, Helena . . . I love you. Family. Thank you all!

THE DARKNESS

PROLOGUE

Several months after the battle at Masada

Eve squatted down and touched the dirt, her elbow extended away from her body, and lifted her forearm to allow a steely-eyed falcon to perch on it. Using every Neteru sensory gift she owned, she followed the nearly imperceptible patterns in the earth, and then she stood in one graceful move that didn't unsettle her winged hunter.

"Fly!" Eve commanded. "It is in the form of a man now. The beast is no longer in its pupa stage." She threw the falcon away from her arm, and it took flight with an angry screech.

"How can this be? I brought you its slain carcass!" Hannibal shouted. His question and eyes were pained as he tried to steady his red battle stallion that pranced in agitation.

The other Kings grunted their assent as they waited for Eve's reply, arms at the ready. Adam's tortured gaze met his wife's.

"We rode hard from Masada through the Judean Desert . . . we missed no trail all the way to Tel Jericho through to the old biblical lands of Amman and Moab, which they now call Jordan, and we circled back to slaughter it here on Mount Temptation." Adam's voice was laden with tension and fatigue as he dismounted from a gleaming white steed.

"Eve . . . my Queen," Adam pressed on when she didn't

immediately reply but kept her gaze to the horizon. "I know the mere thought that her progeny has survived is like a barb in your heart for all that Lilith has robbed from you. You must accept that Hannibal has conquered it. The nightmares will be slow to cease for both of us . . . given all that we have endured." He went to her and landed a hand on her shoulder. "Please . . . let your spirit rest."

She shook her head and turned to the group of Neteru warriors, her eyes glistening with tears of frustration. She cupped Adam's cheek for a moment and then allowed her palm to slide away.

"I am the earth mother. Nothing touches my soil that I do not feel in my womb, which has given birth to every nation. Why would you doubt my inner sense now, after all these years?" Hurt filled Eve's voice as Aset stepped to her side, the Queen resolute.

"Show us the carcass again, Ausar," Aset said.

He dismounted and brought over the blue-white energy containment sphere that had been in his saddlebag. Without a word he kinetically sent it into his wife's hands, one palm up, one palm down, and she received it that way, as had been shown on the great walls of the pyramids at Giza since time immemorial.

"This," Aset said, "is a husk—only the pupa's shell." She jettisoned the orb back to Ausar.

Nzinga tightened her grip on her battle-ax. "Then we ride till we find it, no matter the fatigue."

"How can you be sure? This could very well just be a diversion to keep us expending energy resources to grind us down to the point of exhaustion. That could make us vulnerable! They need evasive tactics like that now that they've lost so many demon legions—and when Hannibal first brought what you call a husk to our Council, we all breathed a sigh of relief." Ausar glanced around at the assembled warriors and found agreement in all eyes except those of the Queen.

"All but Eve breathed such relief, dear husband," Aset said, her gaze holding his. "With all due respect, now she has added reason to believe that her theory was correct. I can feel it bubbling beneath the surface of my Queen Sister's skin."

Eve called over the top three generals from the King and Queen Neteru Councils with a wave of her graceful hand, and then stooped down to point at minute changes in the earth.

"It took my falcon a long time to find this, but here is where it dropped from the sky from your first energy bolt, Hannibal." Like a forensic scholar, Eve drew an invisible trajectory with her finger and then allowed her energy to light the way just above the dirt without disturbing it. "It skidded and left charred grasses, then got up on three legs, not four, in its normal, immature Harpie form."

"It was injured," Hannibal stated firmly, satisfaction resonant in his deep voice.

"Yes. Severely," Eve affirmed, showing them where splashed acid had eaten away vegetation. "Look at the wide, flat sweep against the dirt," she added. "That's where it also dragged its damaged wing."

"That matches the carcass we have contained," Ausar said, lifting his chin and glancing at Adam and Hannibal.

"True," Eve said quietly, lost in thought. "But look at this strange, uneven dark charge," she murmured and stood again as her falcon cried. Eve shielded her eyes from the glaring sun and began to walk toward where her distressed bird circled.

"It just looks like the carnage after a fatal injury," Hannibal said, leaning closer to inspect.

"What is the dark energy signature of the pattern?" Adam

asked quickly as the elite squad of ancestral warriors began to follow Eve.

"Lucifer's," Eve said, bringing the group to a halt. "I would know the foundation of Cain's DNA anywhere, even a generation or two removed." She looked away. "He made this abomination with both Lilith and her Chairman . . . my son, Cain." Eve closed her eyes and hugged herself as Adam's arms enfolded her. "With assistance from that unspeakable source, it stood right up from its own blood splatter in a new form. Guaranteed my falcon has found the footprints of a man."

Lilith stood at the edge of her husband's bedchambers, studying his unreadable expression and mood. He had allowed several months to pass without comment about the total devastation of eight demon legions, an insidious spell that had backfired into the Dark Realms, and a network Light virus sent into their caverns and brain centers by the human Neteru team. Now he'd finally sent for her, and the Harpies had escorted her here—not to his torture chamber, not to his war room—but here.

Knowing that his mood could shift to horrific wrath in the blink of an eye, she remained very still, waiting. She was old and wise enough, had been with him long enough, to know that one of his greatest pleasures was luring his victims into a false sense of security before he struck. That made the shock and terror all the more palpable, the betrayal more visceral, the tears and their cries more bittersweet. Therefore, she would not allow herself to be fooled by his exquisitely handsome smile or his calm repose on the heavy Baroque-style furnishings.

He absently stroked the feathers of one of his glistening black wings and tilted his head as he studied her reluctance to fully enter his domain. "No warm welcome from my mate after these many months?"

She allowed her eyes to travel along the perfect symmetry of his nude, muscular form, and swallowed hard as he spoke to her in a deep, sensual tone in *Dananu*.

"Come to me, Lilith. I know I have had my moments' of rage . . . but not today." He uncovered his flawless, sculpted body by moving a massive wing, and held out his manicured hand. "No claws this dawn . . . no leather wings of fury or cloven hooves to stomp you. Look," he said with a droll smile. "Even my tail is retracted, darling, I am deeply pleased . . . beyond your comprehension. You broke the code."

Somewhat startled by his approach, she hesitated. "But we lost his trail when the second seal broke. They released the red stallion . . . there was nothing more we could do."

"I know," he said with a deep, slow chuckle, and then let out a long sigh. "Don't make me repeat my request. Come to me, Lilith. I've waited a very long time for this."

Her voice caught in her throat as she braced for her final extermination. Lilith's gaze slid from her husband's sensual smile and lush mouth that crested a hint of fang down to his stone-carved chest to witness his calm breaths. His sinewy abdomen was rigid with want, and her gaze briefly considered the massive erection he owned. Just seeing that made her fight the impulse to back away quickly. Whatever torture he'd planned this time in exchange for her failure had turned him on so much that her extinction was imminent.

"Just make it swift," she murmured in *Dananu*, tears rising in her eyes as she finally approached the edge of the huge chamber bed. Her thighs came to a rest against black silk and gold brocade. "While you have every right to prolong my torture . . . I beseech you, for old time's sake . . . as your first . . . the only one who stood with you against Adam and even the Unnamed at the beginning of days . . . be swift."

"Be swift?" Her husband smiled and raised an eyebrow. His dark eyes hunted her. "Why, Lilith, I am completely offended."

Lilith's voice fractured as her breath left her body. His power snatch was so quick and severe that she didn't even have time to gasp.

He smiled and kissed her slowly as he brought her beneath him and extended his onyx-hued wings to blanket them both. "You asked me to be swift and I complied. But I had never considered my giving you pleasure a torturous thing. . . . Should that be swift, too?"

She looked up into his intense black irises that held the depths of all darkness. Unable to help herself, she touched the side of his face, confused when she witnessed raw passion and appreciation in his eyes—something she'd never seen to this degree in them before.

"You did it," he said quietly, nuzzling her throat and beginning to call her jugular vein to the surface of her skin. "You made him. The males who took the lead throne of evil on my most cherished Vampire Council couldn't produce him, but you, my wife, you did." His voice dropped to a sensual whisper. "My own son, Dante, couldn't even do it, but you did."

Relief washed through her and her body relaxed in his hold, but she didn't say a word for fear of ruining the moment. She allowed him to lead the negotiation for now. Dark energy began to enter her pores, infusing her with a slow, inner-leaking pleasure that caused her to writhe beneath him with a feral moan.

"He is not lost, Lilith," her husband crooned as his hands lavished her body, leaving her so sensation-drunk from his touch that she could barely move. "He homed to my energies. . . . Millennia ago I had been there to challenge the one who we never name, and now, my heir has gone to Mount Temptation and slipped out of his birth skin to find the dark chrysalis of transformation. Forty thousand demon troops as a cannon-fodder diversion . . . what you did up on Masada was epic,

Lilith," he said, his breaths becoming ragged. "I will give you what I wanted to give our son, Dante—what he was never demon enough to have earned as a reward."

She arched with a shriek as he entered her and bit her simultaneously in one deft move. It felt as though her heart would explode as temporal colors and scents and sounds from the earth plane erupted inside her. She dug her nails into his shoulders, her talons growing as he sent power into her throbbing vein while he moved against her, causing climatic bursts. When he lifted his head from the infusion, fangs dripping with her black blood, she was barely conscious.

"Give this to your councilmen, and surprise them with the gift. They cannot pass it yet, only my heir will have that right. But you have pleased me, Lilith. . . . This time you have outdone yourself." He kissed her, making her taste her own power-infused blood on his mouth. "Stay with me this morning of your own accord . . . and let me take my time to do this with agonizingly slow precision. Tomorrow, you can share this with them. Is that fair exchange?"

All she could do was nod.

"It's too close to dawn," Sebastian said, looking at his fellow councilmen. His gaze ricocheted between them, the chamber doors, and the goblet of blood he was afraid to touch for fear of being poisoned. "A meeting now, after months of trying to rebuild all the damage . . . what do you think this could mean?"

Fallon Nuit kept his eyes on the huge black marble doors of the Vampire Council Chambers as he spoke in a resigned, philosophical tone. "The caverns murmur that she was called by her husband. After the fledgling from Nod was lost, and given the heavy losses at Masada where the Arc of the Covenant was actually unleashed against us . . . I would say that this is a fond farewell gathering, a prelude to sure assassination." Fallon made a tent with his fingers before his mouth and closed his eyes. "When the Harpies come, do not struggle, *mon ami*. They will delight in it, and that will be added to your torture terrors. Rest assured, I know."

Yonnie leaned forward and filled a goblet of blood from the pentagram-shaped table, his gaze fixed on the golden-fanged crest that revealed all evil machinations beneath it. He absently took a sip. "Then, why worry, Sebastian. If you're poisoned, that's fucked-up, but a better way to go than the wall."

"Because you won't die if poisoned!" Sebastian hissed. "You will writhe and suffer the effects as it eats your insides out, but you will not perish!"

"Aw'ight, so my bad." Yonnie flopped back against his throne. "There were so many things I wanted to do before this bullshit went down."

Fallon reached for a goblet and then knocked his against Yonnie's. "Strange that we are only now coming to a strained peace accord, you and I, when it is so near our end. Ironic, *n'est-ce pas?*"

Yonnie nodded, his gaze holding Nuit's. "*Oui*. But don't get it twisted. I ain't done hatin' your foul ass yet. But given the circumstances, at the moment, we cool."

Nuit smiled. "That is what I most admire in you, Yolando. Rare, that quality of steadfastness and blunt honesty . . . has a ring of the old Councilman Rivera to it. If there was anything I wanted to accomplish before being terminated from office, it would have been settling the score with that impossible-to-kill bastard." Nuit sighed. "Alas, but we are still on a sinking ship together, gentlemen."

"Maybe if we all . . ." Sebastian's words trailed off as the floor began to rumble.

Sebastian foolishly tried to transport out by gathering a dark energy funnel around himself, but the bats refused to respond to the command so close to dawn. They desperately flew counter-clockwise to his funnel directive in an attempt to get him back to his throne for safety. But as he fought to go in the opposite direction, the floor cracked, splattering blood from the rich veins in the marble. The conflict left the bats winded and they simply dropped Sebastian to sprawl in the middle of the floor.

Yonnie just shook his head and took a deep sip from his goblet.

Nuit coolly regarded Sebastian's shriek as Harpies poured out of the floor fissure, their little gray-green gargoyle bodies moving like a swift, demonic tide to cover Sebastian.

"Stop fighting them," Nuit said, resigned. "There is nowhere to run."

Yonnie stood as Sebastian's screams became piteous begging to be released. Poised to begin fighting, he battle bulked and took aim to blow away anything that approached with a black charge.

"There are *millions* of them," Nuit said, standing to walk right into the skittering, screeching Harpie swarm. *"Adieu, mon ami,"* he said with a petulant nod. "It has been, as you say, real."

Yonnie watched in pure disbelief as the forms of both councilmen were overrun by gray-green creatures until they couldn't be distinguished from the thicket of screeching, scrambling bodies that dragged them into the fissure. Cold sweat made Yonnie's suit beneath his council robe cling to his body. He lifted his chin as Lilith's voluptuous silhouette caught his peripheral vision. She sashayed forward as her Harpies began to climb up Yonnie's body.

"You bitch," Yonnie murmured. "One day, me and you . . ."

She laughed and made the crowd of Harpies remove their squirming bodies from his face so he could see. "How about this morning, then? Me and you, topside, lover?" She blew him a kiss and then turned and walked away.

Her laugh collided with Yonnie's echoing yell. "No!"

Carlos propped himself up on one elbow and stared down at Damali. He traced her arm, watching the perspiration he'd left there glisten in the new dawn light. Speckles of radiant white Light energy still danced in her velvety locks and made her cinnamon-hued skin shimmer. Her kiss-punished mouth made his own hunger to taste her lips just one more time, but he would wait.

There was something so absolutely peaceful and yet surreal about watching the colors in her aura float over her soft, beautiful skin while she slept . . . and although he had very pressing, selfish reasons to wake her, he couldn't. Not when she was so sated and unburdened by worry. That was a gift he'd never take from her. The sleep of the innocent was something to treasure.

His wife had rebuilt the team, had gotten everyone to envision a real home in order that it could manifest—and not just a barracks-type compound like before. A real home was what they now shared in San Diego. His baby had even brought back their music after the insane battle at Masada. The healings she'd done on the emotional and spiritual level were so profound that he simply kissed her shoulder and laid his cheek against it for a moment. This woman deserved her rest, he told himself. They'd been at it all night.

Snuggling down next to Damali, he kissed her hair and drew her tighter into their spoon with a slight wince. Her body pressed against his erection, a perfect fit that increased the throb. It was going to take serious concentration and willpower unreal to not move against her warm, butter-soft behind. She stirred slightly and released a peaceful sigh, her hand curling around his the way a baby would unconsciously grip a finger.

Carlos's mind blurted a spontaneous prayer . . . if God would just let there be enough time, let the clock on the scoreboard not run out, maybe he could grow old like Father Pat . . . old enough for both him and Damali to have kids and see them grow up.

In his soul he knew that, fifty years from now, he'd still feel the same way about D. So, yeah, he could let her get some rest. He chuckled to himself—it was ridiculous between them sometimes. Carlos let his head slowly sink down onto the pillows, and he closed his eyes, willing his body to relax. The sun from the skylight was warm against his face. Again, she'd been right to put the bed under it to catch the morning rays and to display the spectacular star carpet at night. Yeah, they were blessed. It was all good.

He drifted off with that thought in mind and pulled the covers up a little higher on his wife's nude body to shield her from the coolness of the air-conditioning.

A sudden thud made Carlos and Damali open their eyes at the same time and sit up. They both started up simultaneously. Carlos was out of the bed, and she was right behind him with a sheet wrapped around herself. The gasp she released could have cut metal. Carlos was in his pants in seconds, tears in his eyes. Blinded by tears and grabbing at anything she could quickly put on, Damali dressed in a flash.

"I gotta go get him!" Carlos said, his breathing erratic as he looked up at the skylight. "That's my fucking boy—I've been there, those bastards . . . oh shit . . ."

"Baby," she said, trying to hold him, as he snatched away from her attempts. "By the time you get there . . . I also remember trying to save you like that. You can't beat the sun. He'll be ash."

"Then I'll go get Yonnie's ashes! That's the least I owe him."

Carlos looked up, the flood of tears winning out as they leaked from the corners of his eyes. Another blood brother had died on his watch. Flashes of Alejandro, Julio, Juan, and Miguel stabbed into his conscience. Thinking of Father Lopez, and then Gabrielle, made him stop breathing. Yonnie's disheveled appearance made it seem like he'd been assaulted by Harpies— his suit was in shreds, and his normally immaculate Afro looked like he'd been fighting wild. Blood leaked from his jugular due to a sloppy vein hit, oozing down the skylight glass to paint it crimson. His body was beginning to smolder, but there was a look of pure bliss on his face. If it had been any other vamp, the fallen would have combusted on impact from Marlene's prayer barriers, but Yonnie was exempt.

"Don't look, baby," Carlos said, defeated, turning away to wipe his face with both palms. "He's two hundred years old. I'm going up to get him before maggots start crawling over the glass."

Damali touched his arm. "Let me go with you, Carlos. I can say a prayer with you over his remains . . . when two or more are gathered . . . remember?"

Carlos nodded, pulled her and the sheet she'd been wearing into an embrace, and folded them away to the roof. He didn't say a word as they stepped out of the nothingness to roll Yonnie over, trying to shield him with the bed linen. But Yonnie kept waving it away.

Carlos called his blade into his grip. "He's in so much pain, D, he's delirious . . . I gotta," Carlos whispered thickly. "Can't wait for ash."

Damali knelt down, trying to get the sheet over Yonnie's head. "Then only like this," she said quietly. "That's one less pair of eyes, one less face to remember having to do this to."

"It feels so good, man," Yonnie murmured. "Don't."

Carlos sat back on his haunches, and Damali stared from where she squatted. Carlos slowly dropped his blade.

Yonnie opened his eyes slowly and squinted, fangs glistening in the sun, and then he laughed like a drunk while crying at the same time. "I haven't felt or seen sunlight in over two hundred years, man." He looked at Carlos, his eyes seeming blind and disoriented as he spoke.

"He's not burning, Carlos," Damali said, jumping up. "Something's wrong." She called the Isis blade into her palm and stepped back.

Carlos was on his feet in an instant and squared off with her, holding a protective shield of Heru over Yonnie. "You crazy? This is family!"

Damali steadied her voice, tears streaming as she shook her head. What she said next came out in a near whisper. "They finally made a daywalker, Carlos. This isn't a resurrection or second chance."

Carlos slowly turned away to stare at Yonnie; the tears that glimmered in Damali's eyes shone with truth. He stooped down next to his best friend of too many years and battles to count. "Talk to me, man."

Yonnie closed his eyes and dropped his head back, smiling. "She bit me, man. I thought the Harpies were dragging us to our deaths by sunlight."

Carlos exchanged a look with Damali.

"Who bit you, brother?" Carlos asked carefully.

"Lilith . . . It was *so sweet,*" Yonnie breathed out. "Better than hump-in-your-back sex." He shook his head and kept his eyes closed with his face tilted toward the sun. "Sebastian practically shit himself when they tied us down—but she had to, man. We were wiggin' so bad, it would have been on to the death. We would've tried to ice her. Nuit tried. He lost his cool and bugged at the last minute. Took about fifty of those little bastards to hold him down, too. By the time she got to me, hey, I was philosophical."

Yonnie opened his eyes with a wide grin and then demonstrated for Carlos, calmly reenacting the scene. "Just turned my head to the side and pointed to the vein. Figured, fuck it. Flat-line me so I don't feel the sunburn, you know." He chuckled and shook his head. "I woke up sun-stupid, brother. Came right here to let my homeboy know I made it." Yonnie grabbed Carlos's hand in an old-fashioned finger grip handshake, and then banged his knuckles. "But I ain't gonna lie, I gotta eat soon . . . gotta come down . . . I'm buzzed like a motherfucker." He wiped both his palms down his face. "Tara home? She gotta see this."

Damali's telepathy stabbed into Carlos's brain. *Say a prayer over him and do him now, baby—send him into the Light proper. There's three of them! Daywalkers! Councilmen. You know what this means!*

No! I can't . . . he deserves the same chance I got. Besides, we learned a lot—don't make me do this, D. I'm asking you as your husband—fall back.

"Everything cool, man?" Yonnie said when Carlos didn't re-spond to the question fast enough. He sat up slowly, monitoring the tension between Carlos and Damali.

Carlos glimpsed Damali and watched her lower her blade. "Yeah, man, everything's peace."

Yonnie stood, making Carlos stand. "Then, uh, why's your lady clutching an Isis? I didn't come this far to get smoked in broad daylight over bullshit."

"When you hit our skylight," Carlos said tensely, his gaze boring into Damali's, "we didn't know you were gonna make it."

Yonnie nodded and then swallowed hard after a moment, slowly pulling Carlos into a brotherly embrace. "Thanks, man . . . I owe you. Always got my back, no matter what. Woulda took my head clean like I'd asked you to, if I woke up burning and screaming. Damn . . . that's a helluva friend."

Carlos slapped Yonnie's back, staring at Damali over Yonnie's shoulder until she glanced away. "Yeah, if it came to that, but it didn't." He withdrew and looked Yonnie dead in the eyes. "Last thing I want, man, is to see you suffer."

PART I

ENEMY OF MY EMEMY IS MY FRIEND

CHAPTER ONE

Damali walked slowly along the beach behind the house, hanging back as Carlos said good-bye to his friend. The battle between her instinct to take the head of a clear and present threat and her desire to honor her husband's request twisted her stomach into knots. She could feel the entire household manning battle stations as each Guardian awakened to their own internal sensory guidance.

No less than she would have expected, Marlene sat up in bed first, eyes wide, third eye vision sweeping and then honing in on Damali's to question the SOS vibration she'd clearly felt. The insistent contact between Marlene's seeking vision and her second-sight unlocked the interior of the house for her in surreal imagery. Like a bad and hazy dream, Damali could mentally see the unfolding chaos in her mind's eye coming to her in fits and starts, and she took in a deep breath to summon calm as she continued trudging twenty-five yards behind Carlos and Yonnie.

Like a giant ebony cobra, in one fluid move Shabazz had slowly unfolded from the lotus mediation position he'd been in, locks crackling with raw fight energy, the look in his eyes deadly. His expression said it all: The house had been breached—unacceptable.

Mike had heard the thud on the roof and was already packing ammo as he came down the hall with Inez. Damali remembered seeing his bald head jerk up when Yonnie first hit the skylight in the roof, but the potential of immediate danger had blotted out the rest of the imagery until now.

She didn't need to watch the trajectory of events mentally, however. The past informed her better than any second-sight ever could. Mike was on the move. Pissed off. A six-foot-eight, two-hundred-and-seventy-five-pound human bear made of pure muscle was in the hall of their compound; Big Mike wasn't having a homestead breach any more than Shabazz was. Her girl, Inez, was right behind him, too, her short self toting a handheld Uzi. Damali groaned inwardly and then turned away from Carlos and Yonnie to head back toward the house before shots were fired.

This was the part that she wasn't sure Carlos understood, as much as she empathized with his dilemma. This was finally *home*.

The entire family had envisioned every room, every detail of the massive San Diego beachfront property. They'd all prayed for a place to call home, and everything had been made manifest, right down to the sprawling ten acres that surrounded the mansion and the pristine mountain view beyond it. It was something to come back to after the battle in the Holy Land. *This* was sanctuary. *This* was what every man and woman on the team, from the eldest to the youngest, had dreamt of for years. A place that was like a citadel, but that was also not like the old maximum security prison–type compound from years ago . . . or the cramped, crazy dwelling they'd survived in during the rough stint in Arizona. *This* was a home where dreams could flourish and peace could reign supreme. And not a Guardian in the joint was having any mess come to their door.

In her soul she knew the brothers were prepared to take a Masada-inspired last stand here this morning if they thought a daywalker had come calling. The vibe reverberated through the air and pierced her skin like tiny knives. Live free or die trying.

"Oh, shit . . ." Damali let her breath out hard, and then picked up her pace and hurried back to the house.

Rider met her at the door with a sawed-off shotgun resting on his shoulder. Tara stood behind him with a 9mm lowered at her side, but the look in her eyes said it all—she knew. Damali held up one hand and let out a weary breath, watching younger Guardians hustling down the steps over Rider's and Tara's shoulders. Couples fell into Full Metal Jacket formation, flanking the windows and doors. For a moment all Damali could do was watch them.

Jose and Juanita parted like pros, clutching weapons while silently doing one-handed leaps over opposite banisters with Jose giving Juanita the two-finger silent signal to take the window while he headed for the deck. J.L. and Krissy hugged the wall and squared off with vents and fireplace openings, splashing each one with holy water before backing up to train a weapon on it. Bobby and Jasmine headed for the back door to lend support to the senior couple, Berkfield and Marj, who were already in the kitchen, strapped. Mike and Inez were out in the pool area, securing the lower decks, and Damali cringed knowing that Shabazz and Marlene had taken the roof. This was ten minutes past real bad.

Everything within the house was in order, the scramble effective and the way it was supposed to happen . . . yet the cosmos was out of alignment and there was no fighting that with conventional demon-hunting weapons. Until Carlos came back with more information, there was no way to know how to take down a daywalker permanently, the range of its powers, or how many had been made. The questions were endless.

"Stand down," Damali said flatly, garnering confused looks from those Guardians within earshot. "Carlos got this."

Incredulous gazes followed her as she brushed past her stunned teammates and headed for the kitchen. She heard the fallback order ripple through the house behind her and knew a near mutiny was close at hand. For this she needed coffee, not herbal tea. Before she could fill the pot with water, the entire team, sans Carlos, had piled into the kitchen behind her.

"That was Yonnie out there! His signature is in my sinuses, tell me I'm lying?" Rider hollered. "And unless my eyes are playing tricks on me and this is a very, very bad dream, D—a fucking vamp councilman is taking a daylight stroll down the beach with your husband!"

"I know," Damali said as calmly as possible, and then added enough water to the huge pot to make enough coffee for everybody. What else was there to say? She didn't have a clue at the moment what was going on, and was trying her best not to freak out. While she gathered her thoughts, she continued making coffee very methodically, and then put on a teakettle for Marlene and Shabazz. Her actions were mechanical, by rote, something she'd seen Marlene do a hundred times, if once, to quell mass hysteria in the compound.

"You know?" Shabazz said slowly, parting the group around her as he neared her. A blue-white swath of electrostatic charge spread across the floor before him like a crackling blue carpet as he approached her. *"You know?"*

Damali closed her eyes and then turned away from the sink in a slow pivot. She'd seen Shabazz upset before, but this was definitely a first.

"Yeah," she finally said, now staring at the senior Guardian whom she loved like a father. How could she get 'Bazz to understand that she had to wait? The look in Carlos's eyes alone was enough for her. As much as her husband had seen, as many bodies as he'd had to drop, rarely had she witnessed tears just rolling down his face at the mere prospect of doing what had to be done. The struggle within Carlos was obviously as visceral as the one now raging within her.

Yet she couldn't explain all of that in front of the team. Nor could she tell them how fearful she was that maybe this time her husband was in more danger than even he understood . . . a newly made daywalker was with him: An entity that had clearly embedded himself in Carlos's heart—the very way the vamps got to you. This entity was like a brother, like Alejandro, and she knew Carlos couldn't make that necessary snap decision to smoke him in a blink of an eye . . . the same blink that could possibly cost Carlos his life. The team had no idea how much she wanted to bolt from the kitchen, Isis raised, and head for the beach. Her husband's life was on the line, and she could feel every regret he owned blistering her skin. But she would honor his request this time, even if it killed her—or him.

"Carlos has a plan," she finally said, stalling for time. "You oughta know that much about him by now."

All eyes were on her, and trigger fingers remained twitchy in the kitchen. This wasn't just her and Carlos's home; it was everyone else's, too. Each Guardian truthfully had just as much right to defend it as she and Carlos did, team protocols notwithstanding. The thin line between an all-out beach assault and this very tense kitchen conference was sheer trust and family respect. Period. Therefore, to keep the peace, she had to give the team a plausible explanation, even if she didn't own one.

"Yolando hit our bedroom skylight about ten minutes ago and we went up to put him out of his misery and to commend him to the Light. But he didn't burn." Damali's gaze raked the enthralled group around her. "Barely smoldered. Carlos is out there with him now, gaining critical intel. He'd made his boy a promise—he'd be the one to take his head if and when the Harpies came for him. . . . They didn't come this morning, and from the little bit I've heard, we definitely need more information. So, we wait."

Jose nodded and was the first to stand down. "C never led us wrong, and Damali is right. If these SOBs are walking by day now, we need to know under what circumstances, how quickly the daylight bite is spreading . . . maaan."

Disgruntled Guardians muttered their agreement with Jose as the team slowly fanned out to lean against stainless-steel appliances and the center island butcher-block counter.

"This is beyond bad," Marlene remarked sullenly. "I knew it had been too quiet for too long. We've gotta figure out where it came from, how they did it."

"Or more important," Shabazz said, his locks still crackling with unspent energy, "we need to know specifically how to kill one of those bastards."

"You ain't said a mumblin' word, 'Bazz," Mike said, pounding his fist.

"If they come out by day, does that mean all bets are off for holy water and other prayer-type ammo?" J.L.'s gaze nervously raked the group and then settled on Damali.

"If so, we're screwed, brother," Rider said, clearing his sinuses.

"From all that I remember," Tara said, her voice tight and quiet, "it is a privilege bestowed by the Unnamed One to the Chairman, who in turn can pass it to his councilmen . . . but that still does not confer a soul into the dead carcass of the vampire entity. Hence, the normal precautions should prevail."

"Good information, Tara," Heather said, her wide gray eyes silently begging for more information. She glanced at Jasmine, who remained mute and had practically welded her petite frame to Bobby's hip.

"So then the only bitch of this is, we can't use daylight as a cover." Berkfield glanced at the other senior Guardians and double-checked his magazine. "No problem. We'll just have to smoke the sonsabitches in broad daylight. We've been in tighter spots than this, not to mention ones where we couldn't see what was coming for us—so what the hell."

Damali watched Berkfield's simplistic logic begin to settle the group, a very necessary thing right now. Comments zinged around the kitchen supporting Berkfield's statement, and she almost didn't hear them, she was so lost in her own thoughts.

But Marlene's knowing gaze locked with hers for a moment. Yeah. There was much more to it than kicking vamp ass in broad daylight. Way more. Like the fact that they had to determine if the councilmen could breed more daywalkers from their bite, or if it still held that daylight immunity could only be passed by the Unnamed One's heir or the Neteru-vamp progeny that Nuit had been trying to create for years. The extent of the contagion had to be immediately understood, with a containment strategy summarily put into full effect.

Then there was the not-so-small issue of collateral damage. This time, just like the battles fought in L.A., Philly, and even in New York, they might not be lucky enough to be able to quarantine a huge firefight to some remote, unpopulated area. And this was definitely the first round of the Armageddon—*daywalkers*. She couldn't even comprehend the scale of an all-out assault by the dark side in a major city. The last thing she wanted to be responsible for was turning San Diego into downtown Baghdad.

The very concept made Damali rub her temples to stem a throbbing headache that was building in a wall of pain behind her eyes. All the cosmic events foretold had already aligned: strange weather, pandemic plagues like AIDS and the bird flu, earthquakes, tornadoes, floods, and tsunamis. People had lost their minds; violence was off the Richter scale. Wars were decimating mankind, with tensions running hot within those regions

not yet at arms . . . economies were crumbling; religious insti-
tutions were being turned inside out by corruption and the
vilest abuses. The National Identification Number was pressing
forward, along with a call for a New World Order by industrial-
ized nations uniting under a single currency. And biblical seals
had been broken.

She needed to talk to Carlos, had to consult with her
Queens—but she didn't dare leave the team before the other
Neteru returned. Damali stared at the whistling kettle, wonder-
ing how long it had been singing without anyone noticing it.

"We've been training for this all our lives . . . guess it was too
much to hope for the Armageddon to pass us by." Dan released
a hard, nervous chuckle and then sat down with a weary thud at
the long oak kitchen table across from Jose. "Guess it's also a
good thing that none of us has any kids, since it'll be a blood-
bath with these suckers out by day."

"Speak for yourself," Inez said, her gaze suddenly frantic.

Everyone stared at her, remembering.

"I have a daughter!" she said, hugging herself and then
pulling away from Mike's attempt to calm her. "Fuck all this—
I want my baby and my momma brought into this compound
now! No more shuttling my kid around under clerics' prayers
and safe houses. If there's no twelve-hour window to shield my
baby, then I'm going out swinging, y'all hear me! *I'll* protect
her."

"I'm sorry," Dan said quietly. "That's not what I meant. I just
forgot because Ayana isn't here with us all the time." Dan
glanced away, catching Heather's sad gaze as the young couple
remembered their recent loss.

"She knows, and it's cool, y'all," Mike said, coming to Inez
again. "We gonna go get Ayana and your momma, okay, suga?
Don't panic. As soon as Carlos gives us the info we need, we'll
make a run and go get the baby."

"Promise me," Inez said, looking at Mike.

He nodded. "I ever lie to you, girl?"

Two big tears rolled down her cheeks as she shook her head. "I'ma get your daughter and momma in here safe or die trying."

This time Inez allowed Mike to pull her into a hug. Damali watched as her best girlfriend melted into her Guardian brother's bearlike embrace. She knew the terror and could feel it stabbing into her chest as Inez's breaths shuddered, making her back expand and contract in uneven bursts.

But the question of logistics shimmered in each Guardian's eyes. How was *that* going to work—two civilians in a compound . . . a toddler and a grandmother, Inez's mom, who hadn't a clue about all this supernatural shit? The only thing that Mom Delores, as she was affectionately called, knew was that her daughter was on tour with a hot band, was on the road, and that Damali was treating her and her grandchild to the best of everything.

The poor woman had no clue that she'd been living under the watchful eye of Covenant clerics, or that every fabulous house she'd moved into had been previously anointed for safety.

Damali wiped her palms down her face. *Jesus.* Carlos couldn't even do a clean, fold-away sweep to pick them up because Mom Delores would have a damned heart attack for sure. Yeah, right, a silver-eyed brother would just swoop into her house and fold her into nothingness with her granddaughter—and the poor baby . . . lord have mercy. Ayana might be scarred for life or left catatonic behind all of that! Which left only one way to go get them: Mike and Inez would have to split off from the team to collect civilians, but then what? And how dangerous was that, given that daywalkers had just shown up on the planet?

Plus, there was that terrible thing that neither she nor Carlos had wanted to think about, much less even discuss, since they'd walked out of the Judean Desert: They'd both seen Lilith's progeny fly away. . . . Without question, that was the Devil's spawn. The silent prayer she'd said months ago filled Damali's entire being: *Please, God, let her prayers be answered*—let Hannibal have gotten that nasty little disease-carrying critter. If it wasn't exterminated by the Neteru Councils, then it could be somewhere, anywhere, churning out daywalkers with its infectious, immediate-turn bites.

For the moment there were no answers. The most she could do was listen to the coffee brew as the Guardians finally sat down with a thud one by one, the magnitude of what they faced weighed heavily on them all.

He had screamed until he'd blacked out. In the back of his mind he heard the titter of Harpies that were still near enough to taunt him. He tried to open his eyes and the glare of sunlight blinded him. Nuit shielded his face with his forearm and rolled over, then covered his head with both arms. Moist earth and freshly mown grass filled his nostrils with the pungent scent of morning dew . . . and life. Suddenly he realized that he wasn't on fire. There was no pain. He slowly removed his arms from his head and opened his eyes. Through his tear-blurred vision as he lifted his head, he saw his old New Orleans mansion, fully restored to its preflood splendor.

His right hand became a fist, and he pressed it to his mouth to stem the sob. He knew that Lilith's cruelty knew no bounds, but to bring him here, at dawn, and to stem the pain temporarily just to tease him before letting him explode into an inferno . . . Nuit hung his head and wept.

"Darling, you are much too paranoid," Lilith murmured, materializing beside him. "I had to wait until you'd collected yourself—you made such a fuss about this timeless gift I was trying to bestow upon you that I had to restrain you before you hurt yourself." She stroked his profusion of disheveled onyx curls and laughed as he jerked away from her caress.

"Just do it!" Nuit shouted and glared at her. Battle-length fangs filled his mouth, but he knew better than to attempt an attack—that would only prolong the punishment.

"I already did," she murmured, a wry smile gracing her beautiful face. "Do you like the morning, lover?"

His confused expression made her laugh again and then she leaned over and brushed his mouth with hers. "Daywalker," she crooned. "How does it feel, Fallon?"

"Non . . ." Nuit tumbled backward and then flexed to a quick stand. "You lie."

Lilith smiled and stood with easy grace. "Normally, I do—and thank you for the rude compliment. But this morning, it's true. That was one hell of a battle at Masada. *Lu* loved it."

"He gave you the key . . . the—"

"Uhmmm-hmmm. Even Dante couldn't deliver for him like I could. He was very, *very* pleased. For your loyalty, I have decided to share his gift with my councilmen."

"You created the Antichrist?" Nuit's voice was a harsh whisper of disbelief.

"Who better than the Devil's wife, I ask?"

Nuit covered his mouth and began to pace with one hand behind his back as though he'd been stabbed. He trudged back and forth beneath the grand bows of the dogwood trees, disturbing the drapes of Spanish moss with each pass. Tears streamed down his face as he stared at the antebellum structure that had once been his original lair, hundreds of years of memories cascading through him with such exquisite pleasure that he was forced to close his eyes. After a moment, he turned and stared at Lilith, finally understanding. He said nothing, just dropped to his knees before her and opened his arms, bottom lip trembling.

She smiled and slowly walked forward. "Yes," she murmured

in *Dananu*. "I thought you might like it after all. No more attempted coups. Deal?"

It was the cruelest of all punishments he could have ever envisioned. Death by daylight. Sebastian kept his eyes squeezed shut as he scuttled into a nearby shadow provided by an abandoned barn. Open, sun-drenched farmland sprawled before him; not even the cover of shrubbery would give him scant oasis between this human-forsaken building and the dense tree line hundreds of yards away.

Terror constricted his lungs as dust motes danced in the shards of light, taunting his intrusion. His gaze tore around the structure—there was no haven. Light found every crevice in the dilapidated wood frame. Pools of the insidious toxin blanched the barn's floor. He looked up, and to his horror, the roof was mostly gone . . . by noon, there wouldn't even be a corner left to cower in. Burning slowly was imminent.

Bereft, Sebastian slumped against the wall, pulling his shredded council robes around him like a blanket. He sensed the earth and closed his eyes. Lilith had brought him home to Bulgaria, how fitting. Once top advisor to the czar he'd betrayed, he would not even be allowed to return to the royal palace within the belly of Mother Russia. Instead he'd be left to turn to ash in a remote hole in the wall . . . left like a vagrant, a lower-level vampire who had lost his bet with the sun.

A mournful wail began the sobs as he remembered his old power, but the slow clucking sound of feminine amusement made him open his eyes and jerk his attention toward the far side of the barn. Fury replaced defeat and he wiped his face so bitterly that he drew blood under his left eye.

"I thought you might enjoy an old-fashioned breakfast of farm maidens in the old country—the way it used to be done, love," Lilith said with a sly smile. "The next farm down the

road is fully occupied, but you were in such a state unbecoming
to a councilman that I thought it best to bring you here until
you'd collected yourself."

"Do not make the indignity of this all the more intolerable!"
Sebastian shouted, bearing fangs. "To tease a dying man with
the thought of food . . . to say it is merely a few miles across *an
abyss* of sunlight—is there no mercy in your black heart?"

"None whatsoever," she murmured and then blew him a
kiss. "But I do feed my pets, darling." She released a bored sigh.
"Haven't you noticed that you're not even smoldering?"

Sebastian glanced around at the places on his body that sunlight touched and tried to squeeze himself farther into the impossible corner he'd been standing in.

"Just be done with it," he said, voice quavering. "Please."

"I heard Dracula's castle is up for sale," Lilith remarked
coolly, studying her manicure as she blithely changed the subject. "I thought that after breakfast you might want to stop by
the fourth-century Thracian tombs in Topolchane—they found
golden masks there, you know . . . and then we might go get
you that castle you've always coveted. But if you don't stop behaving like a big baby, none of that will be possible."

Her smile widened as he opened his hand under a shard of
light and stared at it, slowly turning it over to feel the sun's
warmth without the hissing burn.

"How is this possible?" he whispered with reverence.

"Darling . . . you have no idea the extent of my powers
now."

CHAPTER TWO

So, how'd they take it?"

Lilith stared at her husband's sinewy back with a smile.

"They were positively hysterical."

"I'm sorry I missed that one . . . but you know what they say, I'm always busy."

"You would have loved it, Lu," she crooned, risking going near him.

"Hold it in your mind and show me later?"

"You know you don't even have to ask."

He chuckled deeply as he slowly materialized a white button-down shirt, drawing on the crisp cotton fabric before adding the designer navy-blue suit and sophisticated paisley silk tie. His smile widened as she gaped at his attire, watching black wing tip shoes glisten at his feet as he adjusted his tie and then cuffs beneath his jacket sleeves.

"I must know . . ." she murmured, still enthralled as he smoothed his palms over his once long onyx curls to their now present freshly barbered precision and then checked his watch. "A world conference? A political soiree in Washington, D.C.? Oh, tell me—I love the havoc you wreck when you go topside . . . where are you going this time?"

He gave her a dashing smile. "Where else? To church."

This was so far past bad that his mind couldn't process a point of entry. Where did one begin? Carlos raked his fingers through his hair as he trudged back to the house. The King's Council had to be informed, and a visual on Yonnie had to be given, lest they smoke a brother outright just for breathing. Things were hair-trigger fragile, everything wire-tight. He knew that going in.

When Carlos opened the front door and four senior Guardians drew on him, he just froze for a moment, holding his hands up before his chest until clarity prevailed.

"What's the word, man?" Shabazz said, the first to drop his weapon.

Silence looped over Carlos's head like a noose and tightened around his throat as the team drew nearer to hear the verdict.

"He's cool," Carlos said flatly, his gaze scanning the group and settling on Damali for a moment.

"Dude, you know you're gonna have to come in here better than that," Rider said and headed for the back door. "He's cool? Kiss my ass, Rivera."

"Hold it, man," Mike said, stopping Rider with an out-stretched forearm. "Hear the brother out, *then* we smoke the daywalker. Cool?"

Rider pounded Mike's fist and lowered his weapon.

Sweat beaded on Carlos's brow, and he could feel it making his T-shirt cling to his torso. The adrenaline spike on the team was so crazy that he could practically taste it in the back of his throat.

"Y'all are gonna have to chill and fall back," Carlos said after a moment. "This is a Level Seven high-security breach of the worst kind. My inside man is still cool. . . . He told me that after Masada, Lilith's old man was so happy with the results that he gave her the daylight bite to pass on to them. They can't pass it, though. So far, none but them have been made. She was only authorized to give it to her councilmen—that means three, plus Lilith, can come topside in broad daylight."

"What the hell . . . ?" Berkfield glanced around the team. "I thought we blew forty thousand demon troops to smithereens? Happy with the goddamned results, are you serious?"

"Yeah," Carlos said, and went to the cabinet to get a coffee mug. He poured the dark liquid into his cup very slowly, avoiding eye contact with the team.

"So, what brought on the party?" Jose asked, his eyes following Carlos's every move.

Silence strangled the kitchen.

"Those troops were cannon fodder—expendable," Carlos finally said and then took a slow sip of coffee and winced. "Damn!"

"We didn't get it, did we?" Damali asked, her voice tense and low.

Carlos shook his head and dropped his gaze. It was the thing they'd avoided speaking of for far too long. "The little bastard got away."

"Oh . . . my . . . God . . ." Marlene began to pace.

"Clarification for those of us not reading between the lines," Bobby said quickly.

"Lilith's spawn," Rider said, opening the back door to hock and spit over the deck rail. "Now it gets really fun, folks."

"Rewind that tape," J.L. said, his gaze darting between Jose and Carlos. "The Anti—"

"Yeah, and don't say it," Marlene warned. "Don't even bring the energy up in this house by speaking its name."

"Nobody fire on Yonnie, all right?" Carlos said, setting his cup down hard. "My boy is in a real precarious situation right through here, but he's the only way inside right now. It's too hot for even a Neteru breach at this point."

Tara quietly hugged herself and allowed her gaze to drift out the window. Carlos glanced at Rider and then at Tara.

"But you can't go see him under any circumstances, T," Carlos said gently. "Even though Yonnie's my boy . . . the daylight's got him intoxicated right now and he hasn't fed."

"We'll I'm glad *you* finally see the light, Rivera," Rider said, his gaze hard.

Carlos allowed the comment to slide. He understood where Rider was—he'd been there before himself.

"He's splitting my skull," Tara said quietly, her voice so soft that were it not for the intensity of her words everyone would have needed to strain to hear her. She slowly slid her fingertips up the side of her beautiful face to massage her temples, and then closed her eyes as her fingers began to tangle in her hair.

Tara's outstretched fingers soon became fists amid her dark tresses. Perspiration sheen marred her once even, honey-brown complexion. When she jerked her head to the side as though someone had struck her, the team watched in abject horror as her jugular vein rose beneath her skin, pulsing like an irate serpent.

"Just let me go talk to him," Tara rasped in a breathy, pained whisper, beginning to crest a hint of fangs in her mouth.

"And I can't smoke him?" Rider said. "What, are you nuts!"

"He has to eat soon," Carlos said, keeping his voice flat and matter-of-fact. "Sit her in a chair—do it *now*," he added as Tara began to pace. "He knows that if he breaches this joint, it's all over. I'll be the first one on his ass. He also knows that, if he turns an innocent or feeds buck wild, there's nothing I can do for him at this point. . . . He already has two hundred years of bad history weighing his case in the wrong direction so—"

"Let me go, Jack!" Tara suddenly screamed and began fighting against his hold.

"Either shoot that motherfucker or prayer-banish him," Shabazz said, helping Rider hold Tara in her chair.

A black energy pulse that sounded like a mortar round had gone off hit the house. Instantly tactical sensor Guardians were on their feet, sending a blue-white energy charge against the walls to box in the room.

"I call down the white light of protection and mercy," Marlene said, beginning to walk around Tara's chair. "By all the angels and ancestors of the righteous, barrier this woman's mind and spirit."

"And her body," Rider interjected, struggling to hold Tara down with his full weight while still clutching his pump shotgun in his right grip.

Ignoring Rider's outburst, Damali's voice quickly joined in the low chant with Marlene's until Tara slumped against Rider's shoulder, her body damp with perspiration and her breaths stilted.

"And that was just from a wistful call denied, Carlos," Damali said, staring at her husband. "We've gotta deny him access to the property. He's stronger, baby . . . he's—"

"I know, but he's still on our side, D! That right there was some old relationship bull, but it doesn't mean he's gone dark. It may not be right to lust after another man's wife, but you and I both know that if everyone who did got shot, half of America or more would be blown away—so I ain't going after Yonnie for that kinda shit. Not after the way he's had our back. So, before we just up and smoke the man, we have to know for sure that he took an offer he couldn't refuse."

"Carlos," Damali said calmly, her eyes searching his. "I will go with you on that, but after he just tried to vapor-snatch our team sister out of the house, you have to deny him access to—"

"And leave him ass-out in a firefight, D?" Carlos walked around in a circle. "Do you know who's on his ass right through here?"

"Tell him. Send him a transmission so he knows he's blocked and doesn't get hurt trying to—"

"No. I won't do it, D. I can't go there." He was talking with his hands, his back to the team, pressure splitting his skull. "Barrier him to Tara, you and Marlene make the Light do what it do—but don't ask me to blindside my brother like that over no bullshit, especially not now."

All eyes were on Carlos. He was breathing hard, had begun to pace. The looks on the Guardians' faces spoke volumes.

"Man . . . you know we all got your back," Shabazz said, "but this time, you may be in too deep yourself. You ever consider the fact that you mighta got mind-dazed out there alone on the beach?"

"What?" Carlos cocked his head to the side and stared at Shabazz, his gaze solid silver.

"I'm just saying, man . . ." Shabazz muttered, no apology in his tone. "Everybody's got an Achilles' heel, brother."

"Yonnie ain't my Achilles' heel," Carlos shot back angrily. He pointed toward Damali. "She's that, so I'm not trying to jeopardize the house, if that's what you're saying!"

"Then if D is your Achilles' heel, respect that Tara is mine, bro," Rider said, sending a withering glance in Carlos's direction. "Either check your boy or know that he's a dead man walking."

The rapid-fire exchange of angry male voices ricocheted off the kitchen walls, causing the rest of the team to pivot their attention first in one direction and then the other until eerie silence left an echo.

"Can we have a general's meeting, stat?" Damali asked, her voice calm and her gaze mellow.

"Yeah. Fine," Carlos muttered and stalked out of the kitchen.

She glanced at the team, said nothing, but her eyes told them to just wait and trust her. Slow nods and postures going from tense to at ease bolstered her confidence that they'd hold off any daywalker hunting party at least until she got back.

With swift strides Damali crossed the expansive living room and dining room, finally locating Carlos in the family room. She waited by the archway for a moment as he paced back and forth and finally punched the wall.

"This is so fucked-up, D, I swear to . . . I just can't fucking believe it!"

Damali entered the room and glanced at the plaster on the floor. "I know, baby."

"Yonnie and me . . . maaan . . . that brother has had my back more times than I can count. What am I supposed to do? What, the man is supposed to die just because he has a jones for Tara— Rider oughta let the bullshit go. We've got bigger problems than all that."

Damali nodded and put her hands behind her back and let out a weary breath. "True . . . but you know this is a matter of honor, right?"

"What!"

"Carlos, think back," she said quietly.

He turned away and crossed the room.

"I know this is your boy and all . . . but the situation is dangerous on both sides. Yonnie could go after Rider, too."

"He wouldn't do that."

"A lot of things can jump off in a split second and happen by accident, then people feel bad about what went down after the fact. You know that, baby." She kept her voice well modulated, gentle, as she approached him like he was an injured lion. When she was close enough to him, she reached out and touched his shoulder, all the while watching the muscles in his jaw clench and release. "I love Yonnie, too . . . just like I love Tara and Rider and the rest of this team."

Carlos rubbed his palms down his face. "Oh, man, D . . . what am I gonna do?"

Father Patrick entered the Los Angeles cathedral, stopping at the holy water font to anoint himself. As he passed the alms box, he left a donation, said a prayer, and moved to the rows of flickering votive candles, lighting one for his dead wife and son, as well as one for Padre Lopez, who to his way of thinking still died way too young. Before he could light one for all the members of the Covenant that had died in the line of duty, quiet footfalls arrested his intentions.

The elderly priest stood, his gaze set upon an immaculately dressed man sitting in the pews, who bore the countenance of an international businessman.

"Still questioning the Almighty, Father?" the stranger said with a half smile, standing slowly to exit the pews. He leisurely strolled down the center aisle bathed in multihued light from the exquisite stained glass.

"Where's Father Breckenridge?" On guard, Father Patrick backed up and looked around.

"The Knights of Templar began with nine knights in eleven nineteen A.D., correct? A number twelve year. By eleven twenty-eight your secret members had risen to three hundred . . . again, that was a Holy twelve year for you, yes? Then by eleven fifty you had created your first bank, a seven year, and you no longer guarded the road to the Holy Land . . . if my memory of recent history serves me well." The man before him sighed and clucked his tongue. "Then you ran into conflicts with the church—all over money, the supposed root of all evil, and, alas, by thirteen hundred you all were all but gone. Is this a thirteen year for you, Father, an end-times year, or a twelve?"

Father Patrick made the sign of the cross over his heart, feeling the clamminess of pure evil wash over him. A faint ringing in his ears made it hard to focus on the stranger's words, but the subtle threat was implicit. Although the man's voice remained calm and his tone cultured, his eyes contained such smug hatred that Father Patrick dared not turn away.

"I am not afraid to die, if they've sent a hired human killer to gun down an old man in a cathedral," Father Patrick said, lifting his chin.

"I'm offended," the stranger said with a wide smile. "Human? No . . ." His eyes became chasms of blackness as he slowly sauntered forward. "Your second-sight is failing you, old man. Or maybe you've become comfortable cloaked in self-righteousness." He flung Father Breckenridge's Templar ring toward Father Patrick and chuckled evilly as it hit his robes and then fell to a singing chime at his feet. "Haven't you been watching the news—the Diocese of Los Angeles just had a six-hundred-million-dollar settlement adjudged against it for the molestation of children. Quite a stain and a rather open invitation for me to visit their house, wouldn't you agree?"

"Lucifer . . ."

The man before Father Patrick bowed and offered a droll smile. "Fallen houses of worship are one of my favorite places to meet people. You know what they say, meet people where they are, and so forth."

Father Patrick stopped breathing. There was only one entity with the power to breach hallowed ground that carried a stain . . . only at the end of days. "Father, God, protect me from all that is unholy," the elderly cleric whispered.

"Too late, I got here first," the Beast said with a smile. "Still not afraid to die, old man?"

"No," Father Patrick said, taking a warrior's stance. "And you must be getting desperate if you're going after old priests one by one."

"Never desperate. That is a human condition. But curiosity

is one of my weaknesses. . . . Tell me about these Neterus you guard."

"Yea, though I walk through the valley of the shadow of death—"

"I fear no evil—blah, blah, blah!" the entity shouted over Father Patrick's low, intense murmur. "That is complete bullshit! All mortals fear me!"

Ignoring the angry retort, Father Patrick continued his prayer, undaunted, as pews began to break away from the stone floor. The moment the carved stone font crashed to the floor, the holy water within it spilled in a river of fire down the center aisle.

"Where do they live?" The once ebullient voice had become gravelly and bottomed out with a snarl.

Father Patrick kept his eyes forward on the altar, ignoring burning pews and a wake of destruction as stained-glass windows exploded one after another as though a freight train were passing each one.

"I have given my life in the service of the Most High, and my service remains with you till the end of eternity, Lord Christ. I ask not that you save my body, just take my soul."

"Where do they live!"

Beams and bricks began to rain down from the spectacular nave. Father Patrick turned and looked at the outraged entity and then smiled.

"You cannot touch me, can you? You can only intimidate in this space or frighten. But a man who is willing to die for the love of his family and for the Almighty is a man you cannot sway. Go to hell!"

A black bolt pierced the center of the priest's chest, knocking him down and sending him in a hard slide across the stone floor.

"You may be ready to die, old man, but I bet there's someone who loves you enough to try to save your crotchety stubborn ass."

Carlos jerked away from Damali, instantly battle bulking. The blade of Ausar was in his right grip, the shield of Heru in his left.

"What's wrong?" She stepped back and called the Isis into her hand.

He never answered her, just folded into nothingness with tears in his eyes.

"Battle stations!" Damali yelled out, racing through the house, Isis raised.

"Lock this joint down!" Shabazz called over the scramble as Guardians took known posts.

"Where's Rivera? Is this a daywalker breach, heavy incoming?" Marlene yelled, grabbing a 9mm out of the kitchen drawer.

"He folded-away too fast," Damali said. "I'm going behind his energy trail—don't know what he's hunting, but the look on his face said it was insane."

He slid to his knees and felt Father Pat's neck for a pulse. Wedging his shield and sword in the stone floor, he gently placed both palms against the elderly man's chest, one hand over the other, prepared to try to restart the erratic heartbeat. But the moment he'd laid hands on the man who had been like a father to him, an eerie black tinge wended its way across the old man's chest and began to cover Carlos's hands. Father Patrick was barely breathing, the hem of his robe was scorched, and the cathedral looked like it had been under an air-raid attack—but there were no police sirens on the way.

"Oh, God, what happened?" Carlos asked quietly, sending his silvery · gaze against the darkness creeping up his wrists. "Father . . . come on, you're a tough old dude, man . . ."

"Well, at last we meet."

Carlos jumped up to his feet, but a black bolt of energy separated him from his sword and shield. Immediately he sent a silver warning shot out blindly in the direction of the voice that had spoken.

"Trust me, you don't own that much silver in your veins to counteract what I've got."

The entity laughed and stepped from behind a leaning stone pillar. Instant recognition from his old throne-level experience as a councilman made Carlos know who he was addressing.

"You must have known that at some point we'd meet . . . especially after breaching my wife's lair—not done, under any circumstances." The entity glanced down at the dying priest. "If you want him back, we can make a deal."

Carlos quickly glanced at Father Patrick, amazed that the old man was still clinging to life. "What do you want?"

"Say it in *Dananu*, like you remember it." The entity smiled.

"I'm not agreeing to shit," Carlos said in the vamp mother tongue. "I just want to know terms and conditions."

"Don't," Father Patrick croaked. "You've come too far."

A black-energy bolt made the huge altar candelabra uproot from its stand and whiz toward the priest, but a silver laser shot from Carlos knocked it off its trajectory.

"You can have the old man back if you call off your dogs of war against my heir."

Carlos hesitated. "You must be worried if you're bargaining for amnesty—what, that trick Lilith fucked up again?"

A pew exploded into thousands of pieces of shrapnel, all

whirring toward Carlos and the fallen cleric. The golden disc Carlos called into his grip took the brunt of it, but then oppressive pressure and heat forced him to cast it away.

"Do you know who you're talking to, boy? Have you any idea how little tolerance I have at this moment? The only reason I'm even bargaining with you is—"

"Because obviously you have to!" Damali shouted, filling a naked window with light, her wings spread.

Beams of unnatural white light stabbed into the abused sanctuary from every opening, exploding bricks in rapid-fire bursts as they ate up the floor to where the Ultimate Darkness stood. But he was gone.

Adam walked out of one of the columns of light and looked at Carlos and then the fallen priest as Eve, Nzinga, and Hannibal drew in close to Aset, who clutched the Caduceus. Regal figures loomed tall, casting radiant shadows in their wake, dressed in full Neteru battle armor from centuries gone by. Damali looked up, a question in her eyes.

"It is not this man's time," Aset said, rushing to Father Patrick's side and stooping down above him to begin working on him. "But the damage is severe." She lowered the golden staff over his chest, bringing the entwined serpents to life as she tried to draw the toxin away from Father Patrick.

A lean, quiet young man that Carlos had never seen before stood beside Adam, too reminiscent of Cain to allow the newcomer's presence to go without mention. But before Carlos could pose the question, the stranger spoke in a gentle voice.

"I am Seth, a friend, like the others. It is time for me to fight beside my father, and beside you. Do not worry. Both Councils will convene after this incident."

Too mentally embattled to say a word, Carlos just responded with a nod, his focus on Father Patrick.

"The Unnamed One could have done so much more damage—this was a ruse," Adam said as the ancient spirits gathered around the elderly cleric.

Carlos glanced at the first Neteru king for confirmation, knowing full well that both he and Damali could have gotten their asses squarely kicked by that particular entity. "I figured a topside visit was fishy, man, but I can't figure out what we have to bargain with? Why here, why now, why in a cathedral, and what the hell did Father have to do with any of this? Clearly if Level Seven wanted to break my back, he could have done so right here. Him asking me to call off the dogs of war didn't even make sense!"

"You were lucky that he had a much more strategic agenda than mere revenge," Nzinga said. "Then again, he did exact some of that during his visitation as well."

Carlos looked at his hands, remembering the black ooze that had crept over them. "Yeah, and I think I got tainted."

"Hold out your hands," Eve commanded, glancing at Damali. "Have you touched him?"

"No. I got here the same time you all did." Damali motioned toward Carlos with her chin. "Once I saw Father down, I knew Carlos had tried to revive him—just as I would have . . . so, no, I didn't go to him. Been that route before."

Eve nodded. "Good. Then purge him and his father-seer."

The group remained quiet as Aset lowered the Caduceus over Father Patrick again, this time drawing the black poison out of his heart and causing the elderly man to groan. Searing pain crept up each of Carlos's digits until he panted, and then he watched in awe as the poison left his fingertips to join the inky puddle that was now burning in a pool of white light on the floor.

"In your state of confusion, grief, and rage, you were supposed to call the black horse of the apocalypse, the third seal of widespread human famine, to go after something stronger than yourself," Adam said in a tense mutter. He looked at Carlos and then nodded toward the disappearing murky puddle, watching the haze dissipate into odorous sulfuric fumes. "He has to have all the conditions right before his heir can be positioned for global rule."

"Damn, I was about to get straight played . . ." Carlos dragged his newly cleansed fingers through his hair and neared his elderly mentor. "Father, how you holding up, man?"

"Tell me you didn't agree to anything the beast asked of you," Father Patrick gasped, clutching Carlos's hand.

"Naw, man, I promise you that," Carlos said, trying to comfort the distraught cleric who now seemed so much older for the wear.

"My sanctuaries are no longer safe," the elderly man said, tears slipping from the corners of his eyes. "The Church has failed the people. I am so ashamed of what has become of the Body of—"

"Shush, shush," Damali soothed, hugging Father Patrick. "Don't think it, don't say it. That's not everyone or every church, just some people the Darkness got to."

"But they were *priests,*" Father Patrick croaked, his voice dissolving into an anguished sob. "My Covenant brothers have wars in their lands started by clerics! None of the houses of worship are as they should be. . . . Money is changing hands, there are offenses and abominations—"

"It'll be all right, Father," Damali soothed, gathering him in her arms. "We'll pray, okay? Not everyone or everything is tainted."

Carlos stood. "We need to get him out of here. The Beast penetrated his mind, sodomized it." He walked to the far side of the sanctuary with his hands braced on the top of his head, so angry that his ears were ringing.

"Beware. Human outrage, grief, and pain at seeing one's loved ones and family tortured . . . this was what would have you call the essence of darkness in the name of vengeance. That plague resides within every man's soul and the Beast knows it— since he once had access to your spirit," Hannibal warned. "This is what it was banking on, for you to break that next seal. Once that is opened, he can call the fallen angels that only he has the key to release—the angels of death, hell, and destruction that are to ride on the released horses of the apocalypse. But the Armageddon only advances as each seal is broken and the Most Wicked obviously grows impatient."

Carlos punched a section of stone column as he passed it, sending the rubble to the floor. He almost couldn't bear to watch Damali's wings wrap around the now frail elderly man who'd been his inspiration, a warrior to the end. "Isn't there anything you can do for his mind?" Carlos asked quietly and then swallowed hard.

Aset shook her head. "We don't know the visions that were thrust into his psyche, nor can we endanger the Light by pulling them into each of us. Time will have to heal the rest of it."

"I'll call Imam Asula, Rabbi Zeitloff, and Monk Lin," Damali murmured as she rocked the distraught old man against her. "Their prayers couldn't hurt."

"Then Father Pat comes home with us," Carlos said, pacing, "especially now that daywalkers are—"

"What did you say?" Adam's gaze became hot silver as it met Carlos's eyes and then went to Hannibal.

"Now you know," Eve said, lifting her chin and folding her arms over her breasts. "The time, as I'd said, is nigh. It escaped."

"How many, name the source," Adam said, his gaze tearing away from his wife's to pin Carlos for fast answers.

"My boy, Yonnie . . . he came to me this morning." Carlos sent the Kings and Queens images quickly, now talking with his hands. "They can't pass it, so the spawn isn't transmitting the day bite yet. This came from Lilith directly as a reward for it getting away."

"The one that came to you, did you exterminate it?" Hannibal asked, folding his huge forearms over his massive chest.

"No," Carlos said, glancing away. "Yonnie . . . he's like me— an ace on the inside. He needs amnesty, but the others, not to worry, we're on it."

"Once they return to their compound," Aset said evenly, "we need to convene a joint Neteru Council meeting."

"These are the end of days, young brother. Your alliances must be solid, like your position. No one can take a stand in the middle," Hannibal said, studying Carlos carefully. "That is a very dangerous position to be in."

CHAPTER THREE

The call had gone out, one that lifted heads and stopped the daylight gorging. Within the time span of a vapor whirl, every councilman, including the Chairwoman, was prostrate on the black marble Vampire Council floor. Only Lilith dared to lift her head as the slow, ominous echo of footfalls reverberated off the marble. She cringed.

All the signs of a painful session were there; she knew him that well. The hard clatter against the floor could only be hooves. His topside visit must not have gone as planned. Clearly her husband was in a very foul mood. The silence that surrounded them was deafening.

Bats scurried to safety and hid among the high crags in the endless ceiling above the Vampire Council table. The large transport funnel cloud of the vicious little beasts that always hovered in the vaulted ceiling awaiting commands was gone. Messenger demons and bulking Council Chamber guards were conspicuously absent. Lilith watched it all in her mind as her forehead rested on the warm marble.

As her husband passed the Sea of Perpetual Agony, even the tortured souls stopped moaning and screaming. Yes, he had that effect on anything in his wake. Twisted pride filled her, and despite her terror a smile graced her face. Fear battled with arousal, but she was never a foolish woman.

Before he could even think to reach for the doors, the fanged, golden knockers drew themselves inside the doors, trying desperately to disappear. The doors flung themselves open on their own accord and this seemed to amuse him, regardless of his mood. A low chuckle preceded his entrance, but Lilith knew better than to misread his mirth as a pass. Thrones shuddered behind her, almost coming out of their onyx marble moorings, and the fanged crest in the center of the pentagram-shaped table screeched like an owl before burying itself into the table's interior.

"Rise," a low, even voice commanded. "I have no need of fawning sycophants with so much work to be done."

Sebastian checked with Fallon Nuit and Yonnie as each councilman warily stood, before looking at Lilith for cues to her husband's mood.

"Top of the morning to you, gentlemen." The Unnamed adjusted his white shirt cuffs beneath his jacket and loosened his tie.

The vampires before him just stared at him.

"Oh, come now. Surely one of you has the balls to say good morning?" He shook his head. "Fallon, you're the eldest, did you not enjoy the dawn this morning . . . or should I rescind the gift?"

"Yes, Your Eminence," Fallon croaked, going down on one knee and lowering his gaze. "I was rendered speechless by the power of your presence and the immeasurable debt of your gift."

The Devil laughed and shook his head. "That is such a punk bitch answer, but quite acceptable coming from you. You're welcome. Stand." He walked along the assembled row of councilmen and then gave his wife a dashing smile. "This morning while you were reveling in the sun and dining, I was walking to and fro. I found this marvelous little cathedral to stop into in Los Angeles County." His smile remained easy, his tone casual as Sebastian genuflected. "Yes, I do broken houses of worship, gentlemen. Those are the best sites for stand-up comedy. Nonetheless, it was strictly business this time. It was all about breaking a Neteru."

"You got Rivera?" Nuit breathed out, despite his fear.

"In due time," the Devil chuckled. "I have his heart and conscience through the demise of one old man."

"The priest," Lilith breathed out. "Oh . . . Lu . . ."

"I just had to get him on broken ground," her husband said, straightening his lapels. "Now that I have done the hard part, I trust that you all can keep the pressure on that Neteru team until I safely position my heir?"

"Done," Lilith said, her narrowed gaze raking her councilmen. "We will keep their focus on putting out small fires everywhere, we will fracture them, we will have them chasing their tails and never the wiser of where your heir will surface."

"Good," he replied. "Because right now in this little test run I did, their Neteru Councils are united. This is precisely why I went topside to test for myself. I went after the father-seer, and Rivera showed up—and the moment an imminent threat to his mortality from me was detected from On High, they sent in their A-squad, along with the female Neteru."

"Adam showed up?" Lilith stepped back, aghast.

"With Hannibal, Nzinga, and Eve, as well as Adam's son, Seth."

Lilith began to pace with her hand over her heart. "Lu . . . you could have been maimed."

He waved her away. "Ach—it was nothing. But I needed to draw their fire to see just how tapped into our movements they are . . . and trust me when I say, they are very, very strong at this juncture. Too strong to be hunting my heir, who is still in chrysalis. Therefore, your mission is to wear them down, fatigue them, break their spirits, and keep their spiritual forces of Light protecting the Neteru team—while I move my heir apparent safely around the globe, positioning him to step into his full inheritance."

"It will be our pleasure to serve your desires," Lilith murmured, her eyes burning black.

He nodded, seeming distracted. "Excellent. I need not tell you how failure will be viewed. We are too close, at this juncture, for me to be disappointed."

"You will not be disappointed," she whispered, watching fire burn behind his black, bar-shaped irises.

"Yolando, where do they live—this Neteru team?" The Unnamed One had spoken without turning his searing gaze on Yonnie. A second of silence too long caused fangs to fill his mouth, as the beast tilted his head and addressed Yonnie again in a deeper tone. "Am I speaking a foreign language?"

"I don't know," Yonnie said in a strangled voice, holding his throat. Power choked the words from his mouth, and the Ultimate Darkness hadn't even moved.

"Now, you know they say the Devil is a liar . . . so don't you think I can spot a lie a mile off?"

"I used to know," Yonnie said, struggling as his feet began to lift off the floor. "But I tried to breach the compound this morning and they silver-burned the location out of my head and barred me from crossing the threshold!"

"You did what?" Lilith screeched and flew at Yonnie with claws extended, her black gown billowing behind her. "You tipped our hand; you have jeopardized everything!" She raked his face, opening up five deep gashes that ran the length of his cheek.

"Patience, my dear," her husband crooned. "I'm curious.

"Why were you there?" the Unnamed One murmured, staring at Yonnie until he began to holler, holding the sides of his skull. "I will go through every one of your synapses until your gray matter is jelly—thus we can do this the easy way or the hard way . . . as always, it is your choice."

"While they were partying, eating, and drinking," Yonnie gasped, "I went to meet with Rivera on the beach—to freak him out, to get inside his head and ultimately inside the compound."

The pressure eased as a sly smile tugged at one side of the Devil's mouth. "Admirable. You used your time well, I see." He inhaled deeply. "I can smell the male Neteru's signature all over you—a hug . . . nice. Brotherly. He still considers you a friend, which means he hasn't completely departed from his old heritage with us. Very nicely done." He chuckled and shook his head. "And you also may very well have contributed to them sending the A-squad of the Neteru Council when I taunted the old priest. Now that they know of the existence of daywalkers, they may be edgy," he added with a murmur. "Frightened and prone to excesses of retaliation . . . which will lead to the breakage of the black horse seal."

Lilith backed away from Yonnie, claws retracted, but there was still a glimmer of distrust in her eyes.

"Who owns this councilman? Who turned him?"

"I did," Fallon Nuit admitted cautiously. "He owes me."

"But I have his soul in escrow, due to a little dispute between councilmen that is boring," Lilith interjected, glaring at Fallon.

Sebastian lowered his gaze, trying to remain as inconspicuous as possible as Yonnie fell to the floor.

"Release that trivial debt to his own recognizance for now. We cannot have any dissension in the ranks at this juncture." The Unnamed One glowered at Yonnie and then smiled. "Fair exchange is no robbery, Yolando . . . but if you screw me, you are well aware that I will return the favor in spades."

"Hold your fire!" Marlene shouted, and then sent her vision of the incoming Neteru squad to the other seers in the house.

Inez, Heather, and Juanita picked up the image before Marlene had jettisoned it, creating a quick mental handoff process that caused the full team to lower arms.

The team met Damali, Carlos, and Father Pat in the family room. They stared at the badly disheveled cleric and then Carlos's ripped and bloodied clothing as Damali and Carlos lowered the elderly man to rest on the sofa. Healers in the group immediately rushed forward. Berkfield almost bumped into Marlene as he dropped to his knees to touch Father Patrick's pulse points.

"God in heaven," Berkfield whispered as he looked at the very thin, very frail man who had once owned a robust, vibrant frame. He took up one knobby hand within his and brought it to his chest.

"What happened?" Marlene asked, eyes wide as she stroked long, white hair away from the father's forehead.

"The Unnamed entered a cathedral in Los Angeles," Damali said quietly as Carlos sought a window for refuge. "Carlos tried to battle the beast, but . . ." Her words trailed off as she shook her head. "The Neterus came and white light protected us and did what they could for Father Pat . . . the rest will take time."

"You went up against Lucifer alone, dude?" Rider wiped his palms down his face and leaned against the wall with a thud. "Remind me to just shut the fuck up if I ever have issues with you."

"Word," Jose said, his gaze going between Carlos and the dozing cleric. "But the question is, are *you* all right, man?"

When Carlos didn't answer, all eyes went to Damali. She simply nodded and drew a shaky breath.

"We need to get Father Pat among his fellow clerics—folks that can devote twenty-four-seven vigil around him. His body is healed but his mind . . ."

Damali looked at Carlos's back slowly expanding and contracting, and she briefly closed her eyes as she heard him swallow hard.

"The Beast gang-banged his mind," Carlos said in a thick, angry tone. "Every offense of the Catholic church throughout history—the very thing Father took issue with—is eating his brain from the inside out. He can see it, feel it, smell it . . . just like I can. We're linked, and he was my father-seer. Only difference is, I been to hell and lived there a while, so the shit is ugly but ain't bugging me out. Although some of the scenes from the Inquisition ain't no joke."

"Baby . . ." Damali started across the room and then stopped as Carlos held up one hand without looking at her.

He turned slowly, his eyes closed, lids fluttering. "I'm siphoning it to me, wrapping that shit up in silver, and sending it back to that sonofabitch on a hot wire. That, I'm sure he didn't bank on . . . that I'd been through enough shit on my own to step between his assault and Father P. Father don't have to take the brunt of this, not ever."

Before anyone could protest, Carlos spun around, pointed toward the window, and a white energy jolt left him in a pulse that rattled the house.

"Fuck you!' Carlos yelled, blowing out the windows on the south side of the house. He whirled on the team as Father Patrick opened his eyes. "They would have turned that man into a vegetable! Not having it!"

"Okay, we need to get this man into the custody of Imam Asula, Rabbi Zeitloff, and Monk Lin, stat." Damali rushed over to Father Patrick and took up his hand from Berkfield. "Father, can you understand me? Can you travel?"

Father Patrick nodded, tears streaming down his face, his lips moving with no sound coming out. A thin line of drool ran down the corner of his mouth, and Damali quickly wiped it away and kissed his forehead before Carlos saw his mentor's true condition.

"I'm on it," J.L. said, flipping down a comm board that was encased within the walnut paneling beneath the wall-mounted flat-screen TV. His fingers became a blur as Carlos's incessant pacing left a trail of blue-white flames that scorched the rug.

"Patching through to safe houses 336, 255, and 156. Hello, Brooklyn, you there? Come in, Chicago. San Fran, you there?"

"Shalom. Asalamu alaikum. Namaste."

Three windows opened on the large flat-screen monitor, each with a member of the Covenant within it. J.L. blotted the perspiration from his brow. "We've got a situation urgent. A Covenant seer down. Primary breach of a cathedral. The man took a black charge. One of our Nets is drawing mental poison—Net Council did the body healing. They got Father P."

"Tell them we might need a really high-level exorcism," Rider said, his eyes holding a battling combination of empathy and worry. "Not even Marlene can go in there behind that."

"Patrick," Rabbi Zeitloff yelled into the receiver. "My friend and brother, do not allow the liar to take root in your mind. We will call upon the Archangel Raphael, as in the Book of Tobit, where he is one of the seven spirits before the Throne of God. His name means God Heals, do not forget this! No matter what you were shown."

"We rebuke Asmodeus, the destroyer. Allah will have no mercy upon he who attacks His own."

"My friend," Monk Lin said quietly, so calmly that his voice was like tranquil, flowing water. "I honor in you the divine that still exists . . . that I honor within myself and I know we are one. You are not alone in this."

"Asula," Father Patrick gasped, "I saw what we did, what terrible, terrible things we did!"

Berkfield restrained the elderly man and helped him to lie back when he tried to fight to stand. "Easy, easy there, Father. Listen to your friends, they are telling the truth—you-know-who lied."

"That's just it—it wasn't lies!" Father Patrick shrieked.

"It was truth," Imam Asula bellowed, his voice seeming to calm the upset priest. "But it was not the Almighty. No matter what house of worship, these evil deeds were the misdirected deeds of sick and twisted men. Even as we speak my own faith is splintered in factions that have killed and smote each other in the so-called name of righteousness. This shames me also, but it is not of the truth. It is of the Ultimate Liar. You must see past the horrors and know that these abominations done by man, in the name of your sanctuary, were not of heaven . . . they are not of the All. And, yet, even with these horrors, there are still men and women of good that have moved mountains and helped many."

"Bring him to Brooklyn," Rabbi Zeitloff said with a husky, tear-constricted voice. "Patrick, don't you worry. In Revelations 9:16, does it not say there are two hundred million angels at the ready? If it's war, then we need you in that number—but alive, fighting those rat bastards to the very end. So you keep remembering that."

"Yeah," Carlos said, "Brooklyn it is. I like how you're rolling, Rabbi. That's what *I'm* talking about."

"The brothers will envision you in the purity of the center of the Lotus, and we shall hold you there in constant, unrelenting meditation," Monk Lin said, his voice tight with emotion.

Father Patrick closed his eyes and nodded, too overwhelmed to speak.

"I wanna send some encapsulated messages to the Guardian

teams worldwide," J.L. said, his fingers becoming a blur on the keyboard again. "I need a white-light burst."

"Psalm 91," Father Patrick said weakly. "As my brethren . . ."

"Consider it done," Imam Asula said and he bowed his head in unison with the others displayed on the monitor, and before long they began the solemn prayer in a monotone chant.

"Send it," Rabbi Zeitloff said.

J.L. nodded and pushed SEND. The tension in the room made the static over the system microphone crackle. The three clerics looked up at once, having received J.L.'s transmission that daywalkers were afoot.

"Bring that man to Brooklyn!" Rabbi Zeitloff shouted into the mic. "We have something for them here that they will not soon forget!"

"Done," Carlos said, walking back toward the window. "End transmission, brother. We're out."

J.L. nodded. There was no reason for him to repeat the command; the clerics heard it, and each signed off with a silent prayer. J.L. could feel each one literally coat his skin with a low, buzzing blue charge of protection.

"Point of order," Big Mike said, drawing Carlos's attention. "If we've got a daywalker problem, and the real McCoy is strolling topside—y'all can go to Brooklyn, I'm heading south with 'Nez like I told her to go get the baby and her momma."

"Right now they're in Atlanta, D," Inez said, looking away from Carlos, whose expression hadn't softened to her plight. "When the flooding hit Texas, the Covenant sent them there to higher ground—remember, girl?"

"I feel you," Carlos said in a sullen tone, "but here's my issue. Right now, they are flying under radar. The Ultimate Darkness doesn't know where they are, and just like he can't see where we are, due to the white-light barriers in full effect, they can't see Ayana and your momma. We go splitting the team up, then there's four of you at risk, not to mention it weakens the hub here." He shook his head. "Too dangerous, y'all."

"They went into *a church*, Carlos," Inez said between her teeth, pointing at Father Patrick. "They got to *a priest*."

Carlos rubbed his palms down his face. "They breached a parish and a specific cathedral that had issues. That's how they were able to attack a seasoned veteran . . . so if they did that to him, you've gotta know, 'Nez, that my stomach is twisted up just thinking what they can do to a three-year-old and your mother—I don't want them anywhere near this compound. *Comprende?* Your baby girl and momma are probably in the safest place, with Covenant members who don't have the issues that cathedral did, so their haven can't be breached."

The team's focus followed the slowly escalating debate like it was a tennis match, but no one was ready to jump in. Each member held the line, standing firmly in the neutral zone, agreeing with both sides, not sure who was right or wrong.

"I want you to listen to me, Carlos," Inez said, her hands finding her meaty hips. "You *comprende* this, brother. You said the word 'probably.' Ain't no such fucking word acceptable when it comes to my kid—*or* my mother. Second thing you said which is giving me the hives, you said you don't want to think what they could do to a three-year-old or my momma. You, brother, who done been to hell and back telling me some shit like that means I'm out this gotdanged door right now, you clear. I don't care if all three councilmen show up in Atlanta, they will get they asses beat the fuck down."

Mike shrugged and pushed off the wall, then flipped open his cell phone. "I'll see y'all in New York." He turned to Inez. "You pack whatchu gonna take, I'll get the flight . . . calling for a Covenant lift outta here so's I can bring my shit."

"Oh, Jesus H. Christ!" Carlos yelled. "All right, all right, look . . . if we do a fold-away to Atlanta, full team, then what happens when we get to your momma's, 'Nez?" He began walking and talking with his hands. "I've got a sick Covenant cleric who needs immediate evac. That means, once in Atlanta, I'd have to fold-away your momma and Ayana with us to Brooklyn—because once they're out of the safe house seals, they're targets. They've gotta get with the supernatural real quick, might be in a firefight up in Brooklyn, and gotta be able to hang. I don't want that shit on my conscience—got enough that'll keep me up at night till I'm a very old man."

"What if you dropped us off?" Big Mike said, aiming for an obvious compromise. "We get there, roll up on mom like everything's cool—you know, take a Hummer fully loaded with ammo. Collect her and the baby and drive on up to New York . . . we'll be there to protect 'em, and can break the news to them real easy on the way. The baby's too young to know, so she ain't no problem."

"Mike, listen to yourself, man," Carlos said with his arms outstretched. "How long a drive is it from Atlanta to New York, barring traffic and any drama you might run into on the road? What . . . twelve, fourteen hours . . . longer 'cause you're with a little kid and an elderly passenger that has to stop and eat and pee? We can anoint the Hummer, bro, but what about that eighteen-wheeler they send to crush you in a multicar pileup? What about the bridge they make collapse? How many ways can they kill a Guardian with a baby on board in twelve to fourteen hours, huh!"

"What if I go with them?" Damali said quietly. "Each squad would have a Neteru with them, baby."

Carlos paced away from her, dragging his fingers through his hair. "You were there in the church, right? You saw who's up to bat—or is it just me that has a healthy respect for this particular adversary?"

"I know how to do the fold-away now," Damali said, undaunted. Her voice was serene, just like her gaze. "Ayana knows

Auntie Damali. So does Mom Delores. If they see me coming through the door with Mike and 'Nez, for them, it's all good."

"And after you get them, then what, D?" Carlos whirled on her, his eyes blazing silver. "What're you gonna do, show them your wings!"

"Yeah . . . if it gets crazy," Damali said. She didn't blink and didn't stutter and slowly folded her arms over her chest. "I hear you loud and clear, I know your concern is for their safety—but this is a woman type of thing. . . . Carlos, Inez is going to go get her baby; right, wrong, no matter if it's strategic or not. And, if they see some heat in a battle, I'd rather that baby confuse me with an angel and feel like that's what helped her momma, step-dad, and nana . . . than to have you bust in there with silver eyes and fangs. The poor woman would faint dead away."

"D's got a point, Carlos," Juanita said, pushing off the love seat she'd been leaning on. "I know for a fact that, if they saw Damali's wings come out, they'd be in awe, not in fear, and would be able to hear anything she gotta say after that. But, *hombre,* for real, *for real*—if you battle bulk and drop fang to fight something off, by the time you got back to the innocents you was supposed to rescue, they'd be dead of a damned heart attack . . . sheeit, I know my momma would. An angel, hell yeah, she could deal with that. But the grille you got when you pissed off, Carlos, no way."

"Aw'ight, fine. I don't know what I'm talking about. But what about the drive, the—"

"I'll sit them down," Damali said softly. "I'll explain things in degrees, and since Inez's momma is a praying woman, I'll break it down straight from Scripture . . . then I'll do the fold-away, Hummer and all, to the Big Apple. It will be a miracle."

"And once in New York, outside the seal . . . and when they see the rest of the team? Marj, how'd you handle it in Heathrow airport, huh?"

"I thought I was having a nervous breakdown," Marj said quietly, but folded her arms in defiance. "I cried, I screamed, I freaked out—but my children and husband were with me. And if they had not been, I would have stabbed Richard to death to get to my babies if he thought he was going to keep me from them once I'd learned what was really out there . . . the stuff of nightmares."

Berkfield shrugged. "Give it up, Carlos. Me and Marj been taking bets on how long Inez would last without her kid, anyway. Far as I can see it, she beat the odds making it this long."

Inez walked over to Berkfield and slapped him five. "My point, exactly."

Rider held up his hands in front of his chest. "Don't look at me—I don't have kids, and me and Tara are definitely out of range for that to be a possibility. We're Switzerland on the subject."

"No . . ." Tara said evenly. "We are not Switzerland or neutral." She released a long, emotion-filled breath. "I was robbed of my chance—dead before twenty. If I had a child and I knew vampires walked by day, as well as something so much worse, that child would be on my hip. Period, end of story."

"My bad," Rider said with a shrug. "I was just trying to see it from Rivera's angle . . . a baby in the compound, as well as a civilian changes things dramatically—but, hey, I go with the flow. Y'all gonna make me take up smoking again, though, I swear."

"Anybody else got a problem with it?" Inez said, pecking her neck.

"Not at all," Heather said, stepping close to Inez and then out of the blue, she hugged her. "You're blessed. We'll all share her, okay? Can I be Auntie Heather?"

Inez's gaze held Heather's shimmering gaze for a moment. "Sure, girl."

"Oh, for the love of pete," Rider muttered and walked to stand by Carlos.

"We'll need to give her momma a full tour of the house so she knows what alarms not to trip, and I'm gonna have to work on baby-proofing the artillery room . . . that would be tragic," J. L. said as he stood up and began walking the perimeter of the room. "Need door latches, or maybe retina scans to open certain doors . . . not sure, gotta redesign the whole house . . . I'll be on it."

"It's worth it," Krissy said, nodding toward Inez. "We can make this work." She looked away. "We need to address this subject anyway."

"Why?" J.L. said, jerking his attention toward her, panic in his eyes.

"Because it's gonna come up again," Juanita said flatly.

"Could happen to any one of us," Jasmine said, her gaze going to Inez. "We'll all help take care of her. I know what it is to grow up without my mom. She shouldn't have to."

J.L.'s shoulders dropped by two inches as Dan got up from the ottoman he'd been sitting on and began to pace. Jose simply stared at Juanita without blinking. Bobby stood and rubbed his palms down his face.

"Uh, yeah," Bobby said. "We need a contingency plan."

"Lawd have mercy." Marlene closed her eyes and allowed her head to drop back.

"All right. I guess human nature is what it is, last days or not," Shabazz said in a philosophical tone. "So we do Brooklyn and connect with the Harlem team up 'round 131st while D goes with Inez and Mike to handle their business."

The silver jolt hit the back of his skull like a sledgehammer, and, enraged, his talons extended to catch the offending orb. The throbbing, hot mass made his palm sizzle as he stared at it with a slit gaze. But soon, awareness washed over him in small increments. A wry smile tugged at one side of his mouth as he summoned his wife.

"Lilith—look what that boy sent us," he said, throwing his head back and laughing.

The moment she materialized he held out the silver orb, amused as she hissed and recoiled from it.

"I forgot, you prefer gold, but you *must* share this with me. He sent me back my visions from the priest's mind . . . all wrapped in silver."

"I can't," she stammered, backing away from him. "Have I displeased you, already . . . the day is not even over, my Greatness."

"No, no, no, you misunderstand my intentions. This has been a glorious day."

He sighed and held the smoldering orb away from his body and made a fist to shield Lilith from it. Soon it cooled, dried, and crumbled to a fine powder, and he allowed it to sift from his palm slowly onto the end table by his massive, black marble bed. With a toothy grin he sat down, produced two golden straws, and separated the powder into narrow, white lines.

"All of the iniquity of one of the largest churches on the planet . . . since the Crusades, including the Spanish Inquisition and up to the latest American scandals." He winked at her and licked his bottom lip. "Want a hit?"

"Oh, Lu," she murmured, coming to him and kissing his shoulders as he bent and did a line. She accepted a straw and flicked her tongue over his powdered nostril. "You really are in rare form today, aren't you?"

CHAPTER FOUR

Lilith strolled back into Vampire Council Chambers, blotting her running nose with the back of her wrist. Almost stumbling as she made her way across the expanse of veined marble floor, she adjusted her formfitting black gown before sliding into her throne.

"Damn . . ." she murmured in appreciation with her eyes closed as she leaned her head back briefly, lost in thought. "I swear one day that man will be the death of me." After a moment, she lifted her head weakly and stared at her mute councilmen. "And what are you doing here? Didn't you hear what the man said—you should be out there doing damage, stirring the cauldron . . . something other than gawking at me."

Fallon Nuit made a tent with his fingers before his mouth as though carefully considering his words before he spoke. "I think it's fair to say that the three of us needed a moment . . . to recover. It had been an eventful morning and no one wants to find out at high noon that their daylight powers have been rescinded."

"No lie," Yonnie said, smoothing his palm over his throat where he'd been choked.

"We wanted to be sure we were following orders to the

strictest adherence to your whims—I mean wishes, Madam Chairwoman." Sebastian's pale complexion whitened as he looked down and began nervously picking at his cuticles.

Lilith waved her hand dismissively. "Spare me. Lu is in such a buoyant mood right now that torching you three is the last thing on his mind."

"Be that as it may," Nuit pressed on, his gaze holding hers. "I'm sure that you can imagine how unique a visit like his was . . . in council. In past times, such an event was rare and it meant someone's imminent extermination."

"True," Lilith said, giggling and still high. "All right . . . I admit, he is given to excessive violence, so sue the man. But this morning he was very mellow. This could have been a disaster— *Yolando.*"

A droll smile tugged at Nuit's mouth. "You've learned well from your partner in crime Rivera . . . you've gotten a pardon from the source no one can trump. But I haven't forgotten, Yolando. Rest assured."

Yonnie smiled and raised his middle finger to Nuit.

"Are we free to leave, then, is what you're saying?" Sebastian countered, glaring at the quiet power struggle between Nuit and Yonnie.

"I'm telling you to get the hell out of here before Lu possibly strolls back in here and sees you all sipping blood and not on the job." She took up her golden goblet and leaned it beneath one of the star points of the pentagram-shaped table, filling it to the brim with black blood. "Knock 'em dead," she said, raising her goblet and taking a healthy swig from it. "I'm headed to the Middle East where Lu likes to play—I suggest you boys make nice and wreak plenty of havoc while we're gone."

Nuit blew her a kiss and stood. "My specialty is children at risk, *chérie.* I will make it the best of times and the worst of times." He chuckled when Yonnie stared at him, unable to hide both his alarm and curiosity. But he knew Yonnie could never tip his hand by showing concern in front of Lilith.

Yonnie gave Nuit and Sebastian a curt nod and then turned to address Lilith. "I'm out."

In a grand sweeping gesture, Nuit bowed. *"Au revoir."*

Sebastian stood slowly and looked around Council Chambers and then at Lilith.

"Well?" she snapped, growing annoyed. When he didn't immediately answer, she leaned forward and narrowed her gaze. "I know," she hissed between her teeth, "that you cannot believe you are getting laid this morning?"

"No," Sebastian said, lifting his chin. "I'm talking about rebuilding." He motioned to the two unoccupied thrones. "Full council is six of us, including you as the Chairwoman, yes?"

Lilith brought her goblet to her lips, smiling around its obstruction.

"Then while the other are terrorizing the Neteru team in whatever manner most delights them, permit me to bring you some newly made masters for consideration . . . the best of the covens, Lilith," he said, dropping his voice to a seductive murmur in *Dananu*.

"You caught me at a very auspicious time, Sebastian . . . while I'm high and recently sated by the best of the dark realms. Your request has merit."

"The others didn't think to request it—they are looking at outside conquest . . . spreading themselves and the empire thin without consideration of rebuilding critical infrastructure as quickly as we will soon be growing. I saw this bring Mother Russia to her knees socially and economically, and we cannot afford such a slip in strategic deployment at the end of days."

Lilith set her goblet down with precision, her glowing black eyes never leaving Sebastian. "Keep talking to me like that this morning, and you might get lucky in chambers after all."

A divided mind while on a mission was a dangerous thing, she knew . . . almost as dangerous as splitting the team at a time like this. Damali held Inez's hand as they walked around from behind the manicured hedges onto the front walkway of the property. She just prayed no one saw Big Mike appear like a huge genie. She could hear it now, some poor retiree in the gated community screaming her head off or some little kid trying to make his mother believe that *Kazam* was actually real.

But the thing that disturbed her the most was Carlos's state of mind. No matter what he'd said, he'd absorbed a hellified negative charge today. His nerves were already rattled going in, after seeing Yonnie walk by day. Then add an attack on Father Pat—too much. Now this? Civilians in the compound. No matter how hard he seemed, she knew Carlos, knew her husband's deepest fears. And it was a scenario like this, where a little kid or an elderly woman might be put in harm's way.

That was the only reason she hadn't argued, truly hadn't said much. Right now he so badly needed someone to be on his side, to see his point of view, but by the same token, regarding this—there was no other choice.

"Yaya, you're too quiet in there for grandma," Delores Filgueiras called out from the kitchen as she cut the crusts off a peanut butter and jelly sandwich. "You hear me? You'd better be behaving yourself—come on down here and wash your hands for lunch."

Fascinated, the child watched the tall man who appeared in the window.

He floated! She giggled when he put one finger to his lips.

She looked over her shoulder, somehow knowing that he didn't want Nana to see him. He could put words in her mind that she understood. Sometimes she didn't understand big people, the grown-ups, but him she understood. He wanted her to open the window and say it was okay for him to come in. She never had a secret friend before. Nana was careful about friends.

"Can you open the window for me, sweetie, so we can be friends?"

He made her giggle again, sending tickles across her belly.

"Okay."

She had to climb up on her doll chair to reach the thing Nana turned and it was hard. But she was a big girl.

"I do it myself," she said with triumph, happy when the hard thing turned.

"Yes . . . you are a very big girl," he said in a nice voice. "I am very proud of you. Just lift the edge of the window and say, 'Come in,' and I will."

That was hard, too, lifting the heavy window.

"My room is pretty!" She waved her hand around so he'd see all the Powder Puff dolls and her pink and white bed.

"You have to say, 'Come in, please'; I can't see it so well from out here."

"Oh!" She giggled. "Come in, please."

But something wasn't right. His face was getting scary. His eyes made her want to cry. She should go get Nana! But her legs wouldn't work. His smile was ugly now. He had big teeth. The tickles now felt like buggies were crawling over her. *Nana, Nana, it's the bogey man! Angels, make the bogey man go away!*

A high-pitched scream at a decibel that could shatter glass exited the child's mouth. Fallon held his ears for a moment, stunned, as a knifing pain shot through his temples. Surrounding the brat in a black box, he blotted his forehead with the sleeve of his jacket, glad to have momentarily silenced her voice.

Where the hell had the child learned so young to call the angels with a piercing voice like that?

"Oh, Jesus! Father God, help me! Get thee behind me, Satan!" a strange woman shrieked.

"Silence!" Nuit bellowed and blew her through the door. He heard her collide with something, but had to struggle for composure for a moment after hearing the names of blasphemy hurled at him.

He couldn't believe the woman's foolish nature. She wanted to die, that was clear. She was running at him with a piece of banister post. Nuit outstretched his arm to call her heart into his hand.

A loud bang of wood hitting plaster jerked his attention away from the fallen woman and the black-boxed child. The front door had been kicked in. The translucent shield around the toddler dropped, her screams boring into his ears like a dentist's drill. He cast her aside roughly, the goal to cause her small head to split open against the wall like an overripe melon—anything to stop the incessant screaming. But she hit the mattress instead and scrambled into a corner, still screeching at the top of her tiny lungs.

Behind him, the window crashed. Shards of glass flew toward him like mini razors. Multiple gunshots sounded; hallowed earth shells told him the Guardians had been called. The sickening scent of prayer dirt revolted him. The huge male Guardian barreled through the door . . . he'd wanted to kill that one for so many years, he could taste it. One snatch and the giant Guardian's throat was in his hands. His attention was again jerked to the floor. The old woman had thrown the Guardian the wooden banister piece. Seconds later, it sliced into his side.

Howling with fury, he overturned every piece of furniture in the room, yanking the wood out of his side and sending it whizzing into the palm of the oversized Guardian that had assaulted him, pinning him to the wall. Turning wildly, he looked for his prize—the female Guardian's child. He looked up in time to see the child behind her weapons-bearing mother.

Her two hands holding a single Glock 9mm, eyes lethal, firing off rounds almost faster than he could dodge, the female Guardian was definitely prepared to die. It was in her eyes and in her sweat. Nuit licked his lips. Admirable. He'd feed well on her. The big male had torn his hand away from the wall, leaving flesh, and had broken off a section of bedpost as the furniture flew by him. Cock-strong and insane . . . he wasn't sure which Guardian he wanted to feed on more. But that old bitch had to stop screaming prayers! It was weakening him. Deafening him!

Nuit turned and stopped short, just in time to hear the Isis blade chime, missing his head by millimeters as he fell back and became mist.

"Mommy's got you, Mommy's got you," Inez soothed, clutching her child to her chest with her right arm extended, still wielding the Glock.

"Mercy of mercies, Father hear my prayer," Mrs. Delores sobbed, continually crossing herself as she struggled to get to her daughter and granddaughter. "The Devil almost got that baby—aw, Lord, what is going on? Look at Michael, oh, my God! He'll bleed to death—what's this terrible world coming to . . . this must be the end of days, Jesus! If I hadn't come up those steps, if y'all hadn't come when you did . . ."

"It's gonna be all right, Momma. We knew to come. I had a bad feeling for the last coupla days. I got you, Momma . . . it's all right. Ain't nobody gonna hurt you. Me, Mike, and Damali won't let 'em hurt you or our baby, I promise." Inez sunk to the floor with her child on her lap and began crying hard. "I told you, D! I told you! A mother knows! What, then, if I had listened to Carlos, huh?"

Damali looked around at the devastation and knelt down beside Inez and her mother. Inez was rocking her sobbing toddler and hurriedly trying to feel across her mother's body at the same time, searching for demon nicks and injuries. She watched sadness fill Mike's eyes as he tore off a section of bed linen and wrapped it around his destroyed hand.

No time like the present. She had to get them out of there, but also had to assure the older woman that she nor her daughter and granddaughter would die. Damali touched Mrs. Filgueiras's arm.

"Mom Delores . . . tell me if you're hurt," Damali said calmly.

"Heal my momma up, D!" Inez said, growing hysterical. "Did he bite you, Momma? Did he scratch you?"

"He, he . . . he . . . pushed me real hard, but I don't even remember him touching me. All of a sudden my back hit the banister and I almost fell over it. I hit it so hard that a few posts came out and I almost went over the rail. But the baby was still in there with him." Her voice dissolved into a new round of sobs as she clutched Damali's hand. "I heard something snap inside me, but I had to keep going . . . I used whatever I could, and it was the banister post . . . and I kept coming for him. He would have to just kill me dead, that's all. Not that beautiful child was all I could think. My own daughter had been abused, you had almost been abused—I jus' couldn't take no mo'. Not Ayana! And then it felt like my heart was about to explode out of my chest. I must have blacked out, because I fell again . . . and then y'all started shooting."

"You lie still," Damali said, soothing her. "It's probably a rib, because you were mobile. It's not your back or your legs."

"I can't be up in no hospital with a predator trying to come for my grandchild! I can't live in this house no more, you hear me!"

"You won't have to, Mom," Damali said quietly, and then

looked up at Mike. He towered over them like a massive oak tree, casting a shadow of support, blood running down his arm staining the rose-pink rug, his eyes set as hard as his jaw.

"How you holding up?" Damali asked, gazing up at him.

"I'm cool. Is there a nick on the baby? That sonofabitch flung her. Coulda killed her with the impact against the wall, if the bed hadn't broken her fall."

Damali shook her head. "She's not nicked. Breathe, brother. Breathe."

Inez crossed herself and squeezed her eyes shut, kissing her daughter's soft, cinnamon brown cheek.

"But can I see her for a moment?" Damali asked, reaching out for Ayana.

Ayana shook her head and buried her face against her mother's neck, clinging to her for dear life.

"Aunt Damali just wants to make the bad man go away from your mind, all right, sweetie?" She looked at Inez for support and had to blink back tears as the child wailed when her mother pried her off her body. "Oh, baby . . . oh, sweetie . . . I'm gonna give you right back to your mother—see, she's only an inch away."

Inez wiped her face with both hands.

"My grandbaby's gonna be scarred in her little mind and heart for life," Mom Delores said in a strangled whisper, closing her eyes tightly and forcing more tears to roll down her cheeks. "Jesus, please hear my prayer . . . just blot this stain outta her mind."

"No, Mom, she's not gonna carry this burden," Damali said calmly, stroking the child's profusion of light brown, silky curls. She kissed the top of Ayana's brow and then rested her cheek on the crown of her head, her hand at the toddler's back, feeling her stressed breathing slowly beginning to relax. "He was a bad man and you called the angels, didn't you, sweetie? I know, because I used to do that when I was a little girl." The child immediately popped a thumb into her mouth and began sucking hard.

"Did you know that angels are real and can really come when you call them for protection?"

"That's right," Inez said. "Auntie Damali's been my angel all my life."

Ayana peeked at her mother and then peered at her grandmother for confirmation.

"Yes, baby, you know how Nana says to pray, right? Angels came, musta sent your mommy just when we needed her . . . and Daddy Mike . . . you remember how he fought, hear. He wasn't gonna let anything happen to you, just like me, your momma, and Auntie Damali chased that bad man away."

"Like the other lady did, too?"

The adults glimpsed each other and Big Mike stooped down. "What she look like, boo?"

The child shrugged and spoke in a soft mumble around her thumb. "Miss Christine angel is pretty. She said keep screaming to make him go away. She didn't let me hit my head on the wall when he pushed me."

Damali hugged the child closer and shut her eyes for a moment so that her voice wouldn't quaver when she spoke. "You remember what Christine angel said, but I want you to forget all about that bad man . . ."

"Uh-uh, D," Mike said, standing. "She need to remember what he looks like—not to haunt her, take that . . . but don't take away her understanding of bad men, bad entities. Christine told her right—fight, scream, run, get somebody until she's big enough to kill one of them SOBs herself. You better than anybody oughta know that, D. She gotta learn young, they all do. If she coming to live with us, some of her innocence is gonna be compromised."

Mrs. Delores struggled to sit up but couldn't. She dropped down panting as she winced in pain. "What's he talking about?"

she gasped. "Her innocence compromised by living with her mother and new stepfather? Y'all better tell me something I can understand. You all selling drugs? Is that why that man came to kidnap that baby—swear to me that—"

"No, Mom, I swear to you—"

"Then tell me how y'all got all this money? Ain't that much touring and showbiz in the world when you all was off for two years and just got back up on the road. Now you've got hit men climbing through windows in black suits—we ain't never had this kinda trouble in our lives, Inez. What is he, a mobster promoter—what are you all into that has brought death, hell, and destruction to this door!"

"Mom, the only way I can explain it to you is to show it to you. That man who came to the door was pure evil . . . and Yaya can see angels." Damali lifted her locks up off her neck to let the air-conditioning cool her nape.

Tears filled Inez's mother's eyes. "I can't breathe, my heart is breaking, and I don't understand how you all can live with yourselves . . . money is the root of all evil, and you kids today just don't care how you make it, do you? I thought better of you, Damali. Inez, *you know* I raised you better! And, Michael Roberts, if you are the one who got these girls all turned around, don't you *ever* darken my doorstep again. Carlos Rivera was a drug dealer when I heard about him years ago, Damali—*years ago.* Now you're with his gang and running with all them rappers? Who you in trouble with?"

"Momma, we are in trouble . . . on the run, but not from who you think—it's so hard to explain, and I don't wanna hurt you. I've tried to keep you from it, but now it's at your door and it won't ever go away. I love you, Momma." Inez covered her face and sobbed into her hands.

"Show her, D," Mike said, going to the windows and checking for an intruder, as well as listening to sirens getting closer.

"Inez, I will fight you in court for my granddaughter," her mother shouted, sobbing as loudly as her daughter. Yelling in hiccupping jags, she hollered over Ayana's tears, too, ignoring the child's bleating wails not to make her mommy go away. "I'll take her with me back home to the old country before I see her . . ."

"Let me take the pain, Mom Delores," Damali said as calmly and gently as she could. "Let me heal you."

"D, we need to be on the move before Po Po gets here—ain't no explaining this." Mike looked up and down the street from his post at the window, sure that neighbors who'd seen him would say that some big black man shot up the normally serene neighborhood and abducted an entire family.

"I'm not going nowhere with y'all! Let the police come. Until you have your own, you won't know pain like this . . . to see your child get twisted around and led to the darkness! Every child starts out like my Ayana, every one of them, then this cruel, misbegotten world changes your baby." The older woman sunk even closer to the floor and covered her face and wailed.

Damali yanked up the back of her T-shirt and let her wings unfurl to their full span. Mrs. Filgueiras looked up and slowly covered her heart with her hand. Ayana became calm again as Damali handed her off to her mother. Inez intensely kissed her daughter's hair, rocking her back and forth. As only a child would, Ayana reached out from beyond her mother's clutches, unafraid, and gently fingered the soft feathers in awe.

"Like Christine's?" Damali said, smiling at the toddler.

Ayana shook her head. "I didn't touch hers. They were just sunshine."

"Oh . . . light . . . ah . . . a lot of light. Bright."

The child beamed at her. "Uh-huh."

He carried Father Patrick up the stairs of the Brooklyn safe house like he was an infant, laboring up each step from heartbreak.

He'd had to clean him up before he could transport him. The man had soiled himself, and yet the vestiges of his old self glimpsed through the haze just enough for his dignity to be assaulted.

Carlos drew a deep breath as Jose and Rider flanked him. The man in his arms was getting weaker, as though something was unraveling his life force like a ball of twine. And now there was an SOS transmission stabbing into his mind from Damali. The team had taken fire from Nuit. Carlos ran his tongue over his incisors. He couldn't respond, his hands were literally full. He was standing on the threshold of a synagogue, and all he could do for now was pray that they had enough firepower to keep the Darkness at bay.

Yonnie retraced his steps very carefully, going to the beach, which was now the only place Carlos would allow him along the property line—that and the mountains. But he had to get word to his boy that an all-out assault was about to go down . . . the kind that ruined people forever. They were taking no prisoners. Neither age nor gender mattered. His boss was a respecter of neither. They knew about Inez's baby girl. How, he couldn't fathom, but the Devil knew a lot of shit. Had spies everywhere. And that pussy, Nuit, was trying to gain favor by doing something really foul. Truth be told, the only thing that saved his ass, as well as the compound from a direct hit, was that Carlos and D had prayer blocked him when they did.

As he walked along the shoreline, Yonnie chuckled sadly. Who would have thought that *a prayer,* of all things, would wind up saving his ass from Lu? A prayer, mind you, that got put up as a barrier to keep his horny ass from straight-snatching Tara out of the house at dawn. Yonnie shook his head and then suddenly bent over laughing.

"Oh, shit! I can't believe it. Rivera, where are you, man?"

A silver-tipped arrow whizzed so close to his spine as he stooped over that it singed the back of his Armani suit as it passed him. There was nowhere to take cover on the naked beach. Pivoting quickly, he avoided another one and threw up a translucent black shield against the onslaught of silver fire raining on him.

Fangs dropped, battle bulked and ready for war, he scanned the beach so outraged that a heart-snatch was imminent. But that's when he saw her. She touched down, wings spread, ebony skin drenched with sweat, platinum locks lifted on the wind—a blade in hand. No fear in her eyes. Dressed like a Viking. *Dayum.* He foolishly flung away the translucent shield to get a closer look.

"Yo, yo, yo," he called out, trying to stop her before she took a lunge at him. "I definitely come in peace, baby."

"Be gone, demon! Defiler of the Neteru sanctuary!"

She swung and her blade tip sliced the front of his suit as he backed up.

"Rivera was holding out on you, 'cause a brother *never* told me you were on his squad. Good gotdamn! Where'd you come from?"

She swung wild, fury rising as he pivoted into mist and reappeared, forcing her to expend energy that he loved watching her use.

"To the end!" she yelled, yanking a dagger from her boots.

"To the bloody fucking end . . . whew, baby, sho' you right!" Yonnie whirled away as she swung again, stole a quick kiss, and backed up before she lopped off his head. "Seriously, Ma, where you from? You a new Guardian recruit, Angel Company, or what?"

She released a war cry that made him shudder as she flung her dagger hard at his throat and then gripped her blade with both hands. He stopped the dagger a quarter inch from his Adam's apple.

"Let's talk, baby—it don't have to be all this . . ."

"From the edges of Nod to the ends of the earth, I will protect those I pledged to stand with, demon! Know that!" she yelled, heaving in deep gulps of air between swings. "There is no negotiation, liar, trickster!"

"Whoa, whoa, ma. You've got the wrong man." Yonnie grabbed the hovering dagger out of the air where he'd frozen it and tossed it back to her. "Do I look like I'm trying to fight you, sis?"

She caught the dagger with one hand, breathing hard.

"You ain't no joke with a blade, girl."

She pointed her sword at him. "Who are you—friend or foe?"

"Friend, baby. Me and Rivera go way back . . . me and D, too, kinda."

"Then where are they?" she spat, dragging in huge breaths.

"Their windows are in shambles, a silver energy pulse was released containing toxin. My Neteru Queen's pearl shrieked all the way to Nod that Carlos was being attacked by *the Darkness!*"

"Youse a baad *ass*—gangsta, baby—shit! If you thought that's who I was and came out here buck wild, just swinging crazy, ready to die on the beach for family? Takes heart. Much respect," Yonnie said, slapping his chest. "To see that in a woman . . . uhmmph, uhmmph, uhmmph."

"Do not evade my questions!" she said, frustration making her blade bounce.

"I'm not," he said. "I came here looking for them, too—because I know who's on their ass, but I'm not him, aw'ight?" Yonnie began circling her, watching the sun glisten against her dark skin and enjoying how she turned with him, never giving him her back. "You're really from the forbidden realm and got out . . . like a jailbreak and whatnot, too?"

"We are no longer incarcerated since the first two seals have been broken—we are not criminals."

"Hey, I was just saying, 'cause I found that rather sexy myself . . . that you broke outta the joint over the big edict," he said, pointing upward but unable to elaborate, "just to have Damali and Carlos's back. Like I said, respect. Plus you got a divine transmission . . ." Yonnie stopped circling her and shook his head. "So, uh, I guess if you're an angel, I could really get smoked if, uh, you know, we got to know each other better?"

"If you attempt to molest me, I will cut out your heart."

"No, naw, you got me all wrong . . . I ain't into all that. I know some real wicked motherfuckers who like that kinda thing, but that ain't never been my style. I was just wondering because I half expected a thunderbolt to come out of the sky for the kiss . . . you know, given the wings. But I guess since you ain't really supposed to be here, your people upstairs don't have your back like they should?" He peered around her. "But damn . . . I'd have your back day and night—if you'd let me."

"My people have my back," she said between her teeth. "Valkyries never leave their own."

"Whoa, whoa, whoa . . . what?"

She withdrew and angrily stared at him without blinking.

Suddenly Yonnie burst out laughing. "*Git* the fuck outta here. You're a for-real Valkyrie?"

"That is my name and that is what I am. Do not cast aspersion on my mixed parentage, demon. You walk by day but carry the fangs of the undead—half human, half dreaded ones, and dare to speak ill of my—"

"Hey, I ain't talking about your people, girl. Don't get all salty on me. Chill."

He walked away from her a little to give her space, thoroughly admiring her beautiful features and voluptuous, athletic body. "I'm the last one to speak ill of a person's background, okay. So let's get that out of the way up-front. Next, I'm an old, old friend of Rivera's—before he went into the Light . . . so, I have some issues to deal with still . . . like prayer lines fuck me up. But I can take you to breakfast at this nice little café I know about. Maybe we can talk, girl. I'll buy you some clothes, because as much as I love the view, you're gonna have to fit in with the locals or you'll give yourself away. Then, maybe together, we can find the family? I've got some definite science I need to drop on them."

He watched her narrow her gaze as she ruefully considered her wings.

"They don't retract," she said quietly. "The humans will know what I am. I cannot go on a search for the Neterus without bringing notice their way."

"But you ain't got no silver in your veins or anything that could be hazardous to a brother's health, right?"

"No," she said, looking away with shame. "I'm red-blooded . . . that part is human, if that's what you're asking."

Yonnie cocked his head to the side and smiled, licking his lips. "Com 'ere, baby. I'm a master at illusion."

"Show me from where I stand. I still do not trust you."

"Cool," he said, waving his hand in her direction. "Look behind you."

She screamed and felt her back with her hands, panicked as she dropped her sword. Then she looked down at her clothes. She now wore a sexy red tank top, red mules, and black leather jeans. "My wings!"

"They're there, just blending in really well with the background. You can still knock over people's drinks in a club, but whatever background they're up against, they'll be camouflaged . . . until you say you want them back."

"I wish I could see . . . wish I had a mirror . . . I've always wondered what it would be like to fit in with the true humans . . ."

"Ain't all it's cracked up to be, Ma. I like a woman with a little supernatural somethin'—but that's just my personal taste." Yonnie backed away and left a full-length antique mirror where he'd been standing, careful to remain on the back side of it. He watched the expression on her face slowly give way to awe as she covered her mouth and walked forward, stroking her barely visible wings and staring at her reflection.

"How did you do that . . . the mirror and my wings?"

"Aw, it ain't nothin' . . . just a little sleight of hand, boo." He studied her carefully as she turned around and stared at her image. "You're really a beautiful woman, Val. Fine as shit, with wings or without. A gangsta warrior, too . . . I might not be able to take you everywhere I gotta go . . . but I wouldn't mind hanging out with you while I try to find out what's happened to our friends."

"I can't believe you did this," she said quietly, still staring forward and then looked up at him with her beautiful, wide brown eyes.

"This ain't nothing baby," Yonnie said in a low, seductive murmur. He ran his tongue over his incisors, willing them to stay concealed. "If you think this was da bomb, just wait till after breakfast."

℮ CHAPTER FIVE

There was no reconciling the rage. No escape from it. Fury had burrowed itself so deeply within him that he could literally feel it pulsing through his spinal fluid. How was he just supposed to let some shit like this go? He'd delivered someone a near vegetable—who was as close to his natural father as it gets into the hands of the man's clerical brethren. For a warrior like Father Pat, for any man, as far as he was concerned, that was an indignity worse than death itself . . . and the Darkness knew that.

"It's gonna be all right, man," Rider said, landing a supportive palm on Carlos's shoulder.

Carlos gave him a searing sideways glance that made Rider slowly remove his hand. "How you figure?"

"All right, partner," Rider said, keeping his voice low within the assembled group. "It might not be all right. Ever." He stared at Carlos, trying to reach through the rage to reestablish their team bond. "But we've got your back, though."

"Where I might have to go," Carlos said between lengthening fangs, "I can't ask you to have my back."

"Aw'ight, man," Shabazz said, stepping into the inner ring of senior Guardians.

Shabazz looked around at the assembled team, noting that

Dan and Bobby were still with the clerics, gathering last-minute details. Only the female team members were present. He cut a glaze toward Marlene, who subtly nodded. Yeah, this was man business. Shabazz gave the others the eye to back off so that only he, Rider, Jose, Berkfield, and J.L. remained. Even Marlene stepped back, reading Shabazz's expression.

"Listen to me real good. Where you're at right now is an extremely dangerous place for a man like you to be," Shabazz said in a quiet but firm tone.

"You have no idea," Carlos shot back in a very even voice.

"You're about to allow your anger get you played. Go back to *The Art of War,* man . . . warfare is the Tao of deception. You've got to be strategic and make them think they got you to your core—then come up with a plan . . . not go in there swinging buck wild because fury's got the best of you. That's basic, brother. Even though they did your family—which is all the more reason to fall back and lay for their asses."

Shabazz waited a beat, breaking through in tiny increments. "Your eyes are glowing red at the edges of the silver, and I haven't seen that since you were dead. Bad combination. I want you to think about this place where you're at right now, because we both know it wasn't no accident that you wound up here."

"But wherever this shit takes you, *hombre,* we wit you all the way. Even if you decide to go after you-know-who."

Jose pounded Carlos's fist, but Carlos looked away after the exchange. No. It wasn't about that, taking Guardians up against the beast. That was pure Neteru action, no matter that they were crazy enough to ride or die with him. Problem was, they probably wouldn't die . . . at least not right away. That reality jarred him enough to make him begin to amp down.

Rider landed a hand on Carlos's shoulder again. "This is the rough ride part, dude. We all know they're coming for our family, next of kin, if they can figure out who they are. There's never a way to reconcile a casualty, especially not losing some-body as close as Father P . . . we're all fucked up with you, bro."

"But just like when your partner gets shot . . . and this is what they do, you know they went out their way. Not from some shit like cancer or a worthless DUI car accident." Berkfield stared at Carlos as their gazes locked. "He went down in the line of duty, doing what he devoted his life to. God have mercy on him, and maybe the clerics can do something. But for now, we can't let this rattle our cages so bad that we lose position."

"When it's time, man, we'll rig some real wicked shit like we always do to shove down their throats to leave a smoking black hole," J.L. said, fury simmering in his eyes.

Carlos finally nodded and rubbed both palms down his face, retracting his fangs. It messed with his head no end that, instead of him being the one to give this rally speech, the brothers had to keep *him* from losing it. All this shit was out of order, and he hated every minute of it.

He glanced around the small marble and stained-glass-ensconced foyer that hid the team from prying eyes on the street. "We need to make it over to Phat G's place in Harlem."

He didn't want to talk about Father Patrick's quickly deterio-rating condition. He didn't want to say good-bye to a man who didn't know if he was there or not, or even who he was. Rabbi Zeitloff had him, Monk Lin and Imam Asula were en route, and this place was a prayer citadel as far as he could tell. That would have to be enough for now. There was nothing else he could do—and that was perhaps the most damning part of it all.

"I got G on a prayer-secured sat phone, will make sure we get us a table in the back," J.L. said. "Will do everybody some good to refuel and get our heads together."

"I buy the first round," Berkfield said, slinging an arm over Carlos's shoulder. "I'll show you how we used to do this when I was on the force."

Carlos nodded, his vocal cords wouldn't work. Now they were about to have a good old-fashioned Irish wake. How fitting.

Lilith rolled over and sighed. The warm Vampire Council Chamber floor met her nude back, and she idly pushed the blood along one of the veins within the black marble while staring up at the transporter cloud of bats in the vaulted ceiling. Sebastian lifted himself up on one elbow, stroking one of her Harpies that had scuttled between them. The small, gargoyle-like creature fawned at the attention beneath Sebastian's long fingers, nipping him every so often to get a treat of blood.

"Give me your candidates," Lilith cooed, her voice drifting. "Your style is so much different than Lu's that I often forget how relaxing a primarily cerebral screw can be."

Sebastian smiled and kissed her bare shoulder. "Thank you, Your Highness." He hesitated, anticipation building as he studied her profile to gauge her mood. "I've thought of this for you for some time now . . . I think you'll be pleased."

"I'm growing more curious by the second to see who you'd propose. As one of the most adept necromancers, and now that Lu says I can raise whomever I want from the Sea of Perpetual Agony, I'm sure I'll also enjoy your enlivening demonstration when you bring them back."

"To be sure," he breathed, nipping her shoulder and shooing the stray Harpie away. "Lilith . . . what about Lucrezia Borgia?" He waited as she turned to stare at him.

A slow smile spread across Lilith's face.

"You approve?"

She arched her neck, causing her onyx tresses to spill in a fan across the floor as she laughed hard. "Oh, that is so rich!"

Nervous, Sebastian sat up and snapped twice, causing a golden scroll to appear out of thin air and to hover near her face. "This lush, redheaded, Italian beauty had three husbands—two murdered, one cuckolded and disgraced—plus a number of affairs . . . a true black widow. She is the queen of poisons. The Borgias were notor—"

"Oh, put that thing away," Lilith said, waving her hand and sitting up. "I know her vile resume all too well. Her brother, a *cardinal* with the name *Caesar,* how fitting, was her lover and sired her illegitimate heir, while her first husband was dispatched for allegedly being impotent, which made things *so messy* to annul, unless she would admit to the affair—not. I loved the duplicity in her style. Ah, yes, then they also went about murdering her second husband . . . all the while her father was a *pope,* for crying out loud. I do believe she was also his lover, too . . . and I think she was engaged twice by the age of eleven. In any event, as I recall, she had a passion for white arsenic dispensed from gorgeous rings . . . such a jewelry slut if ever I saw one, but a true Renaissance woman in every sense of the word. I definitely approve."

"I am glad you're happy . . . I think Fallon will like this treacherous European beauty, too."

Lilith chuckled. "I'm sure he'll admire her for her adept utilization of *poudre de succession* . . . inheritance powder, as they say in France. We could also use a poisons specialist to work hand-in-glove with your magnificent spell-casting abilities. But don't get jealous . . . when I'm sure Fallon wins her from you. Prepare your nerves in advance, darling. I can see the handwriting on that particular wall, and she's not even reanimated yet."

Sebastian didn't move as Lilith stood and slowly began to materialize her black gown to cover herself.

"Oh, come now—don't pout," she crooned. "He is, after all, *French,* she's Italian. . . . Both are very passionate, thus you must resign yourself to the inevitable. But the one thing I cannot allow is any further dissension in our ranks at this delicate hour."

"I am already resigned and actually chose her for him."

Sebastian smiled as Lilith sat down in her throne carefully, watching him with the element of surprise subtly shaping her expression.

"Now I am intrigued," she said, taking up her golden blood goblet and sipping from it slowly. "If you chose such a luscious candidate for Fallon, whom you openly abhor . . . then this next candidate must be very special."

"She is," Sebastian admitted quietly, standing and robing in one lithe motion. He began to pace with his hands behind his back. "Initially I thought of Wu Zetian from the sixth century . . . for her power—"

"Oh, hell no!" Lilith screeched, standing and sloshing blood. "That bitch and I would literally lock horns in chambers from the onset." Lilith set down her goblet and folded her arms over her chest as Sebastian gazed at her, seeming amused. "While I definitely admire her ruthlessness . . . to murder one's own infant daughter just to frame the Empress with the crime in order to take her husband, not to mention to ultimately depose her own sons to rule an empire—*that* I can respect. But her ambitions would be—"

"Unmanageable. That is why I'm not suggesting her."

Lilith shook her head and arched an eyebrow. "Toy with me again, Sebastian, and I might turn ugly this afternoon."

He walked to his throne and sat. Lilith raked him with her gaze.

"The thought of this candidate is so titillating that it's given you an erection . . . oh, this one I must know immediately."

"Elizabeth. I want Vlad's Elizabeth."

Lilith's eyes widened as she covered her mouth. "You are insane! And I love it!"

"Vlad the Impaler, our own Dracula, made her his mate a hundred years beyond his death—she is from *Hungary*, Lilith. She is from my same earth, the same Carpathians . . . her hair deep brunette, her features like fine porcelain, oh, Lilith," he said, standing and beginning to pace again. "Fallon cannot have her if I raise her for you. Do you know her triumphs?"

Sebastian stopped at the table's edge and closed his eyes with a shudder. "She murdered over fifty virgins and *bathed* in their blood . . . records at her trial said she'd tortured six hundred and fifty maidens in Castle Csejthe within the province of Transylvania. Her woman servant, Dorothea Szentes, was a witch—Lilith, this candidate knows black magic from the original chasm of Dracula's lair. Then the human betrayers walled this gorgeous, brilliant blood hunter in her bedroom lair within her own castle. They literally put her behind brick dust and mortar, surrounded her with prayer lines so she could not feed, and they allowed her to starve to death. It was an atrocity, a blight on the history of vampirism!"

"Let me think about this," Lilith said with a smirk.

Sebastian dropped to his knees. "Lilith, I have never begged you for anything such as this . . . but she even bit the skin off their faces."

"You know Fallon is a superior lover to you, correct?" Lilith shrugged.

"But Elizabeth is more of a sadist than a sexual being—that's why I want her!"

"Dracula was an excellent lover—insanely creative . . . I was at his coronation." Lilith pressed a finger to her lips for a moment. "Two issues trouble me. One, she may really resent that you aren't her dead husband when she awakens, which gets us right back to the dissension dilemma. Two, Fallon has more of Dracula's style, and she may ultimately go to him of her own volition."

"Not if you help me," Sebastian said, his eyes desperate. "You could enhance my capacities . . . you know my failings."

"You must really want her, my friend, to strike such a deal like that one in hell."

"I do . . . I have fantasized about her since she was created."
He looked at Lilith without blinking and spoke in *Dananu*.
"Name your price."

"Let me get back to you with a rain check—I want an open
ticket to claim what I desire later," she murmured in *Dananu*,
staring at his groin.

"Done."

Lilith tilted her head. "Lucrezia is a better match for him . . .
but to raise Liz Bathory without her mate will create such a stir,
politically. By rights, Vlad, for all his valor, should be raised,
but—"

"Since when have you been politically correct, Lilith?" Sebastian stood and swept over to his throne, fuming. "He was
finally defeated and turned to ash. To the victor goes the spoils
of war, and I still stand in the end of days! I have dreamt of
her, *lusted* for her, *for centuries* . . . but no one would dare cross
Vlad while he was in power. I can raise her, as well as her
sorceress."

"Oh, now, calm yourself. I just wanted to see you beg . . . of
course I approve. Just don't forget you owe me." Lilith sat down
with a flourish. "But my next question is a very simple one, as
my goal is still to keep down all dissension at council, like I said.
What about Yolando? You know he's had two mates ripped
from him very recently; you don't think this will cause unnecessary challenges at the table? And although he is somewhat
more traditional in style . . . my, my, my, he is a natural wonder.
Might Elizabeth take it in her head to—"

"Fuck him," Sebastian snarled, and then took a healthy swig
from his goblet. "He doesn't do sadists and she doesn't do vampires with a predilection for humans after what she's been
through. There are only two open seats at council, and he's not
old enough to appreciate the beauties of the past. Besides,

Yolando likes to indulge in cheap human vanities in Tijuana, last I'd heard. Let him pick one of them to turn."

The storage area in the back of Phat G's joint was just barely large enough to hold the team. Jose caught a metal rack of canned goods and BBQ sauce before it fell. The scent of grilled meats filled the air as they exited the pantry into the galley kitchen in the back. A massive, ebony-hued chef wielding a butcher's knife and hacking beef ribs glanced up, but never stopped chopping.

"What's up, family?"

"It's all you, Mo," Carlos said, pounding fists with the chef.

Fry cooks, grill chefs, and waitresses nodded to the team, and the Guardians took in the stainless-steel environment that was loaded with razor-sharp cutlery and interesting panels that drew J.L.'s attention.

"Yeah," Mo said, chuckling deep in his throat. "We hot-wired up in here. It's all good."

Rider inhaled deeply with Jose. "Mike oughta see this."

"Naw, 'cause he might never leave." Jose motioned to a vat of greens and long metal trays of macaroni and cheese and candied yams as the fry cook dropped a load of battered green tomatoes into a vat. "We got a brother who would definitely appreciate the cuisine."

"The problem would be detoxing both him and Inez after coming through here," Marlene said with a smile.

"Oh, don't worry," Mo said, laughing. "We gonna feed you like family up in here, and we gonna introduce you all around— that's Oscar, Keith, Ty." He motioned toward the kitchen exit with a greasy butcher knife. "Phat G is up front at the bar. It's the weekend, so the joint is jumpin'. Bikers hit us Friday and Saturdays, cops come in during the week . . . families on Sunday, so you know, like I said, it's all good."

A half-smile pulled at Carlos's cheek. There was something comforting in the chaos of the kitchen in a way that felt like home.

"I've got a coupla vegetarians in the group and a couple of brothers that don't do pork." Carlos looked around the kitchen for a moment knowing it was time to water his horses. A menu hit him in the chest and he caught it, still feeling a tactical Guardian's charge coming off it.

"Up here at Monsta Burgers, we got da Big Ass Pulled Pork Platter for those who indulge, the Big Ass Beef Rib Platter, Big Ass BBQ Chicken Platter, and none of the sides are made with meat, so need I go on?" Mo said.

"Thanks, bro—I'm straight," Shabazz said, pounding his fist. "Nice tactical sling, too."

Mo nodded. "Phat gonna introduce you to the team. Mostly tacticals and seers—but we can tune this kitchen up and sling this shit in here like it's a Ginsu knife commercial, feel me. We slices and dices mofos who ain't cool."

"I feel you," Carlos said, nodding. "That's good to know."

"Chantay gonna take y'all to a VIP table we put aside. It's nice to finally meet the legend, you know?" Mo smiled widely, one gold tooth reflecting the overhead lights. Then with a swift pivot that should have belonged to a much thinner man, he sucked in a deep breath and hollered, "Chantay! Yo, git dese folks a table!"

Dan pored over the menu as they walked toward the kitchen door. "It really says Big Ass Pulled Pork Platter." He glanced at Bobby and J.L. "I mean, in writing. Literally."

But before anyone could comment, the kitchen doors swung wide open. A petite, brown-skinned waitress with shoulder-length braids and a sexy, beef-fed figure strutted into the kitchen with one hand on her hip. Annoyance flared in her big brown eyes, and her mouth was pursed in a pout.

"Mo—what I tell you about hollering for me like that? It ain't professional!"

"We got VIPs up in here, girl . . . don't get all new."

"Who VIP?" She crossed her arms and resumed chewing her gum, looking the team up and down, unimpressed. "What group y'all with?"

"You get your e-mail this morning?" Mo countered, frowning.

"No. I pulled a double last night, so?"

"Hi," Marlene said, stepping forward and extending her hand. "Open a channel and I'll send, sis."

The young woman's eyes widened as her gaze shot from Guardian to Guardian. "Oh, my Gawd! Does Phat know y'all are here? Oh, I got your table. Oh, my Gawd—which one is Damali?"

"My wife will be here shortly with some more fam," Carlos said, swallowing a smile.

"Oh, no! Carlos Rivera's up in da house?" Chantay ran to the kitchen doors and burst through them. Her yell mixed in with the din of the lively crowd and the blare of muddy water blues. "Lisa! Nyya, Carmen, Adrienne—y'all are gonna die! Go git Annette and Roshida and tell TayTay to leave the bar for a minute! Where's Anthony and Rene? Make sure Rodriguez blesses those tables good, yo!"

Chantay came back to the chuckling group with a wide grin. "I just wanna shake your hand, brother. Heard all about your squad." Carlos didn't have a chance to answer her before she turned on Mo. "You ain't say VIP-type VIP, man! I swear!"

Marlene winked at Carlos. "So much for a low-key reception."

Damali set them down on the building's roof. She knew coming out of her first fold-away, Mom Delores was going to scream bloody murder. She and Inez waited for the distraught woman to slump against Big Mike's steady hold, but Ayana loved it and simply clapped her hands.

Gently laying the older woman down, they waited. That's all one could do. The poor woman had fainted and it was best to allow her to slowly come to, gather her wits, and then they could open the huge metal door to walk down the steps. From there, they could find a ladies' room to splash some cold water on her face. In the meanwhile, they had to pass entrance inspection protocol.

Mike and Damali nodded at the large Guardian sentry that was obviously already prepared for their arrival. He lowered the assault weapon and smiled, rushing over to them.

"You got injured, sis? I'll get a medic evac stat—how bad is she? Is she nicked?"

"No, this is her first flight," Damali said. "But thanks, brother."

Mike pounded the man's fist. "Even though we fam, under the circumstances jumping off these days, you might wanna make us recite something from a holy text . . . just my recommendation."

"Oh, yeah, oh, yeah, sho' you right," the rifleman said. "But I saw her wings and I figured that was a sign."

"Under normal circumstances," Mike countered. "But like I said, we in some strange times. Seen some new entities with feathers but they ain't hardly on our side."

"I feel you, bro. Good lookin' out. I'll pass the word." The Guardian smiled, his pecan complexion catching the late-afternoon sun. Nodding, he straightened his urban guerilla beret that was jauntily cocked to the side, causing the brass and copper Ankh he wore like dog tags to swing against his fatigue jacket.

"You're Damali, right? Phat G said you'd be here—your family is downstairs. I'm Anthony."

"Pleased to meet you," Damali said, turning to introduce the others. "This is Big Mike, Inez, her Ayana, and . . . well, Mom Delores, who is having a real hard time with all of this."

"You hold tight, I'll get her some water—and will get a couple of brothers up here to help her downstairs . . ."

"I got her, man," Mike countered. "She don't weigh more than two-fifty, two-sixty—I'm good."

Anthony looked from Mike to the large, prostrate woman on the ground, and then his ripped-up T-shirt and jeans that bore bloodstains. "But you bleeding, man . . . dayum—I heard about the Neteru team. Y'all straight, gangsta."

"Thanks so much," Inez said and then lifted her braids off her neck. "My momma's been through a lot . . . she don't need all this, but there's nothing we can do."

Anthony nodded again and then shrugged as he pulled out a cell phone. "End of days, what can you do? She's still standing and ain't nicked, so you blessed, sis. We'll make sure Momma is okay." He turned away from them and spoke quickly into the phone. "Send Rodriguez and Rene up here with some water and a triple-XL T-shirt so the team's strongman won't cause a buzz in the crowd—we've got the rest of the Net squad with two civilians . . . and the momma ain't feeling none of this. Go light on the weapons, ya mean. If she sees heavy artillery, you might have to thump on her chest."

Mom Delores groaned and began to come to. Inez and Mike tended to her and the baby while Damali's thoughts drifted. They were a family within the larger family. The stakes had risen yet again. She briefly closed her eyes and blotted perspiration from her brow. God walk with her husband. His nerves were shot, his father was dying. When was it ever going to stop?

It was only a few moments to wait for water and Mike's fresh shirt, but time was doing funny things in her mind. It was still the same day, and yet it felt like it had been a yearlong siege. The bombardment began at dawn with daywalkers and hadn't let up since. If she wasn't so wired, she would have done what Mom Delores had done and just laid down on the flat roof.

Damali scanned the horizon, watching the low-hanging sun cast late-afternoon gold on the monstrous skeletal structure of train tracks looming above. Long gray columns of steel, stories-high, bisected wide boulevards by the river. Dinosaur bones, they seemed. At one time that species roamed freely, so they say. The bones told the story. That was all that remained. Now they were gone. It left dizzying questions for a thinking mind.

She wondered if humans would finally be wiped out, and if so, then what? A new Genesis as promised? And who would be that first man and first woman to step out of the primordial pool, or out of the clay? Would God even bother again after all this madness? Would husband and wife still share a rib? After the Armageddon, who would tell the story . . . or would the epic be left in the bones and ashes, fossils pieced together by a curious alien species that wouldn't begin to have a clue. Damali looked up as the metal door to the roof opened, thinking about what the last dinosaurs on earth would have told paleontologists about their finals days before the apocalypse.

"This is Minister Rodriguez—he blesses us up and keeps us tight . . . and this is the Professor, Rene . . . brother is tight on the research we need. Lisa, our Guardian sister, also got a son, Rene. It's all fam, you know."

Fists got pounded, bear hugs shared. It was good to be home, and a safe house was just that—a home. Seeing other seemingly regular people helped Mom Delores, as did the bottled water. Damali glimpsed Ayana, who held her mother around the neck, taking it all in.

"The whole building is sealed in prayer," Minister Rodriguez said. "We own the whole thing, every floor. The restaurant on the bottom keeps us going, keeps us in ammo and supplies."

"Minister, we can't thank you enough—"

"No, just Rod. And it's our pleasure to have you in our house." He beamed at Damali and then looked up at Mike. "You're gonna love the grub here, man. Downstairs they told me you put a hurtin' on ribs."

"That be true, that be true," Mike said, laughing.

"Imagine cooking for him and the team," Inez said with a growing smile.

Laughter poured over the small retinue as they walked, serving as balm to everyone's tattered nerves. It was perfect medicine, a necessary release.

"There's a false half floor between the first floor and second," Rene said as they walked through the redbrick structure. "UV hot-wired, ammo stashed, leads out in case this joint gets crashed. We've got a Situation Room on three, backup generators to the backup generators . . . me and your technical man need to do a walk-through. Then we've got suites—just apartments hooked up for incoming family and permanent residence for our squad."

"This is primo real estate, bro," Mike said, impressed.

"Historic, too," Anthony said proudly. "Practically around the corner is the Cotton Club, so like, we ain't trying to blow up this end of Harlem or Harlem period. Our tacticals work with the trains; can show your squad how we jump the cars and pull power off the third rails in a tight spot to hot vamps that come too close to home."

"That is *brilliant*," Damali said, quietly monitoring Mom Delores's composure. "But right now, how about we all fall back, eat, and rest."

Just like they all did, Inez's mother needed a moment of normalcy to balance her mind. Food at a down-home eating establishment would go a long way.

They were ushered into a huge ground-floor dining facility. Damali and Inez glanced around with Big Mike. Inez slipped her mother's hand into hers. As they passed tables, they noticed a huge wall rack being used as a seating divider that was filled with fireplace logs that were suspiciously filed down to stake points. Colorful designer graffiti graced the walls, with scenes of dinosaurs and monsters riding bikes.

"Monsta Burgers," Damali said, pointing out a sign and a menu header before Inez's mom could pass out again.

She watched the older woman release a deep breath and hold Mike's arm tighter.

"Oh . . ." Mom Delores sighed and briefly closed her eyes. "I feel like Alice through the looking glass."

"I feel like that a lot of days myself, Mom," Damali said, keeping her moving toward their destination tables in the back.

It was like walking a skittish racehorse to the starting gate; one needed blinders to accomplish the task. Hells Angels bikers were parked out front. Couples sat at the long, family-style picnic tables set haphazardly outside on the sidewalk, waiting to get inside. The bar was packed, seven to eight deep, with high plank wood tables in clusters that encouraged one to talk to people they didn't necessarily already know.

Between the music thumping and the servers running mega platters from the kitchen to the tables, not to mention the volume of conversations, one look at Mrs. Filgueiras and the word overstimulation came to mind.

"I think I'm going to be sick," she said quietly to Damali.

"Y'all go sit with the team—lemme get her to a ladies' room."

Hustling past a shoulder-to-shoulder press in the bar, Damali broke through with Inez's mother in tow. She hit the door and whirled around, just in time to catch Mom Delores before she screamed.

She clapped her hand over her mouth and held her tight. "Breathe," Damali said softly in her ear. "It's just wall art. You okay?"

Inez's mother nodded as Damali slowly lowered her hand. Both women stared at the wall for a moment. Every inch was covered with bold graffiti, scribbles, splashes of red paint, you name it. But what had drawn the near shriek was the life-size, buxom, female demon riding a motorcycle on the back of the open stall.

"What would possess them to put something like this on the walls!" Mrs. Filgueiras gasped, fanning herself.

Damali turned on the tap. "After a while at this, people get a little twisted. Sorta like painting shark teeth on the nose of a WWII fighter plane when you know you have a fifty-fifty chance of crashing in the Atlantic Ocean, I guess? The name of the restaurant is Monsta Burgers, Mom . . . so I think it's a play on words—you know, we eat them for lunch and dinner . . . er, uh, the way they try to feed on us. I'd put money on it."

She handed Mom Delores a wet paper towel. "You'll feel better in a little while, and I want you to talk to Marjorie Berkfield. She had this happen to her and had to leave the suburbs and join the team with her two teenagers overnight, along with her husband. I think she'll be able to share some of her early fears and how she coped best."

What else could she say? If she sat the poor woman down with any of the old heads, or even some of the newbies, they'd terrorize her already embattled mind with war stories. Hell, even Jasmine would be talking about growing up in Philippine brothels and being indebted to a witch who became a vampire after being bitten by the Devil's wife.

Damali tore a paper towel from the rack and wet it for herself, leaving it on her face for a moment. Juanita—nope. 'Nita's visions even scared her sometimes. Heather, aw hell no . . . a Stonehenger? Krissy . . . maybe—a telekinetic wasn't too bad. But any wizard stuff in that line would freak her out for sure. Marge and Marlene; someone who'd been in her shoes, and an older sister raised in the south, whom Mom Delores could relate to.

"Baby . . . can I ask you something?"

Damali took the paper towel off her face as though suddenly remembering Mom Delores was even in the room.

"Sure, Mom." She leaned against the sink and stared at the woman's tear-glistening eyes.

"That day you ran away from my house . . . because of what my husband tried to do to you . . ." She looked down and hugged herself, her voice faltering. "Did he kill you and you came back as an angel? Is this why I'm being punished . . . because I didn't see the signs and—"

"No, no, no, no, no. Oh, Mom," Damali whispered, going to the woman and hugging her. Soft sobs pelted her chest. "I never died. I'm alive. And this isn't happening to punish you—you aren't responsible for what he did behind your back."

"Then why do I feel like maybe I never really woke up this morning or that maybe I had a heart attack in the kitchen while making lunch for Ayana . . . and this is how it is when you cross over? I keep asking myself if I'm really alive, not dead . . . not trapped in hell like you hear about lost souls, not realizing I'm already gone?"

Tight fists clutched the back of Damali's T-shirt as bitter sobs rained on her neck and shoulders. All she could do was rock the woman, understanding exactly where she was. But there'd be no waking up from this reality, and all she could do was ride it out with her.

"Everything I believed, everything normal is gone," Mom Delores wailed. "I feel like I'm losing my mind and the only thing keeping me glued together is prayers in my head and seeing you with angel wings."

@ CHAPTER SIX

Carlos stared down the long wooden table, listening to the conversation, but not. His focus had shifted for a moment to the tension in the ladies' room. To tell Inez's mother it was gonna be all right was a trivial use of words. It *was not* going to be all right—it was going to be whatever it was. But "all right" didn't begin to cover it.

Still, the old woman's wails cut through the noisy crowd in a way that only he could hear in his mind. It was even out of range for Big Mike—either that or he was doing a really good job of letting it ride. Carlos cradled his skull for a second, his elbows on the table. Her cries might as well have been his mother's sobs. He tried to pull away from the memory of her loss, but couldn't.

The eddy of thoughts had him, the emotional current swift. He glimpsed Dan, remembering meeting his parents—a nice older couple living in the safe bubble of unknowing. Should he bring them in, too? There was no way to know. The person he might have asked was dying from a black-charge hit he should have never gotten where he was. The man had been in church! Carlos's hands left his skull and became fists.

A thick-bodied brother heading their way with static rolling through his locks cut a swath in the crowd. The distraction was needed, was a relief. Carlos had to keep himself from slumping once the wave of rage receded.

"Welcome, family—you met Mo, Oscar, Keith, and Ty in the kitchen . . . well, I'm Phat G," he said, reaching across the table to shake everybody's hand. "Y'all also met the Minister already, Rod, plus who we call the Pharaoh, that would be brother Ant, and the Professor, Rene—our security core. Then our badass seers, Miss Chantay, Adrienne, Lisa, Nyya, Carmen, Annette, Ro, and Tay. LaShonda is on street lookout. The girl is fierce military with a body to go with it—making sure nothing snags innocents coming to or leaving this joint. We're still building after a few firefights, recently . . . you know, trying to get the number back up to twenty-one. But we ain't gonna go there, may they rest in peace. Whatever you want, food and drinks on the house—that's how we do up here."

"Yo man, the hospitality is over the top. Thank you," Carlos said, giving Phat G a slight bow from where he sat. "But you better let us pay for Mike's plates—plural—and Rider's bar tab, or you might not wanna have us back."

The table exploded with raucous laughter. He needed that right now. The noise was a shield, the laugher was, too. It blotted out thought as the Guardians began talking trash and ordering food. It spiked memories of times in hotels after the band did their thing, times after firefights when they'd won. Later, they could take a building tour. It would hold down the stress. Later they could talk about the technology J.L. was kicking back and forth online with Phat G. Right now, he couldn't wrap his brain around reverse-imaging cameras that took cold-reading bit map points, then converted them into digital dot graphics that could be run through 3-D modeling software to build a portrait of something that was supposedly non-photographable. Carlos simply stared at J.L. and G.

His mind was jumping all over the place, couldn't hold focus. Oh, shit . . . Carlos wiped his palms down his face. The conversation at the table suddenly sounded muffled. Where was his wife? He'd seen her come in there and go into the bathroom with Mom Delores. He wasn't a drug dealer anymore—where did that come from? Random thoughts stabbed into his brain out of nowhere.

"Whatchu having, hon?"

Carlos snapped out of the haze and just stared at Chantay for a moment. "Uh . . . what's good? There's so much on here that blows my mind, I don't know where to start."

"Everybody says that when they come up in here," she said with a big smile. "That's 'cause Mo and G really stole my South Carolina secret sauce when I came to N.Y.C. to show 'em how to do the thing right. But we ain't gonna get into all that." She made the crew at the table laugh and then licked the end of her pencil before pressing it down on her pad. "Ribs here are a must-do, if you're a carnivore. Plus, the greens—say no more, and the mac and cheese will give you a food-gasm. Save room, though, baby—'cause we got this pecan sweet potato pie and this banana-coconut bread pudding that'll make you hurt yourself. Lynchburg lemonade made with Jack Daniel's and served in a mason jar crusted with big-grain sugar to top you off. Or you could just get the Big Ass Pulled Pork and fall out, okaaay? That's what I would get, if I was new here."

"Whoooo-weee," Mike said, shaking his head. "I just done fount my *favorite* restaurant—besides my baby's cooking, of course." Mike offered Inez a sheepish grin, making the table erupt with laughter again and then looked down at the menu with longing. "Since Rivera's still deciding, you can gimme all that you just said, *plus* the Big Ass Pulled Pork."

"Hit me right off with the Lynchburg lemonade, darlin'," Rider said with a big grin. "I'd be much obliged. No sense standing on ceremony. How many firefights we been in half-lit?"

Jose laughed hard and pounded Rider's fist with Shabazz. "I believe that's half of what pulled us through, *holmes.*"

"Yeah," Carlos finally said after the order came back around to him again. "Same thing you did for Mike, minus the pulled pork platter." He stared at the ladies' room door. "You can also do a vegan platter with fried green tomatoes, greens, yams, and corn bread for my wife—with a Corona. 'Nez, order something for your mom, too, sis." He stood. "I just need to go check on them."

He excused himself; the team kept talking, but he could feel Marlene's eyes on his back. Something close to panic was drawing him to Damali's energy pattern. But rather than unnecessarily barging into the ladies' room, when he got to the door he stopped—feeling foolish.

"You all right, D?" he called out, hoping she would just come out.

"We're good," she yelled back. "Me and Mom Delores are just talking, baby. We'll be at the table real soon."

"Oh . . . okay . . . uh . . . we're ordering . . . just wanted to be sure we got something you'd like."

"You know what to get for me, but order light for Mom. Her stomach is still a little queasy. All right, baby?"

Carlos held on to the door frame when he heard the older woman hurl. "Okay, I'ma go back to the table and let folks know everything's cool."

"Thanks, baby."

Damali's words rang in his ears, causing him to pivot too quickly to walk back to the table, and he almost took out a server who was dashing back to the kitchen. Two deep breaths, he steadied himself and began walking after the near collision. When he got to the table he made the muscles in his face relax before he met Inez's and Mike's eyes.

For a moment, he didn't know what to do. He had to stop

bugging. The vibe here was cool. The energy flow safe. It was a good place to bed down for the night. A good place to water the horses. But why did he feel like he was ready to jump out of his skin? Worse, why did he feel like if he didn't see Damali or sit in her presence, he'd lose it? Carlos sat down at the table. Everyone looked at him for a report.

"How's she doing?" Inez asked, trying to keep Ayana busy. "I should go to her and—"

"No, no, it's cool. Damali's got her and Ayana needs your lap right now."

Mike put a supportive arm over Inez's shoulder. "It's gonna be all right."

Carlos nodded, reassuring Inez. "D said to order her something light, though."

He and Mike shared a look as Inez closed her eyes for a moment.

"Her stomach . . ." Inez kissed her daughter's curls.

"Just first flight jitters. She'll be fine, Damali said."

Carlos watched the Guardians relax and after a moment Inez seemed to accept the inevitable. It was what it was. Her mother was going to be upset for a few, but just like everyone else did, she'd make the team transition.

"It's all good?" Shabazz asked, not seeming sure.

"Yeah. They're just talking . . . but Mom is adjusting," Carlos said, as though he had more intel than he did. He reached for a piece of corn bread from the breadbasket, not knowing what else to do with his hands while trying to ignore Marlene's unblinking gaze. He wasn't even hungry, truth be told.

"You look a little tense, C. How you holding up?" Marlene asked quietly, once the normal mealtime banter resumed.

"I'm cool . . . just tired, you know. Rough day." Carlos looked up almost startled and accepted his drink from Chantay. "Thanks, my bad."

"Hey, man, it's all good," she said, mopping up the slight spill from when he'd bumped her.

If he couldn't sense incoming that close, right over his left shoulder, then what the hell . . . there wasn't that much relaxed in the world.

Marlene had that look again that said *open up a private channel.* He shook his head and took a deep swig of his drink, shocked to find himself blinking back tears. The request became more urgent, and he set his drink down with precision and shook his head again, tears burning away.

Pasting on a false smile, he leaned around Krissy's back to speak to Marlene while everyone else was talking.

"I can't," he said in a tense murmur. "Something's worming inside my head, and the only one that I could open a channel like that with is laid out from it already. I don't wanna chance it, Mar. I don't even want D near this."

She nodded, their gazes never leaving each other's. "I've been watching you all day. You two need to make a Neteru Council run, given what you went up against earlier. Let them white light scorch it out before it gets too far in you, Carlos."

He sat back quickly and gave her a curt nod. Senior Guardians picked up on it, but let it ride. That was the way things worked on the team. Go with the flow; deal with the details later. God . . . where was his wife?

He moaned as blueberries mixed with pancakes, butter, and syrup to create a sugary confection in his mouth. As it slid down his throat he braced himself against the table for the expected violent reaction. When he opened his eyes, Valkyrie was staring at him with an unblinking gaze. To his surprise, the sweetness created a warm, comforting slurry inside his belly— not the scorching pain of a dead body rejecting normal human nourishment.

"I've wanted to try these since I was a little kid," Yonnie breathed out.

"Why didn't you?" Her brow creased as she watched him shove another heaping forkful into his mouth. "You were on *this* side," she said, her gaze open with wonder. "You were allowed to flee and stay here as a hybrid. I would have tried *everything* my heart desired."

He swallowed, slowing his chewing . . . thinking of how to answer her. "When I was on this side, I wasn't free." There was no bitterness in his tone, just a statement of fact. "Back when I first wanted these, I was a little kid, but a slave."

Her hand went to her mouth in horror. "The humans *enslaved* hybrids?"

He covered her hand. "That was two hundred years ago. Eat your breakfast before it gets cold."

"But you were a *child*." Pure indignation flared in her eyes. "A little boy!"

He put one finger to his lips as patrons turned to stare at her. But he also smiled. The fact that it bothered her so much meant something. At this juncture, he wasn't sure just what, but it did.

"They don't still do that barbaric practice—and please tell me they do not do so to children?"

"Naw, after the Civil War that ended," he said, swiping a piece of bacon from her plate. "Can I have this, since you're not a meat-eater? Damn this is good."

"But you said two hundred years . . . you were able to live that long outside of Nod?"

Yonnie looked up over the edge of his coffee cup and then set it down very carefully. "Yeah. And they fed me, until I learned to feed myself." He looked down at his plate, unable to meet her innocent, trusting gaze. "But I prefer this." To keep from telling her more, he quietly ate, savoring every flavor that covered his tongue and warmed his insides.

However, her unexpected touch made him stare at the graceful hand that had covered his and then look up into her serene gaze.

"On our side there was a Civil War, too," she said quietly. "It left many casualties, many are wounded in their spirits, still, even after the Neterus came to help our bodies. The food there is not this . . . freedom of choices . . . menus. I'm sorry that I prejudged you because of what you looked like. We had been battling demon forces that cannibalize we blood carriers, and yet, some on our side have the same outward appearance as you . . . when your teeth grow. But evil is not in their hearts. Do you understand my meaning?"

"I have come to learn," he said very slowly, enfolding her hand within his, "that this whole deal is about choice, no matter what. Doesn't matter who your people used to be . . . look at Cain. Perfect example. The brother was a king and lost it all for bullshit. His mom was the *first* Queen, and look how he turned out. And my homeboy . . . now that's a brother who made some ridiculous choices and came up in the Light." Yonnie shook his head, his eyes never leaving hers. He couldn't answer her directly, but he could give her a bit of personal philosophy to ponder.

"You mean, Carlos, of whom you speak so fondly?" Her voice was quiet and reverent.

"He'd died, crossed over, took a hell throne, was the baddest mutha in the valley—still is—but his ass was crazy-dark for a minute. Then, he made a choice and it's all about the silver, feel me? So, right now, I'm choosing to eat blueberry pancakes, steak and eggs with a side of bacon, while talking philosophy in the sunlight with the *finest* sister I've seen in a very long time."

She smiled and looked away, but didn't pull her left hand away from his as she began picking at her meal.

"When they sent food allotments over there, did they send

strawberry pancakes with whipped cream and hot chocolate?"
He smiled when she looked up and shook her head.

"Good, ain't it?"

She smiled and licked the excess stickiness from her mouth.
"Yonnie," she whispered. "We *never* had anything like this over
in Nod. We could dream of it, even manifest it—but to truly
taste the full flavor of it . . ." She sighed and closed her eyes for
a moment. "To feel it going down into your belly, oh . . ."

"Tell me about where you used to live," he said, sending pleasure sensations into her palm. "What else couldn't you do?"

She hesitated and then pulled her hand away from his to take
up her hot chocolate.

He chuckled and went back to his pancakes. "Let me tell you
about this side, then." He waited until she looked at him again
before continuing. "Yeah, we have wars and crime and atroci-
ties. But we also party and have fun. The good with the bad. We
dance, eat, drink, and be merry. We make love, we fight, it's all
sensation—and dead or alive, I wouldn't give up on this crazy
plane for all the money in it. Now that's some raw truth."

"I want to experience some of those things," she admitted
after a moment. "We all do. There's not many of us still left in
Nod . . . most have fled and are in hiding. We can't be seen by
the full humans. Those of us who are feather-bearers are bad
enough, but those who . . ." She looked down at her plate.

"It's okay, baby. I know prejudice real up close and personal.
You mean the leather wings, right? Homeboys rocking fangs
and tails and shit."

"Yes," she said in a near whisper. "Those still in Nod are there
because they are afraid and know of no other way to exist."

"Dimmed sensation . . . because you're afraid?" Yonnie
arched an eyebrow as he took a sip of his coffee. "I'd take a bullet first. But then, if you don't know no better, hey. All I know
is life is risk. A damned gamble every day."

"But you are brave, Yonnie. You walk about among the full humans. Most of us have never been so bold. We told ourselves it was because of the Edict, but now that the borders are open, it is hard to imagine such freedom . . . or such risk."

"Hey, be honest. It was real dangerous where you were, so how bad can this be? Plus, you get the perks. Sheeit, me myself, I'd be like—if I'ma die anyway, then I'ma go out loving every minute of being in this joint."

She stared at him and he stared at her. Until he'd said it, he hadn't realized just how much his seductive pep talk to get next to her was really the absolute truth.

"Your courage is admirable," she said without blinking. "I respect that." Then she looked away. "Carlos is blessed to have a friend like you, as is his wife."

Her simple statement did something to him. The purity of her spirit, in the absence of owning one himself, drew him to see beyond her gorgeous face and athletic body, to genuinely appreciate her real beauty. He hadn't felt anything close to that since Tara, and it made him sit back in the booth to consider the dilemma.

"You didn't seem like a woman who was fearful when I met you on the beach," he said after a while, trying to wrest back his game. "You seemed like the type to go for the gusto—the kind of woman who does everything with passion."

She looked out the window and then up toward the sky. "I've spent my entire life in the service of others . . . fighting for right."

"Don't they give Valkyries shore leave or whatever?" he asked, leaning forward to wipe a bit of strawberry away from the corner of her mouth with the pad of his thumb. "You can be on a mission . . . but in your downtime, I can show you some earth plane sensations that'll knock your head back."

"I want to feel real water," she said suddenly, as though the thought had just occurred to her. "I flew over it, the waves, the blue!" She closed her eyes and laughed. "I want to get drunk on life."

"Shit . . . done."

"Really?" She opened her eyes and leaned forward like they were coconspirators in a crime.

He leaned forward and ran his tongue over his incisors to keep them back. "Really. I got this little joint in Mexico with a Jacuzzi . . ."

But his words trailed off as a stabbing call pierced his temples. "Hold up for a second, baby."

"Is everything all right?" Her concerned gaze held panic as he winced and sat back in the booth with an angry thud.

"Damn, Val, I'm real sorry—but I've gotta take this call."

"You're connected to the male Neteru by telepathy?"

He let his breath out hard. "Yeah . . . something like that. But I've gotta bounce."

For a moment, she just stared at him with a look of total confusion on her face.

"I have to go," he said, materializing cash in his pockets and withdrawing a wad to leave on the table. "You go back and stay at the Neteru compound. It's definitely safe there—but be sure to leave them some kinda indication that you're there so they don't hot you on site by accident. If I can . . . maybe later tonight, depending on what's jumping off, I'll see if I can hook up with you. Damn, this gig gets on my nerves!"

She gave his hand a supportive squeeze. "I understand duty. I will look forward to experiencing water with you, then."

She stood when he stood. He leaned forward to kiss her, she gave him a warrior's full forearm grip, looked him in the eye, and lifted her chin. "Be valiant, be victorious."

Yonnie raked his fingers through his thick Afro and smirked. "Yeah, likewise."

"Sebastian, Fallon!" Yonnie hollered as he walked through Vampire Council Chambers. "You bad-timing motherfuckers better have a damned good reason for calling me with extreme measures! I'da came for Lilith, no problem—but she gave you the override code to blow my head up? Why!" He stood in front of the pentagram-shaped bargaining table with his arms folded, fuming. "Where is Madame Councilwoman, anyway?"

"On Seven, clearing the path for a reanimation ceremony. She will be here shortly, if all goes well."

Be valiant, be victorious still singed the edges of his mind, along with Valkyrie's voluptuous body. He was in no mood for guessing games with Sebastian, especially not with Fallon Nuit smugly laid-back in his throne like the ultimate pimp.

Yonnie looked at his Rolex—it was more for show, since he already knew what time it was. "You wanna be more specific, since a brother has places to go and people to see?"

"We're filling two council seats," Nuit said coolly, leaning forward and making a tent with his fingers before his mouth. "Vampire Council Law of the Dark Realms dictates that all existing councilmen must be witness to the installation process, unless dispatched to do otherwise by their current Chairman . . . and I guarantee you, *brother,* you will not want to miss this."

Now they had his attention. Carlos and D definitely needed to know about a one-third expansion of the Vampire Council. More important for him, it also meant two more bastards he'd have to maneuver around just to stay alive. Yonnie pulled his cuffs down and strolled over to his throne, grabbing a goblet off the table, but hesitated.

"Although we are daywalkers," Nuit said coolly with a disdainful sniff, making Sebastian chuckle, "you may find that black blood doesn't mix well with blueberry pancakes or whatever else you've consumed. Like fine wine, the pure essence of life is best savored on an empty stomach and with a clean blood palate. However, suit yourself, *mon ami*. I'm only informing you out of gentlemanly courtesy . . . given that we will have two new members at council, whom I assume you'd rather not see you in a weakened state unbecoming to a senior councilman."

Yonnie stared at Nuit's arrogant smile and then looked down into his goblet as though poison were in it. Ego warred with common sense. If Nuit was warning him, then there was something really foul about to go down. Nuit didn't do courtesy.

"Then as they say in your native New Orleans, let the good times roll." Yonnie lifted his goblet but sat down in his throne without drinking from it.

To raise a glass in a toast and not drink from it was akin to flipping Nuit the bird. But oddly, rather than take the bait, Nuit simply smiled like a man with an ace up his sleeve. Yonnie set his goblet down with precision and sat back. It was now a tense visual standoff until Lilith appeared.

"I hope you boys have been playing nicely together while I was gone?" Lilith smiled as she sashayed over to her throne, subtly nodding to Sebastian and Nuit.

Yonnie stared at her and her smile grew. He was on the outside of their collusion, and that was a dangerous place to be.

Inhaling deeply, Lilith laughed. "Blueberry pancakes, Yonnie?"

"I've wanted some since I was a kid," he said flatly, his gaze on her deadly.

"Don't be so touchy," she said, her good mood making him more wary. She dismissed the subject with a wave of her hand, clearly bored with it in light of her other news. "I know what Sebastian was doing during his first morning . . . now I smell what you've been doing, Yonnie—eating at some pancake emporium. Fallon . . . tell me, have you been a good boy?"

Yonnie watched Fallon sit back, his slender fingers laced beneath his chin. From the corner of his eye, he watched Sebastian lean forward ever-so-slightly. The games had begun.

"Your husband, our Dark Lord, is beyond genius," Fallon began calmly, and then took a graceful bow from where he was seated. "By him attacking the male Neteru's father-seer in a cathedral, this presented yet another opportunity for our side."

Lilith arched an eyebrow. Sebastian offered Nuit a respectful nod. Yonnie remained as still as stone, listening.

"This is my specialty . . . understanding the whims and weaknesses of Carlos Rivera. As I'm sure your husband knew, what he sent the priest would fry a human mind. But, for someone such as Carlos, who had seen the depths of decadence from a Vampire Council throne, these images were mild, by comparison. Therefore, in his heroism, the Neteru would go in, take the images from the old man—as much as possible, and jettison them away."

Lilith released an evil chuckle. "Best coke I've had in a while."

"Precisely," Nuit crooned. "But the part that is of true note is that said attack only infuriated the Neteru. The frustration of not being able to retaliate is causing the old dark vapor within him to rise."

"Yes, yes," Lilith said dismissively. "We know all about it. That was Lu's plan. Piss him off so badly that he breaks another seal . . . blah, blah, blah."

"But the darkness that is beginning to envelop his silver life-force pulse is visible." Nuit sat back with a triumphant smile, waiting a moment to allow the concept to sink in. "Essentially, he's got a GPS locator on him from our side. Therefore, as long as he's not inside a place that is additionally prayer-barriered to us, we can see him. Soon, as the rage further implodes, we'll be able to pick up the white-hot dark signal as though he were beeping on radar."

Lilith lifted her goblet slowly, raised it in Nuit's direction, and then took a sip from it. "Touché, Fallon . . . this is precisely why you are a member of council."

He lifted his goblet toward her, bowed slightly, and took a sip. "And since the male and female Neteru are linked under the one-flesh marriage clause—if he's detectable, she's detectable . . . and because I was aware that one of the Guardians, her best friend from her old life, I believe, had a child . . . I knew that after the Dark Lord breached a cathedral and attacked her husband's father-seer, Damali would go to the preventive rescue of that at-risk child. That, dear Lilith, is how I spent my first morning in the sun after centuries of darkness—in your service, as always."

Nuit looked at Yonnie with a scowl. "I was not eating blueberry pancakes to destroy my vampire palate. Nor was I out trying to get laid by human blood carriers." He turned away from Yonnie to stare at Lilith, raising his goblet. "I was at work for the empire, advancing our unholy cause, attempting to drive a further wedge in the male Neteru's mind by making him know that his family—every far-flung member of it—will *never* be safe. That will enrage a man such as Carlos Rivera, to the point where he might as well have a neon target on his back. It will also ultimately send him over the edge into urban ride-or-die mode, as he used to call it, and that will have cataclysmic results."

Lilith set down her goblet and clapped in a slowly, seductive pulse. "Bravo, Nuit. As always, your treachery completes me." She turned to Sebastian. "You see why I said he is such a good match for your first choice. *She* thinks like that, as well. Both are of the school of Machiavelli." Lilith clucked her tongue. "I so miss him, too."

Yonnie ignored Nuit but keyed in on the word "she," now staring at Sebastian. Dissecting the information quickly, he had to get word out as soon as it was possible. Nuit hadn't lied. That shit that just went down would take Carlos dark in a heartbeat.

Now he understood some of why he hadn't been able to get to his boy. No wonder he'd put up additional barriers at the homestead. Made sense that Carlos and his family had to be behind clerical walls or in a Guardian safe house somewhere.

"Yes, I agree with Nuit's approach to time well spent," Sebastian said, oblivious to Yonnie's inner turmoil. He sat up taller, his tone haughty. "While some people were simply indulging their childhood appetites, I was advancing the cause of the empire as well. My research into viable candidates that had not been slain by a Neteru blade yielded rare gems. Lilith, my hope is that my suggestions have been accepted for induction to council."

"He gets to choose both candidates?" Nuit said, losing his former reserve. While his tone was calm and even, his body was tense. "I had a few candidates in mind, myself . . . hence my earlier comment to Yonnie that he would not want to miss this induction." Nuit stared at Sebastian with a lethal gaze for a moment before taking his petition back to Lilith. "I assure you that my knowledge base of female candidates throughout antiquity is *vast*. Are you certain he is *qualified* to make such a critical selection?"

"In this case," Lilith said, baiting Nuit. "But you will like his selections, I'm sure."

Nuit made a tent in front of his mouth. "Is that due process? I deliver you access to our arch-nemeses, while he only does mere research, and Yolando eats pancakes. Lilith, to say that I am concerned and object is an understatement."

"If I deliver you Lucrezia Borgia, do you still object?" Sebastian asked with a wry smile, and then sipped from his goblet.

"*Non* . . ."

"*Oui*," Sebastian said, his smile widening as he set down his goblet. "All for you, *mon ami*. When I raise her, that will be the condition of her council seat—she's yours."

"Speechless, Fallon? Cat got your tongue?" Lilith teased. "Normally with such a gift presented, a man says thank you."

"*Merci . . .*" Nuit whispered in *Dananu*, still stunned. "First daylight . . . then *Lucrezia?* How can this be—she died a human."

Sebastian stood and opened his arms wide. "I am the master of master necromancers. Respect me for my talents, Nuit! This is why you and I have unnecessarily been at odds. I respect your statesmanship and strategy . . . now look upon my special skills with due awe."

Instantly, a hole opened in the air above Sebastian's outstretched palms, and grains of what appeared to be dark sand, gravel, and ash overran them, flowing through his fingers as he laughed madly. He balled his hands into fists around the silt, catching as much of it as possible until his hands could hold no more. Then he threw his head back as gale-force winds blew the council doors open. Black lightning arced in his palms, and he flung the dirt toward an empty throne. Just as suddenly as it smoldered, lava from the Sea of Perpetual Agony belched up a hot tendril of screaming ooze that slithered along the black marble floor like a wailing serpent to meet the dirt-splattered throne.

"Come back, bring forth your treachery and your wiles. Come back filled with lusts and deceit—I call you Lucrezia . . . from the House of Borgia, I call you to Vampire Council to do its bidding!"

Black lightning hit the throne, igniting an inferno within the seat of it. An awful woman's scream echoed as bits of bone dust and body ash, graveyard gravel, and Sebastian's own blend of sorcery drew it together. Her form rose slowly from the flames, her skin blackened from the pyre. As she screamed and screeched, the cord of ooze from the Sea of Perpetual Agony leapt up her body and drove itself down her throat.

Fallon Nuit was on his feet as the fire died away. Yonnie remained immobile, watching and wary, as Lilith clapped and screeched. Black, crusted skin dropped away from the woman's body as she slumped in the throne, leaving the stench of charred flesh in its wake.

Dewey, pinkish, porcelain skin remained where there had been burned earth. A pair of startled green eyes opened suddenly and she took a gasp, clutching the chair. Thick waves of red hair covered her full breasts, but as she coughed and sputtered to life, her voluptuous form left nothing to the imagination.

"And you say she is for me . . ." Nuit murmured, looking at Sebastian.

"If you elect to do the honors," Sebastian said with a gracious bow. "She is still human, just reanimated without a soul."

Nuit pressed his fist to his mouth for a moment. "Virgin to the bite?"

Sebastian nodded. But Nuit looked to Lilith for confirmation.

"You accept his generous gift with no objections?" Lilith said, smiling a dangerous smile.

"What's the catch?" Nuit said. "What is the soul price for such an amazing feat?"

Lilith laughed. "Oh, Fallon, you are so suspicious. Why can't you just accept a gesture of respect among councilmen?"

Nuit gave her a half smile. "Because that is not how it works in Hell, my dear."

"All right," she said with a sigh. "If you turn her and install her—and you know you want to, just look at your pants . . . there will be no factions in council, and you will respect Sebastian's choice of mate with no poaching." She looked to Sebastian. "Did I get those terms right?"

Sebastian nodded.

Nuit chuckled low in his throat. "*Mon ami,* I knew you had performance anxiety, but had I known it was this bad, I would have exploited it long ago."

"Do you accept or not? She will not last long in this half-state!" Sebastian yelled. "Either make her a vampire now before her breathing expires, or you will have missed your opportunity! The spell only lasts so long!" He looked at Lilith for support. "In a throne, in council, Fallon . . . think of it. Lucrezia Borgia . . . and you will not only have a taste of someone so corrupt, who managed to remain virgin to our bites . . . but you will be able to give her the daylight infusion."

"You would allow that—even though the heir is only supposed to give that?" Nuit's startled gaze held Lilith's.

"Lu said that I could pass it to my councilmen. You can't give it to anyone else, but giving it to a fellow member of council at an installation with me watching isn't going against his intent to contain it to just us. I'm just bending the rules for you, darling, not breaking them." She blew Nuit a kiss from where she sat and it knocked his head back, causing his fangs to instantly lower from arousal. "There. All yours. Now please accept the offer with no more bullshit."

"Offer formally accepted," Nuit breathed, and swept to Lucrezia's throne.

Lifting her slumped body to sit upright, he listened to her expiring breaths as her slender fingers scrabbled at her throat. Tiny gurgling sounds drew him to hold her delicate chin in his palm and turn her head as she strangled on her own saliva.

"I know, chérie, death by natural causes is awful," he murmured, sliding a fang up her jugular as he inhaled her raw scent. "I will be your savior from said tragedy again. You were designed for pleasure," he whispered, sliding his other palm against the small of her back. "And you have come to be made at a most auspicious time in the empire. . . . Your radiance will know daylight, but the power I'm about to confer upon you is beyond what your ruthless mind could have ever envisioned. You will owe me dying loyalty to ash, but love every moment of it."

In a serpent-quick strike, his fangs sank into her rose-petal-soft skin. Her body convulsed, but his firm grip at the small of her back and at the nape of her neck kept her welded to him as he heaved in each siphon of blood. He dredged her until she was limp, arms dangling at her sides. But soon, her flaccid arms responded—first clutching the arms of the throne, then his shoulders. As he drained her completely, whitening her skin, she cried out, but not from pain.

"Damn, I love to watch that man work," Lilith murmured appreciatively to Sebastian. "Now do you see why I was concerned that you might get cuckolded after all?" She shook her head when Sebastian angrily glanced away. "Yolando, watch and learn . . . it takes centuries of practice to want something so badly but to negotiate your terms up-front . . . and to do so with a quickly expiring opportunity. Had she died, he would have been unmercifully teased with no resolution in store."

Yonnie nodded, angry with himself that watching the whole process had given him wood.

Nuit drew away from Lucrezia's throat, dropping his head back, fangs crimson and glistening. "Throne, teach her. Infuse her!" He stepped away from the dead woman breathing hard, trembling.

Never having seen a from-death turn-bite installation, both Yonnie and Sebastian sat forward, watching the process with complete focus. Only Lilith lounged in her throne, amused, with excited Harpies gathered at her feet.

Slowly, the throne came alive, welding itself to the female body that inhabited it. Movement fluttered beneath Lucrezia's lids. Nuit had been taking slow inhalations through his nose, but as she arched and cried out, his breaths came in short bursts through his mouth. Tight pink nipples rose and fell beneath Lucrezia's profusion of red hair as she twisted and writhed. Her creamy thighs parted, giving them all full view of her glistening sex as the throne thrust centuries of decadence into her mind.

Black arc current covered her, causing Nuit to allow his head to drop back, almost too aroused to watch. But when she screamed and opened her eyes, he went to her. Green irises had been replaced with glowing red orbs. Her small rosebud mouth opened to reveal a dainty set of perfect porcelain fangs. She reached out to Nuit and he covered her mouth with his, consuming her bite as his hands found her hair.

But he had to wait, had to wait for the throne to finish transmitting all that had been before her, had to wait until it let go of her spine. Her shrieks of frustration tortured his libido as she reached for him, clutched him wherever he would allow, and then began to sob.

"Don't leave me!" she screamed. "You made me! You have to come to me!"

He held himself just inches out of her reach, shuddering. "I will, *chérie*," he whispered in a gravelly voice, "and I will bring you daylight when I do."

Her laments had become so forlorn and intoxicating that Lilith slowly slid her hand down the front of her gown. "Fallon . . . wherever you take her, do allow me to join you."

Too overwhelmed to initially speak, he simply nodded. Seconds later the object of his desire stood and flew at him. His back hit the table, his suit dissolving immediately.

Lucrezia threw her head back, fangs lowered to a feeding length, and struck him. Nuit's voice rent the air, his nails digging into the marble, spilling blood from his veins as her body sheathed his. The contrast of their skin seemed as though his Creole café au lait was drinking in her milky hue, his blood infusing her with color. Wanton pelvic thrusts inched the entwined couple to the precipice of falling. But as soon as she'd had her fill from his throat, he flipped her on her back, dissolving the table.

A carpet of freshly mown grass broke her fall; dogwoods grew up over and consumed unoccupied thrones, Spanish moss eerily swayed, and a full moon rose. Rose petals rained from the vaulted ceiling until the entire floor was a scarlet wash. Council Chambers dissolved into his bedchamber lair, sheets billowing from an energy breeze. Sweat ran down his muscle-corded back as he fisted her hair and bit her again.

"You're marked as mine," he gasped in *Dananu*, staring at her, blood oozing from his fangs as she spasmed with pleasure beneath him. "*This* is life. What you lived before was a child's dream."

"Magnificent . . ." Lilith whispered, reaching across to Sebastian to hold his hand. "Stop scowling, Yonnie, you must give the man his due." Lilith leaned forward, craning her neck. "He's close—can you feel it . . . just absorb the energy coming off his body. Whew . . ."

A sudden blue-black nova sent a thundering pulse through chambers that rattled thrones. Nuit's voice bounced off the walls in shuddering waves. Bats took flight, and small bits of stalactites and stalagmites fell. As quickly as the charge hit, the chambers brightened for a second, as though the flash on a camera had gone off, and then for a moment everything went dark. Slowly but surely the torches on the walls relit.

"And . . . then there was daylight," Nuit murmured, looking down at Lucrezia with a low, sexy chuckle.

"*Très bon! Très bon!*" Lilith said, standing and clapping. "Welcome to council, Lucrezia." Lilith blotted the perspiration from her brow. "I may have to go topside to feed before you bring back Elizabeth . . . I love how you gentlemen handle your business." She looked at Yonnie and winked, teasing him by stealing some of his slang.

Fallon kissed a breathless Lucrezia, but lifted his head to stare at Lilith. "Elizabeth?"

"As in Bathory."

Fallon withdrew from Lucrezia's body and stood, then helped her stand. "Are you both insane?" he whispered.

"After such a display, you cannot object. It was the agreement!" Sebastian lamented.

"Lilith . . . that is *Dracula's* wife." Nuit raked his disheveled hair and pulled Lucrezia against him to shield her. "He was called Vlad the Impaler for a reason, *oui?* He will come back one night, find the most appropriate orifice on your body, and shove a wooden pike through it until it comes out of your mouth, *mon ami.* This, I promise you. You do not know who you're fucking with."

"Well . . . he's not raising Dracula, so there you have it. This was Sebastian's choice. I felt she would be a wonderful addition to council, so I approve."

"Vlad will raise himself from the dead if he thinks that his wife has been brought back from the grave solely at another man's pleasure. I do not object on the grounds of envy—I object because that is like setting the course for a nuclear missile!" Nuit robed himself and then covered Lucrezia in a new, antebellum crimson gown, then waved away all the visual special effects he'd created.

"Seems like you wasted a barter on Fallon," Lilith said with a grin. "He wouldn't go after your mate, so you didn't have to go to all this trouble. I told you he and Lucrezia were a perfect match."

"You have no troubles from me," Nuit said. "You wasted a transaction, as Lilith said. I would not want to be the one to duel with Vlad, and the possible army he could raise, not even as a councilman. Do recall that he went against the Ottomans with a fair degree of success—while alive and *human.* He did most of his insane impaling while human. Might it not be worth considering what he would do as a born-again vampire? Hmmm? Consult the information resident in your throne,

Sebastian. Vlad was so ruthlessly powerful as a mere Master that even Dante refused to allow him a seat on council for fear of an imminent coup. *I* filled that open seat, thus perhaps am more sensitive to the vibrations of the era."

"Sounds familiar," Yonnie muttered. "And we see how much good blocking Vlad from council did our old Chairman."

"Be that as it may," Nuit said with a scowl. "The Count's skills at dispatching adversaries are legendary for cause."

"He will not come back," Sebastian said coolly. "Vlad was beheaded by a blessed blade, and even I cannot raise him if I wanted to, which I do not. Therefore, if you are happy with your choice, then be happy with mine."

Fallon pursed his lips and put one finger to them before he spoke, and then tapped on the fanged crest in the center of the table until it responded, coming alive. He looked deeply into its ruby eyes that glistened in its golden gargoyle face.

"I want it on the record that I had nothing to do with this, nor did my new bride, the Councilwoman Borgia. And, I want it stated in blood." Nuit held out his wrist and winced when the crest struck him, drawing blood. "From here, do as you like. While you undertake this unthinkable act, we will be topside dining in New Orleans at sunset. Once you are done, by all means, we will come back to council to pay our utmost respect to the legendary lady, scandalous as this liaison may be."

Yonnie stood, walked over to the table, and tapped the crest. "Then I'm out, too." He looked down at the crest as it struck him and drew back. "I ain't party to this one. And you can call me back when you're done and she's all installed and shit. Because if it's bad enough for Nuit's horny ass to pass on an installation witness of Dracula's wife, hey, who am I? I ain't as old as none of you rat bastards—but I ain't crazy. C'mon, man, you trying to raise Liz?"

"She is no longer Dracula's wife!" Sebastian spat back. "She'll be Councilwoman Bathory, under my installation bite."

Nuit nodded. "And this is what the late Count will track through the fires of hell to find the source of."

"He cannot be raised! It was part of my agreement with Lilith!"

"Ah . . ." Nuit said. "But, insofar as we are indeed at the end of days, and should the Dark Lord at some point need to supersede that negotiation for the benefit of the empire . . . and thus figure out a way to raise that particular resource to use at his disposal . . ." Nuit shook his head. "Not good. *Très mal.*"

"That won't happen; he won't need to raise him if we do our job." Sebastian lifted his chin and folded his arms.

Nuit held up his hands before his chest. "As I said earlier, I just want it on the record—in blood, what my position in all of this was. *Nothing.*"

"Hey . . ." Yonnie said, beginning to walk toward the door. "You ain't gotta tell a brother twice. I'm out, you crazy, and we all know how shit goes down here."

"You boys are no fun at all," Lilith said, laughing.

"Let me ask you one question then, Lilith," Nuit said, extending his elbow to Lucrezia. He waited until his new bride took it and then released a slow, calm breath.

Lilith smiled and waited with her arms folded.

"Are you insane enough to help with the installation?"

"Will I fuck her when she comes out of the throne? Be direct, Fallon." Lilith's smile was sly and seductive.

"*Oui.* That is my question."

All eyes went to Lilith, who paused and then threw her head back and laughed.

"Hell no! Are you insane?"

PART II

WE AIN'T HAVING IT

ℭ CHAPTER SEVEN

Yonnie hurried down the beach, turning the dilemma over and over again in his mind. Now that he'd sent Val to the Neteru compound, how was he going to get word to her? If he still had the image of where it was, he could simply mind-stun a passing human to go deliver the message. But that posed two problems: one, it would leave a human witness that could easily be traced, and two, Val might not believe them or say the wrong thing . . . might even accidentally ice them, for that matter.

Time was also his enemy. There was a very narrow window during which he could play this hand. Nuit would be off doing his new bride and probably feeding for several hours; Lilith and crazy-ass Sebastian would be resurrecting Dracula's wife, then installing her. But after that, who knew what could jump off.

This afternoon, however, if time was his mortal enemy, good fortune was his best friend. Val was busily combing the shoreline as though she'd lost something.

"I thought I told you to go where it was safe?"

She snapped her attention toward him and placed both hands on her hips. "I am a warrior. I do not hide from battles. My long sword and bow . . . my quiver, are gone. I must find these before taking temporary refuge in my Neterus' compound. I should be there as an added sentry in their army, not a burden that they must protect."

Yonnie slapped his forehead and let out his breath hard. "I concealed your weapons, boo. Like I said, you can't just go walking down the beach with blades and bows and shit. Off-hand, I don't know what the laws are in this state, but you can't carry weapons out in the open without a permit, in any event—least not since the eighteenth century, aw'ight?"

She lifted her chin and folded her arms over her chest.

"Look. I know you ain't no punk," he said, growing weary. "Coward," he corrected, when it was clear that she didn't know what he'd meant. "And I'll give you back your weapons, but I'm gonna have to do them like I did your wings—make it so you can walk with them without others knowing they're on you. But if you set them down, you'll have to remember where you laid them. Deal?"

A wide, sparkling smile was her answer and then her body relaxed.

"Okay, now that we got that out of the way, here's the thing." He hesitated and looked around. "I went somewhere that is really dangerous just now. Got some inside knowledge that you have to get to Carlos and D."

"You infiltrated the enemy camp . . ." she murmured in awe. "I would be honored to be a messenger."

"Cool, 'cause where the Neterus are right now, I can't go. It'll blow my cover and then the next time I go behind enemy lines, I might get smoked."

She nodded and stepped closer. "I will, as you say, have your back, and will valiantly deliver all that you have to tell me."

"I can't tell you, I have to show you," he said, no fraud in his statement. "This science is too twisted and way too sensitive . . . real complicated. But if you allow me to put the images in your head and you take this straight to Carlos, he'll be able to decode it in an instant . . . and I won't get fucked up if somehow you get waylaid by the wrong side."

"I stand at your ready."

Yonnie walked back and forth for a moment, rubbing the nape of his neck as he studied her. He was more than ready. Problem was, he had to get his hunger in check. Both of the competing desires. After witnessing a coronation with only blueberry pancakes on his stomach, he was getting shaky. He also hadn't fed since Lilith bestowed daylight on him, which was erotic as hell . . . then this beauty had attacked him, hand-to-hand combat with a blade. The adrenaline had spiked her blood and dried in her sweat, creating a layer of sweet allure all over her skin. Not to mention the deeply philosophical conversation they'd just had.

"I am trustworthy," she said, stepping forward, appearing alarmed that he might not believe in her loyalty.

"I'm not," he said, staring at her. "Telepathy is a very sensual act . . . you know that, right."

"I do," she stated flatly. "In Nod, that is all we had."

Damn . . . a woman who gave good head . . . for a moment, he just looked at her.

"Okay, listen, these images are gruesome—and I have to make it look like we were engaged in some mental foreplay and I got sloppy. This way, if the message gets intercepted, it won't seem like I'm playing both sides, feel me?"

She nodded. "I will go along with the ruse to protect your secrets for the cause. I have seen horrors in Nod as well. I can take it."

Yonnie blotted his forehead with the forearms of his jacket. "Good, baby. But once you get to Carlos, have him pull that bullshit out of your head with a silver siphon. The other thing I want you to ask him to do is to override my black box with a silver shield."

She tilted her head in a question. He chose his words with care.

"Right now, there are only two entities that can legitimately override my telepathy to get inside your head. One is the ultimate dark angel and the other one is his wife—you understand?"

She gasped and he pulled her to him and spoke into her ear. "That's right. I went in deep and low, baby. So, if any other demon comes for your head, they'll bump up on my border and figure you're just mine. But C puts an extra mind layer around members of his team that even the lowest of the low can't break. Want you to have that, too, so you can't be used as a pawn. Once he sees these images, he'll know why."

"All right," she whispered, her body fitting against his. "I had no idea it was this bad. Thank you for considering my safety."

Yonnie's hands slid down her back, caressing supple skin wherever he found it. "For the cause, right?"

"Yes . . . for the cause," she murmured as he dragged his jaw up the side of her throat.

"If only I had more time . . ." He let his breath out hard and steadied himself, refocusing on the issue at hand. "After I blow your head up, I'm going to shockwave you to the other side of the country. I gotta do it like that so the bad guys just think I busted a daylight nut and don't come looking for you. But as soon as you hit the asphalt, I want you to get up, look around, find a beef and beer joint. Go in cool, though, sis. They're heavily armed on the Light side. I can't escort you in there without blowing my cover. But you tell them you're from Nod and Carlos will understand."

"Busted a—"

"Don't worry about it, you'll catch on to the lingo once you're here a while. Main thing is for you to get this to the Neterus as soon as possible once I'm done."

"All right, but what about my weapons? If it is a soldiers' den that could come under attack, I should be armed."

"Sho' you right."

He slid his hand down her hip until they both shuddered, making her scabbard appear and then disappear against her left side. Holding his arm out from him without breaking the seal between their bodies, he materialized her blade in his hand and then slowly sheathed it at her side, making it disappear in increments as it slid into the scabbard. She moaned as though he'd entered her, briefly closing her eyes. It was impossible not to drop fang after the morning he'd endured.

When she looked up at him again, they were both breathing hard, but she didn't seem afraid, even though he hadn't retracted his incisors.

"And my quiver and bow?" she murmured, moistening her bottom lip with her tongue.

His hands slid over her shoulders and then he slowly slid his palms between her breasts one at a time, allowing her to see the straps before they disappeared.

"Arrows are in there . . . I can't make silver disappear," he said, staring at the way her nipples had tightened beneath her shirt. "But I can cover the top of the quiver with leather and conceal that. Just open the flap to get to them."

She nodded and swallowed hard. "Thank you."

"I'll put your bow on your right hip, tie it with a leather thong . . . cool?"

She leaned her head against his chest and nodded quickly, her eyes shut tightly. "I've never been armed like this in my life."

He had to look up at the clouds for a moment to remember the message he was going to send Carlos before he traced her waist and upper thigh with the pads of his thumbs to tie her bow to her. Stooping before her, he French-kissed her navel and then nipped her hip, and her bow and its leather tie very slowly dissolved until she cried out.

"Now let me inside your head, baby," he said, sliding up her body to stand. "So I can deliver the message."

She held up her hand, breathless. "Just one moment to regain my composure. I am a warrior . . . this is unfitting to be seen like this by the Neterus."

Yonnie smiled and kissed her earlobe. "Believe me, they'll understand."

Not allowing her the moment she'd asked for, he cradled her skull between his palms, causing her soft locks to spill between his fingers as he took her mouth hard.

Cascading images made her twist to pull away, but then he sent a pleasure balm behind each one that caused her to arch against him with an agonized moan.

He stopped for a moment, panting, and quickly turned his head away from the temptation of her jugular. Reliving the coronation was wearing him out, but not half as much as Val's responsive body. Her pelvis was welded to his in just the right spot, her movements torturous as her hands framed his back, then her palms slowly slid up his forearms so that her hands could shadow his.

"You be sure to let my boy know that delivering this particular message in broad daylight kicked my ass, all right?"

She opened her eyes and spoke softly, trembling. "Tell me you're not done . . . there is more?"

He was rendered mute and had to close his eyes, nodding once, before resting his forehead against hers for a second. "Yeah," he said panting. "There's more. Just give me a minute to pull my shit together."

She fell so hard that she tore a gash in her black leather pants, skinning her knee. Metal chariots with no horses screeched to a stop and angry drivers bellowed foul words at her as she got up, felt along her body for weapons, and looked around semi-dazed. The smell of grilling meats made her run toward a redbrick building, one like Yonnie had described.

Her body hurt, more like ached. The blinding pulse that he'd thrust into her that then sent her hurtling still made her face burn with shame.

Strange two-wheel chariots lined the front of the establishment. It was lively and filled to capacity, but she didn't know where to find the proprietor.

"Yo, sis, you can't just walk in—you see all these people here waiting for a table?" He smiled at her, but it was a gentle smile. "You must not be from around here, 'cause that's a good way to get a beat down."

She looked at the human patrons. "I don't think they can take me."

He rounded the host stand with concern in his eyes. "Who you looking for?"

"Carlos the Neteru," she said flatly. "I am Valkyrie of Nod."

"It has only been *twenty minutes,*" Nuit said between his teeth, slightly leaning over so that only Yonnie could hear him.

"Man . . . I woulda waited at least an hour to call us back, just for the sake of pride," Yonnie muttered.

Nuit nodded but sat back before the new councilwoman took offense. He squeezed Lucrezia's hand as she tried to pat her hair into place.

"Permit me to introduce the newest member of council, Elizabeth Bathory," Sebastian said with pride.

Lilith smirked. "Welcome, how does it feel to be back after all these years, and elevated at that?"

"It is a great honor, Madame Chairwoman," Elizabeth said, her thick Hungarian accent adding to her exotic appeal. She smoothed her hands down the black lace that clung to her lean, statuesque body. Severe hawkish eyes looked around as though she were expecting someone, and disappointed that she didn't see them.

"Countess," Nuit said, standing to bow before her. He smiled a half smile, knowing the use of her old title would pique Sebastian. "The pleasure and honor is all ours."

Following protocol, Yonnie stood and offered her a bow. "Welcome to council. My best regards to your late husband."

Sebastian snarled, but Elizabeth floated over to Yonnie.

"You knew him and were a supporter of his? Perhaps a turncoat Ottoman . . . or a mercenary from the fallen Moorish empire?"

"Naw," Yonnie said, taking up her hand and kissing the back of it. "Just a brother with much respect for the legendary . . . if he ever comes back, make sure he knows me and him are cool."

"I shall do so," she said, smiling to show off a wicked length of fang.

"Might I remind you that I reanimated her, Yolando," Sebastian said, collecting Elizabeth to usher her back to her new throne.

Yonnie held his hands up in front of him. "Hey, believe me. I am not trying to push up on your woman. Like I said, respect. I know who her husband is."

"Was," Sebastian snarled.

Elizabeth tilted her head. "Was?" She turned to Sebastian, dark eyes kindling an emotion that was impossible to judge. "*Dracula* will always be my husband . . . there is no other like Vlad." She had enunciated every syllable, extending the second one for emphasis, making her exterminated husband's name sound like Dra-cuuu-la.

"But I reanimated you and gave you daylight . . ."

"Then, for that the debt is paid in full—I gave you my body. *Once.* Just as you gave me life again. *Once.*"

"Plus, daylight," Sebastian argued.

"Then, when I use the daylight and appear in it, which I assure you will be rare, as I am used to the night . . . I will give you what you most crave. Until then, I suggest you do what the peasant farmers in the old country were forced to do in the absence of willing choices—mate sheep."

"You cannot mean that . . . if you do not take me as a new husband, then at least take me as a lover until your grief over Vlad's continued loss subsides. I know you're overwrought, but our coronation must mean something to you?"

"In twenty minutes, puhlease," Yonnie muttered to Nuit on the side, instantly bored by the debate between Elizabeth and Sebastian. "No wonder she'd rather ride a memory than that bullshit."

"How is it that I find myself in the odd and rare position of thoroughly agreeing with you, Yolando?" Nuit smiled and squeezed Lucrezia's hand, and then kissed the back of it. "You have *no idea* what he interrupted."

"Yeah, I do," Yonnie said in a low voice.

Lilith gave them the eye and sent a private message to them both. *It was so sad, torturous to witness. I should have made you all stay just so that I wouldn't have this tragedy locked in my mind alone. He humped her like a schoolboy would in the back of a car! Five quick pokes right in the throne, no imagination—couldn't hold off, so no wonder our new councilwoman is pissy. After Vlad . . . ? I would have slapped Sebastian's face, clawed out his eyes! Vlad's essence leapt from the Sea of Perpetual Agony at the affront and scorched three messenger demons that were standing too close to the lava . . . but, alas, there was nothing more that he could do but rejoin the wailing masses. I swear, I can still hear his voice cursing above the others.*

I did not need to see that, Lilith, Nuit mentally shot back with a sigh. *Five strokes without ambience?* Non. *I am offended for the poor Countess, but I will not be coaxed into remedying Sebastian's problem. I have already sent my objections to the permanent council session minutes in blood. Therefore, please tell me when it will be appropriate to return to my lair in New Orleans to, shall we say, acclimate Lucrezia to the area?*

Lilith smiled and winked. *In due time.* She then turned her attention to Yonnie, and her gaze raked him. *From the condition of your aura, it seems Sebastian's quick callback left you in a state, darling.*

Yonnie shrugged subtly. *What can I do? Nobody even had the courtesy to hook a brother up, so I went topside . . . this is real fucked up.*

Blowing him a kiss, Lilith licked her bottom lip. *They did leave you out in the cold . . . but I could make up for it before I head to the Middle East?*

Yonnie froze. It was not that Lilith wasn't a good lay, or that he hadn't been with her before. But damn if he wanted her now.

I feel your hesitation, Yolando. I'm not toying with you. I want all my members of council happy and cooperative before I leave.

He made a tent with his fingers in front of his mouth and then allowed her to feel the pent-up desire full throttle. If Fallon was off screwing his new bride, and Sebastian was sniffing behind his new and very recalcitrant mate, it would give Val more time to get word to Carlos and possibly give the whole squad more time to maneuver. Then if he had Lilith good and occupied . . . that was one less headache for the team as well. Plus, the last he'd heard, the Dark Lord was making moves to secure his heir's survival—in the Middle East. He could definitely take this one for the team.

Yonnie opened his gaze to Lilith and summoned every desire he could think of from his core . . . editing out the circumstances but letting her feel the raw emotion of the denial, allowing her to bathe in the heat waves of wanting something so close that was so far away. Hot-stored mental video fed it and hours of being unfulfilled slick-coated it until she finally writhed in her throne.

"Enough bickering!" she snapped, breaking off her transmission with Yonnie, and turning on Sebastian. "Give the lady room to adjust to her new circumstances. Make her happy—somehow! She is the Countess and is used to the best. Give her a blood bath, take her to the old country to feed, whatever it is that brings her pleasure, but my nervous system cannot handle this strife in council."

Lilith stood. Elizabeth bowed.

"Thank you, Madame Chairwoman, for understanding my . . . disappointment. I believed that Vlad had discovered a way to return and that it was he who had hired the necromancer's services . . . only to find out . . ." She covered her face with her hands and then broke down and wept.

"Fix this, Sebastian," Lilith warned. "She is no good to us in such a state. Had you properly—oh, never mind." Lilith ruffled her hair up from her neck. "Council is adjourned for three eves, barring any catastrophe."

Nuit and Lucrezia were on their feet before Lilith had finished her sentence. Yonnie stood slowly, resigned to his fate. Lilith smiled and crooked her finger toward him as she turned to leave chambers.

"I must design a consolation for you, poor Yolando. If you follow me, I think we can work something out."

Sebastian stood in the deafening silence staring at his backfired fantasy. His gaze roved over Elizabeth's body, coveting it, wishing that he could again reach out to fondle the delicate pink nipples that peeked through the sheer lace of her black gown. His mouth hungered for hers, just as his fingers ached to again touch her silky brunet hair and fragile alabaster skin. Her crimson mouth drew him and he still trembled from just thinking of how magnificent her fang-strike had been. That was what made him prematurely lose control. If only she would understand how long he'd wanted her . . .

"I am not Vlad," he said after her sobs subsided. He lifted his chin as she stared at him with angry, bloodshot eyes. "But I can bring things back from the dead if they haven't been mutilated by blessed weapons."

She was about to walk away from him when he caught her by the elbow. Hissing, she looked down at his hand until he removed it from her arm.

"Think about it," he said evenly. "I may not be able to bring Vlad back, but if you treat me with some modicum of dignity I could bring back Dorka, your sorceress. Or even all of Vlad's army to avenge his death."

The Countess turned slowly and stared at Sebastian with much less venom in her eyes.

"Do you want to know my secret, what is at the base of my spell?"

She neared him, but didn't commit, since he'd posed the question in *Dananu.*

"There is an ancient forest in our Hungary . . . in Bukkabrany, in the northeast—where sixty meters beneath a brown coal mine are *eight-million-year-old* swamp cypress trees." He circled her as he spoke in a low, desirous murmur, drawing her in. "The trees, sixteen of them in all, form the number of good fortune, seven . . . are three meters around in size."

Sebastian's voice dropped to a husky rasp, making her lean in even closer. "They are rare and fragile. They literally crumble to dust when you touch them because they've lost their cellulose. Therefore, I had to work quickly to acquire some of this essence before the paleontologists at the University of Budapest seal them away in cement sarcophagi, like they did in Japan—the only other forest of this kind." He stared into her eyes, watching them begin to glow.

"As fellow practitioners of the dark arts, at the very least we should share in the collaboration of such a find. The soil there represents the basal essence of life force preservation. It kept the trees intact for eight million years, Elizabeth—think of it. With my dexterity in spell-casting, which is why Lilith extended an invitation to me to be a councilman . . . and your strategic military mind and wanton lust for torture . . . think of what we could do."

She neared him and stroked his pocked cheek, tilting her head as though considering his offer. "You have this soil, still?"

"I used it to bring you back to life, my love."

"And you would be willing to raise Vlad's army to avenge his death, even though you compete for his wife's affections?"

"I would raise whatever you asked, just to be yours . . . even if just occasionally."

"Eight million years and the trees remained preserved, yes?" she murmured against his throat, making him shudder hard.

"Yes," he breathed. "To the touch, the trees still feel like wood . . . eight-million-year-old preserved life." With trembling fingers, he caressed her cheek. "Just as it brought back your soft, ever so soft, skin."

She took his mouth harshly, causing him to moan as her hand slid across the length of his groin. "This feels like wood, as well, Sebastian," she murmured.

"No," he said on a thick swallow. "For you, I am stone."

She licked his jugular, making it strain against the surface of his skin in an angry pulse until he hissed. "Guardians slew my husband. He must be avenged."

"We can raise your army tonight, at sunset, and give them the demon powers. Nuit told me how to locate the Neterus."

She captured his hand and placed it on her breast with a gasp. "There is more than one?"

"Yes . . . two, a mated pair, with an entire team. They are on the East Coast of America."

"It is an hour until sunset there, darlink. What do you propose we do for that hour to stem the anticipation?"

Tears of need stung his eyes and made her image blurry. "If, for just an hour, to have the fullness of your unrestrained affection . . . even if you believe I do not deserve it, I—"

Her tightening grip stopped his words with a shuddering gasp. Her strike to his jugular was so ruthless that it chipped bone. Pleasure-dazed, he staggered aimlessly with her in his arms, too aroused to immediately sort out where he might bed her.

"Raise the army for me, tonight, to attack, tonight, and this hour you'll never forget."

CHAPTER EIGHT

Yo, Carlos, man . . . there's some chick at the door talkin' about she know you—like in a real up close and personal kinda way," Phat G said in a low tone.

Big Mike leaned forward with Inez.

"You best be glad D's in the bathroom with Momma," Inez said under her breath.

Phat G gave them a sidelong, glance. "Damn, you did say you have audios on your team. But here's the thing, man. This chick seems real outta this world . . . she knew to ask for *the Neterus*, and said she's from *Nod*."

Carlos was out of his seat, gaining curious looks from the rest of the team that couldn't hear. "About five-seven, five-eight, gorgeous dark skin with platinum locks?"

"That would be the one," Phat G said, ushering Carlos to where the woman was. "And did I mention had the body of life?"

Carlos pounded his fist. "I ain't supposed to know all that— I'm a married man."

"True dat," Phat G said, laughing. "But you ain't blind."

"Not at all," Carlos said, rounding the bar to find the small office in the back.

"Oh, thank the heavens," Val said, dropping to one knee and crossing her chest with her forearm.

"Damn, bro, you got it like that?" Phat G said, truly amazed.

"Naw, Val, c'mon, sis—we family," Carlos said, embarrassed, helping Val up quickly and then giving her a hug. "I know if you rolled up on us like this, it's bad. Talk to me."

He stared at her. He'd felt the wings, felt her strapped with all sorts of weapons, but couldn't see them. She stared back at him, her eyes silently begging him not to give away her secret in front of the man she didn't know. Carlos gave her a subtle nod, and Val's shoulders relaxed.

"Carlos, it's horrible," she said, tears brimming. "Yolando said to take this message from my mind and put it in silver and then shield me once you got it."

"You want me to fall back, man, and give you space?" Phat G glanced from Carlos to Val.

"Yeah, man, and do me a favor . . . if my wife comes out of the bathroom, send her back here, too. In fact, can you ask Inez to handle her mom and send my wife in here, stat?"

Phat G looked at Carlos for a moment, and hesitated before nodding. "Brother, when I grow up I wanna be just like you."

Carlos waited until Phat G had left and then he held Val's hand. "I can pull the message out, but I don't trust my silver," he admitted. The truth stabbed at his pride, but Val deserved no less. Openly admitting it made the reality sucker punch him. "Damali will have to silver-coat your mind and prayer-barrier you. I got hit with something from the ultimate darkness . . . I'm not even sure if I can go in to pull Yonnie's transmission without affecting you."

Carlos walked away from her, dragging his fingers through his hair. "If Yonnie sent you, then I know where he was . . . and right now, I'm real susceptible to losing it—if I see any more shit today that's gonna take my mind down a black hole."

"What if I just tell you what I see . . . explain what Yonnie sent into my mind?"

Carlos closed his eyes and dropped his head back, frustration eating him alive. "Yeah, cool, till Damali gets here—then she can pull it." He rubbed his temples and opened his eyes. "But I gotta ask you, even though Yonnie is my homeboy . . . did he nick you?"

"Nick?"

Carlos let his breath out hard. "Bite you?"

She looked away. "No . . . he gave me the message and made my wings invisible, as well as my weapons."

"Cool."

"He doesn't seem evil," Val countered, her eyes haunted. "We ate a meal together . . . pancakes, he called them. He even advised me to hide in your home, for safety. But after he slipped behind enemy lines, he came out with an urgent message. It just so happened that I was searching the beach for my fallen weapons, and he found me to give this important news to you."

Carlos wiped his palms down his face. Yonnie had to be near the breaking point. He'd gotten a daylight elevation from Lilith, eaten food for the first time, obviously fought Val if she was searching for weapons, and gotten close enough to bust a dematerialization move on her and then mind-lock her.

"He's not evil," Carlos said, walking over to Val and taking her jaw in his hand. He turned her chin first to the left then the right, trying to see through any vamp illusion with silver. "He's just a man, pure male. But he is my best friend; that he didn't lie about." He stared at her body outline, silver-scanning her, now able to see her wings and all her weapons.

Val touched his hand before he removed it from her jaw, and then let it fall away. "He is a good friend, Carlos. The man's heart is pure. The risks he took to get these scenes . . . .I cannot fathom."

"Yeah," Carlos said quietly. "My boy's in real deep." He held back telling her more, not sure why.

She nodded. "I have his back, too . . . is it wrong, Neteru, to feel attracted to one's fellow warrior? Is that taboo?"

Carlos shook his head and walked away from her. "Yonnie, Yonnie, Yonnie . . ." He released a hard breath. "Val, he's good people, but the man has issues. That's all I can say."

"You are disappointed that I have lost my focus as a soldier." She hung her head and swallowed hard. "I stand before you, ashamed."

"Naw, sis," Carlos said quickly. "Don't even go there. I just . . . no. It's cool." He came to her and landed a hand on her shoulder. "But you make him tell you more about himself before you take things to another level, feel me?"

She smiled a bashful smile and looked down. "You are like the father or big brother I never had. Now I am truly honored."

Carlos chuckled. "He may be my homeboy, but if he does anything foul to you, I'll kick his ass myself. Hear?"

Without warning Val hugged him so hard he almost lost his balance, making him laugh.

"Please tell me I can stay, Carlos. I am a brave warrior, will fight to the death with honor. I can sleep outside and guard your compound, whatever you say—but I've never felt like this before."

"Oh, my, God . . ."

She stepped back, her eyes frantically searching his until he walked away. "There is muted sensation there . . . refugees who live in fear and half lives. I won't eat much, can earn my own rations, if my burden is too much. There's no one left to guard, to protect, and just for a small portion of my life, I need to feel—"

"Done," Carlos said, his back still to Val. His eyes were closed, his head hurt. "Now I'm gonna get my ass kicked because I didn't ask my wife."

"Ask me what?" Damali said, opening the door. But Carlos never got to answer. The moment she saw Val, she screamed and barreled into her arms. Then within seconds, she drew back, trying to understand feeling something she couldn't see.

"Yonnie concealed her non-human traits and weapons, which is a real good thing in a firefight, D . . . but we just got one more added to the compound—I know we shoulda discussed it, but she can't go back to Nod."

"Oh!" Damali said, jumping up and down, holding Val's arms. "That is so cool!"

Carlos looked at both of them. "Yonnie, uh, likes her, you know . . . and she's got his back, and whatnot."

Damali held Val out, making her blush. "Noooo . . . Yolando?"

Val just nodded. "He is a valiant warrior and I respect him," she said, lifting her chin.

"That is perfect!" Damali's voice hit a soprano decibel that sent a shiver down his spine.

"You approve, Queen," Val said, her voice excited and reverent.

"Do I approve?"

"D, bring it down a notch," Carlos said, rubbing the chills from the nape of his neck. "We've gotta break this to the house, too."

"Rider oughta be cool with this," Damali said, hands on hips.

Carlos raised an eyebrow. "Let's hope everybody else is."

Damali's eyes got big as Val's attention went from one Neteru to the other.

"Oh, yeah," Damali said quietly.

"Uh-huh," Carlos said, walking across the room to lean on the desk. "You know how that shit goes sometimes."

"Yeah, but, she can't afford to go there—even mentally."

"People do things they can't afford every day."

Damali held up her hands and waved them in the air. "Enough. I don't wanna think about team drama. Right now, Val's in the house, which should make our two newest additions very, very happy. She looks like another angel when her wings are out."

Val's attention bounced toward Damali and she smiled, hugging herself. "Yonnie made me look like a full-human. He's amazing."

"Which leads us to the dilemma of whether or not to lift the prayer-barrier to the house." Carlos folded his arms over his chest. "And explaining a . . . Yolando to Mom Delores and Ayana."

"He does look frightening when in battle," Val said, interjecting. "So I would expect him to be able to upset any sensitive members of your team that may have demon battle flashbacks. If you were so generous to allow me refuge in your sanctuary, I would not do anything to violate that honor."

Damali waved her hand. "It ain't you, girl. Your honor is intact. Hell, everybody on the team is gonna have to make adjustments now that we've got a toddler around—plus Inez's momma."

"Sheeit . . . Big Mike's gonna have to make the adjustment," Carlos muttered. "Last I checked I was grown and married."

"A toddler?"

Damali gave Carlos a glare but spoke to Val in a gentle tone. "A three-year-old human baby in the house . . . one of the Guardians—"

"A baby is on the team, in your army?" Val's eyes got big as she took two steps backward and then dropped to one knee again. "The prophecy child . . ."

"No, we don't have the Messiah up in our camp, girl—be serious!" Damali raked her locks and walked in a circle. "Just my niece."

Val looked up. "You do not know of the prophecy?" Valkyrie

stood slowly, appearing confused. "The Messiah is coming this time as—"

"A lion, not a lamb," Carlos said, finishing her sentence. "Full grown—the fire this time. Yeah."

"But the Neteru baby . . ." Val looked at Carlos and then Damali. "The precursor. *The promise* that could possibly avert the Armageddon before one-third of the earth's multitudes is destroyed."

"Whoa, sis," Carlos said, holding his hands up and then staring at Damali. "I didn't hear nothing about that. Did you, D?"

Damali shook her head violently. "Uh-uh. Never heard it."

Val hugged herself. "Maybe because we were in the early days . . . before there were lost books of the Bible? We have the full texts of all the religions up there." Her gaze again went between the nervous couple. "We read so much . . . that was all we had to do for pleasure . . . that and debate the philosophies, speculate on all things."

"The Queens ever say anything to you about this, D?" Carlos's expression held quiet panic.

"Uh-uh—the Kings ever, you know, tell you something after our honeymoon?"

"Naw, I woulda told you."

They both looked at Val at the same time. "We gotta get that missing volume."

"Do you want me to go back and retrieve it now, or give you the message Yonnie sent first?"

"The Yonnie message," Damali and Carlos said together.

"Okay, okay, you go in, get the message and then seal her in silver—then throw it to me."

Damali hesitated. "Baby, why didn't you just go in?"

Carlos rubbed his jaw. "I'm dirty—might be carrying a black-charge residue from the hit Father took earlier today. I went in and tried to drape him."

"'Nuff said," Damali murmured. She turned to Val. "Depending on how bad the news is from Yonnie, all this might be a moot point."

"Yeah," Carlos said in a surly tone. "Just like the tour that's supposed to kick off six months from now might be moot. The future is real tenuous around here, Val."

Damali monitored her husband's escalating tension and the rage embedded in it as she laid her palms gently against Valkyrie's temples. The mere mention of a baby, and the loss that she knew they'd both never forget, had suddenly taken Carlos's mood to a very dark place. She closed her eyes, trying to concentrate, having difficulty with the task. There was no doubt about it, as soon as everyone was settled down, safe, she and Carlos needed to make a Neteru Council run to be sure he wasn't carrying anything toxic that could grow legs and bite them.

But as the images careened through her mind, she knew that might have to wait. "Oh, shit . . ." she murmured, pulling more and more until Val began to shudder. "How you holding up, lady?' Damali asked.

Val held Damali's wrists tightly. "Yolando coated it . . . so it wouldn't be so horrible."

Damali opened her eyes for a moment, dazed.

"Translation," Carlos said, folding his arms over his chest. "He pleasure-packed it."

Val bit her lower lip and closed her eyes, nodding quickly.

"Oh . . . yeah," Damali said quietly.

"What, it's been so long you forgot how this works?"

Damali simply gave him a look. Something was definitely wrong with her husband.

"It won't affect the receiver, since he was sending to me—and me and him don't have that kind of relationship," Carlos said in a sullen tone. "So you'll get a clean transmission, but this is gonna drop girlfriend to her knees in about thirty seconds . . . got a daylight topspin on it that I can feel halfway across the room!"

"Chill . . . I can't do this with a divided mind," Damali said, trying to keep her focus. "Why're you so pissed off about Yonnie doing whatever?"

Carlos walked away from them with his hands on top of his head and his eyes closed. "I don't know."

Val gripped Damali's wrists and spoke through her teeth, in a low, urgent whisper. "No disrespect, Queen . . . but can he leave?"

Damali leaned her head on Val's damp forehead. "I have to transmit whatever I learn to him, girl. You know that."

Val nodded roughly and sucked in a deep inhalation through her nose and bit down harder on her lip. Instant understanding slammed Damali.

"Carlos, do me a favor—take a walk."

He looked at her and headed for the door. "That's why I'm pissed at my boy—he didn't have to send her in here all messed up like that. Darkside bullshit gets on my last nerve!"

The door slammed with a rattle just as Val collapsed into Damali's arms, almost making them both fall. Helping her to the desk, Damali caught Val around her waist as Val stumbled forward and sat on the edge of it with a thud.

"I can never look at the King again, I am humiliated beyond all understanding," Val whispered. "And before you . . ." She covered her face with her hands.

"Girl, Carlos can't say shit about this. He did it to me in front of my whole team—even my mother-seer and a coupla clerics."

Damali smiled when Val's mouth opened and no sound came out. "Yeah, brotherman has a dark side, too . . . but that's what they're exploiting." Her smile faded. "We've gotta get him out of here, away from the team so he isn't a bullshit magnet—and then to the Neteru Councils for a serious purge." She put a hand on Val's shoulder. "*Mi casa es su casa*—you come live with us, all right. Thank you for bringing serious word. Let me get you sealed up in silver, then give me a minute in here with Carlos alone. I'll send Marlene word so you can just squeeze in at the table like everybody else."

Val hugged Damali as she silver-sealed her mind, just rocking. "A true home. A true family. How can I ever repay you, Queen?"

"By staying alive and healthy," Damali said, holding Val away from her. "Seriously. My heart can't take it."

Val nodded and gave her a warrior's handshake.

"Yo, Rivera!" Damali hollered. "It's safe!"

Carlos opened the door and peered in, keeping his gaze to the floor. "Okay, what's the word?"

Val slipped past him and Damali simply chuckled.

"Marlene has on purple, silver locks, you can't miss her. She knows you're coming. I just sent it to her."

"Bless you," Val murmured and then closed the door.

Carlos folded his arms. "How bad is it?"

"C'mere," Damali said. "It's real bad. Like, so bad that I'm beyond hysterical. You know that point where the absurd just takes over and you have to laugh to keep from crying?"

"Been there," he said with a weary sigh and walked over and hugged her.

"Let me show you how bad." She looked up and touched the side of his face. "And it's not you—you have to get a purge, and probably so do I."

"Damn! I knew it! Been off all day!"

"Yeah, well, it was for a good cause . . . was there any other way? Ask yourself, would you be you if you didn't try to step in and take a bullet for Father?"

Carlos closed his eyes, resting his forehead on Damali's. "Sad part is, it didn't do any good."

"The man is still alive, Carlos. He has a fighting chance. The moment you give up hope, they got you—you of all people should know that."

"And here again my wife has been exposed to some toxic shit I dragged in the door."

"Not because you weren't where you were supposed to be. This is what we do, baby. You were in a cathedral trying to get between the Devil himself and one of our family . . . you don't think I respect that?"

He pulled her in closer and rested his cheek against the crown of her head. "I just needed some of your light after it all went down, D. Something to make me see that silver lining, because what's inside me right now is so angry I can barely see straight."

She rubbed his back and kissed his Adam's apple. "I know . . . that's why I haven't been arguing with you." She could feel him smile against her scalp. "I love you. That's the one thing that always chases out the darkness. It may be hard, but until we get to the Neterus of Light, I want you to concentrate on loving Father Pat more than you hate the Nameless. This doesn't mean you ain't mad at them for what they did, or that you don't have the right to be fired up . . . but if Father Patrick needs your love, your hope, your strength; mess the darkside up by doing exactly what they don't expect you to do."

He nodded and swallowed hard, then sucked in a shaky inhalation. "It's hard to shift gears and not hate 'em like I do. When I saw that old man in a hospital bed I thought about my moms . . . Alejandro, Juan, Miguel . . . everybody they came for and took, you know. Damn, they got Padre Lopez . . . I mean, when does it end, D? Got Hubert and Sara, the whole fucking Brazil team, brothers and sister Guardians from that whole ambush in Mexico . . . your mom and dad, start there." He held her tighter. "Even took what woulda been our first-born."

Her body swayed in a gentle rocking motion as her hands traced his back, soothing, healing, trying to staunch the pain. "I know, and when we get somewhere safe and peaceful and pro-tected, me and you are both gonna let all this rage and pain and hurt out. But right now, I have so much to show you, and what feels like so little time."

He drew back and nodded. "You'll now be the sender, and you're female. In a minute you're gonna know why I was so mad at my boy. I know he didn't realize that I wouldn't just go take it from Val without an intermediary . . . but this mind-lock is sender-loaded. You following me?"

"Aw, man . . ." Damali rested her forehead on Carlos's chest. "We ain't got time for this!"

"Yeah. My point exactly."

"All right. Shit. Well, you can talk me down later." Damali reached up and held Carlos's skull. "You ready?"

He smirked. "Making this clinical ain't gonna change things . . . maybe give you a five-second lead on sensation, but my boy took over my old throne, and I know what was in it."

"Just be quiet and let me send you the images." She held his head harder than was necessary and focused on a file cabinet.

"You have *got* to be fucking kidding me," Carlos said as she hard-thrust images into his mind. "Lucrezia . . . we ain't gonna see Nuit for a month!"

Damali didn't speak. She bit her bottom lip and focused on the cabinet harder, noting the tone of gray in the paint, the dull fixtures on it.

"Oh, so they LoJacked me, huh . . . put a tag on me. Wait till Nuit's grimy ass resurfaces. Yeah . . . oh, it's like that—and went after Ayana like wha? See, D, this is what I'm say—" Suddenly Carlos burst out laughing. "Sebastian is gonna get his stupid ass bumped off for sure. Drac's woman—be serious. That—"

Damali crushed the words from his mouth with a kiss. "Remind me to kick Yonnie's ass when I see him." Breathless, she found his jugular with her tongue.

"I don't know whether to kick his ass or genuflect . . . but, uh, D, we can't even begin to go there, till I get a purge."

She backed off and walked in a circle for a moment. "Right, right, compromised silver, bad toxin, bad situation."

"Was that the end of the message?"

She looked at him, squeezed her eyes shut, and squeaked out the answer. "No."

"Okay, baby, just finish it . . . and, later . . . we'll get everybody home, make a run . . ."

She held up a finger. "I can't think that far in advance right now. Let me dump this intel and then go put some water on my face."

He stepped in close and allowed her to gently hold his head again. "Take your time."

She offered him a scowl. "Just be quiet—you're enjoying this, aren't you?"

"Will you be mad if I say, slightly? Rare that I get the tables turned on me so lovely these days."

"Man, hush." She closed her eyes and shot him the rest of the images and then backed away quickly from him. "Damn. Is that what you guys go through all the time?"

"Pretty much, but only if the sister is hot."

She cut him another glare but had to smile.

"You know I'm never, *eva* gonna rest until I step to Nuit about slamming Inez's mom and throwing that baby, right?"

Damali folded her arms over her chest. "You? Sheeeit. I was there, bro."

Carlos nodded. "See how a little violent anger can just kill your libido and make everything all right? I like my anger, not sure I wanna part with it. Gets me up in the morning, helps me manage my day. Wouldn't know what to do as a peace and Zen representative. I just want the Light to burn off a little bit of the super-toxin so the darkside doesn't hot the house. Worst of it is, I hate being LoJacked like a thoroughbred dog. But other than that, the darkside can kiss my ass."

She chuckled. "I don't think the Light is ever gonna be able to burn this level of rage outta my system, and I know there's nothing they can do with you. Thing that messes me up is, they can keep this bullshit going now twenty-four-seven. At least before we had a twelve-hour window of daylight. Damn!"

"Then let's go eat dinner. What else is there to do at the moment?" He wiggled his eyebrows and hurried out the door.

CHAPTER NINE

By the time they rejoined the combined teams at the table, Val had found a spot between Krissy and Heather, and was sitting directly across from Marlene. Phat G's squad was taking rotational visits, popping into a few open chairs, grabbing some appetizers, and chatting it up before they went back on duty. Inez's mother was in a deep, private conversation with Marjorie Berkfield, while Ayana had finally warmed enough to allow herself to be passed from lap to lap.

Female Guardians fawned over her, and Carlos touched Damali's elbow, leaning in to speak into her ear.

"We knew this was inevitable," he said. "And I'm all for it during times like these. But, Damali, my gut just ain't sitting right with it."

She nodded. "I know. But I don't know what else to do."

"Me, either," he admitted. Then, motioning quickly with his chin, he indicated his Guardian brothers. "Cascade effect is about to happen. Krissy got her on her lap making origami out of her place mat, while J.L. is over there having a mild stroke—envisioning the future."

"Oh, shit . . ."

"Uh-huh. And look at your boy, Bobby. Eyes wide as saucers.

That's the look of a man having heart failure. Then I want you to get with Dan. Heather's all snuggled in, the man is sweating bullets, and if we get back home in one piece I put twenty dollars on it he'll make one of his own tonight. Jose is just done— because out of 'em all, 'Nita's bio clock is ticking loudest."

Damali squeezed his arm.

"Yeah . . . and you wonder what keeps me up at night? Ever think about what we'll do if every Guardian female in the house is pregnant at the same time? Only balance beam is Marj and Marlene . . . Tara is still fifty-fifty, who knows. But fact is, since we all live in a group and every woman's cycle has synced up . . . that means the window of fertility is the same, which means all them can—"

"Carlos, stop," Damali whispered. "I can take gruesome images from Vamp Council and sleep better at night than worrying about the horror you just described."

"Me, too. That's why I'm saying, this is so dangerous on so many levels, D. And I haven't left myself out. Every time you hold Ayana in your arms I gotta take a walk . . . can't deal. Because it's one thing to have an image in the back of your mind, but a clear visual makes everything *crystal.*"

"Let's go eat. Go get a purge. Go do that general stuff that we do . . . aw, Lawdy Miss Claudy."

She strode ahead of him, unable to handle any more. Bright smiles greeted them both and Ayana gave her a big grin, holding up the paper fan and bird Krissy had made.

"Look, a birdie an' a fan!"

"That's beautiful, baby," Damali said, forcing a smile and picking at her very cold food.

Val glimpsed the plates and leaned in to connect with Inez. She glanced at Big Mike's stack of bones. "Is your mate half-demon-carnivore, too?"

Mrs. Filgueiras gasped in so hard that three Guardians had to dislodge corn bread from her windpipe.

"No no, no," Inez said quickly, slapping her mother's back. She gave Damali a brief look that contained a plea for help. "Mike eats big. That's all."

Openly curious, Val cocked her head to the side. "He's not hybrid, is all human . . . but built like a cross between—"

"Girl, Mike's just from the South," Damali said, cutting off Val's query with diplomacy.

"I will have to learn these regional differences." She looked at Bobby and J.L.'s thinner, wirier frames. "You are not from the South then?"

"Uh, no," J.L. said, stuffing food in his mouth to keep from laughing. "West Coast."

Val nodded. "I will have to study a map." Then she turned with a big smile and looked at Carlos. "Where is Yolando from?"

"The South," Carlos said warily.

Damali gave the other Guardians the eye and they swallowed smiles. That's all they needed was for Mrs. Filgueiras to have a screaming jag in the middle of Phat G's joint.

Marlene was so tore up with repressed laughter that every few moments she'd wipe her eyes at the corners and swat Shabazz's teasing hand away from her sides.

"Ah," Val said. "Then the South is good."

Jose sprayed Lynchburg lemonade in his plate and started coughing.

"Who's Yolando?" Inez's mother asked, still wheezing and fanning her face.

"A very nice hybrid," Val said. "Honorable—best friend of the male Neteru."

"Is this girl on drugs?" Inez's mother whispered.

Val beamed at her. "No, I do not need medications to visit from Nod, the passage is clear. Your daughter's husband eats like Yolando—but he prefers blueberry pancakes to animal bones."

Jose laid his head on Juanita's shoulder and she elbowed him off her, turning her head away while trying hard to breathe without laughing. When Rider leaned forward with his elbows on the table, Shabazz shook his head.

"Man, don't start. I'm begging you," Shabazz said.

"Now, you *know*, of all people, *I* have to ask," Rider said, looking at Val. "Yolando and blueberry pancakes?"

"Jack Rider, I forbid you to scandalize this table with Inez's mother here and a clearly innocent guest of Yonnie's." Tara cut Rider a glare that could have cut metal. "I mean it. Stop."

"It is all right, Tara," Val said, sipping a Lynchburg lemonade. She made a deep slurping sound as her straw hit the bottom and then she began picking the sugar off the side of the glass to taste. "He really does like blueberry pancakes, plus steaks and eggs and that long, oily meat . . . ah, bacon. Oh, and coffee. I have not seen him eat animal bones yet. I don't think I would like that very much. But I suppose as long as it was cooked and not raw the way demons normally take their carcasses, I could adapt."

Shabazz rubbed his palms down his face and turned away.

"Why does she keep saying demon, Lord have mercy Jesus? Tell me—"

"While we were gone, how many drinks did you let her try?" Damali tried to stem Mrs. Filgueiras's hysteria, cutting her off before her low whisper escalated.

"She had three," Marlene said flatly. "While she was grazing on the different appetizers."

Damali and Carlos both closed their eyes.

Trying to offer a distraction to sensitive conversation, Krissy handed Ayana over to Val.

"Wanna meet a new lady that's gonna be living with us, too?" Ayana giggled. "Anova angel lady."

"Another angel lady," Inez translated. "She's intrigued by angels, now. Long story for another time."

"She can see my wings?" Val laughed and hugged the child. "How did you know that? They're supposed to be invisible. Yonnie made them disappear!"

Ayana clapped and stroked a place near Val that seemed to be four inches from her body. "They're soft. Yours are brown. Auntie Damali's are white. Yours are pretty, too."

"C'mon, boo," Inez said quickly. "Let's go pee pee before we have to give Nana some smelling salts."

Marlene and Marjorie had each grasped one of Mom Delores's hands and were holding her up.

Carlos leaned into Damali and the group got quiet. "The kid can see, boo."

Damali nodded and stared at Inez. "I know."

"Come to Mommy," Inez said more firmly, her eyes panicked. "You haven't been to the potty in a long time."

Ayana hid her face against Val's neck. "I don' wanna go to the scary pictures."

Inez's mother gaped at her granddaughter and then at Inez. The table was silent and the noise of the crowd beyond it seemed so far away.

"She never went in that bathroom, 'Nez. How did she know?" Mrs. Filgueiras opened her arms for the child. "Come to Nana," she said sweetly and then her eyes filled with tears. "You used to be able to do the same thing as a little girl, but I never listened to you. Maybe we make our mistakes with our own, and if we're blessed, we get to make up for all of that with the grands."

Marjorie hugged Delores. "I didn't listen, either, with my two."

"Did the same thing, living in denial," Marlene said. "Lost my girl, you're blessed. You got them both." She swallowed hard and picked up her drink.

Just that fast the mood at the table had shifted. Shabazz let an ice cube fall from his mouth into his glass.

"It's the way of the world. One tiny pebble in a still pond can cause ripples throughout the entire lake. Things are changing again, people. Brace yourselves."

"C'mon, suga. Nana won't let those scary pictures get her baby girl, okay?"

The child refused to budge. "They move, Nana. I don't wanna go!"

Rider took his 9mm out of the holster and checked his magazine. "I'm from coal mining country. I think this little cutie is our canary."

Jose took a deep breath and pulled a Berretta out from the back of his jeans that had been stashed under his shirt. Carlos and Damali were on their feet, as was Val, holding the child to her breast.

"Yo, G," Carlos hollered, motioning him over.

Phat G hustled to the table, his locks crackling with static. "What up, man?"

"Deep concern," Carlos said. "How's your men on the roof?"

Phat G hit his two-way. "You good?"

"Yeah, we cool up here. Got a problem?" Anthony replied.

"Brother Net is feeling some type-a way. That ain't good."

"We on it."

A high-pitched whine made Carlos, Mike, Damali, and Inez turn at the same time. Carlos pushed Val to the floor with the baby and drove across the table to body-shield Mom Delores, flinging a disc of Heru that cut through brick.

"Incoming!"

The blast rocked the top of the building, sending patrons in a screaming frenzy. Phat G's squad came over the bar, out of the kitchen, and from hidden alcoves. "Get these civilians out of here!" he ordered. "Protocol drill alpha!"

Damali swam against a sea of panicked bodies. It had to be an aerial assault, because the roof was being bombarded. Carlos had shattered a window and had a shield up blocking the first floor where there were hundreds of innocent lives at risk. Chaos thrummed in her ears as he folded-away to the roof to assist Guardians there, and tacticals on Level One had commandeered the rack of firewood, sending stake missiles whirring through the door like MLRS shells.

Tables turned over, Guardians hunkered down. Flaming demon arrows whizzed through the front door and windows with black bolt charges, falling at Carlos's shield. It was surreal. Pandemonium would leak into her mind in sharp, quick-stop frames and then erupt in real time.

Valkyrie had her niece clamped between her athletic thighs behind a table while she loaded silver-tipped arrows in her bow. The archer then went up on one knee, firing out the unblocked side windows, while Ayana scrambled behind her. Val's movements were physical poetry, like a choreographed dance, as she popped up quickly, set a target, released instant death to splatter a demon, and then dropped down again to protect the child.

Rider, Shabazz, Jose, and Mike had commandeered the four corners of the establishment, teaming with Phat G's squad to shoot out of side windows as the crowd cleared out. Bobby and Dan covered civilians, helping to usher them out the back exit with Berkfield and several fast-moving brothers on Phat G's team. Fire extinguishers manned by team members were sending white plumes of dense fog everywhere, countering the inferno from flaming arrows designed to smoke the teams out.

Phat had rolled out the heavy artillery with the kitchen crew. From under the cabinets they broke out rocket-propelled grenade launchers, tossing them to Inez and Juanita, while the rest of the New York squad handed off handheld Uzis and assault rifles. Marlene got the assembly line going until every Guardian was strapped. Crowd screams got farther and farther away. Mom Delores stayed with Ayana and Valkyrie as Damali unsheathed her blade. She looked at Inez's mother and Val.

"Val, you got 'em?"

"On my life, Queen."

Phat G dropped down beside them with two Uzis and a shoulder launcher. "I got her back. Y'all go make it do what it do. They ain't comin' in our house like this." He pointed to the train tracks with the barrel of a machine gun. "The third rail's got a lotta juice. Get my roof squad to tell your tacticals when the trains roll—soon as they go by, stand with our squad and bend the beam to fry those fuckers, feel me? 'Scuze my French, ma'am."

"Good look, G. Good look," Damali said, ducking through the arrow assault and heading to an opening in the side windows as the building shook again.

She met Carlos on the roof, shielding three men.

"These guys were lucky," Carlos yelled. "Brother Ant is hit, but if you work on him, he'll be able to use that leg again."

"They're sending up what feels like mortar rounds from catapults," Rene shouted over another rocking blast.

Carlos looked at Damali. "Catapults? What the—"

Another blast rocked the roof, but Carlos's shield took the heavy impact.

"They've got a position up on the train platforms," Rod said, bracing through another blast.

Damali took over for Carlos, trying to piece together shattered bone and torn ligaments while keeping the fellow Guardian conscious.

Lisa and Adrienne hustled through the metal door with Heather and Jasmine, all four women toting heavy firepower. Rushing to the edge of the roof between blasts, Lisa set the launcher down quickly, Adrienne stuffed it, and the launcher was up on her shoulder in a matter of seconds. Heather and Jasmine covered them, sending a spray of Uzi shells toward the offending command post. The blast got deflected by a black charge and, rather than taking out the more densely packed enemy, it took out a section of train trestle with ten demons. But now there was the issue of innocents.

"Damn!" Lisa shouted and reloaded.

"Hold up," Carlos said, looking at Rene and Rod. "What time's the next train through?"

"Four minutes, man." Rod crossed himself and checked his clip. "We can bend the beam, fry 'em, maybe interrupt the power so the train stalls—but at this point, it might be moving too fast. Might still keep coming even if the power shuts down, then the one behind it will ram it. You talking chain reaction, bro, with a lotta people dying."

"Okay, y'all—I need Phat G, 'Bazz, J.L., Dan, any tacticals y'all got to bend the beam," Carlos said. "While Damali is working on that downed soldier, I want three seers on mind-jolt to hit the people that originate the schedule, so they'll check and double-check and delay. It's gotta be so that the train behind this one doesn't ram the one already heading our way."

"Get our Stonehengers setting up blue-white charge on this building, too," Damali shouted from where she sat. "Anything that slithers up the wall, I want it to fry on contact."

"Chantay and 'Nyya can work with 'em, and we got seers that monitor the trains all the time for demon flybys," Adrienne said. "Carmen's got the damned thing memorized."

"Cool. Put her on the lead and our squad will reinforce," Damali said, covering Anthony's wound. "Both squads have enough sharpshooters to pick them off one at a time, if they stay behind Carlos's shields."

"Yeah, but I've gotta go catch a train."

Carlos was off the roof before anyone could draw a breath. He stood on the tracks, assessing the damage, deflecting catapulted black-energy orbs. There was a gaping hole that revealed fragile trestle on the left side of the track. The platforms down at 125th and up at 137th were crawling with skeleton-faced demon warrior archers in black armor and spaded tails. They were the source of the rain of fire. Carlos looked down at the ground through the massive hole in the tracks. Below him, a demon cavalry, riding fire-snorting black stallions, was advancing on the building. Across the street on two building roofs were the catapults. He stared at the crest hard, his old throne knowledge bubbling to the surface of his mind . . . Vlad the Impaler's Hungarian forces?

Then to command them, the necromancer had to be near—as did their mistress, the Countess.

Oncoming train lights returned Carlos to the moment. He added in his pull to the third rails, watching the blue-white power slowly bend. It groaned loudly, the distortion of atmosphere created a haunting sound. *One mind . . .* he was about to broadcast out via telepathy and then froze, quickly retracting the thought. He was viral, could black-shock every tactical on two teams!

The lights went out on the train, but it was already committed to momentum. He could hear the people inside the cars screaming in the dark. He had to get behind it.

Folding-away, he came up behind it, drew a white-light orb into his hand, and threw it as hard as he could. The cord caught and held, but the weight of the train dragged him forward with a violent pop—it was heavier than the dragon Cain had tried to stop in that same manner. He hit the tracks on his stomach, twisting, dragging, almost gutted by the track ties before he was able to untangle himself. There was no way to anchor the rocketing cars. Plan B. Laughter echoed from near the catapults. Good. The generals had given away their positions.

Bloodied and losing energy, he temporarily lifted the shield from the roof team, flung it to the track hole just in time for the train to sail across it. A catapult blast answered the vulnerability, but Phat G's squad, with his, had finally bent the third rail energy and then scorched the offending rooftop attackers.

"This man is whole; get him down below, away from the catapults," Damali said.

"How's the next train looking?" Carlos hollered to Phat G.

"Off schedule. Word is getting back that there's a stalled train on the 131 bisect up in Harlem."

"Tell those seers, good looking, G."

"You're busted up," Damali said, putting a hand to his chest. "Real bad, Carlos."

"I know," he said, heaving in air and spitting out blood. "But we gotta go smoke Sebastian and the Countess—motherfuckers raised Vlad's army."

"What?"

"That's why they've got catapults."

"Take five. You go down, our shields go down, and that can't happen with a baby and an away team in the house."

Carlos nodded, weaved for a moment, and then sat down with a thud beside Anthony.

"Lisa, get Medic up here. Berkfield from our squad. We've got a man down, and I can't heal him 'cause of time."

Lisa nodded and waited for an opening in the rounds.

"Tell Medic it's my husband and to work hard, all right?"

With a crisp nod, Lisa was a flash, dodging between heavy fire while Adrienne took up her post.

Damali's eyes scanned the horizon. So they were fighting old-school, huh? Catapults, archers, infantrymen, and cavalry . . .

fourteenth-century battle tactics. If Lilith had been with them, then it would have been another story. Even Nuit had updated, because he'd been in a council chair long enough. But these were new councilmen—Sebastian only having slightly longer tenure than the brand-new Countess.

If Carlos opened the Ark here it would leave a smoking black hole and too much civilian damage. Police sirens were too far off. Okay, the darkside had co-opted the authorities, too. Had black-boxed this area. Okay, then it was time to find the edge of that sucker and light it up.

Damali came back to Carlos's side and felt his pulse, placing her hands on his chest as Berkfield ran across the roof and dropped down.

"Baby . . ." she said quietly. "I don't know how you even walked over here. It's worse than I thought." She looked at Berkfield and then wiped Carlos's hair from his brow as his head lolled from side to side. "He's got multiple internal injuries, spleen, liver, cracked ribs. He's hemorrhaging."

"I'm good, just need to rest for a minute. Holding the shields is draining me."

"We've gotta get a transfusion going, D—or you're gonna have to do the full Monty. I can patch him till you get back, but he don't look so good. Not like I've ever seen him."

Just as Berkfield was speaking, shields dropped.

"Holy Christ, D—he's passed out."

"Stay with him," Damali said, firing light pulses from the tip of her Isis. "Everybody off the roof. Now!"

She looked over the edge of the building at the increasing black wave of demon cavalry heading toward the now-unshielded restaurant, as Berkfield and Rene pulled Carlos up to hitch their shoulders under his armpits. Phat G and Rod helped Anthony, while female Guardians kept the pressure on with a blanket of shells.

"Jose!" Damali shouted, pointing to the thick line of motorcycles out front with her blade. "You, Dan, Bobby, and any brothers who can ride—on horses!"

"Ride or die, D!" Jose shouted, and then ducked back into the building.

Moments later, a squad of running, shooting Guardians burst out the front doors and windows, hopped on bikes, hard-riding with handheld Uzis, heading directly for the demon cavalry line on the wide boulevard. Horses reared as the bikes drove right at them, and the team flew by steel-girding, spinning out to make a run at them again. They broke the line, avoiding sword slashes, mowing down demons drive-by style, and then led the undead cavalry away from the building toward the expressway. In her peripheral vision she saw a female Guardian lean out the window of an adjacent building, providing machine-gun cover as her men on the ground rode hard. It had to be LaShonda, because as quickly as she'd popped into the window, the woman was down on the ground covering running pedestrians and pushing them to safety.

Damali could see it all in her mind—black bat-winged horses ridden by skeletal troops being taken out by semis and weekend swift-moving traffic while the bikes maneuvered between cars, zigzagging through the lanes. Something unknown was also affecting the people in the neighborhood. Non-Guardians, regular citizens, were shooting out of windows, knocking demons off their mounts with baseball bats, crowbars, and steel pipes. It was as though all of Harlem took to the streets, people who should have been terrified stood with Guardians—eyes blazing with a silent, furious message: *Not here. Not in our neighborhood.* Unsure of what to make of it all, Damali pressed on. The Divine had moved people, she was clear, but she hoped they wouldn't be killed. But she had to stop that reign of terror coming from the far platform. The archers had to go down.

The inbound train had safe room to pass, even as precarious as the track was. The moment it neared, she folded-away and hitched a ride, unseen—holding on to the far side until the very last moment. Popping up, she hit the archer's outpost with a white-light pulse from the tip of the Isis. Demons screamed, incinerating on contact. She flipped off the train and dropped down on their ashes, sending them up in a plume.

Fury in her eyes, she focused on the remaining catapult. That was where the generals had to be holed up. With their cavalry decimated, archers fried, and one catapult down, if she could light up the black box, then she could stop the infantrymen that were about to storm the building. There was no elegant way to do that other than to get over to that rooftop and come out of a fold-away swinging.

But to her horror, the infantrymen rushed the joint. Her focus split as she realized that someone must have called in the kamikaze order. It was no longer about strategy, just straight hand-to-hand combat.

Snarling, hissing, growling entities scaled the walls, propelled themselves from fire escapes, and dropped from the train trestle infrastructure. She could hear Mom Delores scream, hear Ayana scream. Demon bodies splatted green gook and sulfur everywhere. In a flash, Mom Delores popped up, squeezed off a round, and got down. In two-handed swings, Valkyrie was loping heads, while Juanita had her back in 40mm shell single shots.

Inez was out front like a hellcat, hunched down low, firing with everything she got her hands on with Mike, Rider, and Shabazz. Pure hatred shone in her team's eyes. J.L. and Phat G's crew were working knives, up on tables out in front of the building, fly-kicking, then spinning with butcher-knife precision. Phat G and his tactical squad kept stakes whirring to cover them from being overrun. Mo and his kitchen crew sent so much stainless steel through the door to sever heads that streetlamps caught the silver gleam like passing tracer patterns. Sprinkler systems were going off, spraying holy water everywhere. Good.

Damali breathed a sigh of relief. Demons couldn't get in through the prayer barriers. They could send in artillery that could maim or kill, but the building interior was secure.

"Fall back. Hold your fire," she shouted, knowing it would confuse the inexperienced generals.

Demons surrounded the building and waited. It was a stand-off as they contemplated what to assault the open windows and blown-off doorways with next. Another catapult blast hit the roof and shook the building.

If she was watching the progress, so were the darkside's generals. In a quiet fold-away Damali came up behind the small retinue manning the catapult. She hit it with a white lightning blast—stunning Sebastian, and swinging at the Countess with her Isis. The blast she'd sent bounced off the night.

Elizabeth shrieked and caught herself against a hard, invisible force—the same way Sebastian hit it hard. Of course they would be shielded, as commanders. Punk bitches.

Damali was gone, only to step out of a fold-away on the other side of their roof. Hatred-filled eyes met. Damali's Isis chimed in the air. White lightning crackled from its tip as a blue-white charge overtook her arm. She released a Neteru war cry that stilled demons and made them turn to look up. Sebastian yanked the Countess into a vapor escape. Damali hit the rooftop with a traveling white-light nova that sent a blinding prism across the roof, knocked out the catapult, and then made every demon within the black box in front of the restaurant explode.

Just as suddenly as the assault began, it was over. Traffic and sirens could now be heard clearly.

"Casualties?" Damali called out.

"Roll call," Phat G hollered.

Damali counted heads as her team slowly emerged from their makeshift bunkers. Inez had her child in her arms, and her mother had obviously prioritized survival over shock and horror. Mrs. Filgueiras lowered her weapon. Val was collecting her silver arrows from demon carcasses and ash. Rider stood, hocked, and spit. Tara slammed an empty magazine down, while Big Mike gently set down the grenades he'd been slinging.

"We'll get this place rebuilt with the quickness, G," Damali said, looking around at the devastation. "We got some safe houses up in Brooklyn while all that goes down, but in the meanwhile, we gotta cover you with the authorities."

Phat G smiled. "Tacticals—shell casing and bullet removal protocol! Weapons stash in false walls!" He looked at Damali. "A train transformer blew up, and I'm suing the city for business interruption and unsafe conditions, if they harass a brother. We got insurance, feel me?"

Damali hugged him and again counted heads, missing two—Berkfield and Carlos. Anthony hobbled out with the help of Rene.

"Casualties?" she hollered again, beginning to run through the restaurant to the storage room in the back.

Seeing Berkfield come out of a door shaking his head made her come to a skidding halt.

"We got one, D," Berkfield said, holding her shoulder. "His pulse is barely there and he didn't come around . . . and I tried my best to take as much of it as I could. He didn't come around. You've gotta get him to his Kings, maybe."

But as she was about to pull away from Berkfield, she looked at his complexion. His pallor was waxy and cold. He opened his mouth to speak and then simply dropped.

"Richard!" Marjorie's shriek could have shattered glass.

CHAPTER TEN

The moment they touched down in the family room of the Neteru Guardian compound, Damali had the Caduceus in her right hand. Everyone scattered in a mad dash, as though someone had set up a rack of billiards and broken them with the cue ball.

J.L. and Krissy were hot-wiring defenses, getting emergency word to the local Covenant so that windows could be repaired and the house sealed up. Shattered glass still remained from when Carlos had sent a fury pulse out to the darkside, and with a baby in the house, Dan started damage repair and shard clean-up. Jose and Rider swept the house for intruders. The rest of the squad was on prayer barrier and visuals. The team's strongman, Big Mike, and Shabazz helped lower Carlos and Berkfield to sofas, while Marlene and Marjorie stood at the ready for healing and prayer.

Damali only allowed herself two seconds to be torn. Berkfield was straight human—she had to go to him first, or he could die. Holding the long golden staff that had been sent by the Neteru Queens, she closed her eyes and waited until the conductive energy of the metal heated her palms. Blue static energy slowly crept up the rod, igniting the dual serpents that were entwined in the Hippocratic symbol. They fled the staff in opposite directions, entering Berkfield's crown and base chakras with an angry hiss.

"I've never seen them do that before," Damali said, still holding the staff above Berkfield as she glimpsed Marjorie and Marlene.

Marlene shook her head. "Me, either. This doesn't feel right at all."

Marjorie looked like she'd aged ten years as she clasped her hands together. "Tell us what to do, Damali. I can't lose my Richard after all these years." Her voice was a quiet, urgent plea.

"Keep praying," Damali said. "Then, when the healing serpents come out of him, the three of us will join hands, join our energy around him, and hope whatever happened gets reversed. That's all I know to do."

"What do you think happened, though?" Marlene said. She rounded the sofa so that she could stand at Berkfield's head, while Marjorie stood opposite Damali at the back of the furniture. "They were throwing flaming arrows, black-charge mortar rounds, and using blades. He's not nicked, didn't take a mortar . . . I can't figure this out."

Marjorie looked from the team's lead healer to Damali. "He was with Carlos when Carlos got hurt. He never got shot."

Tension wound so tightly around Damali's spine that it felt like it would snap. "If I know your husband," Damali said softly, guilt lacerating her for ever calling for Medic's assistance, "he tried to go in alone and heal Carlos."

"Oh, God . . ." Marlene whispered.

"What were Carlos's injuries?" Marjorie said, taking up her husband's hand and kissing his knuckles fiercely.

Damali's gaze locked with Marjorie's. "Carlos tried to stop a train by himself." She watched Marjorie slowly cover her mouth. "He energy-lassoed it, got behind it, and dug in his heels. But the weight and momentum was too much." She hesitated as Marjorie dropped to her knees, still holding her husband's limp hand. "It jerked him forward and he got tangled up in his own energy tether . . . on his stomach. His spleen, his liver, his breastbone, and his ribs were all lacerated and cracked. If I know Carlos, though, he probably energy-shielded down the front of himself first, which is the only reason why he's probably still alive . . . and if he wakes up, will still have the most important organ to him still intact."

"Marje . . . we cannot afford to panic," Marlene said firmly. "You've gotta get up and focus. Carlos was shielding the roof, the first floor, civilians moving out, and had probably just enough bandwidth left for a thin layer on his body—like Damali said. But that might be all we need. Enough that the injuries aren't mortal."

"I told him not to go in without me . . ." Damali said softly, staring at Marj with an apology in her eyes. "It was so much heat coming at us on the roof that I had to leave them for a minute, get them down in a hole where they wouldn't get their heads blown off. I couldn't stop again, even for my own husband, or the entire joint would have been overrun. The moment Carlos passed out and shields went down . . ."

"Richard is a soldier, Damali," Marjorie said thickly with tears in her eyes. She drew a shaky breath, stood slowly, and bent over her husband's prone body and kissed his forehead tenderly. "He was a man who believed in helping people—that's why he'd joined the force, years ago. And my husband would never sit by and let a man die without trying, especially not one the way he loved Carlos. So, it didn't matter what you told him."

"Marjorie, stop it!" Marlene screamed. "You are using the word 'was' in past tense, over a patient's body!" She went to Marjorie and shook her hard and then slapped her. "He's not dead! He's not going to die unless you put that in the ether!"

Berkfield convulsed. Damali squared herself and held the rod parallel to his body, her wings ripping through her shirt. "I'm losing him, Marlene! His energy is dipping. None of his organs are knitting together."

"Richard!" Marjorie screamed. "Don't you dare die!"

"Lock hands, Mar!" Damali ordered. "Get a Twenty-third going, something's wrong with the Caduceus. Better yet, do Psalm Ninety-one!"

Heat seared Damali's palms and she was forced to drop the golden staff to a thud. Where it landed it burned, singeing the carpet, and leaving an awful acrylic stench. She rushed forward and grabbed Marjorie's and Marlene's hands, and their voices blended in a loud chant of the psalm they knew by heart.

Halfway through the verses, Berkfield convulsed again. His eyes rolled to the back of his head and opened, showing only the whites. Marjorie tried to pull her hands away to hold him, but Marlene and Damali held her hands firmly in their grip.

"Keep praying, don't leave off," Damali said, her voice getting louder with Marlene's.

Berkfield arched and gasped and the two golden healing serpents from the Caduceus exited his mouth in a swift, screaming blur, taking refuge under furniture. Immediately following them was something so large and angry that it split the sides of Berkfield's mouth as its dark head hissed and lunged forward.

Marjorie, Damali, and Marlene fell backward as the huge black serpent spewed from Berkfield's mouth in a seemingly endless length.

"Keep praying!" Damali ordered, calling the Isis into her hand.

The Caduceus snakes leapt at the massive black coils, but looked like garden snakes against an anaconda. Once outside of Berkfield's body, the thing kept growing, hissing and striking at the healing snakes, opening its cobra fan and baring massive fangs.

Damali backed it into a corner while Marjorie and Marlene

kept vigil over Berkfield, who was vomiting blood. Guardian footfalls pounded the floors. Damali's blade chimed as she swung and dipped and dodged away from vicious strikes. She had to keep the thing away from Berkfield and the Caduceus healers, but it seemed to want in to Carlos's body in the worst way. The thing kept trying to maneuver around her until finally she took up a post at the foot of his couch.

"You can't have him, you bastard!" Damali shouted. "Prayer guards," she called over her shoulder. "Juanita, Heather, Inez, on post behind this sofa! Krissy, Bobby, help guard your father! Tacticals, where are you!"

A woman's scream and a baby's cry broke Damali's focus, as well as Inez's. In the split second they'd turned their heads, the serpent lunged, struck Damali, and had her by the leg.

It lifted her, shook her, banging her from one wall to the other, trying to make her drop her blade. Feathers went flying everywhere. Plaster and paint flew off the walls and paintings fell with a crash as Damali was slung back and forth like a rag doll. But a huge black jaguar sailed through the window, and that made the creature drop Damali to the floor with a thud to turn on the lightning-fast cat.

The big cat released a threatening growl, blue-white static rolling over its coat in waves as it leapt, caught the serpent by the back of its neck, and tore into it with claws and teeth. Infuriated, the snake hit the wall to stun the jaguar and then turned on him when he fell. But J.L. and Bobby worked with Dan to get an energy band on it, lassoing its neck with a tactical charge while Damali struggled to get up. The downed cat slowly came to, transforming back into Shabazz. Rider and Mike dropped to one knee with Jose to open up rounds.

But the creature was shrewd, grabbing the sofa that Carlos was lying on, with him in it, within its coils. It brandished him in front of itself like a human shield to the gunfire, making the

Guardians have to lay down their conventional weapons. Inez, Juanita, and Tara fell back, hurling razor-sharp knives that landed in the dark coils, drawing green ooze and demon screams, while Val dropped to one knee and assaulted the entity with silver arrows, blinding it in one eye.

It slung Carlos and the sofa he'd been in away angrily, turning first one way then the other, snapping and hissing wildly. Mike stomped the coffee table, splintering wood, and ran forward in complete battle lust, ramming the broken wood in its open mouth, then dove behind the overturned couch. In two seconds the entity had snapped the wood and was on a mission to get Mike. But when it turned in fury to go after Mike, it had momentarily turned its back on Damali. All it took was one strategic swing and the head came off, jaws open, falling, falling, covering Mike as he covered his head thinking he was a goner—but it all went to ash before it nicked him.

Guardians immediately went to the downed warriors. Jose and Rider had Shabazz; Juanita and Heather worked with Dan to get Carlos on his back and to make sure he was breathing. Damali bent over with both hands on her knees, heaving in air, the Isis on the floor by her feet. She looked up as Berkfield coughed and opened his eyes. The serpents from the golden staff had found their way back to the Caduceus. Her leg was bleeding but she didn't care.

Standing slowly, she trudged over to Berkfield, energy depleted, and lowered the Caduceus over his body. This time the healing rays turned golden green like they were supposed to, and the only sign of repair going on was Berkfield groaning as the sound of cracked ribs could be heard snapping back into place.

Sweaty, dirty, fatigued, Berkfield leaned over the edge of the couch and vomited, but drew a normal breath. Damali was so weary she couldn't even speak, and just patted his shoulder as she turned to go to Shabazz and Mike.

Mike stood and shook his head. "I'm cool. Just got a rug burn. 'Bazz is busted up kinda bad, though."

"I'm good. Just see if my man over there is cool. I don't like seeing Rivera out cold, ain't normal."

Damali touched Shabazz's head as Marlene went to him. "You've got a concussion. Might have whiplash, too . . . but that was an awesome shape-shift. Thank you."

"Old-school," Shabazz said with a smirk and then winced.

"I've got this—a concussion I can heal," Marlene said. "Whiplash, too. We need to get Carlos conscious."

Damali shook her head. "I don't want anyone to touch him. I've gotta take him to the Neteru Council." All eyes were on Damali as she spoke. "That's what happened to Berkfield." She stared at him with a tender gaze. "Sometimes it's dangerous for a healer to go in. What attacked Carlos in that cathedral is way above any of our levels. Even yours, Richard. You have the blood in your veins, but because you were pissed off, once you drew that rage and hurt from Carlos, thinking you were just going in to help fix damaged organs, you got more than you bargained for."

She picked up her Isis and the Caduceus and went to Carlos and knelt beside him, then kissed his brow. She laid out the long blade and the staff as though he were a pharaoh and bent to brush his mouth gently with hers.

"It was beyond even yours," she murmured softly, stroking his hair away from his forehead. "That monster came up in a church. Robbed you of light. Took your hope. Which kills all dreams. Found the bitterness. Tapped into your worst fears. That's what weakened your shields, baby. You could've held that train, otherwise. Before all that, you were invincible."

There was only silence in the destroyed family room as she lowered her cheek to his chest, hugging him, wrapping them both in her wings. Tears of worry, outrage, and frustration rolled down the bridge of her nose and leaked from the corners of her eyes. Feathers were everywhere, a testimony of a battle hard-fought and possibly lost.

"You did what?" Nuit paced back and forth in front of his throne with his hands behind his back as Sebastian sat up tall on his with his arms folded over his chest.

"Yes. I raised Vlad's army for my councilwoman," Sebastian said. He looked at Elizabeth and took up her hand, then kissed the back of it.

She coolly removed it and took up her goblet of blood. "But the losses were immeasurable. The Guardians were well fortified, and we underestimated their tenacity in battle. Next time, we will not be so unprepared." She shot Sebastian a meaningful glare and took another calm sip of blood.

"Perhaps, then, we should use more subtle methods," Lucrezia offered. "They are human, therefore must eat. Might I suggest poison? You did say that they had convened in *un ristorante, si?*"

"Sei un bel genio," Nuit said, bowing toward her with pride. He turned to Sebastian and the Countess, but addressed Elizabeth. "With all due respect, Madame Councilwoman . . . that method has been tried and proven throughout antiquity as a very effective way to dispatch one's rivals. Given our current state of strained resources, it might work as an interim solution while we rebuild lost armies."

Elizabeth smiled and lifted her goblet toward Nuit and Lucrezia. "Very wise. I may have to agree with you, Fallon. Your mate is a beautiful genius."

"Grazie," Lucrezia said with a demure smile and then bowed to Elizabeth from where she sat.

Not to be outdone, Sebastian interjected, "However, the primary goal, in fact the *directive* we'd received from the Dark

Lord, was to keep outright pressure on that Neteru team until it literally collapses from exhaustion. Tonight, I believe, we achieved that."

Nuit took up his goblet with a flourish and spoke through a bored sigh. "Is Lilith aware of this?"

"Is Lilith aware of what?" Lilith sashayed forward with Yonnie behind her, straightening his tie.

"That Vlad's army was raised and subsequently decimated in New York City about an hour ago," Nuit replied coolly over a sip of blood.

Yonnie stopped walking.

"What did you say to me?" Lilith's gaze narrowed.

"Madame Chairwoman, we were following the prime directive from our Dark Lord, which was to keep the pressure on the Neteru team," Sebastian said quickly, defending his position. "Here are the excerpts from the battle," he said, opening his gaze to her as he spoke. "See for yourself . . . Elizabeth's brilliant maneuvers. We took down the male Neteru, he is injured. The female is beside herself with grief—it resonated in her aura and perfumed the air as she charged us. There was outright panic, civilians injured, and the Guardians even had to worry about a baby and the child's grandmother in their midst."

"I'm curious about the one guarding the child, Sebastian," Elizabeth said, not giving Lilith a chance to respond. "Go back in your images. She reaches into her back and pulls out silver-tipped arrows as though wearing a quiver . . . and swings, beheading our troops as though owning a long blade . . . even her movements are odd. In the chaos, she can lift herself from one place to another without the deep push off that one would expect."

Yonnie stopped breathing. The negotiation around this would be extremely dicey with a full council now and female councilwomen adept in picking up the slightest sexual vibrations in a male aura.

"She moves like an angel," Lilith murmured, studying the tapes as she rubbed her chin. "This could be problematic." She lifted her gaze to stare at Sebastian and Elizabeth. "Maybe the expense of that resource was worth it to find that out, and most certainly it was worth it to fell Rivera, even if only temporarily. At Masada, we sacrificed eight demon legions to the cause, so Lu and I are accustomed to extremes to accomplish our goals. Were we not, we would not be in the position we're in today."

Lilith swept to her throne as she flashed through the visual images in her mind again, and nodded. "Yes . . . Lu's toxic hold on Rivera definitely weakened his ability to stop that train— and yet, fool that he is, he tried to save all those worthless, screaming humans anyway."

"But I believe the critical factor we must not overlook this time is—he *still* tried. This means his hope is not completely broken, nor is his spirit. That much I know about him." Nuit paused for dramatic effect, and it worked. Lilith leaned forward and he continued to lobby his point.

"Lucrezia has made an excellent suggestion. Now there've been two full frontal assaults from this council, in follow-up to the edict handed down by our Dark Lord. First mine, to drive a child and non-gifted grandmother into the Neteru compound to complicate their lives and to compromise their battle tactics, then the Countess's, with Sebastian's animation support," he added, subtly diminishing Sebastian's role, "perhaps it is time to then employ a hidden agent."

"Ooohhh . . . I like it already, Fallon. Two hits to the face and then quietly stab them in the back after the bell. Continue."

Yonnie calmly walked to his throne and took a seat, listening.

"Poison," Nuit said. "My beloved's specialty." He lifted Lucrezia's hand to his mouth, brushed it with a kiss, and then nodded to her. "Please. Share."

"They are human, they must eat," Lucrezia said with a calm

shrug. "They must move around to do their music or to even fight us. They are at *ristoranti, alberghi*—hotels—sometimes on airplanes, but Fallon tells me not so much anymore. They must shop for food to feed all those members of their teams. This was how it was done in my time. I do not claim it is effective so much now, but it would help," she said, brandishing a thirteen karat ruby ring that had golden vampire bats lifting it in a high solitaire setting. "My beloved knew my passion," she said with a smile directed toward Fallon as she opened the ring. "White arsenic, my favorite." Then she bowed low in a formal court gesture. "I am at your service, Your Highness."

Lilith clapped, delighted. "I approve." Suddenly she turned on Yonnie. "So, tell me, how will you contribute?"

He knew the question of about results was coming, despite his admirable performance in Lilith's bedchamber. It always came back to what-have-you-done-for-me-lately . . . and he knew sooner or later his alliance with Val would be found out. Therefore, the best way to shield her would be to pull a Rivera move out of his throne and hide Val in plain sight, then evade the council's bullshit detection with enough truth woven in the lie.

He smiled and made a tent before his mouth as the male members of council offered him smug smiles in return.

"Remember earlier when you all were busting my stones for eating blueberry pancakes," Yonnie said casually, and then lowered his hands to study his manicure. When no one answered, he looked up. "Did anyone ever consider that I was on a mission, not just busting a grub?"

Nuit's and Sebastian's smiles faded. Yonnie nodded, glancing at the new councilwomen and then directing his attention formally toward Lilith.

"Why would a brand-new, daylight-delivered councilman not take a sip of blood . . . not even a drop, and go for blueberry pancakes?" He brushed off his lapels and then looked around again. "I know we all have our idiosyncrasies, gentle-men. However, let us never lose respect for each other's skills. We all got here because we brought something unique to the table, and as soon as we recognize that and work as a team, the faster we'll be able to carry out the big boss's directive."

"Yolando," Lilith said in a seductive croon, smiling. "Lover . . . what did you do?"

He dropped his voice and stared into her eyes. "I knew that Fallon going after the child would draw angelic outrage," he said in a bass murmur that made the other councilwomen swal-low hard. He then nodded to Nuit in respect. "That was smooth, bro."

Nuit nodded in return, but his eyes were wary.

"So I laid near where I always meet Rivera. I knew I would be perceived as a demon trying to go after yet another of the Light's Neterus. And she came out of the sky raining silver fire on me." He paused, showed them the edited version of the bat-tle, and then sat back, fading the image to black.

Lucrezia's hand went to her heart. *"Incredibile!"* She looked around. "This was so *coraggioso!"*

"I see why you love her, Fallon," Yonnie said, issuing Lu-crezia an appreciative gaze in a way that would infuriate Nuit. "But that was not the courageous part, baby. You see, a man must have patience." He smiled and then backed off Fallon, whose fangs were lengthening. "Your husband taught me that. In fact, our dear Chairwoman told me to watch and learn from the best on this council during your most elaborate installation. Trust me, I have. I may not tell him, but I do watch his every move, learning."

Fallon sat back, somewhat mollified, his fangs slowly retract-ing to normal feed length.

"Anticipation strums through me," Elizabeth said in her heavy, exotic tone. "Please, release us."

Yonnie smiled. Sebastian would just have to be angry. He was no threat. His wife was the one to watch, so he had to humor her.

"Just like the late and revered Vlad taught us . . . one must study a victim to lure them into an open trap. This is what I did to my feathered friend." He took a sip from his goblet and then winced, and chose his words carefully, never calling Val an angel and leaving her status a question mark. "She trusts me."

"How?" Lilith breathed, leaning forward, eyes burning with passion.

"After I fatigued her in battle and she thought I would attack her, I didn't." Yonnie looked at Elizabeth. "If you want to infiltrate an enemy or inspire their deepest fear, always let one live to escape and return to tell the others." He returned his gaze to Lilith. "I asked her to smell me, I had no blood in my system—but I was hungry as hell. Then I asked her to sit with me and minister to me while I ate my first meal as a daywalker . . . because having seen the Light, I wanted to experience just one sun, one meal, not as a vampire," he said, passion trembling in his voice as he made a fist and pounded the arm of his throne. "And she bought it."

Lilith leapt up from her chair and came to him, held his face with both hands, and kissed him. "What then?"

"I fed her strawberry pancakes and began talking to her about the pleasures of this earth plane . . . telling her about things she never experienced."

Lilith pressed one hand to her heart and the other against her belly. "You were attempting an angel seduction . . ." She backed away until her butt hit the council table. "Only a few have ever tried something so dangerous."

"We are in the end of days," Yonnie said, allowing his fangs to go to battle length for drama. His made his eyes glow red. "By any means necessary."

"Show me," Lilith murmured and then swept her arm around to the others. "Show them how it's done!"

"I told her of my special bond with the male Neteru from our old days running the streets at night together. I shared that I knew Fallon had attacked a child and an old woman, and there would be more to come. I asked her to redeem me by trusting me . . . said I had learned from over two hundred years of this incarcerated life that I wanted to change . . ." Yonnie stood, adding power to his speech, holding the council chambers for ransom. "And I begged her to warn Rivera—yes, I gave her a warning message that I knew would arrive late and useless. She was so far away," he added with a sinister chuckle. "But to get my message, she had to allow me to come in close and mind-lock her. As long as I have an invitation, I can go anywhere. Isn't that how it's done?"

Lilith swooned but remained upright. She licked her bottom lip and nodded. Lucrezia took up Fallon's hand and squeezed it tightly. Elizabeth clutched a fist against her stomach.

"Even I concede," Fallon breathed. "Might, in the interest of war strategy, you consider sharing that image, *mon ami?*"

"Because we are all family," Yonnie said with a sly smile. "I'll more than share it . . . I'll let you feel it . . . hear it, and smell it. Fair?"

"More than fair," Sebastian rasped.

Yonnie dampened the torch lights, infusing the chambers with what seemed like a late-afternoon sunset. Soon the brisk, salty tang of ocean air filled the room and every vampire closed their eyes for a moment and inhaled as Yonnie layered in the sound of waves and gulls on a breeze that rippled through their hair.

"Yolando . . ." Fallon crooned. "You are indeed an artist."

"I learned from you, man," Yonnie replied quietly.

"Michelangelo and da Vinci together, you and Fallon," Lucrezia breathed.

"Her wings are so soft . . ." Yonnie said, not having to cover that truth with a lie. "Just like her flawless, ebony skin . . ." He sent Val's shudder through the members of chamber, causing Elizabeth to gasp out loud.

"Could you tell us what it felt like to go inside her head?" Sebastian asked, practically panting.

"Yeah . . ." Yonnie murmured, becoming aroused himself as the memory played out in stereo. "I pleasure-packed the message like this."

"Damn, Yolando," Nuit whispered. "You have learned much. I shall never challenge you on this topic again."

As a finale, he copied Val's last shudder and then allowed it to die off. Then he suddenly restored the lights and turned off all sensation access to his mind.

Stunned faces greeted him and he began to angrily pace. "But I was so damned close! I almost had her!" he said, pounding his fist on the table and splashing blood. "That was what I was doing when you all called me back here to argue about bullshit! I could have compromised her fully and had a mole like you wouldn't believe in there." He walked back and forth so agitated that it wasn't an act. "I came back here so horny that I didn't want to hear shit!"

"Understood," Nuit said, frustrated enough at the interrupted vision that he bore fangs when he spoke to Sebastian. "The timing, as I told you before, Councilman, was *très mal*."

"Then, Yolando," the Countess said with stilted breathing. "I so wish you would have taken out that frustration in chambers."

Yonnie nodded at her, despite Sebastian's hiss. "It would have been my pleasure . . . but with all due respect to the legend, you know?"

"At times, the past must be laid to rest," she said, eyes beginning to glow. "But that you are also a gentleman, like that of the old world, is beyond refreshing."

"Thank you," Yonnie said. "I am glad someone around here finally sees my value—other than Lilith," he added, to remain politically correct. He bowed to Lilith. "Had you not saved me from myself . . ." He shook his head.

"Oh, Yonnie," Lilith said with a knowing smile. "I am the one who thanks you. It was definitely my pleasure to help you gather yourself."

"The others got to do installation rites while I was working my game . . . then my conquest got snatched. I was fucked up. You have no idea."

"Our apologies," Nuit said, in a rare gesture of extending a truce. "It will not happen again, *mon ami*. No man should have to endure coitus interruptus. It is *très mal* for the nervous system."

"It's all good," Yonnie said, taking a deep swig of blood before returning to his throne. "But I want you all to stay off my back and out of my maneuvering space while I work the chick with the wings. Cool? If they ever dislodge that tracking charge from Rivera, which is likely, then I can get back in through the beach beauty. But if you make me spook her, there's a lost opportunity. So fall back on that one. She's off-limits and mine to work."

Nuit gave him a tenuous nod, as did Sebastian. Yonnie's gaze narrowed as Lilith's smile widened. His voice became harsh as anger flared and he spoke in *Dananu*.

"What, motherfucker?" he said, jumping up, battle bulking and pointing at Nuit. "You giving me lukewarm, when you owe me a mate?"

Nuit smiled. "Ah . . . you remembered our old transaction."

"Hell yeah, I remembered!"

"But the Dark Lord discharged the debt when he—"

"Oh, no, bullshit." Yonnie spun and looked at Lilith. "Pull the records, point of order. The Dark Lord discharged *my* debt, took my shit out of escrow, not yours!"

"The man is right, Fallon. Some things I dismiss, but never the words of the Dark Lord. He becomes tense when people do that."

Fallon threw his head back and laughed. "I was just testing you, Yolando, to see if you really learned anything from me, after all. You have, *mon ami*. You let *nothing* slide—nor do I . . . and we *both* remember *everything*."

Yonnie's and Fallon's eyes met. It was a dangerous moment, and chambers became quiet.

"Settle yourself," Nuit finally said. "It is true. You are owed two mates, actually. Tara and, I believe, Gabrielle. So, no, we will not interfere in your *affaires du coeur*, from this point forward— even, as you say, those that are simple booty calls. Satisfied?"

Yonnie nodded and pointed at the crest in the table. "I want it on the record."

"Fair exchange is no robbery," Fallon said, standing and walking over to receive the blood bite.

"You're in too good a mood, brother," Yonnie muttered under his breath as he and Fallon passed each other.

"A good woman will do that for you," Fallon said quietly with a low chuckle, so that only Yonnie could hear. "Just make sure you don't fuck up and try to drag an angel to a throne. I am not blind. Take care. That could be disastrous. They'll nuke chambers."

Yonnie turned away, unnerved by Nuit's shrewd perception. "Sebastian, I want it from you, too."

"I was not in the original transaction," Sebastian protested. "Why should I?"

"Because I don't want any accidents in the future." Yonnie looked at the Countess and then Lucrezia. "Point of order, of all the feats, we could have a pissing contest about which one was the most insane to try to pull off, which took the most balls, and jeopardized the least resources—and then based on pecking order, or whose dick is the longest, we can reshuffle mates. Guaranteed, if we play musical chairs, I'll have a seat. Will you?"

"Sebastian," Elizabeth remarked coolly, "unless you want to find yourself a bachelor again, I suggest you accept the man's very reasonable terms not to interfere with his personal affairs during our ruthless games of war."

Lilith stood as Sebastian grudgingly went to the crest. "Then it's all settled."

Yonnie smirked. "No offense, but do I look crazy to you?"

She chuckled and rolled up her sleeve. "You don't miss a trick, do you?"

"You did Gabrielle . . . what can I say?"

"That I did," Lilith said with a sigh. "And I suppose you want the wives to also commit?"

Yonnie just folded his arms over his chest. "No offense but, one is good with poison, one has a penchant for torture . . . and anyone I mate will be a Master-level female, with no available seats on the council, therefore at a power disadvantage. This is why I don't want *any* bullshit."

"All right, Yolando. You have certainly earned this one, easy demand. After this, I will be leaving for a while. There is much to do in preparation, and the Middle East beckons me. I trust that now that all dissension has been quashed, you can move forward with subtler, less resource-intense strategies?"

Nods of agreement met Lilith as her gaze slowly raked the expressions around the pentagram-shaped bargaining table. Without further protest, everyone got up, extended their wrists to the crest, accepted the harsh bite, and then sat back down. Only then did Yonnie sit back in his throne and relax. His mind was racing a mile a minute. He had to take his time leaving and endure the politics for a while longer, but his main concern was what was happening with Carlos and the family.

"It seems that there is perfect balance on this council," Lucrezia noted in a cheerful voice. "You may take your leave with a clear mind. We are all prepared to work together to the common goal of Neteru destruction. Following your husband's initial assault, Your Majesty . . . Fallon, Sebastian, and Elizabeth have hit the Guardians hard with variations of a full frontal attack. Then Yonnie has come in through the back door to compromise *an angel,* who obviously had been sent to protect the most vulnerable member of their family—that horrid, screeching child. Then I, with poison, can double back, just as they believe they are safe, to injure and hopefully eliminate more of their family members. Perhaps even Yolando and I can team up, to get the angel to deliver the poison, since he has a way with her?" She waved her hands with sadistic glee. "In any event, it shall be intriguing!"

PART III

PRAYER

ℭ CHAPTER ELEVEN

$\mathring{A}$re you all right?" Marlene knelt beside Shabazz and waited for him to answer, both second-sight and eyes scanning him for any additional injuries that might have been overlooked. She quickly glanced at the spot on the floor where Damali and Carlos had been, hoping that the Neteru Council would be able to help them. But right now, Shabazz was her primary concern.

"Yeah, I'm all right," he said after a long pause and then looked up at Big Mike, who was standing near with Ayana up high in his arms. "Lost my pants in the hall, bro. The shape-shift thing ain't got no modesty." He forced a laugh and began to cover himself before trying to stand.

"I'm on it, bro. Don't nobody care about all that, so long as you cool and ain't nicked." Mike hustled out into the hall with the baby as female Guardians lowered their gazes. He handed Ayana off to Krissy and then tossed Shabazz his jeans, and Shabazz caught them with one hand.

Marlene monitored Shabazz as he unfurled his exquisite ebony body and deftly pulled on his pants. His aura was intact. The blue-white current of tactical energy still crackled through his magnificent dark locks. His eyes were clear and he was completely lucid. He spoke with his back to the group, zipping his pants, but hadn't missed a beat as the senior Guardian team leader.

"All right. We just saw some deep shit," Shabazz said in a matter-of-fact tone, then turned around, folding his arms over his chiseled chest. Intermittent tension still ran through his body and made his biceps twitch. "We've got newbies in the house, and you all just saw live action on probably one of the worst days to join this team. Regardless, it is what it is. But you're going to have to come up to speed real quick, to avoid an incident like the one we just saw in here tonight."

Everybody looked down uncomfortably, especially Inez.

"I'll talk to her, 'Bazz," Inez said quietly.

"Talk to me, talk to me?" Inez's mother shrieked. "Did you just see what happened? Have you all been—"

"Stop," Shabazz said low in his throat.

The sound that came out of Shabazz was so close to a jaguar's growl that Mrs. Filgueiras drew back. Even Big Mike looked unsure. Shabazz unfolded his arms and rubbed the nape of his neck, locks crackling hard with static.

"No, Inez. Tonight, I'm going to break it down for young and old, new and senior—because we don't have time to tap-dance around so-called niceties. Mrs. Filgueiras, you are going to have to pull it together. Pure and simple. You ain't visiting your daughter, moving into a summer guest house with her and her new husband and kid. You are in the equivalent of a damned wartime military facility!"

Shabazz walked back and forth like a caged feline, his grace and swiftness unnerving to the uninitiated. When Delores Filgueiras started to cry, he spun on her. "Suck it up," Shabazz commanded in an even, deadly tone, bearing upper and lower canines.

" 'Bazz—"

"No, Marlene," Shabazz argued, squaring off with Marlene.

"Delores came in here, freaked, screamed, drew Damali's attention at a critical strike point, and our girl got the snot kicked out of her by a demon serpent. The baby took it better than Delores did. Ayana just did what you're supposed to do, instinctively, and she scrambled to a safe spot, hunkered down, and got out of gunfire range." He closed his eyes and counted to twenty, regaining his Zen and composure after a moment. Once his canines receded, he addressed the group, rubbing his palms down his face.

"I don't have to stay and deal with this insanity, and I don't have to listen to whatever he says," Mrs. Filgueiras said, her voice shaking. "He's got the teeth of a demon, oh, my God—and electric, what is he? I am leaving here, getting away from you people, this life, this . . . this abomination! You can't keep me here against my will. I'll go to the police! My granddaughter—"

"Stays," Inez said coolly, unexpectedly rounding on her mother. "You saw with your own eyes what's out there. Ayana stays."

"In here, amid this? Are you insane?" her mother challenged, getting up in Inez's face. "I'll call child protective services on you. I'll get my grandbaby."

"And as much as it will break my heart, Momma," Inez said, lifting her chin, "I will make sure they believe you are insane, getting early-onset Alzheimer's, and you won't stand a chance. Don't make me go there . . . I love you."

"You wouldn't . . ."

"Yes. I would," Inez said, folding her arms over her chest. "Because, here, Ayana has a fighting chance. Out there, with what's happening in the world, without me and my family around her to protect her, she's dog meat. If you can't see that, then I don't know what to tell you. But I refuse to bury my child because you don't want your feelings hurt. You'd better listen to Shabazz and suck it up."

"How can you disrespect me in front of these people? If you went to church more you'd know that you're supposed to honor your mother and father! I am *your mother* and I say we go! You call yourself surrounded by people of faith—what faith? You want to raise a child in this house of horrors? You have serpents in your house, naked people who turn into animals . . . have all sorts of—"

"Listen, let's get it out once and for all," Inez shouted, making her mother back up. "Honor? Honor! *Don't you dare throw stones.* I had the same gift as my daughter. I told you things were happening to me at the hands of your husband, but you didn't want to see it. You wanted to be blind because at that time, blind was convenient. It's only because Damali saved me from it happening even more by almost killing that rat bastard and running away that you had to finally see for yourself." Inez walked back and forth and slapped a wall. "That said, I have and still do respect you—but I'm not taking no unnecessary guilt trips and drama along the way, Momma. I'm a soldier and good and grown . . . yeah, Momma, I grew *a lot* while away from you. I came into my own and I like who I am now. Plus, I came with serious squad to pull you and my child out of harm's way. But since you wanna talk about faith, let's go there!"

"Don't go there, baby," Mike said softly, trying to calm Inez down. "Some things you say can't be took back."

She snatched away from his touch and whirled on her mother. "*This,* right here, that I'm about to say—I don't wanna take back!"

Inez circled her mother, her voice dropping low and lethal. "You went to church day and night and lived there to avoid seeing the truth and to avoid living your life. But you were hiding! So-called in the world and not of it, but talking about people, who's wearing what, who ain't tithing like they should, whose kids are bad . . . not helping a soul, not advancing any cause other than the social. That's how the Devil gets up in a church in the end of days, ain't you figured that out by now?"

Her mother turned away, but Inez followed her, circling her as Delores Filgueiras tried to shut out her daughter's words by closing her eyes as the team silently watched.

"You claim you have faith, Momma . . . and every time something kicks off on the news, you holler, 'Girl, just look at how these folks act—it must assuredly be like pastor says, the end of days.' But now, when Scripture comes to life, when it is as real and tangible and up in your face as a live demon, a true spiritual battle between good and evil that's not some theoretical future-tense possibility, when it boils down to what are you gonna do and what are you willing to sacrifice—you want out." Inez stepped back. "It don't work like that, Momma."

Mrs. Filgueiras wrapped her arms around herself and swallowed hard, seeming too stricken to even cry.

"You always talking about how you living in the world but not of it . . . how you believe in angels and the power of the Word. Yeah, okay. Well, it's show time. Here's how it works, Mom. If you *truly* believe and you have on whatever is the symbol of your faith—in a firefight, you might be able to hold that up and back the demon up. But if you've got what we call up in here, 'Sunday morning faith,'" Inez said, making little quote signs in the air with her fingers, "that demon will laugh at you and snatch your lungs out. It's a lotta different faiths on this team, a lot of different races and cultures, but we're all *one family* and the glue is, we all believe in good winning over evil. Period."

Inez walked away and lifted her braids off her neck, perspiring. "Make a choice now and tonight, Momma. We have to reinforce these busted-out windows, get you and Ayana in a safe room down the hall in a guest suite, and, because Carlos is injured, we can't just whisk things in here. We have to do it the old-fashioned way . . . lean on the Covenant to have construction crews in here, drop off groceries and ammo, along with clothes for you and the baby."

"I didn't choose this," her mother whispered.

"You think any of these people here did? Look around. You think anybody in here is having fun tonight? Poor Dan's got a mom and dad outside of here. My brother—that's right, I said *brother,* because he is . . . white, Jewish, and all, he's my brother, my team tight—he's worried about his people, this I know. It's a privilege to be here, Momma. Everybody's parents ain't so lucky." Inez glanced at Dan. "I'm sorry I rubbed a sore spot, but she gotta know the truth."

"I'm good, Inez. Thanks," Dan said, his eyes holding hers with a private bond. "When we took Father Pat in, I told Rabbi Zeitloff how worried we all were . . . they sent a team to scoop them, to bring them in till this blows over."

"They coming in, Danny boy?" Berkfield asked. "We can make room. You're the only other kid on this team that's got parents alive, and I'd hate to see anybody have to go through a funeral caused by the darkside."

Dan shook his head. "They think that they're being put in temporary protective custody because of my supposed job in White House security." He smiled a sad smile. "*General* Rivera saying that I worked high up will give Mom bragging rights. They have her and Dad secured and prayer-barriered in the equivalent of the Ritz-Carlton, so they'll be fine."

"Well as long as they're cool with it, and you're cool with it, man," Jose said. "But if you need to bring 'em home, let us know. We all fam, and I've lost my moms . . . so I know."

"This is my point," Inez said in a gentler tone, staring at her mother. "No one here chose for this to be their life. Every person you see here came in here, just like you, Mom. They were chased into this family . . . scared, alone, seeing things that made them think they were crazy. Leaving the life they knew. Leaving normalcy, whatever that is. Leaving dreams, sometimes, and having to come up with new ones here because the old ones just didn't fit anymore. Lord knows, my best friend and team sister, Damali, did . . . you wanna hear a tale of woe, talk to *her*. Then you go sit with Carlos, and if that brother's stories don't turn your hair white, I don't know what will. He lost *all* his people. *All* of 'em, Mom."

"Damn sure did," Marlene muttered. "When you come to sit with me, I got some for you, too . . . and can bring them with images and sound effects. Huh . . . don't get me started."

Inez nodded. "So you're gonna have to learn to fit into a new reality, gonna have to learn to fight, pray from that real place down in your soul—not just for show—carry a weapon, and learn protocols to keep you and the baby safe from demon attacks. . . ." Inez let out a weary breath. "There's so much that I can't even begin to go over it all in one night."

"Demon what?" her mother whispered in a squeak.

"Yeah, ma'am, like not opening the window for vampires, and such. I'm with Shabazz," Rider said, rubbing his palms down his face. "Starting tomorrow, you go through basics because we cannot have you mess around and accidentally get a team member hurt or killed. That cannot happen again." He looked at Tara. "Maybe you seers can help speed up her and Val's process. Just do a mind dump and then we can run 'em through ammo skills. My patience is real short right now, but the knowledge needs to get embedded stat."

Tara nodded her chin toward Valkyrie who had remained silent, just watching the fray. "Val, welcome, too. You don't need formal combat training, as you fight like a true seasoned warrior. I'd be proud to have you on my flank."

"Thank you," Val said, crossing her forearm over her chest.

"But we're gonna have to get you up to speed on new

weapon technology, how this house is wired, and do some heavy cultural immersion so you don't sound so much like a foreigner."

"I stand at the ready," Val said. "I stand with great pride."

"Cool. Then I'll get her phony docs," Dan said, "everything from birth certificate to passport, so she can travel with us. New identity."

"You da man," Shabazz said, giving Dan a nod.

"Me, J.L., and Dan, with some wizard help from Bobby, can get the windows blue-energy wired hot till the Covenant crews get here to replace them in the morning." Shabazz looked around. "Better tell them that this room got jacked up, too, J.L."

"I'm on it," J.L. said. "I'm also up with Phat G—he told me about some new photo technology they had up in the Big Apple, so I can add that to our security cameras."

"Like 'Bazz said," Juanita threw in, "you da man."

"Okay," Marlene finally interjected in a weary tone. "Everybody needs a hot white bath, needs some rest. 'Nez, just tell your mom how to bathe herself and the baby for security, and I'll explain why to her later. One of you ladies get Val square and in a room with bath stuff. We'll just have to pray they don't come at us again tonight. But you can rest assured they won't, because the house is tight."

"Val, I'll help you," Jasmine offered with a smile. "You might also want to tag your weapons on your dresser, so you can find them in the morning."

"Bless you," Val said, and bowed.

"But that thing just came in, plus the panther," Mrs. Filgueiras gasped. She looked around clutching her heart.

"Jaguar," Shabazz muttered. "And I was on your side. Don't forget that."

Inez's mother looked at Shabazz and then her daughter. "Then, then, the snake . . ."

"It came in with Berkfield, because it was embedded down deep in Carlos's system, and Berkfield unknowingly pulled it up and out into him, ma'am," J.L. said. "Otherwise, the way we've got security systems locked and loaded, a hostile fly can't come through here undetected without getting fried. If our alarms sound, you head for your daughter and Mike, and they'll tell you where to hunker down with the baby—until we can get you acclimated to defense protocols."

Delores shook her head. "Me and Ayana aren't sleeping in some room alone. We're all gonna be together."

Mike looked down at his boots. "That's no problem, ma'am . . . until you all feel safe. All right?"

Inez simply nodded and looked away.

"Nope," Marlene said, placing her hands on her hips. "Not all right."

All eyes went to Marlene, especially Mrs. Filgueiras's.

"Here's my problem with this on many, many levels, Delores," Marlene said flatly. "While this looks like something out of *MTV Cribs,* this is a barracks. Number one, you are eventually going to have to pull your own weight in here. Crying, running around wringing your hands, and otherwise being hysterical won't cut it. Two, the baby is going to have to learn her limits real quick—even at her age, because we've got ammo in here and all sorts of child-unfriendly hazmats. Third, you have to learn the basics, because God forbid, one day your daughter and Mike aren't around, just like that morning when a vamp crashed in on Ayana, you're going to have to know what to do. Then there's the not-so-small issue of rest for two soldiers. Mike and Inez are beyond exhausted. They are critical members of this Guardian team. If my big audio is off, or one of my seers can't see because she's fried, then that puts the team at risk."

Marlene strode away from where she'd been standing to come

closer to Delores. She looked her dead in the eyes and didn't blink and didn't stutter.

"Woman to woman, mother of a grown daughter to mother of a grown daughter, last but not least is this—your daughter is *married*. If we go by biblical law, since you're an aficionado of Scripture, her *husband* comes first, just like your daughter, his *wife* comes first . . . yeah, before *all* others, it says. So hell no, I'm not allowing you to be in their room after they just came out of a harrowing, traumatic battle, keeping them up all night, bitching, crying, and feeling sorry for yourself. Not having it. Mike and Inez need a married couple's space. End of story."

Marlene walked away, then stopped as though someone had slapped her, and she cocked her head to the side.

"And, no," Marlene said, fury in her expression as she turned to stare at Delores. "Don't even begin *that* guilt trip. This ain't about the baby; it's about what your stubborn ass wants. The baby is not suddenly going to start sleeping with them, either, giving you a reason to be running into their room or their business at will. Before you showed up, we had peace in this house. It's gonna stay that way, trust me. I have second-sight like you wouldn't believe, sis—plus a whole lotta hard-earned wisdom to go along with it . . . therefore, I can and will say stuff to you that your daughter just can't bring herself to say and that Mike is too much of a sweetheart and a gentleman to say. But see, I gave up being a lady a long time ago—and I will ride your ass like a cowboy if you start some shit up in here."

Marlene folded her arms. Delores angrily looked away.

"The baby is going to bed at regular hours—starting at eight P.M. so the child is on a schedule and isn't cranky. At three years old, yes she *will* take a nap during the day, too. In addition to your basic boot-camp information drills, you and Val will be added to the house chore schedule. Everybody in here pulls their weight. You're also going to get a rude wake-up call in the kitchen. We only do the heavy meal, heavy fat thing for *real* special occasions, because we're not trying to have warriors in the streets coping with diabetes, heart disease, cancer, you name it. So we do healthy. And we don't do subversive. Everybody here works in harmony—we've already had our trials with that, and I'll turn your ass out into the street and let the werewolves feed on you before we go through that again . . . this way, it won't be on your daughter's conscience—and I can live with it."

Shabazz landed a hand on Marlene's shoulder and then kissed her cheek, chuckling. "Retract the canines and the claws, baby. Damn, if I was bad cop, you're RoboCop."

She didn't care what anyone on the Neteru Councils of Kings and Queens said, she wasn't moving any more than an inch or two from Carlos's body. Damali leaned down and kissed his forehead again and held his hand tightly while Eve and Aset laid hands on the sites of his wounds.

As Aset and Eve carefully stripped away his ragged T-shirt and cut away Carlos's bloodied jeans, she could see how thoroughly angry, bloodied, blue-black welts covered the entire front of his torso. Places that weren't the dark-stained hue of bruised blood trapped beneath skin had a yellowish-greenish tinge. She hurt for him; what he must have endured brought fresh tears to her eyes. When Aset gently lifted another strip of fabric away, that's when she saw a rib move in an unnatural way beneath his skin. Yet they worked without ceasing, cleaning him off as they laid strips of delicate linen across his groin.

Surrounded by opalescent alabaster walls that throbbed with pulsing white-light energy, they had brought him to what could only be described as a Kemetian ER. Hieroglyphics of Ausar's conquering death with the help of his wife, Aset, frescoed the ceiling. Damali tried to steady her breathing. The Neteru energy was so all-pervasive that she felt disoriented by it, almost woozy.

Silver and alabaster canopic jars delicately decorated with colored faience and carnelian made her nervous, though. She knew what those were for. In the days of mummification . . . Damali briefly closed her eyes and disallowed herself to even think it.

Light was everywhere. Adam and Ausar stood at the ready to lend an infusion of necessary, balancing male energy. One carried the ceremonial Pharaoh's crook made of gold, while the other grasped the traditional flail—their stance symbolic of the joining of upper and lower Kemet, the Smai Tawi, the Great that could not be divided, just as Carlos's spirit could not be divided, from his mind, nor his body.

The male Neteru Kings had spoken through the *Book of Coming Forth by Day*, Ausar's original copy of the *Pert M Heru M Gher*, and had renounced Set, then placed the all-seeing eye on the long white marble table above Carlos's crown chakra and the feather of Ma'at at his feet. But this delicate work of healing the spirit remained in the province of women. The Caduceus had rendered futile results, and that terrified her.

"*Neith, Selkis, Nephthys, Isis*," Eve murmured. "From the sacred *Amduat* I call the *shabti* of life and Light, those who labor for the Pharaoh in the Light in the afterlife to bring forth healing, to convert pain into knowledge, heartbreak into joy, destruction into creation . . . where life is ebbing, let it flow. Where the moon of his breath is waning, let it wax."

Aset breathed out a slow breath, opening her hands to form a glistening amethyst ray of light between them. She stood on one side of Carlos, left palm up, right palm down. Eve mirrored Aset, standing across from her with left palm down, right palm up, pulling the light across him in a wide band that they slowly brought down the length of his body as though giving him an MRI.

Perspiration beaded on Aset's regal forehead, her golden robes beginning to cling to her flawless, cinnamon-hued body. Eve's moss-green robe darkened with moisture against her ebony skin as they worked in tandem.

"Damali," Aset finally murmured. "Your mother's line is that of Powers angels—this we now know. Your father carried the Neteru gene. You must join us . . . you are Carlos's wife. From here, your prayers and energy will be heard throughout the realms."

Damali stood where Adam indicated, at Carlos's head. As soon as she joined hands with Aset and Eve, creating a physical pyramid around him, a gentle, healing green glow spilled from her heart into the center of their outstretched arms. Slowly and carefully, Aset led the movement down Carlos's body, forcing Damali to step around the table and walk with her and Eve.

Aset finally released Damali's hands and then looked at Ausar. He simply nodded with Adam, and both male Neteru Kings stepped forward and placed a silver Eye of Heru on Carlos's forehead and the feather of Ma'at over his heart. They took up his hands and gently placed the crook and staff within his grip, folding his arms over his chest.

"The judgment is up to the All," Aset said quietly, drawing Damali away from Carlos's side. "Whatever is decided for your Pharaoh, you must accept it, and rule on in dignity and honor."

Damali clutched Aset's hand and stared at her, blinking back tears. "I don't understand what happened to him . . . why this time . . ."

"The attack stripped away the Neteru fortification *inside* his body," Eve said quietly, touching Damali's cheek. "Outwardly, he was still Neteru . . . but inwardly, he was becoming more and more human . . . more normal mortal, the more the hate festered. And he sustained mortal injuries, beloved daughter. His Guardian brother took some of the brunt, and the healing serpents of the Caduceus tried to chase out the poison, but the

healing of his body took so long. We just do not know the out-
come, and have called upon the Divine Creator, Neter, and all
the angels, even by their ancient Kemetian names."

Tears filled Aset's eyes. "This was not supposed to be that
young king's path," she said in a harsh whisper, suddenly hugging Damali.

Damali pulled away. "You've given up, haven't you?"

Eve shook her head. "We have called the *Sunnutu* . . . the divine physicians, and Imhotep, the physician-healer to whom the
Caduceus first belonged. Even as his breath expires, we will labor in spirit to fight this tragedy."

"We continue to pray for *Seneb*—his health, soundness, and
wellness, from the *Metu Neter*," Aset said quietly. "But he may
experience *Khepera* . . . ultimate transformation, daughter."

"No . . ." Damali whispered. "He already died and came back
to me from the darkness into the Light. That is not his *shai*."

"None of us believe it is his destiny," Ausar said, his regal
Pharaoh robes billowing as he came to Damali's side with Adam.
"I, of all Neterus, believe in resurrection, even after battling
Set—the wicked one."

"But we have prepared Carlos's body," Adam murmured,
touching Damali's shoulder. "Just in case . . . if what is in his
heart is not the weight of the feather of Ma'at or lighter, her
scales will not balance and his Ka—his soul—and his Ba—his
heart soul, which dwells in the Ka and has the power of
transformation—cannot reunite with his Khu—his spiritual
soul. He has been scattered within. Before, when Set, also
known by many other names, attacked Ausar, he'd scattered his
body. This is why Aset could find those pieces and heal the
physical. But in time Set learned that the body matters not; to
kill a man forever, scatter his spirit. Thus the body dies, energy
imploding as the soul flees its shell. At this moment, Carlos's organs are healed . . . but there is much more involved."

"If I had gotten to him sooner," Damali whispered, hugging herself. "I should have never left him, even for a moment to secure the teams."

"You could not properly heal his body while on the earth plane," Aset said sadly. "Until we purged you of the taint Carlos had, you could only minimally reverse the damage. This was the one time when the one-flesh marital rule worked against you. Even as a Power, your Guardian brother, the healer Berkfield, could do more than you could. The taint from the Unnamed is truly unfathomable."

Damali looked over at Carlos's body, which had been prepared for the possibility of burial. Tightness filled her chest, a dread so profound that it stole her breath. She moved to him in mechanical, jerky steps, unbelieving. They had given him the all-seeing eye, so that he would not be blinded to the truth or his enemies on the other side. They had put the regal staff and crook in his grip, that he might walk into the Neteru Kings' Council already bearing the symbols of office . . . and they had left Ma'at's feather so his heart could judge him. But that was the place that the Darkness had attacked.

More fine linen was waiting to wrap him. Damali shook her head and gently cradled Carlos's head between her palms. Drawing on all the love within her, she murmured into his ear, "Say it in your mind, baby . . . *Rex a em Ab a sekhem a em hati a . . .* I know my heart, I have gained power over my heart. *Ba ar pet sat ar ta . . .* soul is of heaven, body belongs to the earth. Carlos, are you ready to depart this earth? Are you ready to leave me? Say it! *Un na uat neb am pet am ta . . .* tell Ma'at as she weighs your heart that the power is within you to open all doors to heaven and earth—because you *are* a millennium Neteru and you've got work to do," Damali urged, beginning to sob.

"Tell her you were already baptized by the fire, and came back in the water—Father Pat took you to the water and opened your heart to a second chance that can never be taken back . . . *Sekhem a em mu ma aua Set*—I have gained power in the water as I conquered Set. Put this man in the spiritual water, Ma'at, put his heart there so that it's weightless! He was even born a water sign . . . give him a spiritual bath that he may gain power in the water and conquer this thing that has a stranglehold on his heart,"

She rested her head on his forehead, trembling, her voice becoming a fragile whisper. "Please, baby, do it for me, Carlos. Cast that demon out of your heart and come back to me tonight."

⒞ CHAPTER TWELVE

He heard his wife's voice like a distant whisper in his mind. He felt her tears—warm, a soft pelt against his face. He repeated the words that were muffled, trying to decipher what she was trying to tell him. A dark void suddenly splintered with light. Pain shot through his breastbone and he literally felt and heard it crack.

Carlos sat up gasping, clutching his chest. Metal objects were in his hands. Something fell from his forehead and clattered to the ground. He dropped what he was holding. His chest hurt so badly that he couldn't open his eyes. The room was spinning. He almost fell. Strong arms caught him. He couldn't breathe. Agony roared inside his head like a lion. The sound of his own blood rushing within his skull was deafening. He heard the blade of Ausar chime, felt the backdraft of a purposeful swing—then smelled sulfur. The putrid scent made him clutch the edge of the table, lean over, and hurl.

Then the pain eased to a dull ache. Hot flashes and chills fought for dominance in his body, making him shiver. A cool palm wiped perspiration from his brow. Panting, he rolled over on his back and shielded his eyes from the bright, bright lights.

"*Tua Neter*," Ausar said in a thundering voice. He knew that voice anywhere, and he heard Adam's refrain.

"Yes . . . Praise Divine," Damali whispered as she kissed his forehead. That made him slowly open his eyes.

"*Tua-k, Tua-Tu*," Aset said, and then Eve repeated her words for him in English.

"Thank you," Eve breathed out and closed her eyes. "Thank you Divine All for bringing our young Pharaoh back alive."

Damali rounded him so that he didn't have to see her upside-down. Ausar still had his blade in his grip, bicep pulsing.

"They got it," Damali said. Tears were streaming down her face, but he couldn't even lift his arms to wipe them away. "That was the last of it . . . it came out of your chest and Ausar took its head." She gathered him in her arms, holding him like he was a fragile treasure. "You keep dying on me, Carlos, and one day I might have to kill you."

She made him smile, weakly, but he really wanted to laugh. But his smile broke her tension and he felt her cheek move against his with a slow smile of her own.

"You oughta know, dead or alive, you can't get rid of me, boo," he croaked.

He'd meant to make her laugh, to further ease her trauma, but instead it broke loose torrential sobs. His foxhole humor had opened her dam.

Little by little as sensation flowed into his arms, he was able to slowly lift them to hold her. All he wanted to do was pet her back, rock her in comfort. It wasn't until she lost it and he glimpsed where he truly was, saw the tear-stained faces of Neteru royalty, that he realized just how close he'd come to lights-out. He'd been two seconds from Ma'at's final judgment scale.

Shell-shocked by that reality, he held his wife a little tighter. Up until now, he'd felt pretty close to invincible. But the harder

Damali cried and the more he took in his environment, the more he knew . . . damn . . . after all, he was mortal. If she couldn't heal him down there in the family room, and had brought him to a Neteru OR . . . shit . . .

"I tried," Damali said hard against his neck. "It was so bad, Carlos—you were busted up on the inside so bad, and even the Caduceus couldn't fix it all fast enough."

Her words came against his skin in hot, wet bursts of quiet hysteria, escalating, building like a wave that he knew would soon consume her.

"I called Heaven, wings out, asked them in my soul to take me instead," she said in gasps. "There was a whole building, two teams—my husband was dying and there was nothing I could do!"

"Baby . . . it's all right . . . it's—"

"The black mortars kept coming, civilians were everywhere—men, women, and children, families . . . but my husband was dying and no angels came to give us backup! The Guardians . . . they, they . . . everybody was doing everything they could—and—"

"Baby, it's—"

"I shouldn't have left you that long without closing the hemorrhages! You could have died!"

Her voice had become shrill, so unlike Damali that it set his teeth on edge. He could almost feel how much the pain inside her was like a knife, lacerating her insides as her hands became fists at his back.

He pressed her to him tightly and held the base of her skull as she lost it. He looked around at the attending ancient Neterus. "Sedate her. Take this from my wife. It's not her fault." He stroked her hair as she began to hyperventilate. "I love you." Three simple words made her begin to scream.

Eve and Aset surrounded her. Aset kissed her temple, Eve touched her back. Damali went limp in his arms.

"Battle fatigue," Ausar said flatly, and then turned away and swallowed hard.

Adam rubbed his palms down his face. "Your wife loves you dearly, young brother. Never again do you allow the Darkness habitation within you like that. Not for anyone. You are too valuable to your family unit."

"He didn't realize he'd done that—given it habitation," Eve countered gently. "He drew it in him out of a powerful love. That was not wrong—to give one's life for another."

Adam grudgingly nodded and took a deep breath, then spoke in a faltering rumble. "But he is a young man with a family . . . like another of my sons. His father-seer is elderly . . . Carlos's purpose is yet to be fulfilled . . . and I admit that I am biased in my Neteru brother's favor. I want the young Pharaoh to live well and prosper . . . and I never, *ever* want to see his wife in ruin over his demise like this again." Overcome with emotion, Adam turned away and left the chamber.

"We did not forsake you—tell her that," Ausar said thickly. "Our resources were deployed hunting down the true nemesis halfway around your world, and when we arrived, the battle was done. Yet we sent reinforcements to cover the elderly priest, your father-seer, to be sure he was not harmed as he heals." Ausar stared at Carlos with silver burning in his eyes. "You are our most favored. Your wife is like my daughter. We would never leave you." He lifted his regal chin higher and strode out of the room.

For a moment, silence enveloped Carlos and the two queens. He held Damali's limp body even closer to him and nuzzled her hair.

"I didn't mean to offend them," Carlos said quietly, searching the faces of the older women that stood near.

Aset allowed a single tear to spill from her exotic Egyptian eyes. The moist bead sparkled like a diamond as it trailed along the long black kohl liner to finally roll down her cheek.

"They are not offended, young king. They are so vastly overwhelmed that you survived your ordeal that, they do not quite know how to express the warring emotions within them under the masculine principle. These are old Kings, son. They have been very male energies for a very long time. Even they could not heal you, because they were so outraged that their thoughts splintered from the task at hand to the singular thought of destroying. They needed to kill something to redress the unspeakable wrong that had been committed against you and your family. But we needed to heal something—you— to keep you from dying. This remains the struggle of our polarities. It is the genius of the Divine. We do not question such differences in our designs, as each is needed under different circumstances."

"That's where I was," Carlos said quietly, hugging Damali against his chest. "I needed to stomp the snot. . . ." He closed his eyes for a moment to steady himself. "Like even now, when I see what's happened to my wife. . . ." He looked down at Damali. "How can I change what I am?"

Eve and Aset helped take Damali's limp form from Carlos. Aset materialized a golden robe of the finest filament and gave it to him, and both Queens turned away, holding Damali as he pulled it on and tied it.

"Come with us," Aset said. "You do not have to change who you are. Your rage will be needed in the future. Your righteous indignation was a catalyst. You were tricked to allow something dark inside you that fed on it. Had that not been inside you, the rage of the righteous would have burned as pure silver. The Darkness knew this, knew that you hunting his heir is the greatest threat to it. This is why the beast had to figure out a way for you to invite it inside you, in order to attempt to destroy you from the inside out. Now that you know, and are wiser about shielding yourself, it will never be able to penetrate you again.

This was another good lesson that you survived, young king. This, too, you will share with your wife."

"It is no less than becoming immune," Eve said, her gorgeous eyes serene and hypnotically tranquil. "As we draw any residual poison away from your queen, she will also build her immunity."

Eve sighed, gazing first down at Damali and then toward Carlos, with tears beginning to fill her liquid brown eyes. "Children . . . as much as you love us, as much as your parents mean to you—you are the future. We are never meant to become an impediment to your progress . . . to do so would be selfish and would undo all of the hard work and every sacrifice we'd ever made on your behalf. You are our future, our hope, our lighthouse. Your father-seer knows this deep in his soul, and if you could ask him whether or not he would have rather died in that cathedral than to have you harmed in any way by Satan—as a parent, I know his answer. He would have even taunted the Devil to draw whatever horrors he could hurl his way, to give you and your wife time to escape. It was never his own survival that concerned your father-seer, it was *yours*. But you do not have such wisdom yet, Carlos, because you do not have a child. However, coming from a mother, trust me . . . believe what I say is true."

"But he was suffering . . ." Carlos whispered.

"As a parent, you would give a vital organ for your child that they not suffer." Eve stared at Carlos. "If that old man awakened to find you dead so that he could live . . . if Satan's blast didn't kill him, that surely would."

Carlos locked his jaw hard to hold back the tears. It was bad enough that he'd come into Neteru chambers all busted up, had upset his wife so badly that after all these years she finally had to be sedated . . . he would not add insult to injury by allowing tears to fall. After a moment, he'd composed himself enough to speak to the elder Queen without his voice betraying him. "I just wanted to give that old man a fighting chance . . . after all he'd given me." That was as much as he trusted to get out before emotion reclaimed his throat.

Eve's eyes searched Carlos's face and her voice was calm and tender. "We that precede you will eventually pass away to become ancestors on the other side. This is the grand design. Therefore, we assist, even from On High . . . and when you honor us with a life well lived, we are proud beyond measure. This makes the sacrifice worth it—to see you flourish. This is how you best honor thy mother and father, with respect. If we are lucky, we shall predecease you—the natural order is currently out of phase, with children dying before parents in the greatest heartbreak of the cosmos."

Eve's voice faltered and the building tears finally fell in quiet streams down her regal ebony face, but she did not turn away. She lifted her chin and bore the glistening moisture like they were jewels. "This was how *I* knew it was the end of days. It was a deeply personal heralding for me. I buried my son, Carlos, and there's not a day that goes by that I don't wish I could have chosen wiser choices for him, given him my Light, and taken the darkest influences that beset him into myself for his sake, so that he would flourish . . . so that he would have lived on . . . so that his children's children's children would come to inherit the promise. But that was not to be. I could not, even with all my power, do that for him—because it was his choice. This is what I know Father Patrick would tell you . . . that he would have taken any horrors delivered so that you could keep going and your future could flourish. Do not renounce his gift. He loves you. All is in Divine order."

Aset reached out to Eve with her free hand and touched her cheek with trembling fingers. She then looked at Carlos. "Don't you see, son? You and Damali belong to all of us up here. Just as you belonged to your parents down there . . . you have been claimed in love by us, too. This is why Adam and Ausar were beside themselves with near-grief, and are over-wrought with relief. You are our dreams deferred, our sacrifices paid forward. Eve lost Cain, but she gained you, just as Adam lost Abel, but gained you . . . and Damali. A daughter *and* a son which means legacy. Thus, when it is your father-seer's time to transition, as long as you are flourishing, you will allow him to smile in his heart and spit in Satan's eye as the angels come to collect him. That is the ultimate last laugh."

"It is a blessing to close one's eyes on the earth plane before one's children, dear young King," Eve said quietly. "Our love never dims; it only increases in the Light. But no parent dead or alive who truly loves their progeny would want their child to suffer, to give their life for theirs, to experience any indignity that they'd lived. Not if they are a real, evolved parent, they wouldn't. They would want to spare you all they'd been through and more in unconditional love sublime. Carlos, haven't you come to understand that by now?"

"Let us allow the young King's mind to rest," Aset said in a gentle voice, staring at Eve. "They need to rest, recuperate, and be still for a while outside of the pressures of their responsibilities. It will all be there waiting for them upon their return."

"We have to get back, though—no disrespect, but we've already been gone too long," Carlos said, feeling panic suddenly surge within him. "The team, the safe house where Father Pat is . . . the darkside LoJacked me, had a tracer on my whereabouts . . . my boy told me. I have to make sure the house is safe or they could smoke the entire team while I am up here—"

Eve held up her hand as Carlos tied his robe sash tighter and began glancing around for his clothes. "Shush . . . quiet your conscience. Time is not linear, have you forgotten? A few hours away there can be a few days here, and vice versa. We have your home protected. The Kings drove off any predators from the safe house, which remains under guard. We saw what tried to breach your citadel—the black serpent of household destruction and inner turmoil. We also saw the vampire that tried to snatch one of your Guardian sisters. Do not fear. Upon the next attempt, we will white-lightning-strike him. We will not allow some abominations, even in the end of days."

"You must heal. That is all that is important. We will set lions on the beach, in your gardens," Aset warned. "Nothing shall be allowed to take your palace, young Pharaoh . . . not while you are healing. Your sanctuary is safe because there is no evil intent indwelling there. It was built on love."

"My boy!" Carlos jumped down from the table and almost fell, tightening his sash again quickly and then rushing to the Queens to pick up Damali. He held her around her upper back with his other arm under the bend in her knees, trying hard not to allow her head to awkwardly loll. "Listen, this is nonstandard . . . by now, you know I don't necessarily follow the rules to the letter, but usually it all works out."

"You are having a son? You know this for certain?" Eve's eyes widened. "We didn't know that—"

"No, no," Carlos corrected, stammering. There was so much to explain, but his mouth was working slower than his mind.

"You said your boy," Aset replied, shocked. "If there is a Neteru child in gestation or in hiding . . ."

"No, my buddy, friend, tight, ace, *hombre*—he's beyond the wall. He's my inside man, always comes through. He's in a bad spot, and his transmissions are blocked. I haven't heard from him and I blocked his access to the house . . . because he was having some issues. But if I'm up here, I can't leave him blocked, but right now, I don't know his status . . . like, if I can actually let him in—but I don't want him smoked on sight just because of what he is. Oh, man, this is complicated. I didn't even get a chance to explain all this at the archon's table."

"Put Damali down on the table," Aset said coolly, "and talk to us, Carlos."

"Should I call Adam?" Eve stared at him, but the previous serenity she'd owned had fled her gaze.

"No, no, listen, it's sorta crazy, but I need to get my boy's incoming calls," Carlos said, walking quickly to the table he'd been on and gently laying Damali down on it. He kissed her forehead and then turned to look at the Queens. "All right. Let me come clean. My boy is . . . a vampire."

Both Queens drew an audible gasp and Carlos held up his hands.

"Let me explain. There's definite war strategy going on here."

"Speak quickly and clearly," Aset said, beginning to pace. "You tell me such insanity and then I will have to translate it to Ausar for *his* understanding?"

Carlos raked his fingers through his hair. "Me and Yolando go way back. I got out of the life, but he was trapped behind the wall. My man, though, always has my back. Whenever he goes dark—like I can't hear from him for a coupla nights—he always brings me back accurate information when he surfaces. In fact, he was the one who tipped me off about daywalkers. I have to be able to let him go into my mind."

"Are you *insane?*" Eve breathed. Instantly she called Damali's pearl into one hand and into the other she called Damali's platinum necklace that held the six other divination stones she'd collected in her Neteru initiation.

"It has taken *months* to restore this dragon's pearl to her full health after just seeing Cain descend to a dark throne. Zehiradangra has even grown strong enough, through rest and healing, that she no longer requires water to communicate. And you are just off the burial table, after inviting the Ultimate Darkness into your system, and now you want us to allow a council-level vampire to communicate with you?"

"Yeah," Carlos said, not sure what else to say.

"Pearl was so overwrought that this Yolando had tried to breach your home and she felt the tremors of the Darkness taking root in you, that while we were away she sent a message to a Valkyrie. This so-called friend tried to seduce *a Valkyrie* from the forbidden zone of Nod on the beach in front of your house!"

"Eve . . . I know it looks bad—"

"Looks bad?"

"It must be the residual from the charge, Eve," Aset said, dismissing Carlo's request. "The young Pharaoh is confused. We should have sedated him as well."

"No, I'm real clear about all this. Crystal," Carlos argued.

Both Queens folded their arms over their chests and stared at him.

"Then clarify," Aset said evenly.

"Make it beyond crystal," Eve murmured dangerously. "Make it diamond."

Carlos rubbed his hands down his face.

"Hi, Carlos," the pearl said with a giggle. "We were all so worried. Whew!"

Eve swept over to him and plunked the pearl down in his hand. "She's supposed to be *your wife's* oracle, but she's taken with you. Not much I can do about that. I do not even want to fathom how you could have compromised Damali's pearl— don't even tell me. My nerves are already shattered glass. Speak Zehiradangra."

"If Carlos holds me to his temple, I can show him what I know . . . but Val really, really likes your friend."

"Oh, man . . ."

"This is *exactly* why we do not consort with the darkside!" Aset shouted, losing her composure.

"If I can get my man's side of the story . . . maybe that would clear things up?" Carlos shrugged. "Then again, knowing Yonnie, maybe not. Depending on what he's tried to send by mental voice mail, the Kings might hot him on sight. These are some really tense times."

"I saw the images from Pearl of what he tried to do to the Valkyrie," Aset said between her teeth. "Spare me any further indignity."

Carlos hung his head. "Queen . . . it's not always the way it looks. But my apologies on behalf of my friend for anything you saw that didn't . . . that wasn't. I'm sorry."

Eve stared at Carlos, pressing one finger to her lips for a moment as Aset took in deep, cleansing breaths. "You could not receive any transmissions from any source from the darkside, Carlos, once you got tainted by the Ultimate Darkness. Your Neteru defense systems went into overdrive, surrounding the primary threat to your existence. The silver galvanized around all your major points of entry . . . your mind, your spirit, your body, like white blood cells trying to surround an insidious cancer. Add that to the protected hostels you were traveling to, and this is what kept you from getting his signals."

She let her breath out hard and looked at Aset. "I've had three sons, two who made it to the Light . . . but even they, at times, had friends I disapproved of, Aset. You also had a son, Heru." She waited until her Queen sister looked away. "Might we claim that we are testing Carlos's immune system . . . to, uhmmm, open a slight channel to his mind. If it is an attack, we can certainly light-scorch it away quickly . . . and then he'll know. With male children, you cannot tell them; always, they must know for themselves."

"Up here?" Aset said, incredulous. "Allow a vampire transmission to reach here during the end of days? Have you lost your mind!"

"It must pass through our filters; think of it, Aset," Eve lobbied with a smile, giving Carlos a sly wink when Aset paced away. "If the information is dark and meant to maim him or his family in any way, it will incinerate on contact. But if it is indeed sent in friendship . . . in love of their bond as true best friends, then that part will come through . . . even if the message is garbled, he will be able to get enough to ease his mind so that he may heal."

Eve walked over to Aset and hugged her. "Isn't that what we want, to fully *heal* this young King's mind?" She glanced at Damali's calm, prone form. "Isn't that what we've dreamt . . . peace in their lives . . . just long enough?" Her eyes sparkled and then she backed away as Aset's gaze softened.

Aset nodded. "That is indeed what we want . . . in the larger view." She let out a hard breath. "All right. Contact this *Yolando* and tell us what he says."

Carlos kissed the pearl, making it giggle, as he handed it off to Eve. Then he watched the two older Queens, who seemed to be sharing a secret. They had somber eyes but it was as though they were quietly swallowing smiles. Excitement radiated off their skins . . . but he shook it off as he looked around, realizing that he was in a King's burial preparation chamber and not an OR. That fact, in and of itself, was sobering. This time, Yonnie really owed him.

"Are you ready to open your thoughts?" Aset scowled and shook her head, and issued a hard snap of her fingers before Carlos could even answer.

Bleating calls filled his mind, causing him to wince. There was so much information coming at him so fast that the Queens stepped forward, worried. But he held up his hand to stop their intervention.

"He was blowing up mental voice mail, third-eye video phone, brain two-way, and gut-instinct cell . . ."

Carlos closed his eyes, allowing the garbled message to come in fits and starts. Major sections were burned out, but in a few minutes he'd gathered enough to make him want to tweak the prayer shield on the property surrounding the house. Yonnie definitely needed a fallback position now, a place to go during a firefight—but, still, out of respect for Rider, and never *ever* being quite sure of what Yonnie might do . . . the house itself still needed to be off-limits.

"I need to ask Ausar and Adam to come in here. What I've seen isn't fit for Queens, and I'd never transmit this kind of information to another man's wife. But they've installed new councilwomen—Lucrezia Borgia and Elizabeth Bathory, Dracula's wife."

"Ausar!" Aset yelled, dropping all Queenly dignity and rushing to the chamber door.

Both Kings came in dressed for battle, brandishing blades. Adam stood by Ausar's side holding white stallion reins, clearly ready to ride.

"Mind-lock, open a channel," Carlos said. "Male Neteru sensitive data given to me, through a light filter, straight from Hell."

Ausar and Adam looked at each other.

"Is his purge complete?" Ausar asked, unsure. "This could be residual synaptic contamination from the Beast."

Aset shook her head. "He's clean. This came from his friend, whom he wants given special wartime courtesies."

"I need to show you everything my homeboy shared with me—from there, you can decide how to edit the images to share with your wives and the rest of the Neteru Council. But Yonnie's intent is in there, too . . . as well as his image, his position . . . the tight spot he's in . . . and why he did what he did on the beach with the Valkyrie—"

"Speak it out in the open no more, young brother. Not in front of our wives," Adam said, taking off his helmet. "Damn. A Valkyrie and a vampire . . ."

"Where does this man select his alliances?" Ausar said, shaking his head. He lowered his blade and stepped forward.

"I know, I know," Carlos said. "But check it out for yourselves. This is *serious* information. Solid sterling."

Both Kings closed their eyes as the broken images transferred from Carlos's mind to theirs in jags. Ausar rubbed his jaw and shook his head. Adam took in a deep breath and walked away. When Carlos opened his eyes to end the transmission, the three male Neterus simply stared at one another for a moment.

"Kinda leaves you speechless, don't it?"

Adam and Ausar nodded, but said nothing. Adam rubbed the back of his neck beneath his long dreadlocks. Ausar sheathed his blade.

"Well?" Aset said, her gaze expectant.

"Give Yolando courtesy and safe passage, and send a representative vision down to make sure none of the Guardians accidentally fire on him in Carlos's absence, should he need sanctuary at the compound," Ausar said flatly, his eyes on Carlos. "As well as give that young man my utmost respect."

Tara sat quietly in the dark staring at the moon, sipping Jack Daniel's neat. There were still some nights where she couldn't sleep. Her biorhythms had never self-corrected. There'd always be a part of her that would remain nocturnal. The argument she'd just endured in the bedroom required space. Some issues simply needed the combatants to find mutual corners, lest something get said that couldn't be taken back.

But the vision was clear. It came directly from the Neteru

Council that Yolando could seek refuge on the compound outer grounds in the event of a firefight. Barriers were to be dropped, the drawbridge effectively lowered. Rider was going to have to make his peace with Yolando, one way or another . . . sooner or later, and it just seemed that now was an auspicious time.

So she waited, knowing the vampire life by second nature. Yolando would call for Valkyrie as sure as the moon would continue to light the night sky.

Tara kept her gaze on the fluttering sheets that Jasmine had drawn intricate dragon patterns on to shield the house. Sacred blood spirals from Berkfield's veins made elaborately fierce creatures that seemed already alive and added the faint scent of human blood to the breeze.

Each dragon-emblazoned sheet was suspended in a spiderweb-like maze of blue tactical energy, holding dragon images waiting to come alive like compound watchdogs. Tara sat so still that her lungs barely moved, and it wasn't even necessary to blink.

Night vision was a gift that had never fled her when the Light spared her. What her husband didn't understand was, her heart broke—no, bled—for Yonnie . . . bled that he hadn't been pulled over to a full life, given back his soul, and offered the chance to live out his mortality with the love of his life. Jack Rider had to ease up. She and Jack had been blessed. Now this newcomer spoke of Yolando with a purity of passion that he'd never even gotten from her. Not even as his vampire mate for a time. It had been a marriage of convenience . . . and of deep friendship, but it wasn't what Valkyrie could give him now.

Tara brought the rim of her glass up to her lips and took a delicate sip, thinking. She'd already violated house rule number one—team seers weren't supposed to go into the thoughts of fellow housemates uninvited. But there was still so much of her that had old habits from her past existence. This was an emergency. She needed to know if this *thing* between Yonnie and Val was all a part of his normal vamp seduction bullshit, thus potentially endangering a fellow team woman's life—or if this was the real McCoy.

She lowered her glass to study the moonlight dancing in the crystal, glad that the windows were busted out so that the breeze could lift her hair. Oh, how she loved the night . . . no matter how bad that life had been there was something so electrifying about it. She briefly closed her eyes and inhaled deeply, allowing a collision of scents to tantalize her old palate. Ocean on one side, redwood forest not far off. Plus blood. Dry, brittle land struck barren from the worst drought in centuries. All of it made her quietly sigh.

As expected, the soft pad of near silent footfalls marked by the hesitation of a woman unsure drifted into her stellar hearing range. Tara opened her eyes and waited. The moment Valkyrie crossed her path, she stood.

"Good evening," Tara said with a sly smile.

Valkyrie whirled on her, drew a blade, and squared off. Tara didn't have to see it to know what it was. She'd heard it and smelled the steel alloy.

It took a few seconds, but within moments Valkyrie recognized her.

"Forgive me," Val said and lowered her weapon, placing her hand over her heart. "You startled me. Of course there would be sentinels taking shifts."

Tara smiled and lifted her glass. "I'm off duty tonight, but I should have warned you that I was here. Old habits die hard." She parted from a shadow as though she were part of the night itself. In complete silence.

Val gaped. "How . . ."

"I learned from the vampires."

Impressed, Val walked closer. "You must teach me."

Tara arched an eyebrow. "I can't. To show you how I do it, I'd have to kill you."

Val stepped back and subtly gripped her blade tighter.

"I'm just teasing you because I'm in a semi-foul mood. My apologies." Tara dragged her fingers through her midnight-hued hair and stepped into a wider shaft of moonlight. "You didn't deserve that. But I did want to be sure you understand what you're in for with Yolando." She took another careful sip from her glass and then stared at Val for a moment. "That is where you're headed, right?"

It wasn't a question. It was more of a statement of fact. Val looked away.

"I know we are not supposed to leave the house without alerting the others, so that no one is lost to the enemy. It was not my intent to violate the hospitality of the Neterus or this team on the very first night of my sanctuary . . ."

"But, he called," Tara said flatly. "I know. What can you do?"

Val shook her head. "That's just it. He never called. I feel as though I must search for this brave soul who may be injured . . . he's behind enemy lines. He could be trapped. Where he'd been was . . . I cannot describe."

Tara lowered her glass and her expression softened. She swallowed hard. "Where he is, hon, you can't go retrieve him. You have to wait until he surfaces, or you'll compromise his cover. Or, worse, you could be taken as a hostage and used as a lure to bait him to his certain death. If he hasn't called, wait."

Val sheathed her blade. "I feel so helpless—and as a warrior, that feeling is completely unacceptable."

"I know," Tara murmured. "I have wished from the very marrow in my bones that Yonnie didn't have to be in this unrelenting quagmire. His predicament haunts me, too. I have prayed on it; I know Carlos and Damali have. Maybe with you having some angel in your bloodlines, they'll hear you? Who knows?" She tossed back the rest of her drink and swallowed it with a wince. "Try to get some rest. Day and night have become eventful around here."

.   "It is comforting to know that you also care for him and think well of him. This tells me so much more of his character." Val's eyes searched Tara's face, staying her leave. "He is beloved to you, just like he is beloved to Carlos and Damali?"

Tara hesitated, but as she stared into Valkyrie's eyes, sudden hot moisture filled hers. "Yes. He is beloved. A dear, crazy, ridiculous soul—who is wanton and passionate and funny and decent . . . who will give his life for you, if you're his family, and that is *all* that man has ever wanted. They'd made him a slave and then took everything from him, even his personal dignity. But he is still a class act, because he chooses to be. I will always be his friend. Always."

"I care for him, Tara," Val said, lifting her chin. "I've never known this kind of caring, and it happened so quickly that it frightens me."

"Continue to care for him, Val," Tara said, banishing anything else she was about to say prior to this. "He needs someone like you to believe in him, to fight for him, to wail for him, to hope for him when no one else can. To love him from the depths of their soul. To love him when he doesn't even love himself. And if his luck runs out, he will need someone who will never forget what he meant to this world to bury him."

"I will not rest until I know that he is back safely with our side." Val's voice shook with quiet emotion but the warrior within her would not allow tears to fall.

"Then go to the window in your room and bathe in the moonlight . . . and pray for that man without ceasing." Tara swallowed hard and drew a shaky breath, thinking of the many nights that she'd wanted to do that very thing, but could not.

"I will keep vigil," Val said quietly. "Those prayers will come from my depths. Thank you, Tara, for being such an honorable friend to him. He must love you terribly much, and I can see why."

Now she knew. Yonnie had the right to disclose his life status, or the lack thereof, himself. The honorable belief Val had shining in her eyes, the purity of her trust . . . it was rare and clean and good . . . and she would never rob Yolando of that.

CHAPTER THIRTEEN

Slowly the room came back into focus. She was groggy but her head didn't hurt or pound. Damali's sight zeroed in on movement behind an ornately tooled papyrus and silver screen. A male shadow drew her attention, and as she rustled the bed linen to try to sit up, Carlos walked around the room divider with a wide, foaming, smile. A toothbrush was jammed in his cheek.

"How long have I been out?" she asked, testing her voice, which came out in a rasp. She glanced around the room. This was not the burial preparation chamber they'd been in.

Carlos hadn't answered her. In the distant echo of her mind, she heard water run, heard him spit, but her gaze roved her new environs with awe.

Four solid alabaster columns rose from the corners of the sumptuous bed she was lying on. The ornately carved stone was etched with gold and silver markings that, if she stared at them long enough, seemed to breathe with a pulse of their own. Sheers draped the top, creating a canopy that was gently hued in dissolving pastels that were oddly backlit like butterfly wings in the sun. But she dared not trust her legs to stand yet. Where she sat felt so high up, and each side of the broad carved platform that held the bed flaunted rows of pyramid-like gold steps that terminated at the foot of the massive structure into a silvery pool.

Blooming lotus blossoms floated aimlessly over the surface, and thick ferns seemed to grow right out of the marble. There was an alabaster vanity and a huge white marble armoire, as well as several thickly cushioned loveseats and a chaise longue embroidered with the finest white silk.

"Fly, ain't it?" Carlos said, coming toward her with a fluffy white towel. "It's the New Pharaoh's suite."

"Whoa . . ." Damali pushed her locks back from her face, feeling too dirty and grimy to even touch the lush silk goosedown duvet. At least someone had taken off her Tims. Slow terror began to kindle in her stomach. "This is gonna sound like a silly question, but . . . if they're allowing us to see and use New Pharaoh's chambers, did we accidentally get smoked on the battlefield and just didn't realize it?"

Carlos laughed, but it wasn't his normal, booming, raucous brand of laughter. It was gentle as he sat down next to her and began wiping dirt off her face. "Almost . . . one of us did. Remember? So, yeah, they said I was so close and had died, and almost died, so many times that, at least for now, I could see what was in store for me later. Sort of a preview."

Her hand flew to her mouth, but he gently pried it away as tears rose.

"But I didn't. This is Neteru shore leave, so they said."

She closed her eyes and allowed her body to fall back against the mounds of fat silk pillows. Several slid to the floor and she didn't care.

He leaned over her and kissed the bridge of her nose, continuing his ministrations of cleaning battle grime off her face. "My dirty-faced angel," he said with a passionate rush of words. "You're beautiful, you know that?"

She opened her eyes and reached out to touch his cheek, feeling

it as though she were blind. Just contacting the realness of his
skin, the heat of life within it, made new tears rise along with
her embarrassment. Never in all her years had she fainted dead-
away like a girl. Her Neteru pride was injured from the experience, and the fact that she couldn't stop the relentless tears or
make them burn away tortured everything warrior within her.
It was also the first time she'd tasted real failure—the inability to
save someone who was closer to her than second skin made her
crazy.

Carlos kissed her before she could utter any words of self-
defeat, and when he pulled away, she touched his chest. She
didn't have to say it. He seemed to know what she was asking
even without telepathy. He opened his robe to show her. She sat
up and pulled the golden fabric off his shoulders, inspecting.

Gently, her fingers played across the once-damaged skin,
finding no injury. She bit her lip to hold back a sob of relief
and then opened her palm wide to splay it across the scar she'd
left there while holding her Baby Isis so many years ago. She
watched his lids slide closed under her touch and he pulled her
into a loose hug, but kissed the crown of her head hard.

"I'm all right, baby," he said into her hair. "They got it all
out, and purged you, too. Lemme clean you up so you can rest."

She held him tighter and spoke against his chest, a place that
had almost split in two while she'd helplessly watched. "I can
bathe at home . . . we have to get back to the house to protect—"

"Shush . . ." he whispered. "And that's exactly why you're
wrung out and can't stop crying, and why I did some really stupid shit that laid me out flat on my back. We're burnt out,
D. Face it. The Kings and Queens assured me that they'd put a
reinforced barrier around the compound, plus have Father Pat
on twenty-four-seven surveillance. They're giving us twenty-
four free ones . . . said to sleep, eat, just chill and get back to
center."

She relaxed and nodded slowly. "Twenty-four off duty . . ."

"Twenty-four off duty," he repeated, kissing her head again. She felt the warmth of his breath penetrate her scalp. "Eve said the twenty-four will feel like a week in cosmic time, and when we get shipped home it'll be tomorrow morning, our time."

The weight of his words made her body slump against his. Once she gave into the concept and stopped fighting the fatigue, the profound sensation of peace flowed through her until it felt like her bones were melting.

"C'mon, baby," he said quietly. "Let me get you out of the battle gear and into the pool. All I've gotta do is drop your clothes outside the door and they'll send staff to collect them, and then leave them for you, all clean, when we get the boot outta here."

She looked up into his warm smile and fresh, natural mint filled her nostrils. "I'm so dirty I can't stand myself," she said, cupping his cheek. "You should have put me on a bench with a towel when I passed out." She glanced at the bed. "This is so clean . . . and me . . ."

"You didn't leave a mark." He stood slowly and scooped her up with the towel in her lap.

"How . . ."

"Seems they don't tolerate dirt up here in Mid-heaven." He chuckled and used a nod to indicate the towel. "Check it out. I just wiped away enough grime to plant potatoes, on a white towel no less, and you'd never know it."

Damali picked up the towel and inspected it, turning it over and over. "Deep . . ."

"Ain't it just?" Carlos said, putting her down easy to stand.

"You shouldn't be picking me up and doing stuff," she said, concerned. "And I should be giving *you* a healing waters bath . . . not fainting like somebody who's never seen blood." She closed her eyes. "Carlos, I am so, so—"

A slow, easy kiss stopped her words.

"You are so, so important to me," he whispered against her mouth. "And I will try to be more careful from now on, if there is such a thing in our job descriptions."

"I—"

His mouth covered hers. "Owe you an apology. You never fainted, and no you didn't go all girlie-girl on me. You straight wigged, just like I have in the past when I thought you were dying . . . and I asked them to sedate you before your nervous system fried and shut you down in its own defense."

"Oh, God . . ." she murmured against his shoulder as she closed the gap between them and held him. "I'm so tired, baby. Tired from days and nights of fighting the Darkness since I can remember."

"I know," he murmured against her temple. "Me, too. In the early days, it was different. Now with a full family . . . civilians, kids . . . it's—"

"Taking a toll," she said into his mouth, finishing his sentence. "Let me tend to you," she said after a moment, breaking their long, soul-deep kiss.

"I already got fixed up, boo . . . you need—"

"To allow me to do for you, sometimes," she said, having cut him off with another kiss before pressing her point against the side of his neck.

"I could fight like this all night," he murmured, leaning into her gentle suckle at his jugular vein.

"Remember how we used to fight?" she whispered. "About nonsense. Now here we are fighting about whose turn it is to do for the other."

"Change is good, sometimes," he said as his breath hitched when she nipped his old vampire sweet spot.

"Like the gift of the Magi, us two . . . she cut her hair to sell it to buy him a gold chain for his cherished watch," she murmured into his ear and then gently pulled the lobe of it between her teeth.

"And he sold his watch to buy her a set of combs for her beautiful hair," he said in a quiet rasp, allowing her locks to fall between his splayed fingers. "God . . . I love your hair . . . let me wash it."

"How about a compromise?" she offered in forbidden *Dananu* into his ear, ruining him.

Even in this place, she knew conversations between man and wife were a very private matter, so the slight risk was worth witnessing his reaction. Who would know? As long as there was good intent behind it, anyway, she reasoned, no real feathers should get ruffled. But all of that skittishness to use the forbidden tongue evaporated when she'd felt Carlos's body come alive against her thigh beneath his robe. The look on his face made her ready to accept any fussing she might have to endure from the Queens. Yet, she also felt restraint ripple through his system like a slight tactical charge, and could tell that he was trying to allow her time to fully relax into their new environment.

"Name your terms," he said in a low rumble in *Dananu* after a moment, his eyes slowly going silver. "You're about to get us both in trouble, you know that."

"Like that's ever stopped us before." She stared at him with a sly smile, aware that the very fact that they'd just done something which wasn't completely sanctioned, while contemplating taking it to a whole different level, had been enough to turn him on.

"You lie back and relax . . . and watch. I'll go down the steps and take a bath. Then, we'll see if you're fully healed . . . if so . . . who knows what could happen?" She shrugged, baiting him into the game, but also telling the truth. "I still don't like the fact that I couldn't help you when I so desperately wanted to. I want to make that up to you—so let me."

His half-smile slowly faded as full silver overtook his irises. "I accept your terms," he breathed out in *Dananu*, then slowly began to peel her destroyed tank top up her torso. But when she winced as she raised her arms, he stopped, worry blotting out the silver in his eyes. "Baby . . . I'm sorry. Hey, look, maybe we need to just chill. I had no business—"

She put a finger to his lips. "It isn't an injury, it's—"

"Yeah, right, D," he said, and then kissed the rest of her argument out of her mouth. "I saw it all, even while out cold, third-eye snapshots. A damned serpent banged you against the wall so hard it left plaster on the floor. Then back in N.Y.C.—"

She'd grabbed his jaw with both hands and shoved her tongue in his mouth. "They healed that," she said, coming away from the kiss breathless.

"Then tell me about the wince. I ain't blind, I saw it, baby. Don't much get past me, and I know what I'm—"

She kissed him hard as her hands untied his robe sash, stopping his words midsentence. "It's tension in the muscles between my wings," she said in a breathy rush when he broke the kiss.

"Oh . . ." he said, silver glinting at the rims of his irises again.

She turned around and slowly pulled off her shirt with her back to him. He surrounded her waist with his arms and pressed first his mouth, then his cheek, to that hard to reach spot between her shoulder blades.

The moan she released came up from her gut and caught low and deep in her throat. "Yeah, right there," she said in a husky voice, turning into his therapeutic touch as his hot palms slid across her belly and then ribs. "It all hurts," she finally admitted, now feeling the body blows one by one. "I thought they got it all, but they didn't."

"That's 'cause they're merciful and wise," he murmured, allowing the heat from his hands to slowly rake up her back and then over her shoulders, kneading them gently. "They saved something for me to heal . . . because they know I love to be the one to make you feel better."

She closed her eyes and dropped her head back against his shoulder. "You definitely do that best."

"Yeah?"

She nodded as he found a set of bunched muscles in her right shoulder. "Oh . . . yeah . . ."

"Can I still watch?" he asked in a sexy tone.

"Uh-huh," she whispered, unbuttoning her fly.

"I bet your wings got dirty, too," he murmured against the top of her hair, sliding his hands over her hips to make her panties and jeans pool at her feet. "They might need a good soak . . . if your back is sore."

"Then I might just have to open them while I'm in the water," she whispered and stepped away from him just enough to torture him, then bent to pick up her soiled clothing.

The moment she felt his palms trace over the lobes of her behind, she pivoted around and held her jeans, underwear, and tank top up to cover her breasts, walking backward down the steps into the pool. Then suddenly she tossed her clothing at him, pushing them away from her chest as though passing a basketball. He caught the knot of jumbled fabric, but didn't take his eyes off her. She stepped one foot closer to the mercury-like water and nodded toward the door.

"Better leave them for the staff before you forget."

"Then, don't move," he said quietly, all playfulness gone from his voice. "I don't want to miss any of it."

She smiled and watched him walk across the room. For a moment he'd hesitated, looked toward the door, and then almost seemed to physically jolt himself out of the daze in order to move. He could have simply jettisoned her clothes to make them materialize on the other side of the door. But that was what she loved about him most—his ability to read her intentions just from her eyes, knowing that she was thoroughly enjoying messing with his mind.

When he returned from the task, he stopped at the large armoire and collected a new, thick, fluffy towel and brought over a silver robe that seemed to have the weightlessness of gauze. He carefully laid them at the edge of the large bathing pool, and then sat down on the top step to sprawl out like a huge, sunsoaked panther.

"*Now* you can get in," he said, his expression still so serious that it made her wonder.

She stepped down into the water, feeling tiny tingles claim her feet and ankles and then begin to slowly overtake her calves. She stepped a little deeper, and when the sensation captured her thighs, her eyes widened. That's when he smiled.

"You spiked the water with current, didn't you?"

"A man's gotta do what a man's gotta do . . ."

She stopped just short of submerging her upper thighs. He allowed his gaze to travel along her torso, stopping at the V between her legs covered in soft down that partially eclipsed his Neteru tattoo. She'd willed it back to the surface, every silvery-hot line of it. The sight of her offering made his mouth go dry. His gaze sought hers, stopping en route to admire her breasts. His palms ached to be filled with them, just as his tongue hungered to taste the tight, hard-pebbled flesh at their tips. She broke his concentration yet again as she gave him the gift of a breathy "Oh," of surprise when she dunked herself beneath the surface up to her navel.

"What's in here?" she asked, her lids becoming heavy as she hugged herself.

"King's Ransom," he murmured, watching her slowly drop her head back.

"Seriously . . ." she asked again, beginning to tremble. "What's it called?"

"I told you . . . that's the name they gave me."

"The Neteru Kings?" she said, lowering her body with her eyes still closed. She cupped the iridescent waters in her hands and then drizzled it over her breasts. "Oh . . . God."

"Yeah," he said so quietly that, for a moment, he thought he'd said it in his head.

"What's in it?" She lowered her face to the pool's surface and inhaled then shuddered. "It smells *so good*. But it feels . . ." She looked up and then closed her eyes tightly and spoke in an urgent murmur. "Like you're touching me everywhere at once . . . gentle caresses. How . . ." Another soft shudder claimed her as she submerged to her neck.

"A brother can't give up all his secrets."

She inhaled sharply through her nose and then allowed her head to drop back until her hair was fully submerged. Her voice became a deep moan that traveled through his groin, and then suddenly she dipped her head under the water and came up shaking, her glorious white wings spread.

He materialized shea butter soap in his hand and leaned forward. She opened her palm and called a strangely blue-white-lit oval into it. Within seconds the scent registered in his sinuses. Oil of Hathor. He briefly closed his eyes and set down the soap he'd been holding.

"You said we'd share this," she murmured, lathering her palms. "A little for you, a little for me." She smoothed her soapy palm along her arm and then shuddered so hard she dropped her soap. "What does King's Ransom do? Warn me a little at least."

Watching the silvery sheen on her skin and her trembling, nude body temporarily stole the function of speech. Agony shimmered in her eyes as she waited for his answer, but slowly she brought her soapy palms over her breasts with a gasp.

"It ransoms your sanity for pleasure," he finally said in a

hoarse murmur. Spellbound, he watched her palms slide across her caramel, sun-glazed skin, teasing her nipples until it made his cock bounce. "There's healing crystals in the water for the injuries . . . but to help you relax, they gave me this."

Small beads of perspiration were forming on her brow and upper lip, and he watched Damali stick out the tiny pink tip of her tongue to moisten her lush mouth. The heat in the chamber felt like it had suddenly risen to sauna levels, and condensation had begun to form over the pool's surface in a fine mist. As she stared at him with her large, pleasure-haunted brown eyes, it took all he had not to go to her—but that had not been their bargain. So he honored it.

This time when she submerged he felt it, shuddering so hard he had to clench his jaw to keep from biting his tongue. When she broke the surface, she had the Oil of Hathor in her hands again, the sensual fragrance nearly lifting him from the steps with a hard arch.

"I'd like to renegotiate terms," he said in *Dananu*, not caring if anyone heard. The throb in his groin was a skin-splitting pulse now.

"No," she said, soaping her hair and covering her naked breasts with her wings. She leaned back, massaging the suds into her locks, breathing through her mouth, and then slowly rubbing some lather into a feathery appendage until the sensation buckled her.

He stood, had to before he slid down the steps. But she shook her head and then rinsed her hair and wings by going under again. This time when she came up for air, she cried out, waded toward the shallow end, and held on to the side heaving in breaths.

"Okay," she whispered, looking up at him, clutching the marble.

He was in the water before she could change her mind, robe

and all. The gossamer gold fabric floated to the surface around him, disturbing the lotus blossoms. Within seconds, the mixture of Oil of Hathor in the water stunned him in a blinding shudder that made him drop fang.

Her hands seemed to touch every available surface of his skin as she waded to him and climbed up his body. The Oil of Hathor was wearing him out, the elixir soaking into his skin, tightening his groin in pulses beneath the water's surface the moment Damali welded herself to him. She was trying to kiss him, but he couldn't even get himself under control enough to retract fang. He literally had to turn away from her soft, soft lips, not wanting to cut her, to find her neck to punish, making her cries more insistent as she tried to position herself to take him in.

Super slick from the Oil and her own emulsion, every near miss made him grip her tighter, made them crazier, while he began to walk them backward, blindly searching for a wall. The scent was all in her hair, all in her wings, all in the water, all in his sinuses, all over her skin, *por Dios.* Her tight fist around him made him begin to stutter, *oh, baby,* the Oil of Hathor was all in her palm.

She was burning up, he was burning up—he dragged his nose along the bend in her throat and stopped moving, hoping she would try to mount him again. *Where was the damned wall?* Panting against her throat he realized he'd been so messed up he was walking in circles.

"*Mi tesoro, por favor,*" he said harshly into her ear, unable to tell her more.

Wings spread, fanning the water in small, splashing waves, she circled his neck with one arm and guided him into her slowly with a groan.

The pleasure shock buckled his body from the midsection as a low moan thundered from his insides. Short, shallow pants seized her and suddenly she pulled her head back and stared at him, irises slowly turning silver.

Just witnessing that made his tattoos feel like molten brands. Her mouth suckled the one at his throat while her body hot-sheathed the other, causing him to stumble back, his spine finally hitting the wall. His hands slid over her slippery, soft backside, her toned calves pulling against his ass, guiding their rhythm, her breasts bouncing against his chest. Tears leaked from his eyes as he fought not to bite her—not up here, this was raw enough. Then she bit him hard on his sweet spot and made him see stars.

Pure animal instinct made him round on her, knock her head back with his jaw to find that place he knew would send her over the edge—but he only nipped her, making her cry out and fist his hair.

"Do it," she said between quick bursts, moving against him hard.

He shook his head, eyes shut tight. "Not here, we—".

She took his mouth hard and he tasted her blood, but couldn't resist the urge to put his tongue halfway down her throat. He needed to release so badly his sphincter twitched. She'd snuck him, had soaped herself under the surface. The Oil of Hathor sent jags of lightning through his scrotum every time he slammed against her mound. He could feel the tattoo at his base literally coming alive, pulsing with its own need to return to her sheath on every thrust. Unable to stand it any longer, he flipped her to press her hard against the marble, then at the last second remembered her wings. A quick transport to the bed remedied the problem.

Disoriented when her back hit the soft duvet, she wrapped her legs around his waist and held on for the ride. He hadn't missed a beat, had dug in, tightly gripped her around the waist for leverage, practically snorting silver. Golden-silvery sweat leaked from his pores. His voice had become a hard staccato refrain of guttural utterances with each hard return. She could feel him building, his body trembling so violently as he stroked that it sent blue-white pleasure currents to race over her skin, through her hair and feathers, until she screamed.

Her Sankofa tattoo felt like it had fled the small of her back, melting into her spinal fluids. Silver left his eyes, running the metallic spectrum, first darkening to bronze, then gold, and finally settling on solid platinum. The images he sent split her head in blue-white pleasure novas—quick-moving snapshots of everything he appreciated about her, but was too overwhelmed to say right now.

The beach, her laughing, their first time. *La casa,* her music. Their first time. Her mouth, her legs, her taking off her bra. Their wedding, her *I do,* their first time. Her pulling her Isis, her opening her wings . . . their first time. Vanishing point dovetailed into Creation Point, then their first time. Her nails scored his back. *Jesus compassion!* Water was evaporating from the pool; wet, heavy mist blanketed the entire room. Colors from the sheers cast hue on the mist. She could feel the pulse of the bedposts quicken to meet theirs. Weeping, hollering, their first time. She thrust a song into his mind—"Remember, Baby," then "Wounded Lover" . . . and he shot back, their first time on an audible groan. She opened the cosmos, knocking his head back with galaxy shudders. He brought her the mountainside in Tibet, a burning kiss against the compound wall . . . his fingers splayed against the glass from outside, hers mirroring that . . . returning them to their first time.

She was crying, writhing, reliving their past in acute cellular memory, his thrusts relentless, creating cascading orgasms so blinding that all she could do was arch and hold him. She wanted him to have everything within her; *Just take it,* her mind shrieked as her voice fractured in soprano.

Then it became so eerily still as pleasure seemed to rapidly draw back, receding from her body so harshly she gasped like a woman cut.

For countless heartbeats, all she could hear was their breathing and erratic pulses. He stopped moving for a moment, causing her to stare up into his agonized gaze. He then stopped breathing. His eyes slowly slid shut as he turned away from her almost in slow motion. A quiet storm had gathered, blue-white charges releasing hard in the mist around them. Three seconds of torturous delay felt like thirty.

"Mi esposa, te quiero."

"Husband, I love you, too," she whispered, her voice failing as it dissolved into a broken sob.

As the words left her mouth, the tattoo at his neck lit with pure blue-white energy, as did his eyes, and an arc from it splintered through the mist all around them. It connected with the energy bouncing off the posts, dissipating the fog in a fast-rolling, white-light scorch. Silver rain swept them as though they were barren savannah. His voice rent the air; the hard orgasm thundered through him first and then slammed her.

Mouth open, head back, tears streaming, his body heaved against hers as wave after wave of pleasure poured from him into her. Her hands at his back caught muscle spasms climbing up his spine, heating the fluid housed in his vertebrae. His mind had seized hers, bluntly pounding it the same way his fist had become an anvil against the scattered pillows—*with all that I have and all that I am, oh God, woman, I love you!*

Then he dropped, gasping, his full weight crushing her. Intermittent blue-white charges flickered over his skin, twitching his muscles and making his eyelids flutter. Tears rolled down the bridge of his nose with golden-silver sweat. It took several minutes for him to come to and shift his weight so she could breathe while hard, teeth-chattering shivers consumed her. But when he finally eased up, arms trembling from his own weight, she tightened her legs around him, arching to the strangely pleasurable sensation of uncomfortable warmth deep inside her.

He rolled them both over without withdrawing, so that he could gasp air and save her badly crushed wings.

"I'm sorry I lost it in here," he said with his eyes still closed, taking in huge breaths. "You were supposed to be getting a healing bath and resting . . . I don't know what—"

"Shush," she said quietly between deep inhalations. "I started it. I wanted to give you a gift."

"The King's Ransom was over the top . . . but my real plan, I swear, was to give you pleasure and let you relax. I was gonna fall back and just do you."

She kissed his chin and then the center of his chest with her eyes closed, listening to the powerful thud of his heart slamming against his breastbone. "That's all I wanted to do, too." She kissed one of his tight brown nipples. "You hear that?"

He stirred, having dozed off just that quickly. "Huh, what?"

She smiled. "That," she said in a soft voice, as her breathing normalized, then she placed her hand in the center of his chest. "Your heartbeat."

He relaxed again. "Trying to crack a rib right though here . . . yeah."

"That is my most favorite sound in the universe, Carlos, to hear your heartbeat, literally, inside me," she said, lifting herself to be able to look into his eyes. "I thought this time . . ." She shook her head. "That's why I wanted this to happen, and I didn't care where we were. I *needed* to make love to you," she added quietly. "Wanted you to feel how much you're a part of me."

His fingers trembled as they traced her cheek. Silver was everywhere, making both their bodies glisten. "It wasn't until I realized where I was . . . and how scared you were this time, that it finally got through just how much my doing crazy shit affects you. I was trying to say I'm sorry and that I love you in the only way I sometimes know how." He closed his eyes and stroked her damp arm, releasing a weary sigh. "But you turned me out so bad that I even sorta messed that up."

"What in the world are you talking about, man?" She rained kisses all over his face, making him smile. "Are you crazy?"

"I had plans, old-school plans . . . like back in the day when I could hold my shit together for a minute." He chuckled softly and kept his eyes closed. "Problem was, every image I was holding for you was blowing my mind, and I could no more project us there than I could stop the inevitable—I must be getting old, girl. Damn, that don't make no sense. That was sloppy. Mind stuttering, no foreplay, just straight animal." His hands trailed down her shoulders and then covered her breasts. "I'll make it up on round two . . . I promise."

"You are *crazy*," she whispered softly against his mouth, loving his touch. "You almost had me swallow my tongue from a pleasure seizure, rained down King's Ransom on me till I shrieked like I was being murdered, and shot white lightning so hard that static was arcing between my fingers and toes . . . and you're doing postgame highlights?" She shook her head and dropped against his stone chest. "Go to sleep, man."

"White lightning—for real?" He pulled her up and looked in her eyes.

"Blue-white charge jumped from your tattoo to the mist to the bed and back, lit your eyes, and felt like it was blowing my back out when it hit."

He sat up a little more. "Yeah? I guess I was working so hard I didn't notice at the time."

"Yeah," she said, laughing. The expression on his face was like that of a little kid. She cupped his cheek. "Trust me on that; I can still feel it warming my insides. Go to sleep."

"No shit?" He flipped her over and then kissed her slowly.

"You wouldn't play with me about something like that, right?" He kissed her ear. "Baby . . . I was trying to give you everything in me to remember me by, in case one day something does happen to me. Know what I'm saying?"

She nodded. He'd definitely cascaded all her favorite images, ones she'd never forget, as well as some that she didn't know were so completely special to him.

"In our line of work, sometimes it just ain't your day, or night. So, I gotta know . . . no shit, you ain't just saying all this to make me feel better, right? The burn is way deep, right?"

"No shit," she finally said, chuckling. "*Si, Señor* Rivera, I can still feel it, *muy caliente*. All right?"

He closed his eyes and nodded and then rested his forehead against hers, pulling her into a slow, tender embrace. His voice became so soft that it was a mere murmur against her ear as he spoke.

"*Bueno.*"

His thoughts drifted as he peacefully slid away from her body and gathered her against him to rest. That was all he could do, he was spent, left merely a husk. Even money said it would be a boy . . . if she got the shivers, she'd probably have a girl.

ℭ CHAPTER FOURTEEN

Marlene tied her robe sash hard as she walked down the hall scanning the house for Rider. She could sense his energy coming from the kitchen, and had waited all night—on Shabazz's advice—to approach their Guardian brother once he left his suite. Rider didn't normally function at the crack of dawn; why he was up now truly disturbed her. It took all of the self-discipline she owned not to do a mind-invasion and just see what was going on. But she knew it was deep, given the vision directive she'd gotten from the Neteru Council camps. Yonnie was no longer barred from the property, even if the premises were off-limits. All of the seers in the house got word, which meant Tara got word . . . which meant Tara and Rider most likely had *words*. Second-sight was not a prerequisite to know how that particular news flash was received.

Passing each couple's suite in the house, she was so glad that Big Mike had insisted on soundproofing. Marlene kept her pace swift as she rounded the grand, sweeping staircase that led to the first floor. Yeah . . . leave it to the audio-sensor to point out that critical detail. This way every couple had their own bedroom, mini–living room, and master bathroom where they could argue at the tops of their lungs . . . or do whatever else, and now the added complexity of little ears didn't have to be in grown folks' business.

As she crossed the expansive dining room, she thought back on the early years, when she and Shabazz were first scuffling. When they had no resources, and vampires were hunting them, rather than the other way around. Thought back on the blessing of a brainstorm that she was sure an angel of inspiration whispered in her ear. That became the Warriors of Light. From there, she and Shabazz built a small citadel, the first compound. And one by one new Guardians running for their lives got brought in and schooled. Not so surprisingly, each one had a skill that could be used in the new record label—not surprising because all of this was divinely orchestrated. Rider was next in, after her and Shabazz, and then came Mike. The old heads. After that was Tara, by extension to Rider . . . and then poor Jose, searching for his mentor, Jack to Rider, who he thought was dead. The good old days. Uncomplicated days. Now this was akin to a hot mess.

Seeing Jack Rider hunched over a to-go cup of coffee broke her reverie. She stared at his rumpled white T-shirt and the way his shoulders slowly expanded and contracted. The poor man was asleep at the kitchen counter, and only the pitch of his elbows against the tiles held him upright. His gray sweats looked like he'd snatched on his clothes in a hurry. His hair was jagged spikes all over his head. He was barefoot. But she did notice that he'd gone out and gotten a paper. He'd even left the TV on in the other room, and the too-cheerful melody of cartoons filtered in with the dawn. The whole scene became suddenly surreal.

But given the very long status of their friendship, she didn't directly rouse him. She decided to treat him the way she did Shabazz when she wanted him to wake up so they could talk about a difficult subject. Marlene banged the kettle, so-called making tea.

"Whoa!" Rider was up, off the stool, grabbing a bunch of fabric at his hip.

"Mornin', partner," Marlene said with a mischievous smile. "I hope you left your gun in the holster upstairs, because it's a little early in the morning to be shooting up the joint."

Rider wiped his palms down his face and sat back down with a thud. "Mornin', Mar. Damn, that was a heart jolt."

"Better than caffeine." She chuckled, he slurped his coffee. "Whatchu doing up at no o'clock in the morning after a Jack Daniel's kinda night, man?"

"Couldn't sleep."

Marlene filled the tea kettle. "Oh, so it's going to be that type of conversation. Why don't I just put on some music so we can dance?"

Rider closed his eyes and slurped more coffee. "It would be so much easier if you just went in and took whatever you wanna ask me from my already jellied mind, darlin'. C'mon, Mar. Can't a man have a cup of coffee in peace? I'm already babysitting, for chrissakes—trying to do the right thing."

"Babysitting?" Marlene set the kettle on the stove and flipped on a burner.

He indicated with his chin toward the family room. "I needed some air. Got up and went to get a morning paper and a real cup of coffee that only a diner can make. Don't worry, although I didn't have a gun I was in a bad enough mood to smoke a daywalker solo, all right. Anyway, when I came home, that little bird in there was wandering the halls looking for somebody to help her with the TV. Said, and I quote, 'Nana said she was too tired and to go ask Mommy.' Problem was, Nana didn't tell the baby where her mommy's room was. So she's aimlessly wandering the halls . . . and I scooped her up before she could get a real serious education."

"Oh, Lawdy B!" Marlene said, closing her eyes and holding onto the edge of the sink. "We're gonna have to set up some whole new house rules, gonna have to tell folks to lock their doors . . ."

"Uh-huh," Rider said through a loud slurp. "This had been a grown-folks-only establishment since the beginning. None of us would dare to just wander into a room unannounced, especially after post-battle adrenaline is—"

"I know, I know, I know," Marlene said quickly, cutting him off as she waved her hands. "Jesus."

"But the kid can see, Mar," he said, taking his cup down from his mouth slowly. "She was walking with her hands out as though she was feeling energy patterns . . . had her cute little lip poked out looking for her mommy and Daddy Mike. So I let her wander a bit, just to see, ya know?"

Marlene came closer to him, awed. "Did she figure it out? Did she know?" she asked excitedly.

"Get this," he said, leaning back on his stool. "Not only did she guess the room, but caught me in a lie."

"What?" Marlene whispered.

"Man, it was the freakiest thing to see in a kid that young . . . but she found the right door and smiled this smile that just wrapped me all around her little finger and pointed. I nodded that she was right, but told her Mommy and Daddy Mike were asleep, so I'd get her some cereal and would put on the cartoons."

Marlene hugged herself, listening to Rider's account of the child's gifts with wide eyes.

"Then she told me, no, Mr. Jack—Mommy's not asleep. She's awake . . . but is making a funny sound like she's hurt."

Marlene cupped her hand over her mouth as Rider began to laugh.

"So I said, aw, little lady, your mommy's just snoring, that's all, let's go get some cereal."

"Oh, my God . . ."

"Oh, it gets better, Mar. You'd better have a seat."

He waited for dramatic effect, and Marlene obliged him, pulling out a stool and half-sitting, half-leaning against it for support.

"The kid shook her head and tugged on my arm. Told me to get my gun, because her mommy must be hurt." He smiled wider when Marlene closed her eyes. "I said, how can you be sure—since you know I'm testing for multiple gifts here, Marlene, wondering if the kid has super hearing or something. Know what she tells me?"

"I am afraid to ask."

"She says, 'Mr. Jack, Daddy Mike is praying to Jesus and is holding Mommy, like she's hurt. I can see it in my mind; you have to go help them.' "

Marlene jumped up out of the stool like she was being chased by wasps. Her hand was waving, shooing away Rider's words as she laughed. "Oh, no, oh, no, this is . . . this is—"

"Outrageous comes to mind," Rider said with a droll smile. "So, what's the protocols, oh wise senior seer of the house? The kid cannot cruise these halls if her gift works while she's in range. And what if she can pick up at a distance? When Rivera gets back here—"

Marlene slapped her forehead. "Rider, I can't even begin—"

"Just for grins, not to make your job as housemother more difficult, but uh . . . you know the old vamp style when they go to work. Special FX, thunder and lightning—you know what we lived through with those two in the old compound, right?"

"I'm going to have to do a divination and consult the ancestors on this, will have to go back to the Temt Tchaas and see what my old black book has to say, 'cause, *chile,* no! And I don't know if I should try to block her, for fear of potentially damaging her new, growing gift. But one thing's for sure, that child cannot be trolling these halls unescorted. Me and Delores are gonna have a come-to-Jesus meeting this morning, trust me on that." Marlene folded her arms over her chest.

"Tea water's boiling, Mar," Rider said, chuckling and taking another deep swig of coffee. "Not to worry, the kid is completely tuned into Nickelodeon right now . . . but boy-o-boy, when Mike finally gets his rusty ass down here to forage in the fridge like a bear coming out of hibernation, I am going to rib him until he threatens my life. Trust me on that, hon. It's just too rich to pass up."

Marlene laughed. "He'll kick your ass."

"Yeah, that he will, but it'll be worth it," Rider said, laughing.

She smiled and began making tea, flipping off the burner. Rider sat back, much less tense, but theirs was indeed an old dance. He waited; she put loose herbal green tea in a bamboo tea ball. He watched her process calmly, knowing that she had to think while her hands worked.

"So, you went out to get a newspaper and a cup of coffee without any backup and without a sidearm, in this time of daywalkers. Musta been a helluva argument."

Rider let his breath out hard. "There's breaking news that warranted knowing first thing."

"Ah . . . and CNN might not have it on cable. Are we out of coffee?" She kept her back to him as she spoke, but her smile threaded into her voice.

"Check it out," he said, opening the paper. "Get this, Mar— a *rare tornado* touched down in Brooklyn. Flooded the subway systems—on the same day we had our little skirmish in Harlem, but after we dropped Father Pat off to a safe house in Brooklyn. I love the media spin on these cosmic events. It sounds so much better to say that a natural act of God occurred, like a twister, than to say that maybe a swirl of demons looking for a priest

after they got their asses fried in Harlem were seeking retaliation. Just like the steam—see, page thirty-five: mysterious steam
rising in Manhattan is not another attack by Al Qaeda. Authorities claim an underground steam vent somehow burst, sending
downtown workers and residents scrambling."

He closed the paper hard. "That is such a crock. That was the
leftover cavalry after Damali flushed them onto the expressway—
they traveled as far as they could and probably had to gather to
blow out a blocked portal underground or something."

Marlene stirred raw honey into her tea and came to the
counter with Rider. She sat down calmly, without saying a
word. He grunted and opened up to the science section. "Not
impressed with the weather? All right, then how about this. Last
night was a new moon. Mars, the planet of war—my sidebar
editorial comment added for emphasis—was visible from the
northern sky . . . the big red dot, while we were fighting. Sci-
entists say that from midnight onward, the Perseid meteor
shower was the most impressive this year than it had been in
years past . . . sixty meteors fell per hour."

"Let me see that," Marlene said, taking the paper from him.

"Oh, so now I have your attention."

"That's a meteor per minute that our side was lobbing—talk
about a shock and awe campaign." She glanced up at Rider
from the paper and then flipped to the weather. "Only one human casualty, a car accident—tragic, but think of how bad that
could have been . . . a frickin' tornado hitting New York City,
c'mon, Jack." She handed him back the newspaper.

"People could have drowned in the subway, or gotten elec-
trocuted from falling power lines . . . trees had been uprooted
and smashed houses and cars, but no civvy got hurt." He sat
back, vindicated. "I told you I had to go get a paper."

"All right," she said with a gentle smile, sipping her tea.
"And it was safe, relatively . . . word came down, we're under

protection until our Neterus get back—but that doesn't mean we can just be going buck wild without precautions."

He raised his to-go cup to her. "I know. And you'll be proud of me, I left without a weapon because I didn't trust myself. Figured I wasn't going far; Tara told me we had a sorta temporary shield, and if I bumped into somebody who was gonna piss me off, it was best that I couldn't draw on him."

Marlene nodded. "Wise man."

Rider raked his hair with his fingers. "You know how I feel about this," he said, losing all mirth from his tone.

"Yeah, I do." She landed a hand on his shoulder.

"Fucks me up bad, Marlene."

"Which part? The part that he's no longer after Tara, or the part that he's found somebody new?"

Rider looked at her and a half smile began to tug at his left cheek. "The part that still wants to empty a clip in his vampire ass for making my heart stop a few times over my lady."

"Who is now your wife."

"Yeah, yeah . . . true." Rider let out a hard breath and then looked out the window. "But it's a real challenge knowing . . . okay, you're right, I've gotta let it go."

"All right, Jack Rider," Marlene said, folding her arms and lowering her voice. She leaned in toward him to make him lean in toward her. "Listen," she said, as though someone else might hear. "You are never going to be able to make it rain rose petals in the bedroom, or whatever else vampire lovers tend to do— but never forget, you did something none of them can do . . . you loved that woman back from the grave. She sat up off a slab in a church, or did I get the story wrong?"

Rider sat back, awe in his expression. He looked away and then rubbed his jaw, and then stared at Marlene as though seeing her for the first time.

"Yeah," Marlene said in a conspiratorial whisper. "That's

some hard-down, *crazy* love. Tara never struck me as a foolish woman, and if she was going to Yonnie, I know it had to be to threaten his vampire ass, not to jerk Val around . . . and to tell him she'd hunt him down herself 'if he got carried away and turned that innocent. Then, who am I to say, but I think my gut is right on this . . . she probably was gonna lay so much guilt on him, remind him about how she was turned while innocent and wide-open sexually, blah, blah, blah so that if that man had a glimmer of a conscience, he'd think twice before he bit her. Not to mention, she had to be sure he wasn't just playing with Val's head to try to play with hers—you know that old make-her-jealous-so-she'll-come-to-me move. If I know Tara, she was going to waltz out there and put her hands on her hips and tell Yonnie to go stroke himself. She'd never violate you like that, Jack. Be serious."

Again he rubbed his palms down his face and then just shook his head, looking at the floor. "How come y'all are so damned complicated? I would have never figured all that out . . . when she headed for the door, I sorta lost it."

"When he called her before, on a new daywalker high . . . yeah, you had a right to be worried. But since then, he went wherever and handled his business, so much that he was cool enough to pass Neteru Council inspection."

Rider's gaze traveled out the kitchen door. "I'm in the dog-house, Mar. Jack Daniel's will make you say some shit that is really, really hard to take back."

"Uh-huh, I hear you," she said, sipping her tea. "Hence, why I'm always telling you brothers to chill on that particular rem-edy when you're angry."

Rider held up his hand. "I know. You're right."

"I don't want to be right," she said, meaning it. "I want you to be peaceful . . . who knows how this day is gonna go. So, how about if you go back upstairs and get some, uh, rest, and I'll watch the baby. Throw your hat in the door, fall on your sword, eat crow, but come down here in a few hours a much happier man, will ya?"

"I love how you think, darlin' . . . but I really . . ."

"I know you ain't no punk, Jack Rider," Marlene teased.

"Been called many things, but not that," he said, slipping off his stool. He downed his coffee like he was downing a beer and set the empty cup down hard like they'd been sitting at a saloon bar. He then hitched up his saggy sweatpants in a way that made her laugh and swaggered toward the door. "I owe you, ma'am, much obliged."

Marlene waved him away. "Aw, shucks, sir. It wasn't nothing . . . besides, I already got mine."

"This time, Mother, I insist." Abel stood across from Eve in her royal chambers with his arms folded. "You have allowed Seth to join the battle, why not me? He is my junior; I am now eldest and it is my birthright to fight with the Neterus at the end of days."

Eve stared at her second son, whom she'd lost so many years ago, and then let out her breath hard. He'd caught her in chambers alone before sunrise and wore only a simple white linen wrap around his loins. *No longer a baby,* she thought, *no longer a gangly teen.* . . . he had Adam's tall, proud carriage, and his skin was deep ebony, just like his father's. Thick Nubian locks the hue of midnight interlaced with gold threads hung down his straight back. But rather than owning Cain's thick, muscular frame, Abel was long and lean, his muscles moving beneath black skin like a leopard's. Her hand went to her mouth, her fingers nervously drumming her lips as she contemplated the inevitable.

"I lost you once," she said quietly, and then gathered her golden robe more tightly around her body. "I consoled myself by knowing that I'd have Seth with us his entire life, but you were cut down before you could even . . ."

"They cannot eradicate me here."

"You are young and think you are invincible. This is why I worry." She stared at her baby boy, now a man, a full spirit in his own right. "They can damage your spirit, set the Darkness upon it to twist it like it twisted your brother's." She pushed her Nubian locks off her shoulders as her voice dropped to a pained whisper. "You saw what they did to Cain's spirit. You know what that did to me. If they harm you again, I shall pass away from all existence. The earth shall have a mother no more."

She went to Abel and hugged him and laid her head on his shoulder. "And yet I know that, no matter what I say, you are going to war."

He petted her hair and nuzzled his face against her temple. "I love you, Mother, and respect you . . . but yes, I am going to war."

She held him away from her and then cupped his cheek. "You loved me best and respected me the most . . . and for all these years, you stayed with me here, despite your need to see the world."

He covered her hand with his own and stared at her with the clearest gaze. "I knew you couldn't take it, and there was time. This, Father taught me. There is a season for all things, and prior to now, it was not my season."

She nodded and hugged him again tightly. "What is the plan?"

Abel hesitated and then walked away from her. "I have the same Neteru tracer in my DNA that they need to track from the darkside, from Cain's blood ties to you. Since Carlos and Cain shared lineage as well, albeit from the wrong source, we can mask enough of the differences to cause confusion."

No apology in his startling gaze, he turned and stared at his mother. "I have the same rage as the newest Neteru," he said in a quiet, tense voice. "I watched my mother break down, wail for centuries at their hands. Let me help end this new dark line. It comes from the same pit that whispered in my brother's ear and stoked enough jealousy within him that he murdered flesh of his flesh."

"How can you ask me to thus put you in harm's way, yet again? You must know how this creates agony inside my heart." She walked deeper into the chamber and, hugging herself, spoke with her eyes closed. "Tell me your plan. Make me have hope that it is not an all-out assault on Hell."

"It is what they now call guerrilla warfare, Mother—but what we called shrewd strategy in eons past. I will shadow the male Neteru, making them send and waste valuable resources after me . . . I will act as a decoy, an energy body-double for Carlos Rivera. Seth will also help, but his rage is weaker, as he was never lost to you. Your wails for him were never as profound. Seth gave you grandchildren and made you happy . . . but he is outraged for his mother's sake, as am I. He and I will work in tandem to confuse the enemy. When they send retaliation toward Rivera, it will be Seth or I that will redress it, and then our father and the armies of Ausar will return fire—while the living brother is always in the shadows. This way, Rivera can hunt the Antichrist with some added measure of protection."

"It is a sound and approved plan," Adam said in a low rumble, entering the room. "The archon's table convened, and even Hannibal agrees with this approach to keep the darkside chasing after spirits to allow the living room to live. It is especially critical now. This also avoids the need to open another seal so quickly."

The two elder Neterus exchanged a meaningful glance that left Abel with a question in his mind.

Eve slowly nodded but her heart was heavy, making her words spill from her lips with weighted emphasis. "You will tell them, the young Neterus?"

Adam smiled. "Yes, my beloved . . . but not right now. Perhaps in a little while."

"So, what is the verdict?" Rabbi Zeitloff asked in a weary tone. He stared at the clerical physicians assembled around Father Patrick's bedside, blinking rapidly through his Ben Franklin glasses. He peered up at the gaunt faces that nervously looked from one to another before speaking, growing peevish. Each man before him had the best of credentials and the Ivy League background to go with them, but he silently wondered if they had any real *chutzpah.*

"Listen," the Rabbi said, beginning to pace. "We have endured a tornado, meteor showers—so much that our other members from the Covenant have not been able to even get here in one piece. Delays, delays, delays, and our dear colleague is running out of time! I must know the extent of the horrors we're still facing, and the New Yorkers are going to have to fill in until we can get more assistance. I refuse to have this man die on my watch!"

"The only way I can describe what is happening to him medically, as well as spiritually," one cleric said, "is to liken it to the theory of black holes." He rubbed the nape of his neck, ruffling the soft blond down there, and stared at Rabbi Zeitloff with crystal blue eyes. He was only a few inches taller than the Rabbi, but stood with the bearing of a much larger man.

"Come again?" Zeitloff stared at the threesome for a moment. He appraised the other two clerics, both young brunetts that looked like they belonged at a country club rather than at a healing as serious as this. If only the older, more seasoned clerical veterans were able to get through the weather delays. The frustration was making his nerves brittle. Finally, when no one spoke, he took a potshot at their expertise. He wanted answers, straight answers, not to be mollified!

"You sound like my late brother, with this scientific crazy-making."

"Black holes, the example my colleague, Dr. Linder, was trying to express to you," another cleric pressed on, undaunted, "occur when a star implodes. Everything folds in on itself into a very small, very dense black hole where the gravitational pull into the darkness is so profound that not even the light can escape."

Rabbi Zeitloff took off his glasses for a moment to wipe the perspiration from his face. His glasses had begun to slide down his nose and his face felt oily and uncomfortable. They'd been up all night, had his dear colleague and friend hooked up to the most state-of-the-art equipment, but at the end of the day it still all came down to prayer. At past eighty years old, he understood this. Men in their prime would not.

"Sir, his mind is slowly pulling into that tiny black spot of implosion from the black-charge blast he took. That is what began the implosion. The outer edges that slip over what we call the *event horizon*—the edge where the darkness begins to suck the gray matter into itself—is what we're trying to save now. If the draw inward continues, it will first pull the mind in to collapse into itself . . . then as that density continues to draw inward, it will siphon the spirit in . . . and ultimately the body will be an empty shell that will go right into pure darkness. He will simply disappear."

"No," the Rabbi said, shaking his head. "That is *not* going to happen, because we have something that is going into that black hole as we speak—prayers. Let them suck down as many as they want! Are you measuring his brain mass? Has it changed in the hours since he was brought here and we began our vigil? You must employ faith as you work on the medical and preternatural answers so that it is a blend. His case is not run-of-the-mill, and a general exorcism for this did not work."

"You attempted an exorcism, even knowing what caused his condition?" the lead physician gasped. "Sir, you could have been seriously injured."

"Hey, this is New York," Rabbi Zeitloff said proudly, adjusting his squat frame while lifting his chin and crossing his arms over his chest. "And half of the staff here grew up in Hell's Kitchen. So we're not taking any crap."

How was it that almost getting his liver and vital organs stashed in Kemetic canopic jars for all of eternity had made him unable to keep his hands off his wife?

Carlos slowly took in his environs as Damali slept quietly beside him. The silvery mist had evaporated, causing the rained-down bathwater to disappear. Everything was drying. A glittering residue of King's Ransom painted the sheers, giving their butterfly-wing hues an entirely new spectral prism. The ever-present light had burned away all of the dampness, and he'd watched the pool refill on its own, as though this magical, wonderful place just followed the ebbs and flows of cosmic energy . . . using it, replacing it, expending and replenishing. It was a rhythm, a pulse, just like the one he could subtly feel making the bed hum.

If this was the afterlife, then, hey . . .

But he was so not ready to die. Being here, seeing how close he'd come to that was more than enough. He had things to live for before, but now . . . damn, he'd be a crazy man keeping the Darkness from his doorstep—and most assuredly away from his family. He brushed Damali's cheek with a gentle kiss so as not to wake her, loving how she'd wrapped them both in her wings as she slept the sleep of the innocent.

His prayer was a quiet one, issued not just from his mind, but from his heart, Por Dios, *please don't allow them to injure my wife like they did before.* As he stared at Damali, her face became blurry and he blinked back tears. *This time,* Madre de Dios, *hear my prayer. Let her be able to carry to term, if it is Your will . . . let her be able to hold our baby in her arms . . . let that child come into the world healthy and strong and whole. . . . And just give us enough time to fight long enough, to make it through enough battles, so we can see our kid grow up.*

Carlos closed his eyes and slung his forearm over them. Breathing through his nose, he tried to settle the roiling emotions within, overcome with the gravity of it all. This morning went beyond an epiphany or even the normal vague awareness that something in his life was changing. It was a turning point, one that required action . . . problem was, he wasn't exactly sure what that might be.

For the first time in his life he realized that he didn't have a strategy, didn't have enough game to play this off, if things went awry. He was vulnerable, wide-open behind this. A man with something to lose didn't even describe it. Until this moment, it was hard to imagine being even more vulnerable than having Damali to lose . . . it was incomprehensible that he could love her harder than he already did.

If they came for him this time, and if they got Damali or the baby, he would lose his mind. There would be no fallback position. They said a man with nothing to lose was a dangerous thing, but a man with everything to lose was something frightening to encounter, indeed.

She'd tried to tell him that's why she wasn't ready . . . told him the first time she got pregnant how this was gonna go. But there was something so surreal about that previous experience. The reality of it hadn't had a chance to sink in and marinate in his mind before she'd miscarried. And when he'd made love to her, this time, just like when it had happened between them before, his intent was all messed up . . . his heart overriding his head . . . silver shot, nowhere to be found, no damned protection, willing life through his body into hers . . . now what? Up here in Mid-heaven, no less.

"*Por Dios,* what have I done?"

CHAPTER FIFTEEN

Daybreak eased her from slumber like a gentle kiss. Even in the perpetual light of the Neteru chamber, an internal sensory awareness lifted her from the deep sleep that had overtaken her, leaving her fully refreshed but so oddly serene. Perfect peace had stolen every anxiety, so much so that it was initially hard to move her limbs. Carlos's reassuring warmth radiated through her entire body. His steady, rhythmic breathing was a constant reminder that they'd yet again beaten the odds.

She lifted herself carefully to allow him to continue to sleep undisturbed. . . . Lord knew the man needed to. Vague memories of prophecies and strategies pelted her mind, then simply evaporated as she leaned on one elbow and caressed his chest, admiring the masonry of it.

Bronze skin drawn tight over carved marble is what his body seemed like to the touch. Her brand was still there in the center of his chest, a raised keloid scar from a silver burn years ago that protected his heart. She wanted to kiss his eyelids, but knew that would rouse him. Instead she allowed her eyes to drink in the subtle contours of his face and how his long, jet-black lashes created a beautiful dark fringe against his sun-golden hue. The tips of her fingers hungered to feel the thick, velvety texture of his hair, but she wouldn't allow them to disturb him. She stared at his mouth and sighed, wanting to run the pad of her thumb over it and then allow her lips to claim his. But, again, she refused to steal even a sliver of his peace for selfish reasons.

It seemed so impossible that she could have found a way to love him more than she already did . . . but somewhere during their passionate night, she had.

Damali briefly closed her eyes as words echoed in her mind and then tumbled down from it to overflow her heart. *Dear God, I love him so much sometimes it scares me.* Carlos stirred, his hand dragging a lazy pattern across her skin and claiming the same hip it always did by rote the moment he became conscious.

"I didn't mean to wake you," she said quietly, and then kissed him the way she'd wanted to for minutes.

"You can wake me up any time you want to like that," he murmured, tracing her back with a warm hand.

They stared at each other for a long while and then he simply nodded.

"I thought so," she said just above a whisper.

"I couldn't help it," he said softly, his gaze searching her face. "You mad at me?"

She closed her eyes and hugged him. "Mad at you? Oh, God no . . ."

He let out a breath of relief and kissed her temple. "I didn't ask you first . . . we never discussed it."

"Your heart asked mine and mine said yes," she said quietly in his ear. "We've both wanted this for a long time, but . . . I just hope . . ."

"Don't say it, baby." His voice was moist and warm against the side of her face, and his kiss against her neck was just as gentle. "With all that I have, and all that I am, I swear to protect you this time."

She nodded and held him tighter. "I know that, always knew that . . . but I think we should wait until we know for sure."

"You're right," he said, his tone slightly dejected as he loosened his embrace so that he could look at her. "There were times when we thought it had happened and it hadn't."

She cupped his cheek, gently stroking it. "I know . . . that's why I want to be one hundred percent sure."

"Yeah, we shouldn't get ahead of ourselves with wishful thinking or worrying about what might not be. Right?" He sat up and then turned away from her to find the edge of the bed so he could stand.

"Oh, Carlos . . ." She caught his hand, staying his leave, and sat up. When she was sure he wouldn't bolt, she let go of his hand and scooted over to him, then made him turn to look at her. "I love you. I want it to happen, too. We can hope."

Her voice hitched as she held his face between her palms and stared into his deep brown eyes. Within them she was positive she could see eternity, the color was so pure, the gaze he offered so clear. And she knew that they were both afraid on so many levels it was impossible to articulate. Maybe that's why neither spoke the words or gave "it" a name, and danced around the topic, even while open and naked and vulnerable in bed—that was just too hard after the losses and disappointments.

She kissed him slowly and tasted salt in his mouth. "It's going to be all right," she told him with fierce conviction embedded in a whisper.

"Promise me," he said in a barely audible tone, hanging his head and drawing in a deep, shuddering breath.

His request shook her to her core. It wasn't until that moment that she fully realized just how profoundly the losses had carved at his heart, too. All this time he had made it about her, how she'd felt, how she'd taken the losses so hard, her physical, mental, and spiritual well-being . . . all the while her husband was quietly hemorrhaging on the inside from the same emotional blows. This man had been hurt to the bone. Perhaps on many levels his wound was deeper, because no one had truly gone to him to help him purge it. The inequity was incomprehensible—he was supposed to get over it alone and with time, while she'd been surrounded by support and cleansing women's tears.

Her arms gently encircled his neck, then a palm cradled the back of his head, her fingers threading through his hair as she brought his cheek to lie against her breasts. Defeat left his arms loose at his sides. But her slow, relentless kisses against his scalp, in time with her gentle rocking back and forth, soon brought life into his limbs enough for him to return her hug.

"I promise you, baby . . . with everything that's in me—it's gonna be all right. This time will be different. This time I'll be more careful. This time . . ." Damali let her head drop back as she closed her eyes, fighting tears—then she gave up and let them fall. "This time I'm gonna call in every marker, call all the angels, okay?" she whispered. "I won't let the other side do this to you again."

He knew and she knew that it was a hollow promise. No one could control the vagaries of fate, much less know the grand design. But the fact that she'd said it, was willing to fight to make their dream manifest, and wanted what he wanted with as much passion, made him hug her tightly and add to the rocking.

She knew he was so close to meltdown that he couldn't speak. And if she said another word he'd lose it, so she held her peace. It was the touch that told her, the rough handling of her back as though he was trying to pull her inside of him to keep any and everything away from her, even the air. Each breath he dragged in and released was as ragged as the sob he refused to allow . . . wet and thick, his face burning up against her breasts.

God, make it be all right. . . . The stress this man had been under for years tore at her. Something other men took for granted, the ability to sire, had been hunted by militias of darkness. Carlos could never assume he could father a child without incident. His woman's womb had been targeted, coveted, ransomed, gored, his child massacred and sacrificed to the cause—all while his hands had been tied, all while he'd been staked to a wall in Hell. She rocked him harder, her wings cloaking them both from the cruel memories.

Every kiss she landed against him now made him stop breathing. He had to let it out, once and for all in private, just man and wife. She broke her silence to break his dam.

"I swear to you, baby, I have enough hope for us both."

He stopped breathing, stopped rocking, and then his shoulders shook. It all came out in agonized gulps. She saw what tortured his mind, her large-bellied and vulnerable, the house under siege . . . her raising an Isis with him outgunned and outnumbered, just out of range, just out of reach as a huge, black claw gored her, leaving her stunned, glassy-eyed, and dead. An infant's wails, an overturned crib—him running through the house searching, taunted by pure evil and unable to locate their child. Her hysteria, screaming at him that the baby was gone, him paralyzed by not knowing where to look first.

"Baby, no . . . shush, no . . ." She held his head, grappling with his hair, trying to force good thoughts to override the bad.

His hand slid down her belly between their bodies and settled over her womb. "What have I done to you, D? I . . . had no right—"

"It's going to be all right," she repeated, cutting off his hoarse whisper. Every image that had been embedded within him she light-shocked the moment it surfaced in his skull until he dropped his head back and began to hyperventilate.

"That's poison," she said quietly, firmly, now up on her knees to hold his head tighter between her palms. "They lied to you, from the day they first took you down into the pit. They knew this would fuck with you more than anything else in the world, baby. It was encoded into a throne. Dante used it, Nuit used it, Cain wallowed in it, Lilith horse-whipped you with it, and the Nameless probably bathes in it. So give it to me, once and for all. Right now, Carlos, give it to me and let me follow that dirty thread to the root and then choke it off with silver."

He held her wrists, trying to dislodge her hands. "Don't go in, not that deep—I never wanted you to know how—"

"I'm your wife!" she shouted. "I've got your back!"

Silver streamed down his face as his grip loosened around her wrists. "D, I'll be all right," he said in a thick whisper. "Baby, I swear you don't wanna see what's been on my head about this subject for all these years. I'm begging you."

She inhaled a deep, steadying breath, braced herself, and ignored his words. Flashes of blinding light like hundreds of camera bulbs went off in her head as each gruesome image opened. The light burned the center of the image out, scorched it to the edges as though a match had been set to a Polaroid. But then she saw the dark tendril that connected each image. She let go of his head with one hand and called the Isis into her right grip. Carlos squeezed his eyes shut as she rested the sharp metal gently against his temple.

A thick, coiling, dark mental rope unfurled in his mind like a serpent. Suddenly she was running alongside it, following it, trying to find the base. To her horror the base was as wide as a mature oak tree, with hundreds of twisted black roots partially exposed in his gray matter. She sheathed the Isis long blade and called the Isis dagger into her palm, then reached back, hauled off, and stabbed the largest root she could find.

Carlos's yell coincided with the black geyser as the root let go of his cerebral cortex and flailed wildly. But she got a glimpse of what it had been connected to. A horribly deformed, half-demon changeling. The gargoyle-like fetus stared up at her with slit-shaped green eyes and snarled. She was on it before it could un-curl, driving the dagger into its unbeating black heart.

From a remote part of her mind she could hear Carlos's sobs. But her focus was laser as she watched thick black root branches disconnect from the burning ball of putrid flesh. Both hands on her dagger, she pumped white-light blasts through it, cleansing the area like a hazmat team. She burned everything in her wake, and then set her own mind to remembering their hopes.

Flash—his laughing and picking her up, swinging her around. Official news called for celebration. Flash. Him laughing at her and complaining about being sent on yet another craving run. Flash. The brothers in the compound teasing him about being henpecked. Flash. Him sitting beside her watching TV, just rubbing her belly as it moved. Flash. The look on his face when she came out of the shower, heavy laden with life he'd planted. Flash. Kissing her belly and talking to the baby. Flash. The look on his face when she put the wet, wriggling child in his arms for the first time.

She came out of his mind breathless. He sat calmly, looking off in the distance, and then wiped his face. She lowered herself to sit beside him and then took up his hand.

"All those years, you carried that all by yourself. . . . Baby, you don't ever have to do that again."

"It was so ugly, D," he admitted quietly. "I never wanted you to know."

"It's gone."

He nodded. "You always amaze me . . . I never know all that you can do." He turned and looked at her. "Thank you."

She smiled. "You're welcome."

His expression remained serious. "No. Thank you, for real . . . for loving me like you do, and for remembering those very old dreams I had of us. You took those flash shots from

when we were just kids—from when we first met . . . before I
even died or came back."

"How could I forget those?" She kissed him slowly. "Those
were coming from the pure essence of your heart, Carlos."

"It's been so long since I had pure essence in my heart
that . . . I wouldn't have known where to begin."

"Not true," she said, taking up his hand and laying it against
her belly. "Last night you found it."

She'd meant to make him smile, but his gaze remained serious as it searched her face.

"Last night, I gave you everything I could. And, now, because
of what you just gave me . . . a clear mind and a clear conscience,
which washes my soul . . . even if you aren't pregnant, I don't
have to worry about what used to keep me up at night." He
shook his head as he touched her face. "If you are, I won't worry
like I did . . . Damali, do you understand the depth of that gift?"

She couldn't frame an answer using words; the only thing she
knew to do was seal what had just happened with a kiss. The
worry was also gone for her, despite the realities they faced.
There was never a good time to conceive, per se . . . what about
living human life was convenient? People had walked by faith
and taken families through slavery, holocausts, wars, and famines,
and yet the indomitable human spirit endured. They would endure, whatever, come what may. They had to. The options were
limited, and to do otherwise was unacceptable.

They sat together quietly for a long time, holding hands, her
head leaning against his shoulder, both of them staring down at
the clean, clear pool water that had replenished itself.

"I guess we should get dressed soon," she finally said, hating
to break the stillness of their rare peace.

"A part of me wishes we didn't have to go back, but then the
other part of me knows that—if we didn't, it would be because

we were dead." Carlos let his breath out hard. "That said, I guess we oughta get washed up and put on some clothes."

"All right," she said in a dejected tone, and slowly pushed herself to the edge of the bed to stand.

"I'm sure they left our stuff for us by now," he said, not taking his eyes off her as she walked down the steps.

When he almost bumped into a love seat, she had to laugh. But she stopped walking down into the water long enough for him to open the door, grab the neatly pressed bundle of clothing that had been stacked on a silver tray outside their chamber, and come back in the room.

"You'll let me wash your back?"

She laughed quietly and shook her head. "Yeah . . . but isn't that how all this got started?"

He wiggled his eyebrows and offered her a dashing smile. "True, but I'm going to chill, I promise. We've been gone a long time, ya know."

She did know. As nice as the break had been, there was a crest point, a horizon where the joy of being away from the team pressures began to slide over into the mental realm of guilt, worry, responsibility, et al. She knew he'd simply gotten there first, and would probably be there from now on, given the new potential responsibilities he felt coming down on him.

"Turn around and let me wash your back," she said, knowing that if she kept her touch therapeutic and set the conversation to the right dial, they could get out of the water without further incident.

Again, he seemed to be reading her mind, as he didn't put up a struggle and simply handed her the soap.

"They said they had them covered through the night," Carlos said as her hands soaped his shoulders and hurriedly slid down his spine.

"Yeah. If something had kicked off, I think they would have come to get us."

Carlos chuckled as she turned him around to do his chest. "That would have been really messed up, too."

She watched him build lather in his hands to begin to wash her. "You know what, we're not even going to talk about last night until we get home." She turned around quickly so that he would only soap her shoulders and back, not her breasts.

"Good idea," he said, sliding his hands down her back, then over her backside.

"Turning around or changing the subject?" She couldn't resist the question.

"Both."

They laughed, parted, and dunked themselves.

"This reminds me of those free days during our honeymoon, you know that?" she said, wading in the water up to her neck.

"C'mon, D. Why'd you have to go there?"

She held up both hands in front of her. "My bad."

"You know, you need to stop messing with a brother," he said, coming closer to her and making her back up. "I've been under some serious stress."

"I'm not trying to stress you," she said, evading his grab and then laughing as she stumbled up and out of the water.

She ran to the huge armoire dripping wet, delighted to watch the puddles she left with each footfall simply burn away. "Is that cool, or what?"

"Very cool, especially if you're a dead man walking." Carlos pulled himself out of the water and caught the thick terry towel Damali flung at him. "Trust me when I tell you, having seen both, this side lives way better than the other half."

"I'll take your word for it," she said, snooping in the many alabaster jars and pots lining the vanity. Carefully sniffing each one, she selected a fragrant body cream. "Oh . . . man . . . smell this."

Carlos shook his head, tugged on his jeans, and definitively zipped them. He turned away quickly and began pulling on his Tims. "Uh-uh. *Please* get dressed, baby. For real."

"Oh, I'm *sorry*," she said, hurriedly slathering on lotion.

He put his hands on top of his head and walked away to the other side of the chamber to stare down at the gorgeous meadow below. Listening to the cream hit Damali's damp skin was nearly enough to make him drop fang. But he stilled his mind by remembering what she'd just done, thinking of all the hurt over the years that she'd siphoned, healed, and drawn out of his soul. He was truly blessed, especially given where he'd come from.

The more he stared at the jewel-green meadow painted with wildflowers, and the more he became aware of the cool breeze wafting off the surface of the winding, clear stream that ran through it, the more reverent he became. The peaceful lull of pristine nature was so close that it felt like he could reach down from the balcony and touch it, and a familiar refrain jumped into his consciousness.

. . . *He makes me lie down in green pastures, He leads me beside quiet waters, He restores my soul . . .*

His wife's touch wasn't jarring, but he hadn't heard her come up behind him. She wrapped her arms around his waist for a moment and then laid her head against his shoulder blade. He brought her around his body with a gentle lead, and then turned her to stare out at what he saw, encircling her.

"Look at it, D," he said in an awed rush. "If this is just Midheaven . . ."

"Can you imagine being so arrogant and so out of your mind that you'd start a war up here?" she said with a quiet gasp.

He shook his head. "Not at all."

"The angels wept," she whispered. "And so did God . . . and a third of the entire company of Heaven fell to start the legions of darkness."

"That's why we've gotta go back and do our part." He planted a kiss on the top of her head, but her palms covered his, lowering them from her waist to her abdomen.

"This is why I can tell you, through faith, it'll be all right." She turned and stared at him without blinking. "Carlos, if I am pregnant, this time our child was made in heaven. We've got two-thirds of an angel company left to protect it, not to mention both Neteru Councils—since it was made in their Pharaoh chamber." Her gaze burned as she continued to stare at him. "How many children of destiny were spared by the minute so-called happenstance of fate? If this kid comes through us, with all the love and all the struggle . . . this child has a purpose."

Her simple truth rendered him mute for a moment. "I believe you, D," he finally said, once his vocal cords would respond. "That is so profound . . . I wasn't really focused on the venue when, you know . . ."

"Look around, baby," she said, extending her arm. "We were brought into the womb of where all creation began, up here . . . when I saw the meadow and the stream, the Twenty-third Psalm jumped into my head."

"It jumped into mine, too," he said quickly.

" 'He preparest a table before me in the presence of mine enemies. He anoints my head with oil, and my cup overflows.' "

" 'Surely goodness and love will follow me all the days of my life,' " Carlos said, gathering Damali into his arms. "You heard it, too, at the same time as me?"

"Yeah. I did," she said, nodding. "It's a sign, a message."

"Okay, you've always been better at the info coming from the Light than me . . . I sorta had more skills on the other side of the coin, but you really think it's a direct message?"

"I do," she said, breaking their hug to step back and hold his hands. "I also think we should use this opportunity very wisely.

I don't know about you, but, when I've come up to Neteru Council before, I never got this high up, this deep into their chamber system . . . I don't know if this is a part of that 'My Father's house has many mansions' thing, or what. But I know they brought us in deep this time."

"Okay, like, what should we do—what do you think we need to get in order while we're here? I'm down for whatever at this point, D, you know that."

"We should go outside, stand face-to-face, put our blades in the rich earth, drawing on the nature and booster from the water, and we should call the Archangels."

"Okay, baby, listen, let's not get too crazy—we don't wanna stay, just to say thanks for having our backs and for the great evening of R and R."

"The water is the river of life, which never stops flowing . . . in fact, I think we should take off our shoes, stand in the water . . . you know, wade in the water, thrust the blades into the fertile soil, and hard-down pray for everybody we love and the world at large . . . while we're up here."

Carlos dropped her hands and rubbed the nape of his neck. "We might accidentally get the real Boss on the conference call, you know . . . and I don't know if my scenario is ready to go before Him, boo . . . seriously. It's two of us that would be out there, and you know how they say, when two or more are gathered in His name . . . D, I don't know—you've got wings, I've still got a lotta bad boy in me plus fangs. What if there was a technicality and they find out, ooops, this one wasn't supposed to make the cut?"

She chuckled, but she also knew he was dead serious. "They would have gotten you by now, if you were supposed to get hotted by sunlight."

"It's not funny, D. I have some baggage that's way different than yours."

Her smile faded. "I want to call them to pray for Father Patrick . . . and Yonnie."

"Yonnie . . . you'd actually do that up here?" He walked away from her. "Father Pat I can see without question. And Yonnie is my boy, don't get me wrong, but I don't wanna see my wife smoked by a thunderbolt for asking for something outta order."

"What can be out of order about asking for a burden to be lifted from my husband's heart?"

He stared at her. She folded her arms.

"All right," he finally said. "We do this together."

It was easy to slip over the low balcony wall and hit the soft grass. It was so pristine that they agreed before the jump to not put on shoes. Cool, sweet green carpeted their footfalls and sprouted between their toes. Oddly, the living plants seemed to coo with pleasure and sent gentle pulsing waves of joy up through their feet.

"Whoa . . ." Damali murmured, holding Carlos's hand as they walked. "You feel that?"

"Yeah," he said quietly as he looked down, and stopped. "I thought I was tripping."

The fragrance coming up from the grass and flowers was nearly intoxicating, and the pungent smell of rich earth made one want to dig one's fingers into the dark, fertile silt just to bring it closer to one's face.

"This is so different than Nod," Carlos said quietly. "There was a pretty replica, but plastic by comparison."

"That's because here is alive," Damali said, closing her eyes and breathing in as they walked the short distance to the stream. "It resonates with life, life force, creation energy, and Divine intent." She turned and looked at him. "This is what it was originally supposed to be about. How can such a place be devoid of sensation or joy or abundance?",

"You can say that again," Carlos murmured, just thinking back on the previous night. He was so filled up with peace that for a moment he even had compassion for Cain . . . no wonder that brother had lost his mind. Then he censored himself, but Damali shook her head.

"The pleasure you feel coming from the grass is peace," she said, leading him by the hand to stand under the wide canopy of a tree she couldn't name. "It is also resonating *love*. The frequency of Heaven is Divine love. Here you can forgive anyone and anything, because you can see how separation from this, from the Divine, is what twists them into ugly behavior, into tragic beings."

He touched the bark of the ageless tree and then quickly drew his hand back, unsure. "It was in a joint like this where my brother, Adam, got in trouble because his wife said that everything would be cool . . . so, uh, I'm just taking it slow because I already know what I don't know. I'm not talking about your Queen or anything . . . I'm not casting aspersions in the least, but, uhmm, you sure we're even supposed to be near this tree, boo?"

"According to the way I read it, there was a command that was not followed. I think we can explore as long as no one says we can't. But the moment we hear an off-limits, do not walk on the grass, don't touch the tree, don't wade in the water, or eat the fruit, I'm out. Cool?"

"That's exactly what I'm talking about. For a minute, D, you had me worried, because, be honest, sometimes you don't listen to authority figures—and I have the same problem."

"Up here? You crazy? I know my limits."

Carlos nodded and relaxed. "Cool . . . but if you hear something before me, you'll let a brother know?"

She laughed and stepped closer to the tree and then pressed both palms against it. "Oh . . . feel this," she murmured, then opened her arms wide and hugged it, placing her cheek against it, then lifted her tank top in the back to spread her wings.

He hesitated. "I feel kinda out of my element, hugging a tree. I know some things stay between man and wife, but . . ."

"Oh, come on, Carlos. Feel it—it's deep."

Grudgingly he came near the tree and placed both palms against it. But the sensation that rippled through his hands and then traveled up his arms to send a warm implosion into the center of his chest made him sigh.

"Whoa . . ." he murmured and stepped closer to open his arms. He laid his head against the smooth, dark wood and the entire tree felt like it shuddered.

"Didn't I tell you?"

"I feel like I could go to sleep standing up, girl."

"It's love flooding your system, infinite joy," she said in a breathy whisper.

"I never felt anything so profound in my life," he murmured. "Like everything that ever messed with me is just draining out of my body through the soles of my feet, and the grass is sending renewal back up into a closed loop . . . till I just wanna lie down."

"I know . . . the warmth is comforting, isn't it? My belly feels so good and tingly that I want to laugh and cry at the same time."

"Stay there as long as you want to, D . . . maybe all that is good for the baby, you know?"

"You finally said it," she whispered, her voice cracking.

He lifted his head when he heard her voice break. "Said what, *corazon?*"

"Said *the baby,* not *it.*" She swallowed hard and drew a shaky breath. "Words have power, especially this close to the Source."

"Then I'm ready to step into the water with you and put up a prayer," Carlos said quietly. "If words have power, up here, and intent is everything since they can see your heart . . . and there's battalions of angels keeping everything cool . . . yeah—I want a word sent."

He slid around the tree and clutched Damali's hand. They both peeled themselves away from it with effort, and the tree groaned in discontent.

"You hear that?" she said in a delighted squeak. Then she went back to the tree and stroked its trunk and kissed it. "Bye, tree . . . bless you . . . thank you for sharing the love with me and my family." She turned to Carlos with a wide smile. "Say good-bye."

For a moment, he just looked at her.

"Everything living has the life force of God in it. Everything alive is divine . . . you must honor it all, especially while up here."

"How do you know all this stuff?" he said, walking back to the tree to pet its trunk. "Bye, tree . . . thanks for being so cool and sharing the love." He gave the tree the kind of hug he would have given one of his brother Guardians, which tickled Damali no end.

"I guess the tree knows what you mean," she said, laughing and then stepping down into the water.

He watched her eyes cross as she hugged her body and her eyelids went to half-mast. Sunlight dappled her wings through the thick canopy, and he wished he were an artist and could draw what he was witnessing.

Golden sunlight hit her dark locks, sent prisms against her sun-fired skin, and rained speckles of fluttering sunbeams across her white wings. Pollen spores bowed and curtsied before her like tiny pink fairies, nature's ladies-in-waiting. There was a collision of color all around her, his possibly pregnant angel in jeans rolled up to her knees. The sight stole his breath, shook his reason, but made him walk forward.

The moment his feet hit the quiet water, he hugged himself and closed his eyes.

"Oh, God, Damali, what's happening?" he whispered.

"All of life, the abundance of it, and the infinite possibilities in it, is at your feet."

"You feel that?" he croaked through a gasp. "That current?"

"Yeah . . . the All One connection." She flapped her wings to stay upright as Carlos came closer and hugged her.

"The love is . . ." He opened his eyes and stared at her.

"I know—there are no words . . . and your eyes are silver."

He kissed her so hard he almost chipped a tooth, and then pulled away. "I'm sorry. Don't know where that came from."

"I do," she said and then returned his kiss just as hard. "It's part of the abundance, part of the gifts of nature, of living, of procreation, of marriage . . . that, too, is part of the Divine."

He was about to say damn, but censored himself. She nodded. Her eyes said not out here, not in this holy water. Her eyes didn't have to tell him twice.

"This river has a lot of current in it, D . . . you still wanna do the sword thing?"

Damali materialized her Isis long blade in her grip. He opened his palm and the blade of Ausar filled it. Reading each other's eyes, they rammed their swords into the lush silt between them at the same time. She led the dance, placing her right hand over his heart and her left hand on the handle of her blade. He matched her positioning and stood waiting for instructions.

He watched his wife go old-school, into hard-down prayer, and then closed his eyes. She opened with a litany of thanks, calling out everything in the world that they were thankful for, down to the last breath she just took to speak. His part was minor, he felt, by comparison, in that he was merely support and backup with nods of agreement and well-timed *amens*.

But he also felt every word she'd said in his spirit; there was agreement in the name of the Most High for every word she uttered, and then she got specific—started calling for people's healing by name, going down the team list, going down the friend list, going through folks they didn't know, speaking on world crises, families beset upon by tragedy and evil. She spoke on people who knew loss and pain and heartbreak and financial woe, asked that they be lifted up, even before her own family.

His *Amen* here or there started getting rowdy, got down right off da chain. He heard himself going from *Amen* to *That's right, tell it, boo!* He could hear what she was calling out in his bones. Could feel the empathy draining out into the water and coming back to fill them up. He could feel for that person who could be accidentally caught in harm's way, knew the terror of the innocent victim caught in the cross fire of good and evil. Knew what it was to be the vanguard for a family only to watch it be decimated one by one. Felt for the soldiers in every country and their wailing families.

Oh, yes, his wife could take it to the wall, could send it through his marrow, could make the angels sing. The words Damali was delivering had her sweating, tears running, wings beating a cadence till she was foot-stomping and jumping up and down, splashing water everywhere.

It was everything he could do to keep his hand against her heart. When she spoke on him, though, he was so full that there was only one word, *Yes.*

Each impassioned stanza ended in, *my husband.* If he never knew what he'd meant to her before, he definitely knew it now. Her voice was brittle, husky, and worn-out. Her body shook, sweat making her tank top cling. She called him by name, Carlos Rivera, and told anyone in Heaven who would listen all that the Devil had done. Asked not for her own sake, but for the sake of her husband, that Satan be sent from their door.

Then she got to calling Archangels out by regiment and specialty—asked God to send Raphael for healing for Father Patrick and asked that Michael bring his blade to take heads and take names. She wanted some good news from Gabriel and begged him for a word. Asked for mercy sublime for all her shortcomings and her husband's, too . . . and asked for the wisdom to know the difference between the things she could change and the things she couldn't.

Of all the spoken word he'd ever heard Damali do, he was sure this was the most profound. She might have played Madison Square Garden, but *this* was the invisible audience that could change their destinies.

He could feel her winding down. They were both breathing hard, sweating, tears streaking their faces. The waters were crackling with blue-white charge and it raced over their sweat-damped skins in intermittent waves. But before she closed out, he had something to say. He hadn't really had a lot of practice; most of his conversations like this were always in his head—not out loud. Something moved him beyond thought, just jumped up in him and had him. He pulled his wife close and buried his face against her neck.

"I have no right to ask for anything, given all You gave me—but I just want her and the baby to be safe. I'd give my life for this woman right here, this gift. I'm ready to change my life, give it to You in full service. Your will this time and forever, not mine. Amen."

The moment Carlos closed the prayer, heat swept through both blades so quickly that it forced him and Damali to part. A blue-white beam shot up, exploded in the sky like a nova disc, and then sucked back down through the blades, shaking the earth beneath their feet before they could even draw a breath.

Massive ground tremors toppled them, sprawling them in the shallow water. They came up coughing and sputtering, and stared at each other. Their blades were glowing and vibrating in resonating tones. The cloudless sky flashed pastel hues and then suddenly large cumulous clouds gathered and then exploded in a sparkling confetti-like rain.

Damali and Carlos stared up, gaping, and then slowly looked at each other.

"I think they heard us," he said quietly.

"Yeah," she whispered. "I'm pretty sure they did."

CHAPTER SIXTEEN

Adam and Eve ran into the meadow, barefoot, with Aset and Ausar right on their heels. Two young men were with them that neither Carlos nor Damali had seen before. Too disoriented to get up without assistance, the young couple allowed themselves to be pulled to their feet. Elder Neterus splashed into the water, creating a commotion, as Damali and Carlos just stared at them.

"Are you hurt, children?" Eve said, her hands touching their faces and then scanning them with panic in her eyes.

Aset was right beside her. "Please tell me you are all right?"

"No," Damali said. "We just got the wind knocked out of us."

"Are you unharmed, brother?" Adam asked, patting down Carlos's body like he was about to frisk him for weapons.

"Yeah, I'm cool—just like D said, just got blown away. I'm good."

Ausar let out a hard breath of relief, but from the command in his voice and the speed at which he delivered choppy sentences, Carlos could tell the man was shook.

"Good. Excellent. Battle stations are scrambling as we speak. We got the Word, lest you dash your foot against a stone, we are to hold you up." Ausar paced back and forth in the stream.

Carlos rubbed his palms down his face. "Tell me we didn't bust a seal, man."

"No," Ausar said, "but Heaven is going to war on your behalf."

"Whoa, whoa, whoa," Damali said, holding out her hands. "We asked for—"

"Protection," Aset said, cutting Damali off.

"After all they've done to you and the prayer you lobbed, child . . ." Eve shook her head. "I'm suiting up in armor, myself."

"But—"

"The Law of Attraction," Ausar said to Carlos, not letting him finish. "You know what you focus on, you get?"

"Okay, okay, school us fast," Carlos said, glancing nervously at Damali. "We don't want any accidents, like setting off a nuke up here."

"If you have poison down in the deep recesses of your mind— toxic thoughts—and you keep thinking of those, focusing on those, that is what you'll attract to you," Adam said flatly. "This is why one of the first things the darkside tries to do is co-opt your mind and make you turn your focus toward it and away from the Light. But if you think of good things, seeing people healed, seeing yourself in abundance, seeing yourself victorious, seeing your family safe and well—that is what you attract. This is why you have to focus on the Divine." He shrugged. "It is simple."

"It takes practice, man," Carlos countered, raking his wet hair back with his fingers. "If you grew up like me, you had toxic thoughts implanted in your head from the time you were a baby—parents screaming and yelling, nonsense going on in the neighborhood . . . all sorts of sh—stuff." He looked over at Damali. "If it wasn't for my lady, I'd still have some really bad toxin all up in my head. Regardless, I'm not understanding how battle stations got called?"

"You asked for protection at the Highest level." Ausar folded his arms over his chest. "Your wife wanted everyone on your team safe, people healed, the planet uplifted, anyone being attacked by demonic forces helped . . . believe me, that will take millions of angels working day and night. She called in the warrior squadrons. Her focus was justice and defeating the enemy by asking for love and good things to come to all people. She focused on the Light of victory, not on the Darkness. She called for this with all her heart and soul, in agreement with you, while standing in the river of life, under the tree of life, in the meadow which surpasses all understanding . . . need I go on? We got the Word, and the call was clear. Infantries are deploying as we speak. It may not be visible to the average human, but you were heard."

Carlos let out a long whistle. He and Damali shared a glance.

"Permit me to introduce you to my sons," Adam said proudly. "Seth and Abel, your personal bodyguards and energy doubles. We will explain before you return."

Damali lifted her locks up off her neck and glanced at Carlos. "Wow . . ."

"One last request while we're up here," Carlos said, needing a moment to take it all in. "On the way home, can D and I just stop in to see Father Pat?"

Ausar walked over to Carlos, landing a firm, broad hand on his shoulder with a wide smile. The two men stared at each other for a moment, and after a few seconds Carlos felt the elder Neteru's request to open a private channel.

So, how's it feel?

Carlos frowned, not sure what Ausar meant. *How's what feel?*

Ausar pulled him into a hard embrace that almost knocked the wind out of Carlos. He held him back as Eve put her arm over Damali's shoulders and walked off a bit with her, talking to Aset. Adam came in closer with his sons, beaming.

Some things they're supposed to find out the old-fashioned way, Adam said, looking at Ausar, then laughed.

Confusion made Carlos's line of vision scan from one face to another. *Going to war ain't no joke in a regular human body, man . . . you brothers need to get out more—because this ain't no laughing—*

The Pharaoh's chamber, man? King's Ransom?

Carlos stared at Ausar and blinked twice. With everything that had just happened, last night had been shoved to the furthest region of his mind. "Oh . . . yeah," he said, caught so off guard that he answered verbally. Then, slow shock registered. Surely his elder brothers weren't asking about details regarding his wife—that was so out of order and up here?

"We would never, that's not what we were asking," Adam said, clearly taken aback.

Ausar looked five ways, drawing the huddle of men closer. "I was asking how it felt to know you've sired?" He released a long, pleased breath as Carlos simply stared at him, shell-shocked. "I remember my New Pharaoh's chamber . . . I couldn't go back to my life, as sadly I had lost it on the treachery of the battlefield. But my Aset carried Heru away from that glorious night. There is no other joy quite so profound."

Adam cuffed his sons' shoulders. "Abel, Seth—this is my legacy. Find good, strong names that can resonate through history. Fruit of your loins will have a role, we are certain."

"I'ma, I'ma . . . you know for sure?" Carlos's voice came out in a rasp.

"Ausar, hold that man up before he passes out," Adam said, laughing. "Why do you think we called for war?"

"But, I'ma, I'ma . . . really, I'ma . . ."

"Didn't you feel it?" Ausar said, slapping Carlos's back hard. "If you don't know, then I most certainly cannot speculate. But we gave you all of the tools . . . Ransom, the pulse *of life* through the bed."

"Redirected from the living waters over there," Adam said, pointing. He looked at Ausar. "The living waters always work, yes, brother?"

Ausar and Adam extended their arms, opened their palms, and slapped the backs of their hands together in a loud crack that drew sparks.

"Yes!" Ausar said in a booming laugh.

"Every time!" Adam said, walking away, laughing hard.

"All I know," Seth said with a sly smile, "is that it was thundering and lightning so badly in chambers that my mother was walking the floors sending up intercessions."

"We do not know you well enough to tease you, young brother," Abel said, swallowing his laughter, "but our dear mother kept flipping a Kemetic coin saying, 'Heads, it's a boy, tails, it's a girl.' "

Adam playfully punched Abel in the arm. "Oh, she did not. Do not harass this man's sanity so badly."

Carlos hadn't heard half of what they were saying. His hand was over his chest as he slowly paced, dazed. "I'ma, I'ma . . . this time, I'ma . . ."

Ausar and Adam slung heavy biceps over Carlos's shoulders to get him to stop pacing.

"Yes, man," Adam said with a dazzling, white grin. "You're going to be a father."

Ausar folded his arms over his barrel chest. "Excellent. Now that that's settled, let's go to war."

Eve kissed Damali's cheek and Aset touched her lower belly. The women simply looked at one another, no words necessary. They knew.

"Now do you see why there is a bit of a commotion up here?" Eve said, her voice like calm, clear waters.

"Surely you didn't think the child of two Neterus in the

millennium, during the end of days, would be sent into the clutches of the darkside?"

A soft kiss met Damali's cheeks from both sides in unison.

"Daughter," Eve whispered in her ear, "the first one's body was corrupted, we had our reasons. This is different. But we saved its tiny soul. It will have a second chance to come back to you."

Damali's palm flattened against her heart. "This is still our first?"

"We cannot disclose the prophecy in total, which is why you never got wind of it before," Aset said in a gentle breeze against her ear. "Some things must unfold in fate and choice and we are not at liberty . . . but you need not worry. This child is shielded." She looked around and nodded to the question that Damali had asked and then clasped her hands together in excitement. "The living waters work every time, daughter. Wait till Nefertiti finds out! Nzinga will dance a jig!"

"Wait until your first trimester passes to inform your team, however," Eve said softly. "There are wounds on your team that must heal, and this could cause some of your sisters pain, even though there will be the mixed emotion of joy . . . but you can tell Marlene the faithful. Just not the younger ones."

"Oh . . . no . . . Heather," Damali said, looking from Queen to Queen.

They nodded.

"But we are not finished with her yet," Eve said with a wink.

"Or some others," Aset murmured with a sly grin. "Timing is everything."

Then both Queens hugged her tightly, kissing her, and then said three words in unison: "No foolish risks!"

"Why are you in my war room?"

Lilith stared at her husband for a moment, completely

unprepared for his outburst. "You sent for me, said we were to go to the Middle East together and—"

"Do not dispute me!" he thundered, whirling on her as he smashed a section of the globe. "Tornados, hurricanes, there!" he yelled, pointing at regions of the suspended sphere and sending a black jolt into it. "Why would I take you to the Middle East with me?"

"To help ensure the safety of our precious cargo, Dark Lord."

"There is a war going on over there, you stupid bitch—or don't you watch the news! Why would I leave my son to incubate in a war zone? My mention of that region was to draw the Light's forces into chaos and destruction and to increase the human collateral damage on all sides. That's the potential epicenter for the world's big three religions to collide! You make me insane, sometimes!"

Lilith dropped to one knee and lowered her head as he passed. "Tell me your bidding, Your Eminence, and it is done."

He leaned back and roared with frustration, his angry form blistering through his human one to sprout the more terrifying version of himself. When she heard the clatter of his cloven hooves and smelled sulfur, she knew something had gone horribly wrong.

"What's happened?" she whispered. "Send me on your errand and I shall vanquish any inconvenience that has befallen you."

"The priest's brain is not imploding as it should have," he said between his teeth, causing her to look up. "Somehow, they got a prayer all the way up to *Raphael* for this man, and he's *healing!*" He began to pace. "I so loathed Raphael when we used to work together—simpering, sycophant, healing son of a—"

"Lu, Lu," she said quickly with outstretched hands. "We don't want them to send redress before we're prepared . . . to call an Archangel's mother out of her name, given they came from—you-know-who . . . uh . . . darling . . . let us be wise and strategic. The priest is not that important, given your overall objectives."

He rubbed his palms down his face snorting fire, spaded tail lashing the air as he paced. "The Neterus have gone off my dark radar. The priest is healing. A white-light charge hit the atmosphere and singed it. I don't like it, because I don't know what's going on."

"We have a councilman who is close to penetration of their hideouts," she said quickly. "I will send Yolando in, with our new councilwoman, Lucrezia, right behind him to poison the lot of them. The others can apply pressure, as planned, while you move the heir."

"Make this so," he snarled, flames curling at the edges of his nostrils. "We are too close to the end of times to have this bullshit going on. This is not the Genesis era in the least."

Carlos stood on one side of Father Patrick's bed, with Damali on the other holding his hand. Rabbi Zeitloff, Monk Lin, and Imam Asula were at the foot of it. Machines hissed and thudded, bringing liquids and oxygen into his frail body, sounding like straining sump pumps.

"How's he doing?" Carlos asked quietly, brushing back Father Patrick's white hair from his brow.

"He's resting easier," the rabbi said. "Much easier than before. He'd been feverish and beginning to hallucinate, and then this morning, it was as though a storm had passed."

"Patmos," Father Patrick croaked and squeezed Damali's hand.

Carlos leaned in close. "Steady, steady, it's all good," he murmured.

The elderly man's eyes fluttered and he was becoming visibly agitated. "Patmos," he groaned again.

"He's asking for somebody," Carlos said, looking at the clerics for help. "Who is Patmos?"

"Where is Patmos, is the question," Rabbi Zeitloff said.

"Greece," Imam Asula confirmed. "Where John penned Revelations during his exile. The Cave of the Apocalypse."

"The beast was in his mind," Monk Lin said calmly, coming to the side of the bed. "If it fled, it could have left important residue for this seer. Let us employ the standards of *The Art of War.*"

"No, man," Carlos said. "One beloved cleric down is enough."

Monk Lin stared at Carlos. "No . . . son. We are old men; you have something to look forward to." His gaze went to Damali, and the other clerics nodded. "Have your wife stand back from this bed, you shield her body and stand back, as well." He glanced at the imam who unsheathed his machete. "We will reach our friend. He is in there."

Rabbi Zeitloff picked up a small dagger from a side tray that was ornately etched with gold and silver Hebrew words along the blood gutters. "From the House of David," he said, and stood at the ready.

Monk Lin gently cradled Father Patrick's skull and then closed his eyes. His smooth, unlined face became flaccid and increasingly serene as his breaths deepened. Soon the two men were breathing in the same rhythm, Father Pat's withered chest rising and falling in the same steady motions as the elderly monk's. Then Monk Lin's face unexpectedly contorted, and Carlos threw up a shield blocking him and Damali.

"*. . . The great prostitute sits on many waters . . . with her, the kings of the earth committed adultery and the inhabitants of the earth were intoxicated with the wine of her adulteries . . . I saw a woman riding the Beast's back that was covered with blasphemous names . . . she was dressed in scarlet and was glittering with gold and jewels . . .*

she held a golden cup in her hand, filled with abominable things and the filth of her adulteries!"

"Lilith," Damali said through her teeth and her hands became fists.

Carlos nodded and put a hand on Damali's back. "Tricking to the very end."

Monk Lin's voice became strained. Veins stood out on his temples as his body shook. His face turned red as he stuttered out the words, drooling and panting. Suddenly Father Patrick sat up and screamed with unseeing eyes.

"Mystery. Babylon the great. Mother of prostitutes. Abominations of the earth." Father Patrick fell back, beginning to pull the tubes out of his arms as the other clerics tried to restrain him.

A black fog began to rise from the priest's chest, and Rabbi Zeitloff stabbed it. The force flung him back, but the imam caught him and hacked at it with his machete. The blade of Ausar was in Carlos's hand as fast as the Isis hit Damali's palm. Three blades sliced at the rising demon mist, severing it from its hold on Father Patrick's chest. Carlos quickly opened a small, black, translucent box lined with silver and captured the three angry serpent heads that were forming. Damali delivered the death blow to the headless body that continued to rise out of Father Patrick's chest.

"I'm keeping these heads," Carlos said, as he carefully set the box down on the floor. The creatures inside it snapped and hissed, and Damali gave him a quizzical look. "They'll home to their source, and if we're hunting the Unnamed One's heir, they might home to him. They black-tagged me, and I learned from the best of them how to do it. I'll just silver-tag these demon heads, so when they try to reincorporate with the host or similar energy, we can track 'em."

"Yeah, sounds logical, but—uh—what are you gonna do with them until then, you know?" Damali peered around the edge of the shield at the snarling box on the floor. "That's not exactly something you can bring home and put in the family room to use for later."

"I saw the woman," Monk Lin croaked in the unnatural voice of the near-possessed. *"She was drunk with the blood of the saints . . . the beast will come up out of the Abyss and go to his destruction. Watch the seven hills—the seven heads, they are seven kings . . . five have fallen, the other has not yet come, but when he does come, he must remain for a little while. The beast . . . who once was, and now is not, is an eighth king. He belongs to the seven and is going to his destruction."*

Monk Lin slumped on the bed, and Imam Asula and Rabbi Zeitloff rushed to his aid. Carlos and Damali helped the gasping Father Patrick, who waved them back.

"We wiped out the first five councilmen," Father Patrick wheezed. "Then they reinstalled a full council again—that's six, plus the beast, makes seven. The eighth is the one Lilith orchestrated by riding the beast's back . . . and the eighth one of them belongs to the seventh. If the seventh is the Darkness, the ultimate eclipse on Level Seven, then the thing that comes from him, the eighth, can only be his heir."

Carlos caught the old man around his back as Monk Lin slowly came to. "Easy, easy, just lie back."

"No," Father Patrick wheezed again. "I don't have time, son. The Light is purging all of it away, but I must tell you now—I saw the beast, and locked in on his ultimate plan so I could tell you."

"Oh, dear, God," Damali gasped. "He mind-locked with Satan?"

"Keep her back!" Father Patrick said in a strangled rush. "Shield her."

"Talk to me, Father," Carlos said, putting up a shield in front of Damali again, even though she peered around it.

"The seven hills refer to old Rome," Father Patrick gasped. "The focus is on the Middle East, but the seven hills are where the old dark empire got its stronghold. Religious and economic sway will come from there, but right now, what you seek is hidden in Patmos—where John the Theologian was exiled. Go to the Monastery of St. John . . . there is a library there. The Greek Orthodox monks will help you and it is built like a citadel. But know that the beast is toying with us. The Greek islands, the Dodecanese, are made up of twelve larger islands, plus one hundred and fifty smaller ones—which equals the number six. Twelve and six is the beast's number, eighteen, which divided evenly, becomes . . . six-six-six. His heir will be able to island hop in the Mediterranean where there is peace, tiny communities with little technology, gorgeous landscape, balmy climate, and lightly populated villages where he can *eat*."

The elderly priest's hand fluttered against Carlos's cheek. "I am losing what I knew, Carlos," he cried out, arching with tears streaming. "I must remember, I have to remember!"

"It's all right, it's all right. Rest. We'll work with what we've got." Carlos looked over to Monk Lin and the other clerics. "How is he?"

Monk Lin waved his hand. "I am fine. We will all be fine, now. Next, we prepare for war."

"Glad you're back and looking healthy. I've been working on this all night, guys," J.L. said, walking with Carlos and Damali as everyone gathered in the living room. "Our tactical team members can use this while we're out in the field. It's based on the same principles that the Sandi National Laboratory in New Mexico has under wraps. It's a generator where the initial burst of electricity creates a magnetic field that compresses charged particles. That compression and quick release is like an e-bomb, yo. It'll send out an electromagnetic pulse that will stun an invisible entity. The Sandi Lab's version is much weaker and real huge. But with our tactical guys essentially being walking batteries, theirs can pack a sweet punch."

"In English, J.L.," Marlene said, talking with her hands.

Damali and Carlos looked at each other.

"There's four of us. Me, Dan, 'Bazz, and Carlos have the zap juice, right. The handheld generators would compress charged particles—our noses always smell it before the entity appears, so we aim and hit 'em with a quick compressor jolt. Then a hard release zap, and whatever the handheld is aimed at will interrupt the entity's electromagnetic field—it's aura, essentially, knocking that mutha out."

J.L. looked around as though confused why everybody wasn't standing and cheering. "I also got a serious imaging schematic from G in New York. He borrowed some of the process from the magnetic resonance imaging technology, MRI machines, you know . . . hydrogen atoms are highly magnetic, and entities move around, going from solid to vapor because of the volatile nature of hydrogen—and we can draw images from that, bit map it, and get an outline."

Carlos gave J.L. a fist pound. "You make it do what it do, man. We trust you on the details."

"I got you on this," J.L. said, his tone pleased as he sat down hard on the sofa and folded his arms over his chest.

"Everybody's good?" Damali asked, looking around the group.

"We had a good, restful night after the little home invasion drama died down. And a good morning. As things generally go around here, can't complain. Nobody's injured or dead, so that's a blessing," Marlene said, her gaze raking the team. "Val and Delores had the day one speech. Ayana had cereal—"

"Yup. Mr. Jack made it for me."

All eyes went to the three-year-old. Carlos and Damali

shared a look. The room became eerily silent. The only sound that could be heard was Guardians nervously fidgeting.

How are we gonna talk about killing shit with a three-year-old in the war room? Carlos looked at the child and smiled a tense smile, but then began to pace.

Damali fought not to shrug, in answer to his mental question. *I know . . . and we're gonna have to figure out how this is gonna work, long term, for us, too. You know?*

"Rider was up early enough to make Yaya cereal?" Damali shook her head and tried to make light of things before the little girl became uncomfortable. "Oh, yeah, this is the end of days."

"To which Mike owes me," Rider said offhandedly with a smile, but he gave Damali a look.

"Forever indebted," Mike said with a sly chuckle, talking over Delores's head in subtle doublespeak.

Carlos and Damali looked at each other again and then focused on Val.

"How're you doing, sis?" Carlos said, walking forward.

Val stood, dropped to one knee, and crossed her chest with her forearm.

"No, no, no, I told you, we're family." Carlos helped her up and Damali came to her side.

Damali hugged Val. "No more of that, all right? Especially not in public. People can't know who we are while we're on the road."

"I just stepped to you because I'm concerned," Carlos said, tilting Val's chin from side to side. His eyes blazed silver for a moment as he studied her neck. "You look tired."

"I am ready for war," Val said, lifting her chin.

"She's not nicked, just up all night holding vigil," Tara offered. She glanced at Val, whose expression bloomed with silent thanks. "A private word in the kitchen, after the general update?" Tara's expression was unreadable.

"Yeah," Damali said. "No problem."

Again, she and Carlos shared a look.

"Glad to see you hearty and hail, man," Shabazz said. "I ain't gonna lie, the way you went out of here on an angelic stretcher, didn't look good."

"Right," Berkfield said, and then all pandemonium broke lose.

The team rushed Carlos, passed around hugs, and it took a full ten minutes to restore order.

"Now, we can have a meeting," Marlene said. "First things first."

"Ya mean?" Jose said, rubbing the back of his neck. He looked at Carlos. "We woulda all been f— . . . messed up if you hadn't come back."

Marlene smiled and looked at Delores and then Ayana. "Do you know how *long* I've been telling these folks on this team about cussin'? And it took a baby in the house and her nana to *finally* clean up their mouths. Heaven couldn't do it. Have mercy!"

"Yeah . . . well . . . after where we've been in the last twenty-four hours," Carlos said, "a whole lotta things are gonna change."

Damali shot him a look.

"But I'ma let D explain the mission."

"First off, after Carlos healed, we went to go check on Father Pat." Damali glanced at Marlene and a silent understanding passed between them.

"How is he?" Rider asked. "I love that old man, swear I do."

"Yeah, we all do," Berkfield said, nodding toward his son, Bobby, and then toward Jose.

"Tell me they got whatever attacked him," Marjorie said.

Krissy reached up and threaded her fingers between her mother's.

"We can keep vigil," Jasmine offered. "Me, Heather, Krissy, 'Nita, and Tara, while Marlene trains the new team members."

The women passed supportive glances between one another, but Damali shook her head and sat on the edge of an over-stuffed chair.

"It's deeply appreciated but won't be necessary." Damali took her time describing what happened at the safe house in Brooklyn. "And, by the way, there's this real strange black box from it out in the driveway . . . uh, my suggestion is nobody go near it until Carlos figures out what to do with it."

The room went silent again, the only person saying anything was Ayana, who was humming a merry tune.

Finally Dan spoke up, breaking yet another strained silence. "Are Zeitloff, Asula, Imam, and Monk Lin all right?" Dan's eyes searched Damali and Carlos's faces.

"Rabbi believed in me," Heather said, twisting the edge of her shirt. "If anything hurt that old man . . . any of them . . ."

"They're all right and some bold old men. Gotta love 'em," Carlos said. "But we've gotta take the heat on the road."

Damali looked at Inez and then Mom Delores. "We have to go to Greece. Patmos, to be exact. And we've gotta go fast, with heavy artillery to meet the Greek team over there in a surprise attack of the Antichrist, while it's in chrysalis form. This means no airports this time, pure fold-away. Together, Carlos and I are strong enough to do the full team transport that far."

"Before the one-flesh rule kicked in, I mighta dropped us in the ocean, if I ran out of juice trying to go that far with so much weight, plus artillery . . . but with D able to work it with me, we're good ta go." Carlos folded his arms over his chest and ignored the horrified look Mom Delores shot him.

"The clerics have a word going to the monks over there to receive us," Damali said, not missing a beat. "I think Val can hang . . . but I would honestly feel better if Carlos dropped Mom Delores and Yaya to the safe house in Brooklyn, where seasoned spiritual warriors are, than to have them only day two on the team and in a firefight with the ultimate darkside. Your call, though."

"You're going where to do what?" Delores whispered.

"Take her to the safe house," Inez said, closing her eyes.

"Don't I have a choice?" Delores argued.

Carlos walked away to lean on the wall. "You want the politically correct answer or the truth?"

PART IV

TAKE NO PRISONERS

CHAPTER SEVENTEEN

Man . . . did you ever think me and you would be standing up here in the hills, looking down on your house in the daylight?" Yonnie laughed and came up to Carlos to give him a brother-to-brother chest bump hug. "Not exactly how I envisioned the thing, but this works for me."

"Yeah, man," Carlos said with a sad smile. "This works for me, too."

"Oh, so you trust a brother now, huh?" Yonnie opened his arms and laughed.

"Why? Shouldn't I?" Carlos smiled and shook his head.

Yonnie stepped back and appraised Carlos while rubbing his jaw. "You one crazy motherfucker, you know that? Got yourself busted up pretty good in Harlem. Wasn't sure you was coming back from that."

"Shit . . . me either," Carlos said, chuckling from the memory. "But I wanna thank you for the heads-up on a lotta details that coulda got me and my lady smoked, feel me."

Yonnie's smile faded. "We ain't gonna discuss that. You woulda did it for me, so I did it for you. But even thinking about getting caught in that particular lie gives me the shivers." He pounded Carlos's fist and turned his gaze toward the house.

What was there to say? Even though they were standing out-side in broad daylight, his boy still worked for the Darkness, and messing with Lucifer in a double-cross was probably the stupid-est thing anyone could attempt—dead or alive.

"Appreciate the property sanctuary, too. It's nice to have a fallback position, if a brother gets ass-out." Yonnie hadn't turned when he'd spoken; his gaze was on the house.

"I can't drop the house barrier, man," Carlos said. "Not with the hybrid in there and my Guardian brother still having issues."

Yonnie nodded; his back remained straight and his voice was nonplussed. "Yeah, family politics. I can dig it . . . but she's fine, though. Who woulda thought that *both* of us dawgs woulda wound up with some serious good girls?" He turned to Carlos with a big grin and shrugged. "Now that's some crazy cosmic shit."

"That *is* some crazy cosmic shit, man." Carlos had to laugh. But as Yonnie crested a little fang to begin staring at the house again, his mood sobered. "So, did you tell her yet?"

"Tell her what, man?"

"C'mon, Yonnie. Sooner or later you're gonna have to tell Val about your condition—ask me how I know."

"Yeah, yeah, I hear you. I was just waiting to let things get a little more solid between us, then I'd drape it on her."

"More like put it on her," Carlos scoffed and then rounded Yonnie.

Yonnie gave him a sly smile and materialized a toothpick in his mouth.

"I remember not so long ago when you were telling me to be real. So, this morning, before me and the family bounce, I'm going to return the favor."

Yonnie shrugged and studied his new manicure. "Fair ex-change is no robbery."

"All right then, here's the thing . . . she doesn't have Neteru antibodies and girlfriend is wide-open for you—you know it. I don't even know if she's ever been with anybody, except on an intellectual basis, seeing as how she came over from Nod, and they didn't roll like that."

Unable to resist, Yonnie turned to glimpse the house. "She's hot as hell, man . . ."

"Yeah, that's my point. So, if this Viking-angel female warrior drops shields for you, and climbs up your torso, if you bite her and turn her, you and I will cease to be boyz. You know that, right?"

"Okay, Daddy Rivera."

Carlos hesitated. "I'm serious, Yolando."

Yonnie held his hands up in front of him. "Yo . . . we cool. But I'm Yolando now? All right, I respect her as family. I won't bite her, but that's about all I can promise."

"She ain't a quick lay, either," Carlos said, folding his arms over his chest, eyes beginning to burn silver.

"Hey, hey, watch the angry-eye, *holmes*. You need to chill, relax a little. I know she ain't no coven ho'," Yonnie said, backing up. "You look like you're under a lot of stress, but I ain't the one stressing you, man."

Carlos rubbed the back of his neck and walked away, trying to make his fangs retract and his eyes stop burning silver. "You ain't the only one that has to answer to a management team that doesn't play. My side will hot me in a minute, if they think I knowingly allowed an angel hybrid, with a human soul, to get turned right out of Nod by the darkside."

"I feel you, man," Yonnie said carefully. "Awful ironic how we also both wound up in the same situation—you dancing on the edge, me dancing on the edge, the rules real fuzzy, about to be smoked at any time. Just a case of which side gets us first."

"Don't bite her, man," Carlos said, letting out a weary breath.

"I'm not going to bite her. Damn."

Carlos closed his eyes and inhaled slowly before speaking. "*That* is a lie." He opened his eyes and they were pure silver, but no beam hunted Yonnie. "You are talking to me, remember? You want to bite her so bad that just thinking about it makes your dick hard. Now I'm only going to say this once, she has no immunity. Her system is like a human's—red blood carrier, no silver tracer to back the vamp plague up." Carlos dropped his voice as he came closer to Yonnie. "I'm her big brother and therefore her silver carrier. If you get any vampire bullshit into her system, I will silver hot yours."

"Damn, man, and I thought we was boyz!" Yonnie walked away and began pacing. "What am I gonna do, Carlos?" His voice became strident and all amusement was gone from his tone. "She's . . . like . . . different than all the others. First off, she's about *me*. You hear me, man? Just about me. For once, I'm not coming behind some old baggage from her previous life. You know what that feels like, brother."

Carlos did understand, but his face remained impassive as Yonnie paced.

"None of them, especially Tara, cared about me to this bone-deep level. I haven't even touched Val yet . . . and she's got this pure love-jones that's—"

"Intoxicating," Carlos said flatly, remembering Damali.

"Yeah . . ." Yonnie closed his eyes and allowed a brief shudder to claim him. "You know what I'm saying."

"That's why," Carlos said, his voice calmer, "I know that if you get with her, you'll bite her. Problem is, she won't wake up in the morning . . . worst yet, if you can't pass the daylight bite, you'll have her banished to the Darkness. Man, as much as she turns you on, I can't sanction it. I just can't."

"Can't you do something?" Yonnie said, arms outstretched. "Like, give her some kinda silver seal, something, I don't know?"

"I know I can do a lot of shit, man," Carlos said with a half-smile. "But I do not know how to make a silver dental dam, if that's what you're asking."

"Kiss my ass," Yonnie said, walking away peeved. He spit out his toothpick and dragged his fingers through his Afro. "I really care about her, man."

"You just met her."

"Don't discount my shit like that, Rivera. Don't."

"All right, my bad," Carlos said, holding up his hands. "I just want you to think about this and to care about her enough not to throw caution to the wind. She's really good people, Yonnie. Really good, ya know?"

"Yeah, I do," Yonnie said quietly, now staring at the house with his hands behind his back. "You know what she said to me when I was on my way to council?" He didn't wait for Carlos to respond, but pressed on as though speaking to himself. "She said, 'Be valiant, be victorious.'" He shook his head and chuckled sadly. "Funny thing is, she really makes me want to be that."

"That ain't funny," Carlos said, causing his friend to look at him. "That's real. Now you're being real. So, as boyz who go way back, let me be honest and tell you the truth about me and Damali." Carlos let out a long breath. "I had to wait for her for five years."

Yonnie winced.

"Yeah," Carlos said. "If you're dealing with a sister with wings, and you're bad to the bone, you've got one of three choices—wait for her, and do what you've gotta do on an extremely discreet basis; ruin her, which you and I both know is unacceptable and a punk move at best; or walk."

"Guess I'll be headed to Tijuana this morning."

Carlos chuckled. "Sheeit, that's where I used to go."

Yonnie pounded his fist. "It was worth it though, right? The wait."

"She turned twenty-one on me at midnight in Hell, man, in a demon firefight with Fallon Nuit, and I wasn't even a councilman." Carlos looked back at the house, the memory full in his mind. "She was trailing Neteru ripening—blazing it, but all those people in that house were about to get slaughtered. And she looked up at me, a vampire then, man . . . with those big brown eyes, blade in her hand, and begged me in her eyes to save her family."

"Tell me you hit it, man, and then saved the family." Yonnie closed his eyes and leaned his head back, laughing to keep from crying.

"No," Carlos said. "It woulda been her first time, and to ruin her in Hell with her family in body parts—come on, brother!"

"Aw'ight, what's the very insane moral to this story?" Yonnie stared at him, not amused in the least as Carlos started laughing.

"I got fucked up by demon legions. Disemboweled, arm tore out the socket, face crushed, jaw busted, and flung topside in the time before daywalkers, into the sun in the desert."

"Oh, this is getting more romantic by the minute." Yonnie spit and Carlos laughed hard, landing a hand on his shoulder.

"Then I crawled my bloody dying ass into a cave, after a very foolish coyote thought I was carrion—"

"Eeiiw, stop! That's *nasty*, Rivera!"

"Uh-huh, but I was trying to live. I had a love-jones for my wife so bad I didn't care. I got in a cave, laid up until I knitted back together, and the rest is history—but believe when I came outta that cave, and she was old enough . . . sheeit . . . a brother was on a mission."

Yonnie nodded and pounded Carlos's fist again. "That's what I'm talking about!"

"That's what I'm talking about," Carlos said, grinning. "So, until you can find a way to have you cake and eat it, too, I suggest Tijuana."

"You keep working on cosmic loopholes, is all I'm asking," Yonnie said, flipping Carlos the bird when he laughed harder.

"All right, man, so . . . if I let her know you're up here, ten minutes, no nicks, and we're out." Carlos stared at him hard. "Don't make me have to come up here and get her, either."

"I hear you."

"Say it in *Dananu*," Carlos said in their old vampire contractual language.

"So, it's like that now? Damn!"

"Man . . ."

"Oh, and you never answered me when I asked you where you were taking my lady and how long you'd be gone." Yonnie folded his arms over his chest.

"You know I can't do that for your own good, and for the team's safety, should you get busted in council. But you still haven't answered my question—no nicks, ten minutes, and she comes back unmolested." Carlos waited with his arms folded, smiling. "I ain't got all day."

"No nicks, ten minutes, but don't ask me not to put my hands on her, man." Yonnie turned away and stared at the house.

"Ten minutes ain't a whole lotta time, bro . . . no sense in going there," Carlos said.

"You, my friend, are putting a serious strain on our friendship." Yonnie had spoken between his teeth but hadn't turned around.

Carlos swallowed a chuckle and began walking.

"You're not even gonna transport her up here?" Yonnie turned and walked behind Carlos, fuming.

"Saving my energy for the flight. Plus, I have some real wicked shit in a box in my driveway that's taking a toll," Carlos said, sounding amused.

Two huge, snarling dogs with black muzzles and bodies the

hue of tea and milk blocked Carlos's path. He looked at Yonnie unconcerned.

"Hell dogs disguised as Fila Brasileiro Mastiffs—the national dog of Brazil. They can guard whatever you've got in the yard, if you just hurry up and send my lady up here."

"I'll go get her, but, damn, man, that's the second or third time you've called Val your lady. You can do what you like, but before you go there in your mind, I suggest you talk to her about all that. Just my two-cent tip for the day." Carlos shrugged and Yonnie snapped his fingers, removing the dogs.

"You really need to talk to her," Carlos said, his tone serious. "You can't hide the situation from her forever."

"Let me break it to her . . . I'd appreciate it if nobody in the house did."

Carlos nodded. "You'd be surprised at how many people in the family got your back and are pulling for you, man. Tara didn't tell her while I was gone getting patched up. Damali didn't say a word, neither did Rider—who, of all people, I expected would. None of the other Guardians got in it. So . . . it's all on you, bro."

Damali leaned back against the large butcher block center island in the kitchen and listened to Tara's recount of the predawn hours in the house. All she could do was hug her Guardian sister, understanding what being torn was like and deeply appreciating Tara's loyalty to her husband's best friend. Yet, as part of the dual Neteru leadership, she also had to look out for Val's welfare, another person she loved. Yonnie, as much as he was like a brother, was a potential hazmat to Val's life.

She wiped her palms down her face as Tara slipped out of the kitchen. Damali stared behind her, knowing that very, very soon she was going to have to have a long sit-down conversation with Val. But at the moment, the team was packing ammo, and

Carlos had something ridiculous in the driveway—something that was like a nuclear warhead. Hell, she wasn't even sure how to ship it! Mom Delores and Ayana had to get dropped off in Brooklyn, and it wasn't even ten A.M.

When she pushed off the counter, Marlene was standing in the doorway. The two exchanged a look. A slow smile spread across Marlene's face. Marlene made the gesture of a key locking a lock in front of her lips, and then she hugged herself. Damali smiled and nodded and hugged herself from where she stood across the room, making Marlene silently jump up and down. Then both women opened a channel.

It's official?

Yes!

Oh, my goodness!

Mar, I'm scared. We can't say anything until after the first trimester and I start showing. . . . We're about to go hunting again.

Marlene's smile faded, and she crossed the room.

"This time won't be like before, but it's your news to tell, not mine."

Damali hugged Marlene hard and spoke against her neck. "Pray for us, Mar. I promised my husband this one would hold—but I have to keep working up to the end, can't stop doing what we have to do."

Marlene held Damali back and stroked her locks away from her face. "You might not see the angels working, but you have to know they're there." She kissed Damali's forehead. "You're *my* child, baby. I've been your mother-seer for how long . . . all these many years, and I have never been so sure about anything in my life."

"Really, Mar?" Damali whispered. "Because even though they told me not to worry, I—"

"Shush, shush . . . words become thoughts, and thoughts become things. We're not even gonna speak no negativity out into the universe about what could possibly go wrong. We're going to stay, mentally, in the Light," Marlene chided. "What's more, when it gets too serious, if they tell you to put your feet up, then that's what you're going to do . . . evil's been around for how long? Since the dawn of time," Marlene added, answering her own question. "So, if one sister needs to take a little time off, hey, it'll still be there when you get back on your feet." She hugged Damali tightly. "Don't let 'em steal all your joy, baby. If you let them do that, then they've won before the battle has even begun."

"Okay, I'm going to try to remember that." Damali kissed Marlene's cheek. "Thank you, Mar, for being my mother-seer and my earth mom."

Marlene cradled Damali's face between her palms. "I wouldn't have it any other way."

"Just don't start treating me differently in front of the team," Damali said with a soft smile.

"Huh . . . you better tell that to your husband," Marlene said, beginning to laugh. "I knew something was wrong when he came out of that fold-away bringing you home, holding you by your elbow and asking if you were all right. Puhlease."

"He's going to be a hot mess,' Damali said, laughing quietly with Marlene.

"Carlos Rivera ain't got that much black box or silver lining in his head to hold that info. Brother's got that deer-in-the-headlights look happening," Marlene said, shaking her head. "Big giveaway. 'But I'ma let D explain the mission,' and then held his breath like he wasn't sure how much of whatever you were going to disclose. I *knew* something was up."

"Yeah, something is up all right," Rider said, sauntering into the kitchen, giving Damali and Marlene a start. "I hope you ladies have finished laughing about the antics of Miss Ayana, aka Yaya, because there's a serious PG-13 problem in the house . . . more like a triple X, no one under twenty-one admitted, not even with an adult. You have no idea how dicey it was in here, D."

Both Marlene and Damali relaxed, once they were sure that Rider was prattling on about Ayana. Suddenly, Marlene's eyes widened and she stared at Damali.

What if the baby picks up on it and blurts it out?

Oh, my goodness!

"Yeah," Rider said, vindicated. He folded his arms over his chest. "Not so funny now, when you think about it, huh? It's not just a privacy issue, but a security-breach issue. I love the little darlin', but if we all have mission-sensitive information in our heads, and she can just go flitting around the house unlocking people's deepest thoughts, then one day when her nana has her out at a store, or whatever, what happens then if a daywalker or general-purpose demon goes trolling inside that three-year-old's head?"

The potential ramifications made both Damali and Marlene pace.

"So, I don't know what the protocols are, or even how you might want to silver shield the kid's head—if she's going to be living with us . . . and I know Marlene probably feels some type of way about stunting the natural abilities of a child—but until she learns what is appropriate and not, I for one am having a hard time with this." Rider dragged his fingers through his dark blond hair. "I don't even know the right answer, but you all didn't have to do the two-step and ole soft shoe routine this morning when she broke in mentally on her mom and Mike."

Damali cupped her hand over her mouth and Marlene fought not to laugh, despite the serious nature of the problem.

Marlene nodded and spoke in a flat tone, but her eyes sparkled with merriment. "Yeah, uh, she thought her mommy was hurt and Daddy Mike was calling Jesus for help."

"Oh . . . no . . ." Damali said, bending over with her hands covering her face.

"Yeah," Rider said, his tone peevish. "That about sums it up. So, you might want to tell Rivera that if he's gonna go all-out in here one of these ye old nights, that you've got a seeing kid in the house and he might wanna damp down the thunder and lightning!"

"You all are never gonna let us live down that *one* time things got out of hand at the motel—jeez, Rider!" Damali was laughing and walking in circles. "I have to talk to my girl, Inez." She stopped by the sink and the mirth slowly dissipated. "Bigger problem is the security issue you brought up, Rider. I hear you. Houston, we've definitely got a problem."

"You're all right," Valkyrie gasped as she came out of Carlos's transport jettison.

She hurried up the hillside to where Yonnie stood and it took a great deal of restraint on his part not to go to her.

"Yeah, I'm good," he said, his gaze raking her.

The Guardians had given her some clothes. She wore a turquoise-blue halter top without a bra to make space for her wings, a pair of white capri pants that showed off her lovely, athletic calves, and Viking sandals. It was an eclectic mix and he loved it. Her long platinum locks were pulled up high in a blue elastic band, and her face was exquisite in the sun. He could feel the excitement brimming just under her skin: relief, desire, and curiosity an intoxicating mix in her bloodstream. Yet, she was holding herself back, seeming a little afraid of something—most likely him. That was a wise thing.

"I also heard your squad took a lot of heat . . . had a serious firefight in Harlem. I'm sorry you had to go through that. Glad you're okay."

His words were coming out in halts and jags. Everything he

wanted to say was bottled up inside, and he spoke to her formally, like someone he didn't know.

"Are they watching you now?" she whispered, glancing around. It was clear that she felt the distance he projected, too.

He shook his head. "I'm just trying to honor my word to Rivera. You're like his sister, family—and he told me to keep my hands to myself." Yonnie put his hands behind his back and let his breath out hard. "You're really beautiful, Val . . . never met anybody quite like you. And I don't want to hurt you or mess over you, you understand?"

"The male Neteru thinks of me as a blood relative?" Val placed her hand over her heart. "He actually challenged you to be honorable . . . and because you are that, and you are his friend, you will not dishonor me." She looked up at him and stepped closer. "But you make me afraid, and that is something as a warrior that I am not proud of, but it is my truth."

Yonnie stiffened. "Why do I make you afraid?"

"It is not because of what you have done, or the dangerous mission you undertake for the sake of the Light . . . but I am afraid that I could dishonor the Neteru."

He tilted his head to the side and stared at her hard. "You're not playing both sides against the middle, are you? Because let me be clear, Rivera's my boy, and if it's anything shady, I'm not down with all of that no matter how fine you are."

"Oh, no, no," she said, holding up her hands. "You misunderstand my meaning. I am not in league with those hybrids that betrayed the Light, Cain loyalists that allowed Lilith's demon legion beyond our realm. Heaven forbid!"

"Then . . . I don't—"

Her sudden kiss stopped his words and his hands sought her hair, at first gently, then more aggressively. Her mouth opened to accept his tongue and the fragrant hint of pineapple and mint from toothpaste rolled over his palate. She smelled like rosewater lotion and chamomile soap. But her skin was like smooth, dark chocolate melting under his touch as though he were her personal sun. He swallowed her groan and filled her mouth with his.

She broke the kiss breathless, her eyes heavy-lidded and filled with desire. "I don't trust my willpower around you, Yolando . . . and it is shameless. That is what frightens me. I have just met you and the Neteru has admonished the wrong one. He should have challenged me, not you. I feel things I haven't ever—"

His kiss swallowed her words as his palms trailed down her back, sending pleasure through her spinal fluid until she arched. He palmed her bottom and slowly lifted her up his body, wanting so badly to dissolve her clothing that he had to turn his head away from their kiss.

The heat of her body alone was cresting fangs in his mouth. He hugged her, trying not to move against her, frustrating them more. But then she kissed his neck . . . the side that was the original site of his turn bite. He kept his eyes closed, sure that they had gone to a deep crimson glow. Vampire instinct was on autopilot. The sound of the blood rushing through her veins blotted out everything else. The scent of adrenaline in her perspiration and of wet, willing female made him wanna holler. He could literally feel her heart thudding against his chest, she held him so tightly. He raked her mind, opening pleasure centers as he found her mouth again. This time she threw her head back and wailed.

It happened so fast that her hair was in his fist, her jugular exposed, his pelvis welded to hers. She thrashed and rubbed herself against his length and he tore his gaze away from her exposed throat and settled on suckling her breasts instead.

He'd promised not to bite her, made a bond to Rivera in *Dananu*. He lifted her halter top, allowing her agonized breasts to finally bounce free. His tongue immediately began to lave her sensitive skin, and every lick drew spasmodic, jerking motions from her hips as he attended her tight, dark nipples.

She had handfuls of Afro between her graceful fingers; he had both thick lobes of her backside palmed in each hand. She was so close to an orgasm that it took everything he knew not to just FX mist her into a bed, and be done with the torturous ordeal. Instead, he blew in her ear, let her feel it in her mind, then let it slowly implode between her legs, his kiss a sound barrier as she let go.

He pressed her to him as she came out of the daze; he was so hard that he had tears in his eyes. Her hand slid between their bodies to touch him. He winced.

"Don't," he breathed out. "I ain't got that much self-control, at the moment."

"But, you're in agony," she whispered, her hand cupping his cheek. "You're body is cold . . . you're shivering . . . I can't even feel your pulse."

He let her go, immediately hit with reality. "I'll be all right. All the blood just rushed to one place. I just have to walk it off."

"I cannot understand how you . . . the way you make me feel when I'm in your arms." She fixed her halter top, then hugged herself, and looked at him wide-eyed.

He came to her, checked his watch, and kissed her quickly. "Rivera said ten minutes, and the brother is being real peaceful, because this has been more like fifteen."

"Are you coming on this mission with us?"

He hesitated, knowing he wasn't supposed to know where they were going, but he did. He'd been all up inside her head. "Not this time. But if you get jammed up, you send me a mental SOS, and I'll be there for you, girl." He walked back and forth for a moment and then stopped. "Damn, I can't believe I got all caught up and forgot to tell Rivera this." Yonnie let his breath out hard. "You and the team be careful what you eat right through here. Pray over every meal and look for signs of white arsenic if you don't feel right—I can't go into it, but trust me. All right? If it gets real bad, call me, and I'll be there."

"I will inform the Neterus . . . but you can do fold-away movement like they can?"

"More on the black tornado, mist-vapor, tip, but I get around. Call me, if you need me . . . or . . . if you want me." He stared at her, knowing he shouldn't have put that last part out there, but he couldn't help it. The sadness in her eyes made him trace the edge of her jaw with his thumb. "Be valiant, be victorious . . . my Valkyrie. If you're who came for soldiers at the end when they didn't make it, then I understand why those men weren't afraid to die."

@ CHAPTER EIGHTEEN

The team landed on a small jewel in the Aegean Sea that seemed to be lost somewhere in early biblical time. Balmy Mediterranean breezes blew light wildflower fragrances in all directions. From the top of the mountain where the monastery was perched, small, rolling hills of green dotted by white houses were surrounded by a gorgeous, azure sea.

"Oh, this is so beautiful, Damali," her pearl crooned from the platinum necklace she hadn't worn in months since her oracle's illness. "Greece . . . where the Temple of the Goddess Diana was built—the ancient cities. Oh! Isn't it just breathtaking?"

"It is," Damali said quietly, "but no talking and scaring the monks. I'll take you to the sea, if there's time, okay, honey?"

"Oh, I'd like that . . . bathing and joy is good for—"

"Shush," Damali whispered. "Remember our talk?"

"Yes, yes, just when it's you and Carlos around . . . but I am *so excited.*"

"No more outbursts, unless there's an emergency."

"I understand. Bye," the pearl cooed good-naturedly, then became dormant again.

Damali looked around, marveling with the team. Pretty rock-strewn beaches and coves too numerous to count fringed the island. They'd been told by Imam Asula that with only a tiny, highly religious population of three thousand residents, there would be no heavy traffic, no nightclubs, and the streets rolled up at night. The island had been invaded and changed hands since five hundred B.C., from Romans to Turks to Ottomans and Persians; practically every force in the region had stopped by to beset this speck of land.

Therefore, just as the clerics had warned, the monastery at Patmos was indeed a fortress that looked more like a medieval castle than holy retreat.

Fifteen-foot-high stone walls enclosed the citadel from the outside world, and winding, narrow, intentionally confusing streets provided escape routes during hostile invasions. The open balconies were not victims of wood rot or neglect, but were floorless by design. This encampment of monks had a long history of sieges against pirate attacks, and the lack of flooring was to permit hot boiling oil to be poured down on invaders. Buildings annexed buildings as though the fortress had begun as a single cell and then split repeatedly within a predefined footprint. There was one door in and one door out to the huge network of structures.

Damali and Carlos glanced at each other. The seers in the group were scanning the premises, too, and were bouncing mental signals to those in the group without the gift. Yet despite the severity of the exterior, the interior was beautifully Byzantine with a bell tower and cells built around the chief nave. Ten chapels, the cave where St. John was exiled and received his visions for the last book in the New Testament, a massive library, a bakery, and a museum—a small city within a city had been created here. Pretty whitewashed stucco buildings, well-kept gardens with brilliantly colored flowers, and serenity that echoed from the stones made Damali sigh. Why here? Why would evil bring its vile carcass to this paradise?

They'd disturbed the monastery's serenity in the quiet town of Hora today for sure. This was a place where driving wasn't even allowed. A ring of Eastern Orthodox monks quickly rushed in to greet the team, profusely crossing themselves and welcoming them in an agitated linguistic flurry. Though clearly prepared by the Covenant for the team's arrival, their hosts still obviously found them a subject of awe.

"Greetings and blessings, welcome to the Island of the Apocalypse," a tall, rotund friar said as he ambled forward. "I am Koustsanellos." He wore sandals and traditional monk's robes, and had a wide, friendly face and wiry salt-and-pepper hair that had receded in the middle into a shiny horseshoe. His eyes sparkled with excitement and there was a keen intelligence in them, too.

But the team simply gaped at his description of the island. Island of the Apocalypse didn't sound good at all. While the man might have been talking about a metaphorical apocalypse, as in where St. John wrote his apocalyptic vision, the Book of Revelations, the statement visibly worried the team.

"Father Koustsanellos, thank you for having us," Damali said, trying to restore civility throughout the unnerved team.

"We appreciate it, sir," Carlos said, and then went around the group making introductions.

"Our brothers can settle your things in your rooms," their gregarious host said, but then he hesitated. "Although you are married . . . the ladies must stay at the nunnery. I hope you understand?"

"Yeah, sure, Father," Carlos said slowly, reading the concern in everyone's eyes. Splitting up the group was not part of protocol.

"The Nunnery of the Annunciation is within the same town, only a fifteen-minute leisurely walk from our Monastery of St. John, and on the southwest side of Hora overlooking the Bay of Kypos," the monk said, and he smiled as bodies relaxed all around him. "Then, we lunch!"

He waved the team forward, but Big Mike hung back. He cringed as two monks lifted a trunk and dropped one end.

"Uhmmm, not to be overly cautious, but some of this ammo should only be handled by folks who know what they're doing," Mike said quietly to Carlos. "That has the launcher and grenades in it. Don't need no incidents, feel me?"

"Uh, Father," Carlos said, stopping the man's long strides. "We have some pretty hazardous materials for the job we've gotta do. Any chance there's somewhere safe our guys can stash it, where no one will accidentally get hurt?"

Just as the large friar was about to object on the grounds of hospitality, two monks tried to lift a silver case, but dropped it and ran as it squealed and hissed. The case bumped up and down on the ground as though a Tasmanian devil were locked inside it. The monks made the sign of the cross over their chests, which only seemed to agitate the unseen thing in the case more.

"I *told you* to leave that mess in Brooklyn or let me kill it, Carlos," Damali fussed in a low tone.

"Might need it for later, boo." Carlos looked at the case and then at the concerned monks. "We got it during an exorcism to use it like a hunting dog . . . and it's probably really agitated being cased in silver and sitting on hallowed ground right through here." He went over to the case and kicked it. "Serves your nasty little . . . serves you right, now shut up!"

For a moment the gathered monks said nothing. One whispered to the lead friar and pointed to a large clay pot that sat in the courtyard, filled with water.

"My brother friar suggests we dunk it in the holy water here, which should sufficiently subdue it," Koustsanellos offered.

Carlos kicked the case again. "You hear that? We're up here where St. John did his thing and these guys don't play. They're seriously talking about drowning you in holy water from wells that go back to Christ's time, so what's it gonna be?" He folded his arms over his chest as the silver case went still and released a little squeal of terror. "Yeah, I thought you'd see it my way." He turned to Father Koustsanellos. "You better let me move that case, but lunch sounds real good."

Damali rolled her eyes and then tried to allay the monks' fears as much as possible. "Fathers, we're only here to get some information, and have no intention of opening up a firefight here . . . in fact, if you just want to move our things to a safe place, temporarily, as soon as we tour the facilities and visit your library, we'll leave you wonderful gentlemen in peace . . . I'm sure there are rooms we can rent closer to the shore points."

"Yes, yes, we will accommodate your relocation for your comfort—this is a much better plan," Father Koustsanellos said, appearing totally relieved. His fellow friars' shoulders dropped by inches, and friendly smiles again replaced sheer-panic-laden expressions.

"Come. As is customary in our homeland, food shared with guests is a way to show our warmth. You will not have to eat at a local taverna, no. Here we have the freshest meats and vegetables. Our brothers have made *mezedes* of all flavors—as we were told some of your team are kosher, some are vegetarian, and that others eat meat in your group . . . we made fried meatballs, squash balls, octopus and squid, olives, cheese, stuffed vine leaves, and our famous *tzatziki* . . . this is, hmmm, garlic yogurt and cucumbers, yes? You will like. Eggplant dip with small sausages. They also made lamb kabobs, and *pastitsio*— macaroni pasta and tomatoes . . . *stifado*—braised beef with onions, and grilled lamb chops—*paidakia*. Our bakery is literally divine, and our breads—oh! The butter and cheeses will make you weep."

They followed behind the ecstatic friar who spoke with grand, sweeping waves of his hand. It was not lost on the group in the least that the man was practically jumping for joy that they wouldn't be staying at St. John's, but who could blame him? After what happened to the joint in Harlem, there'd be no way to replace the level of religious antiquity here if a firefight broke out.

Hours passed as the meal was consumed in wave after wave of aromatic courses. The large group took their meal in the refectory, where the monks ate their meals together at two long, marble-covered tables. Beautiful frescoes and paintings dating back to the eleven hundreds covered the walls. Rushing the friars was not an option. Something embedded in their cultural DNA made the whole process of eating and breaking bread an experience, not just an act of nourishing the body. It was holistic, including the mind, body, as well as the spirit. The team gave in to the process without a struggle. They'd already been through the ringer the night before, and no one was too anxious to begin a new mission.

But between creamy yogurts made from the freshest ingredients and sautéed vegetables seasoned like she'd never had in her life, Damali was able to glean basic information from the friar without giving the poor man acid indigestion.

They'd learned that Psili Ammos was the most beautiful beach, one that was also the most remote, exotic, and surrounded by wilderness. It was only a twenty-minute walk by way of the little footpath over the mountain. The friar also let on that if one were discreet, one could bathe in the skinny. That level of seclusion meant that said beach sounded like a good place to set up temporary camp and have a full team meeting without eavesdroppers. After the tour, that would be good. One thing for sure, they'd have to get moving before everyone fell asleep where they sat.

But first, she needed to see the library, even though she

hadn't a clue to what she was looking for. Father Patrick had sent them on a mission to Patmos for a reason, even though he wasn't sure exactly why. Maybe he thought that at this particular citadel, if the Darkness came calling, it was their best stronghold against it. Who knew?

"So, then we must go to fulfill your curiosity," Father Koustsanellos said to Carlos. He stood patting his belly, making the group smile, and everyone slowly got up and stretched, commenting on how fantastic the meal had been.

"This library," their host said with pride, "is today considered one of the foremost libraries of Christianity. Manuscripts, vellum codices, even books written on cotton . . . works include Xenofonta, Plato, the Great Philosophical School of Mystra, and the classic text, Aristotle's *Accuses*. By the thirteenth century it was stocked full and kept on growing . . . it is called the Soul Hospital."

Damali's and Carlos's attention jerked toward each other at the mention of the place being a soul hospital. They entered the massive room that had every wall lined with grand, carved wooden bookshelves. The center was supported by stone columns, and plaster arches loomed high.

"We like to believe that St. John also blesses this library, as he is the patron saint of booksellers and the fine arts . . . remember his trials and burdens," the friar said, folding his hands over his barrel stomach. "He was arrested and thrown into a vat of burning oil, from which he emerged unhurt. Then he was exiled here in the company of an eagle, where he wrote Revelations . . . then upon his return to Ephesus eighteen month later, he survived yet another ordeal set up by the high priest of Ephesus—they poisoned the man," he whispered, drawing Guardians in close. "They offered the saint a golden chalice, but John blessed it, and the venom—in the form of a snake—was drawn from the liquid."

"This is what he must have been trying to warn us of," Val said excitedly and stepped back.

"Pardon?" the monk said, confused as his gaze roved the team.

"Yolando told me to be careful what I eat and bless it for everybody." Valkyrie walked over to Damali. "May I share with you?"

"Yeah, girl, c'mon—if you've got info, spit it out."

"Father, do you have docs that date back to that time we can see, so we can see what John actually said over the chalice?" Carlos was already scanning the walls as he asked the question.

"Absolutely," the monk said, rushing about the shelves as Damali stepped to the side to privately confer with Valkyrie.

"Talk to me, girl." Damali's gaze was unblinking.

"Some of this is very private," Val said and then looked away. "I should not like for the more intimate details to be shared with the male Neteru."

"I'll respect that—your source is Yonnie, right? I understand more than you know."

The two women shared a look.

"Yes," Val said quietly. "And at some point, if you deem it within your heart, I would appreciate *any* advice you would graciously share with me on how to manage these . . . feelings and my role as a warrior. I am so beset by conflict. You have balanced your role with dignity and grace. I aspire."

Damali hugged her. "We'll talk, lady—I promise. Let me in. I cast no judgment. But if there's something dangerous we need to know, we can't tap-dance around it."

Valkyrie immediately relaxed and the brief comment from Yonnie filled Damali's mind. She looked past the broiling scene and kept focusing on Yonnie's words. Then white arsenic surfaced from the passion haze that had buried it in Val's consciousness.

"Lucrezia!" Damali breathed. She dropped her hold on Val and all eyes turned toward her. "The queen of poison—white arsenic being her specialty, is a new councilwoman and Nuit's latest . . . wife." Damali looked around and blew a stray lock up off her forehead. "That means water, food, even toothpaste, gang, you've gotta say whatever St. John did over your stuff until we get past this drama. But that's part of why we came here. They could have taken us out without even firing the first warning shot."

"You do not have to worry about anything you had here. There's a flour mill on the premises, we make our own wine, all of our food is made from here." Father Koustsanellos said, seeming nervous. His brow seemed feverish and Damali looked from him to Big Mike.

Carlos stepped away from the shelves. "How you feeling, big guy?"

"Just a little dizzy, you know, the hot air and eating like a champ . . . I'll be cool in a while," Mike said.

"Anybody know the reaction time of arsenic?" Damali said frantically, going to each team member as her mouth went dry.

"From my old cop days we had a murder case where a wife took out her husband—forensics said you start feeling sick anywhere between a half-hour after ingesting it to twenty-four, but it sneaks up on you." Berkfield looked at Damali and Carlos, then his wife and kids.

"Symptoms, Medic? What were the symptoms?" Carlos said, his voice escalating in the quiet, vaulted room.

"Nausea, vomiting," Berkfield said. "Same things common to travel in a foreign country if you drink the local water." He wiped a palm over his now sweaty, bald scalp. "Visual impairment, dizziness. Rashes, burning pains in the hands and feet."

"Everybody line up," Damali said, rushing to Jasmine who had a large red rash beginning to spread over her throat. "Carlos, you got that doc?"

"On it," he said, holding a fragile parchment.

"But I don't understand," the monk exclaimed. "How could evil cross here? We said a blessing on the food!"

"They didn't send supernatural forces, Father," Damali said, reading the words as she talked to the distressed monk. "That cannot cross into hallowed ground. All it takes is one kitchen staff member or one guy at the market to give you a bad batch of whatever food you ordered, and have it tainted. If it's a natural element, like arsenic, it can cross into the Vatican, and we know popes in the past have been assassinated like that."

The monk crossed himself as Damali and Carlos studied the writings and began to speak in unison.

"We could sure use your help, Father," Carlos said, getting the monk to join in.

Within moments of completing the words, every member of the team, as well as the friar, dry heaved and belched up twisting, angry serpents. Blades drawn, Damali and Carlos made quick work of severing the snapping heads. Witnessing monks dashed to find holy water and returned, splashing the gore until it was thoroughly incinerated.

Team members leaned back against the bookshelves, breathing deeply and slowly recovering.

"Damn . . . that was so messed up," Inez said. " 'Cause I really, really loved their bread."

The team trudged into the Cave of the Apocalypse, winded, but on a mission more than ever before. A dim stone grotto surrounded by a sanctuary and filled with priceless icons greeted them. Heather's and Jasmine's hands immediately went to the stone walls, pulling in impressions. Damali's gaze raked the interior. Why did Father Patrick mention this place, just to keep them from getting poisoned?

"Over there," the much-subdued friar said. "The three fissures in the wall are where St. John received his visions."

All was still . . . nothing penetrated their psyches. Disappointment loomed heavy, even as they entered the main chapel and stared at the breathtaking sculptures and glorious friezes. There were thrones with mother-of-pearl inlaid in rich mahogany wood, and the holy altar which was built from the ruins from the Temple of Diana had inlaid jewels of impossible-to-estimate value, but no additional clues leapt forward.

The question on everyone's mind remained—how did they get tracked here? Where was the leak, the weak link in the chain?

"The woman who left the house in Brooklyn and went to the store with the child," the pearl whispered into Damali's tortured mind. "Lucrezia is very shrewd. She knew the baby could not go on this mission but you were sheltered. This I learned after the snakes were released. Once you began to ingest the poison, I felt woozy, too, and my ability to know things was impacted. Had I known, Damali, I would have warned you."

Damali sent a hot glare to Inez and gave her the report from her pearl, then shot it to Carlos. The information ricocheted through the group via the seers within seconds.

"J.L., when we get to the main administration offices here, get on a prayer-secured line to the safe house in Brooklyn. I want 'Nez on the phone with her mother to let her know what just happened here and how she could be next if she doesn't follow what the clerics there tell her to do!" Carlos's voice bounced off the walls. "Then, I want you to give the rundown on what just happened to one of the clerics in charge while Damali and I move the ammo to the beach."

"Do you have a fax machine, Father?' Damali said, looking at the friar and then Inez. "Because we need to fax that prayer to the Covenant—who knows, they might have been poisoned, too."

"The Greek isles," Lilith said nervously. "That is dangerously close to where Lu has moved the chrysalis. Even with a hundred and fifty islands that could keep them searching for months, I don't like it."

"This is why I've poisoned the entire team, Your Majesty," Lucrezia cooed. "It was a simple matter of finding their weakest link and exploiting it. Once is enough. Human helpers are easy enough to bend to our will, and, let's face it: Humans need food to sustain them. A supernatural attack would be impossible against the citadel of St. John . . . however, a little tainted food is a whole different matter."

"She bided her time, Lilith, as a shrewd and brilliant murderess," Nuit said with pride. He handed Lucrezia a golden goblet filled with blood. "Now we wait."

"How long?" Lilith's gaze narrowed as she sat forward expectantly.

"I administered enough to give them three hours before they would begin to experience discomfort."

"Why so long!" Lilith snapped and rose from her chair.

"To allow them to eat, take the normal Mediterranean midday nap, and die quietly before the Neterus could apply any healing techniques. They should go quietly in their sleep, or convulse while having a midday rendezvous . . . but if I were too heavy-handed, and allowed them to begin to have violent episodes right at the table, then our plan would be discovered and foiled."

Lilith sat back down and took a slow sip from her goblet. "Then we wait." She looked at Nuit and Lucrezia. "Together we wait."

"Am I required to be here?" Sebastian said. "Given this is not my strategy?"

Lilith's lip curled. "No . . . but where is Elizabeth?"

"Bathing in the blood of ten maidens I slaughtered for her this morning . . . milk carton runaways. I should like to attend her bath, if I might?"

Waving her hand, she dismissed him. "And Yolando? What of his whereabouts?"

"The last I spied," Nuit said dryly, "he was in Tijuana."

Damali submerged her pearl in the sea and immediately Zehiradangra laughed like a small child, her gleeful shrieks an odd contrast to the morose team all around her. Carlos stalked back and forth and then punched one of the many tamarisk trees that gave the beach its exotic green fringe.

"Yo, yo, yo," Damali said, tossing her necklace to Val and rushing toward Carlos. "What did we learn about trees when we went to see the Neterus?" She was distressed that he was so distressed, and she was trying to keep pace with him as he worked the rage out. The comment, while true, was really meant to diffuse some of his anger, but it wasn't working.

They tried to poison my pregnant wife? Carlos shot her so hard mentally that she thought her nose would bleed. "Oh, hell no!"

I know, baby, but I'm all right—besides, if you ingest a little of the substance you build immunity to it—so they played themselves.

Carlos just looked at her. Clearly he wasn't buying her attempt to mollify him.

"D, be serious. Maybe some other poisons work like that, but not arsenic."

"Sorry, tree," Damali said, rubbing it, and watching Carlos pace. She had to deflect this conversation.

The team's male members had the same looks on their faces. Everybody was sitting on crates and trunks—all except the silver one that had something alive inside it. But their expressions held a dangerous brand of repressed fury—the kind of thing that could make people jump up and go after the enemy buck wild without a plan.

"Listen," Heather said, glancing around. "Me and Jasmine have been talking . . . we're stone workers. At the risk of offending anybody, I think we have to say that there are two polarities working back at the monastery. The old Diana energies—because after all, she was Goddess of the hunt—and of course St. John."

"Okay, I'm not trying to get in trouble here," Damali said, trying to figure out how to fuse two totally different cultures. She looked to Marlene for support, but her mother-seer just shrugged.

"Information is power, Damali," Jasmine said, glancing at Carlos and then Marlene. "Doesn't all the Diana information predate the other biblical text—so they don't overlap—but we definitely felt female energy rising in those stones . . . good energy, as though she were trying to help, too."

"We could use all the help we can get," Damali said with a hard sigh. "I also find it fascinating that they built the altar right over the temple altar of Diana . . . you would have thought they'd totally demolish it and clear it out."

"Maybe that's why we're supposed to be here," Tara offered with a shrug and then looked at Marjorie and Krissy.

"It was the females that tried to kill us this time out. Last time, too, with Liz Bathory's army. And I don't even want to talk about that skank, Lilith." Damali looked at Carlos who had stopped pacing and was listening. The male Guardians sat up and focused.

Val came running up the beach from the water's edge, holding the pearl. "She's saying interesting things, Damali."

"Pearl, what's up?" Carlos said, making the pearl giggle.

"Hi, Carlos . . . you know the Aegean Sea completely rejuvenates oracles, oh! This is where it all began . . . the Oracle at

Delphi; all of us have Greek and Roman histories. I was talking to Egeria, Diana's servant—she's a water nymph and midwife, but more on her later—we've always been friendly. Anywho . . . I told her what happened, and Diana is on the warpath in the cosmos. Damali is viewed as special, given she's a huntress, Diana is a huntress, blah, blah, blah—so Diana took this very personally."

Damali looked at Carlos. "You think it's possible we were supposed to get the antidote from the prayers of St. John—since he drew the venom of poison out of the chalice before—but the war strategy from Diana?"

Carlos walked away.

"Where are you going?" Damali ran behind him, peeved.

"To go apologize to Diana's trees . . . I know Greek and Roman history from my other life, boo. She loved her tree groves and would hunt a man down for messing with her environmentals, feel me?" He stroked the tree. "Hey, I'm sorry—tell Diana, peace. I was just mad because the bad guys poisoned my wife and family."

"Okay," Berkfield said to Marlene, "I want you to go in with me to try to get the rest of the poison out of this man. Rivera was sick yesterday, and it could have hurt his system worse than the rest of ours—the man is *talking to trees,* hallucinating."

"It's cool," Marlene said and then shot Shabazz a look. "It's the Tao of the tree, right?"

"Okay," Berkfield said, holding up his hands. "I'm just an old-fashioned Irish Catholic, and I'm waaay outta my league with all of this."

"Can you get word to Diana?" Damali asked the pearl, gently taking her from Val and staring down into the choker necklace in her hands.

"Already done, Damali . . . she advises that you pick off their weak links one by one. Elizabeth is bathing in blood right now as we speak. She killed maidens—and you know Diana is the protectress of virgins." The pearl clucked her tongue. "Diana will send emissaries, her warriors. They can lead you to her, and you, or they, could slip some silver nitrate into Elizabeth's tub if it was mixed with blood. Plus, since she is working with Aset and Eve, I'm sure they can lift the silver scent taint just long enough . . . this is war, now, after all."

"Oooh . . ." Marlene said, squinting. "And add some holy water . . . we could bag it and tag it and then if Diana lifted the scent . . ."

"Uh-huh." Damali smiled. "Same deal with Lucrezia. Couldn't a sprite get to her goblet and dump a lil something-something in there?"

"I'd really prefer that we form an alliance with Diana, so you can fall back, D," Carlos said very carefully. "If they've got sprites and whatnot that can deliver poisons . . . I'm just saying." They shared a look and his gaze didn't waver. "We should save the big guns for the all-out offensive."

She accepted his position with a nod, knowing that he was trying to state his case in such a way that let her save face as a general while also not tipping off the team to her condition.

"I can assist," Val said. She lifted her chin. "I am a Valkyrie and a warrior. My blood may have a more exotic scent, given my parentage and that I have lived in Nod for so long. Plus, I am a virgin. This is what the she-devil craves. I have felt her ravenous impressions from my interactions with Yolando." Val held out her arm and unsheathed an invisible blade. "Bring a chalice and I shall give it to Diana's emissaries to taint. Serve this cold to both Lucrezia and that Bathory bitch!"

"You betta go, sis!" Juanita hollered, jumping up off a crate to slap five with Inez.

"The girl's been with us, what, a day or two—and she's straight gangsta," Inez said, laughing.

Val smiled. Carlos and Damali nodded. The rest of the team bristled and murmured with a new, more positive outlook.

"Just hold up and put your blade away till we make contact, Val," Damali said with a big grin. "But we are *loving* your style." She walked away, raking her locks. "This is what we needed: fresh ideas, new perspective, something to open up our heads to the possibilities . . . guerrilla."

"Then, if Seth and Abel body-double me and you, and we send extra life force pulses in a fold-away, we could make them think the team got so sick that we left here," Carlos said, finally calming down enough to strategize. "The moment they realize their fellow councilwomen have been hit—Nuit and Sebastian will come looking for us wherever Seth and Abel are."

"They gonna get their asses kicked by those two brothers," Mike said, folding his arms.

"How about if their fathers come as backup, too? Dang," Damali said with a wink.

"Then, meanwhile, I let this monster out the box and we go find that sucker who's incubating. It's nearby, closer than his daddy in Hell, so it's gonna home to it—we do a drive-by, old-school." Carlos pounded Jose's fist.

"If the monster you caught eludes you, Carlos," the pearl said in a sweet voice, "you can always look to Damali's necklace. I'm voice guidance, but before you left Neteru Council chambers, Aset had us all fine-tuned."

"Whoa . . ." Carlos said, going over to stand closer to the pearl; he stroked it with the pad of his thumb. "Baby, how do you work now?"

The pearl released a long, sexy sigh that made the guys on the squad chuckle. "Those entities you track are carbon-based like the diamond. That will light and warm her throat when one is near, but the other stones in Damali's necklace will light in depth or distance relationship to danger. . . . I'll say, 'Coming up from Level One,' and the first stone will light; or 'It's so many yards away.' Aset thought this was necessary now with there being a baby—" The pearl cut off her own statement, glowed pink, and went silent.

"That is so cool," Inez said. "They installed an Amber Alert for my boo?"

The pearl cleared her throat, and Marlene looked at Damali. The muscle in Carlos's jaw pulsed.

"Sorry, Carlos," the pearl whispered. Then she made her voice a little louder so the rest of the team could hear her. "Yes, we have an Amber Alert embedded in us. If a child on the team is in jeopardy, especially if no Guardians are around, we will all light and flash wildly, and you can believe that I will be screaming my head off."

"Cool," Carlos said, and then wiped his brow.

"You didn't think the ancient Neterus would forsake you, did you Carlos?"

"Naw, Z," he said quietly, and then kissed Damali's necklace, causing the pearl in it to release another deep crimson glow and a breathy sigh. "Thanks, baby. Good looking out." He handed his wife the jewelry before he got in trouble.

"So let's go kick some demon ass," Mike said, standing and opening the case that had his shoulder launcher. "They messed with my food . . . you know I'ma hafta address that shit."

Damali smiled. "Uh-huh. Sounds like a plan. *That's* why we came here."

☙ CHAPTER NINETEEN

They moved in single-cell death squads. Gone were the days of the full-team frontal assault. That had become a predictable, dangerous pattern. This time the Neterus would hold back precious resources. They would coordinate with beings in the Light, relying not solely on their own human understanding. New team circumstances required new battle strategy, something the enemy would never suspect. The daywalker females had gotten sloppy: they loved the sun. In times gone by, councilmen stayed underground and were therefore hard to ambush. But these newly made rulers flaunted their abilities, and their mates were drunk on the excesses of power.

Diana's ground forces moved between the ether and hunted like individual predators—hit women with a score to settle. Then they stepped back and waited. The strike against the darkside was smooth, calculating, and oh-so-femininely vicious. Damali held her necklace in her hand, her thumb absently stroking the precious stones within it as though they were worry beads. Patience would reward her soon . . . she could feel it. Better than that—she could taste it.

———

The hooded human servant added more blood to her bath. Elizabeth sighed at the new fragrant, exotic blend. She gazed around her old lair in the Carpathian Mountains, wishing for Vlad's return. For now, Sebastian would do . . . until she could steal some of his reanimation spells. Then she would attempt to call forth her real and only true love. But a slow, agonizing pain began to paralyze her limbs and scorch her skin.

Shrieking, she stood, convulsing and trembling as servants scattered. Sebastian jumped out of bed, coming to her—then he backed away.

"Silver nitrate!" he hissed. "I will have the head of the human who—"

"I'm burning!" she screamed. "Help me, you fool!"

He jettisoned her from the tub onto the floor in a hard, bloody crash and then showered water down on her smoldering form. He kept away from the tainted blood that spread in a blue-white flaming carpet along the parquet wood floor, eating up the plush Persian rug to leap into the tub as though a match had been touched to a gasoline spill.

Elizabeth lay naked, shuddering, her hands bloody claws inches from her face. Third-degree burns covered her body, and what had once been her perfect, bloodless white skin now oozed yellow puss in a sulfuric stench that made Sebastian heave. He turned away and sent a white sheet to tent her as she screamed and wailed. Yes . . . he would feed her . . . yes . . . she would unfortunately survive. But he also knew that she would never look the same. There would always be the visceral reminder of severe scars. Silver always left its mark.

He had called for another body to be drained. Feeding Lucrezia had become his passion. Nuit took the golden goblet from the tray and waved the servant out of their chamber. New Orleans moonlight favored his new mate so. He brought the goblet under his nose as Lucrezia's beautiful green eyes lit with a fiery red glow.

"They've outdone themselves this time, darling. They found a virgin . . . I believe you'll love this particular vintage."

"You spoil me," she murmured, accepting the goblet from him with a toothy smile.

"After your latest success in poisoning the entire team, don't you think that a virgin is the least I can give you?" He kissed her over the chalice. "Tell me what else I can do for you, *chérie?*"

She took a deep sip from the goblet and coyly batted her lashes. Then flung the goblet away, sputtering and convulsing, scrabbling at her throat. Nuit jumped back, out of bed, on his feet, frantic as his wife screamed. Smoke bellowed from her mouth, and a long, black stain covered her mouth and ran down her throat all the way to her stomach, where her skin began to collapse in on itself with a smoldering stench.

"Silver nitrate . . ." Nuit hissed.

Lucrezia's body arched and heaved against the mattress. With no option, he came to her, opened her mouth with a powerful grip, and reached in to break off the bottom part of her jaw, extracting her tongue, esophagus, clawing away the damaged soft tissue until he could finally scoop out her stomach. He looked at his ruined wife with tears in his eyes. His right hand was smoldering from touching the residue, and he quickly materialized an ice bucket of water to ram his fist into before the third-degree burns were too severe.

"Forgive me, *chérie,*" he whispered, bereft. "I had to, just to save you . . ."

A snap of his fingers brought a hose out of thin air, and he focused a stream of water on her open passageways as though cleaning out a gutted trout. Horrified as she gurgled and flailed about, he held her arms and legs down with a black-energy cord. Even if he fed her, she would always be disfigured . . . her once perfect, rosebud mouth would be misshapen, the gorgeous, creamy skin at her throat marred by deep twisted burns . . . her torso a wreck. He turned away and walked to the window as he made blood rain down on her within the frame of their ante-bellum rice bed. Silver always left its mark.

Tonight, he would find the Neterus once and for all and leave his!

Damali looked down at the lit stones. "It's done."

Carlos called his blade into his hand and two younger Neteru males stepped out of a golden splinter on the beach, dressed for war.

"Damn . . ." Shabazz murmured, glancing at Rider and Mike. "Is it my imagination or does something seem a little bit more serious about Rivera and D?"

"They ain't playing," Mike commented in an awed whisper as Seth and Abel walked up to Carlos and gave him a warrior's hug. "Not that they were before, but something's definitely different. I ain't never seen D this cold, either."

"I think it's the kid," Rider said, chewing the end of a twig he'd found. "They know they've got a baby to protect and the darkside kicked off something parental in them . . . bad move. I think our fearless leaders are going for broke." He nodded toward the silver box still sitting on the beach. "Ever see Rivera bring something like that home before, and Damali let him?"

All sidebar conversation ceased as Damali and Carlos turned toward the team with the two golden Light warriors.

"Just confirmed," Carlos said. "Nuit and Sebastian are on the warpath. They've got night vamps coming in from all regions to descend on our old compound in L.A.—the one that's aban-doned. Our Neteru brothers have them thinking it's been re-built and that we fell back there. I got a jumper signal going from them, to Yonnie, to me, and got my boy doubling back this way so he ain't in the drama when it goes down. We need a blood sample from every member of the team for an authentic signature."

"So, let's do this," Mike said, pounding Shabazz's fist and then holding out his wrist as he hoisted his launcher on his shoulder.

Carlos shook his head. "All we need is a blood sample, bro. You can put the launcher down for now. This is Light squad only—we'll get in on the other firefight as soon as their forces are crippled at the old joint."

The windows were open at the old compound. The steel gates were in rusted disrepair. Bodies in white medical coats could be seen hustling about, seemingly attending the sick. There was no prayer barrier. The scent of human blood was thick in the air. The team appeared to have returned home in a rush, with human Covenant staff doctors trying to help them recover.

Nuit looked at Sebastian, and both generals stared out over the legions of vampires they'd called from every corner of the earth. One nod in unison sent hundreds of black tornadoes whirring toward the house. But behind it, splinters of light ringed the dark funnels just as the house lit in a blue-white nova.

Ashes fell everywhere as demons screamed and tried to escape the fast-moving carpet of light.

"Retreat!" Nuit yelled, shielding him and Sebastian with a black translucent dome.

The heat was so pervasive as the nova rolled over their shield that it sucked the oxygen out from it with a staggering quake that crumbled the dome. Nuit and Sebastian were on their feet in seconds. The chime of a Neteru blade made Nuit instinctively duck. But Sebastian foolishly outstretched his right hand to block it. The limb was severed so quickly that for a second it didn't even bleed.

"For my mother, Queen Eve! May that bitch, Lilith, you serve rot in Hell!" Abel hollered, advancing on Nuit, sending white energy pulses from the tip of his blade like mortar rounds.

Seth ran forward, releasing a Neteru war cry, blade drawn, coming for Sebastian, who clutched his amputated limb and then disappeared. Nuit was right behind him, melting into the ground like fast-moving black water. Seth stood in the middle of the swirling sulfuric ash and raised his blade over his head. His brother whooped and then raised his blade, touching it to his brother's weapon, drawing them both up into a splinter of golden light.

"You can open the box and let the monster out," Seth said, leaning on his knees with both hands, gulping in air. His smile was brilliant and he glanced at his ash-stained brother who caught his breath against a tree.

"You must see—even Father did not have to assist. This was beautiful. Their outrage made the vampires careless." Abel looked at Carlos and Damali, his expression containing obvious joy.

Abel's silver eyes crackled with blue-white static charge and then he pointed his blade just above the sand, replaying the brief battle for the team like a QuickTime movie. Cheers and hoots echoed on the beach as Guardians high-fived and hollered out encouragement. But Damali and Carlos looked at each other, knowing that while it was good to get the mood hyped for the big one, early wins in a long war weren't to be confused with sure victory.

"Who authorized such a complete and devastating deployment of resources?" Lilith shrieked. "Just as we're recovering from Masada, are you insane?"

"See for yourself the injury to our councilwomen!" Nuit challenged, blood in his eyes as he waved his hand to show Lilith his and Sebastian's wives. "They cannot even tolerate the sun until their injuries heal. How could we allow this to go un—"

"Because we are at war, there is a bigger picture than your own inconveniences . . . collateral damage is a basic reality, and those two bitches are worth an empire," Lilith seethed. "And where were you, Yolando!"

"In Tijuana," Yonnie said, holding his hands up in front of his chest. "I didn't know they were going to war, nobody ever called me . . . I ain't have jack shit to do with this fucked-up mission."

Lilith stood from her throne and paced. "We are calling in the upper levels, from werewolves to Amanthras, to phantoms, as well as all Harpies and the one-third fallen angel company that allied with my husband when he was banished."

"He is sending the black angels?" Sebastian winced, clutching his forearm stump.

"To protect his heir?" Lilith scoffed. "Of course, you fool. Is any price too great, any resource more valuable than the Antichrist?" She looked at Sebastian with disdain. "Seal up that wound and leave it. After a Neteru blade swipe it will not regenerate. I should kill you myself, because you allowed one of them to take your conjuring hand. Isn't that your right hand, the one that you used to cast your spells with . . . the one that used to hold your sorcerer's wand?"

Sebastian drew back in his throne. "I am ambidextrous, Your Eminence."

"You'd better be," she seethed. "Because if there is a sudden call to arms, injury or not, you will join the battle . . . and if you cannot, you are worthless. You know what happens to the worthless here in Hell?" Her gaze narrowed when

Sebastian didn't immediately answer. "They become *food* for our troops."

"Everybody ready?" Carlos looked around and then his gaze settled on Damali.

"Ready," she said, clasping her choker necklace on and calling her Isis long blade into her hand.

Damali looked around at the fully armed team. Prayers had been lobbed, and the team stood behind a golden shield of Heru that Carlos had erected, just in case what he released tried to double back and hide in a human body. He pointed his blade at the latch. The trunk bounced and snarled in agitation. Carlos opened his free palm and stared into it until three orbs of white light filled it. Then he sent a power pulse into the lock from the tip of his blade.

Instantly the lid blew off. A three-headed black cobra with acid-dripping fangs careened out. It kept coming and coming, as though the trunk had been bottomless. The creature had obviously regenerated while trapped and it was fighting, spitting mad. The first thing it did was wheel around on Carlos. He hit it with a white-light pulse, causing it to scream. Then when it saw two Neterus advancing on it, the creature let out a loud hiss, jumped up high, and did a nosedive into the sand.

Before the three agile necks disappeared, Carlos flung the light orbs as though hurling fast baseball pitches, embedding the orbs at the backs of the angry serpent's skulls. Its tail flopped and twisted, its shriek near deafening, and then it thundered under the sand, tumbling Guardians on the beach like bowling pins.

"Go, go, go!" Damali shouted, hitting the sand with white pulses from her Isis so hot that the sand turned to glass wherever the charge went.

Carlos hurled a flat, golden disc to blanket the sand as the serpent resurfaced, trying to snap at running Guardians. "Hit the deck, get onto the shield!"

He and Damali kept pressure on the three-headed creature as Guardians dodged fang strikes and made it to the golden island of safety on the beach. Infuriated, Mike stood and aimed his launcher.

"No," Carlos shouted. "I want it to go home—let it run!"

Damali and Carlos rounded on the creature, and as its heads focused on Carlos, she got a stab in that made the monster squeal. One of its heads dangled, dripping acidic black blood, and the other heads tried to nuzzle it back to life. But after a few seconds it realized that the Neteru blade could fatally injure it. That's when it ran.

"Fold-away time, people! This thing is gonna run hard and fast—will be a bumpy ride!" Carlos shouted as he and Damali ran into the water behind the fleeing serpent.

Carlos threw a white energy line on the disc. Damali sent a tactical charge to create a small fence. Every tactical member of the group reinforced it. Then suddenly there was a hard yank, Carlos put down another shield beneath his and Damali's feet, and they left the beach.

Airborne for a few seconds, they hit the azure water with a hard splash. A black serpent dragged them like a speedboat, and white, turbulent surf sent shockwaves through their knees, quaking their bodies. Guardians fell back, tactical charges and sheer strength the only thing keeping them on the disc and alive. Carlos tossed his blade to Damali, who caught it with one hand. She rammed her blade and his into the floor of the shield and held on tight. Needing both hands to keep the beast from diving, Carlos pulled hard on the energy reins in each hand, straining with his foot on the lip of the shield to prevent it from towing the whole team under.

Infuriated, the creature leapt like a snared marlin, dragging the entire squad in the air to smack down on the water repeatedly.

Were it not for the steady, blue-white concentrated effort of all tactical squad members, the discs would have flipped and the impact of the capsize would have stunned and drowned every member of the team.

Screaming, hissing, and dragging one dead head, the creature sped toward the only safety it knew. Land was in sight—so were jagged rocks along the deserted cove. The mouth of a cave loomed.

"I gotta cut the line!" Carlos shouted, two seconds before too late.

All tactical members sent out a blue-white net, catching the team as the discs they'd been riding hurled beneath them and slammed into the rocks, exploding.

Guardians came to a soft thud on wet sand.

Rider was on his feet first. "Whoooo-weee! Ride 'em cowboy—let's do *that* again!"

Carlos stood slowly, helping Damali up, flexing his hands and rubbing the soreness out of his biceps. "You all right?"

"Yeah. I'm good." She felt her necklace, and it warmed under her fingers.

"Due north," the pearl said in a calm voice, "then make a left at the first big boulder. Thank you."

Damali shrugged as the team checked their weapons and collected their wits. "Okay, you heard the lady."

"Everybody look alive," Carlos said. "You know this joint has gotta be heavily guarded."

"Can you pull in whatever weapons we dropped, C— especially those handhelds and the imagers?" J.L. said. He looked at the mouth of the cave. "Would sure help to be able to see an outline before it struck."

"I got you," Carlos said, bringing their gear from the trunks on the beach. It hit the sand with a thud, and Carlos rubbed his neck.

Guardians armed themselves as J.L. sent a scan toward the door.

"Hate to tell you this, but it's like about a hundred and fifty black-winged, invisible motherfuckers walking toward us," J.L. said, reading his scanner and then looking up as Damali's necklace lit.

"This is correct," the pearl said calmly. "One hundred yards and closing. Two hundred and twenty-five black angels, to be exact."

"Now?" Big Mike said with an angry smile.

"Now," Carlos said with silver in his eyes.

Mike released a shell that seemed to explode against nothing, but within the flash one could see flying body parts, followed by waves of advancing demon troops. From there, it was a free-for-all.

Guardians released hallowed earth rounds from hand-held Uzis. Juanita's and Inez's bodies shook from the shell discharges, as Tara employed snub-nose blasts each time a demon materialized to create a charging target coming into her peripheral vision. Dan and Berkfield lobbed grenades at the mouth of the cavern. Using the hand-held devices, tactical Guardians sent out pulses in all directions, making forms visible in a flash as they fell back, stunned.

Team sharpshooters Shabazz, Rider, and Berkfield picked off the fallen with silver-packed hollow-point rounds before they could get up. Jasmine and Heather lit the stones with white-light energy, incinerating black-charge snipers where they stood before they could even get off a shot. Marlene and Marjorie fired relentlessly as they kept open visuals for the team, barking out directions, alerting everyone where the invisible onslaught was charging from next.

Krissy and Bobby worked in tandem as a brother-sister team, moving Carlos's shield in quick rotations to cover the shooters' backs, their flanks, and overhead. The onslaught came by land, air, and sea. Val would pop up, sent a flurry of silver airborne, and then Krissy would shield her as demon bodies rained down. Marlene ran to the edge of the water and prayed over it, calling the angels to join with her in anointing the sea, sending a white-hot charge along the surf that stopped black dragons and serpents in a sizzling, sulfuric burn.

Death was all over the beach. Invisible bodies became visible as they expired or sustained mortal wounds. Carlos's silver gaze scorched a path to the cave's opening. One nod to Damali and they rushed forward, shields raised. The team was handling the beach—they had to get to the target.

Darkness so pitch-black closed in on them that it was almost impossible to sense direction. Even with their Neteru night vision and Carlos's silver beam, the chilling absence of sound and substance slowed their adrenaline-hyped advance. Low snarls and a familiar scent made the Neteru team instinctively stand back-to-back. In a flash they saw them. Werewolves attacking.

Damali's Isis chimed at the same resonance as Carlos's. Blue-white pulses exploded charging beasts, opening a path to run forward, with huge werewolves on their asses. Carlos threw up a shield, causing the infuriated beasts to collide with the hot golden disc and roar in pain as they burned.

Harpies flowed over the crags like a gray river of maggots. The Neterus held hands and sent out a blinding charge that lit like a flashbulb going off, liquefying the onslaught. Gray-green goo dripped off of stalactites and stalagmites. The stench was almost unbearable, but they ran forward gagging.

A swift-moving rock narrowly missed Carlos's head and he ducked, pushing Damali down. Bats swooped in, baring lethal, gnarled fangs. Another flat disc of rock whirled over the couple's heads.

"Fucking phantoms," Carlos muttered, as he shielded himself and Damali with a golden disc.

"Silver-dust 'em, baby," Damali said, jumping up quickly between hurled objects, exploding the next rock that came at them into tiny particles with a blast from her Isis. She held the shrapnel in stasis in the air for a second while Carlos's silver-eyed beam coated it, then he sent it hurtling back in the opposite direction. Ghostly moans and wails thundered through the cave. The couple was up in a flash, running forward before the darkside's security squadrons could reposition.

But they skidded to a halt as they came upon a large, slick, gore-covered chrysalis that was suspended from the roof of the cave by an eerie network of bulging veins.

A fully grown, naked humanlike male was inside it. He peered at the Neterus through the transparent, glowing red chamber that pulsed to a slow heartbeat. The blackest of eyes, the depths of which Carlos and Damali had never known or witnessed, stared back at them. His eyes were dangerously hypnotic, his face so tranquilly beautiful. Only the slight hint of fangs could be seen pressing against his perfect bottom lip. His face and hue changed with each pulse . . . the creature was African, then Asian, then European, then Latino, then Native American . . . and on and on, each heartbeat changing its face and ethnicity in a dizzying kaleidoscope. He stirred like a fetus would, trying to get comfortable in a tight-fitting womb . . . his glistening black wings partially covered his nakedness. It was apparent that he was so very close to being born.

They had only been stunned by the horrible magnificence for a few seconds, but that was apparently enough for its guardian to awaken. A huge black serpent uncoiled from the nothingness of complete darkness, its head the size of a minibus as it hurtled forward.

Damali and Carlos touched their blades together and fired a pulse which hit the creature dead-on. It exploded, rocking the chrysalis and tearing a section of it away. They trained their pulse on it, released, and then there was complete blackness.

They hit the beach with such force that had they not been Neterus, they would have broken their backs. Warrior angels lit a path from the sky and filled the black hole with a surge so swift that they seemed like one long beam. Hannibal yanked Carlos to his feet and slapped him hard. Eve and Aset drew Damali up, covering her womb, and then nodded and set her on her feet. Black and white mortar rounds were going off above.

Damali turned quickly with Carlos to see their team was still in the battle. Adam and Ausar had Lilith backed into a corner. Eve left Damali's side, half-flying, half-running to reach Lilith before the ground opened and a great black claw snatched her away. The three ancient Neterus sent pulses of white light into the ground behind her, releasing battle wails. Seth and Abel advanced on Nuit, who power-snatched Sebastian out of the way and then dodged their blows. He saw an opening, his gaze narrowed on Yonnie—suddenly noticing that Yolando was blocking shots and not advancing their cause.

In a shrewd move that Damali saw in slow motion, through the chaos Nuit sent a black charge toward Valkyrie. Yonnie turned at the same time Carlos turned away from the entity he was battling. Carlos threw a disc to save Val, but it narrowly missed the black charge. The dark energy deflected from the shield, saving Val, but it hit Yonnie. The direct heart hit blew Yonnie onto his back.

Carlos beheaded the attacking Amanthra that had been on him and began to slash his way toward Yonnie's body on the beach. Val was already running to him, stabbing, cutting; she was a wild woman in motion, flying, she reached him first.

"Let him go!" Damali yelled, engaged in fighting so many

adversaries at once that she could only make minor progress to get to Val's side. "The black claws will come and take you both down!" Her voice cracked as she watched Val cradle Yonnie's body, sobbing.

Carlos fought to get to her, his blade out to behead his best friend. It was a promise, the only thing he could do, but demon after demon blocked his path as Nuit escaped, laughing. Then, as they always did, *the reckoners* came. Their evil black claws sent up from Level Seven to give the Devil his due parted the sand, making it fall inward like quicksand as Valkyrie stabbed at them, refusing to let Yonnie's body go. Frantic, Carlos took blows he should never have allowed as he watched in horror as his best friend and the innocent hybrid who loved him began to sink.

"Valkyrie, for the love of God, let him go!" Carlos said, his voice breaking under the strain.

"No!" Val screamed, still struggling with the entities. "I am a Valkyrie; we do not leave our honorable on the battlefield."

"He's a vampire!" Damali shouted. "We love him, but by rights, he's theirs! Release him and save yourself before it's too late!"

"No!" Val shouted, burying her face against Yonnie's smoldering chest. "I don't care what he was, he was valiant and he will be victorious! I call my sisters of the sky! I call my mother's people to have mercy! Do not let this abomination occur on this beach—he was tricked, he honored me, he never laid a hand on me!"

Swift-moving light rained down on the beach. From every cometlike flash, a winged, fully silver-armored Valkyrie stood with a blade. They rushed to Val's side, frantically slicing at the screaming claws.

Lilith appeared a distance away, shouting, "You are in violation of supernatural law—he has been ours for over two hundred years!"

The lead Viking angel with broad, luminescent white wings

lifted his blade, and a smaller, platinum-blond version of Val stepped forward and spoke as lightning crackled from the big Viking's blade.

"My daughter says deceit took this man's valiant life, and at the end of days, there is only justice—no technicalities will serve you now! Her incessant prayers called for his review. We cannot bring him back to life, but we can remove him from your clutches! Begone, demons!"

The crack lit the sky, and a black seal fell to the beach, broken and smoldering. A black horse rose up from the split disc, reared up on its back haunches with a glowing warrior angel on its back, whinnied, and then plunged into the sand.

"Tell Lucifer that we have released the black horse and this one vampire is ours—we are reclaiming our lost, those who were deceived but who kept the faith!" the large Viking roared, his eyes blazing silver. "His heir has been injured, and we have sent hunters to track it even into your bowels of Hell."

Warrior angels fanned out in numbers too numerous to count. The beach immediately emptied of demons, Lilith leading the instant retreat. The claws holding Yonnie grudgingly released their death-grip and receded. Neteru Council members nodded good-bye with expressions of deep satisfaction on their faces, and then pulled back into splinters of gold and purple light. Val struggled to lift her and Yonnie out of the sand. Splinters of light rained up in reverse, causing angels to vanish. Ash and sulfur were everywhere. Guardians stood dazed, clutching weapons, looking at the broken seal that still smoldered.

Yonnie coughed and slowly opened his eyes.

Val touched his bloody, dirty face. "Be valiant, be victorious," she murmured against his lips, and then cried.

Next day: Back at the team compound in San Diego

Carlos lay back on the sofa in their suite propped up by a mound of pillows, watching TV. Damali was curled up next to him, providing calming warmth as they watched the news.

The Dow Jones is still plummeting, and analysts say that the housing market is expected to remain soft as banks begin to tighten regulations on mortgage lending and credit becomes—

"Good," Damali said. "I'm glad you cut that mess off."

"Yeah, ain't nothing we can do about it but ride it out anyway," he said, releasing a long sigh. "I'm just thinking about all the people who ain't got it like we got it."

"I know," she said softly. "We've gotta help where we can, pray where we can't. You saw the power of that."

"No lie . . ." Carlos shook his head, wincing from his still-sore muscles from the body blows he'd allowed to try to get to Yonnie and Val.

"Why don't you let me heal that?" Damali said, leaning up to kiss him.

" 'Cause this ain't nothing," Carlos said, tracing her cheek with his finger. "I don't want you exerting yourself any more than necessary . . . not after that crazy bullshit we just went through—you sure the Queens said everything is all right in there?"

"Yes, for the hundred-and-fiftieth time," she said with a smile. "Then let Berkfield work on you—your ribs, baby . . ."

"Naw, that man needs to rest, too." Carlos kissed her nose. "You know how lucky we all were to make it outta that one?" He closed his eyes and let his head drop back. "What was I thinking, tying a white-light line to one of Lu's monsters . . . that was insane."

Damali laughed. "Yeah, it was, but at least this time we weren't the ones to break the seal."

"You know, I was just thinking that." He opened his eyes and peered at his wife. "I'm not even sure why we were trying to hold back the inevitable . . . it says in the Good Book, man, this thing is gonna blow—so all anybody can do is hold on and get ready."

"Then, uhmmm . . . I guess it doesn't make sense to walk around worried about the sky falling, huh?"

He kissed her nose again, avoiding her mouth, making her pout. "Nope. Gotta live life to the fullest, do as much as you can to help people, and pray for the best."

"Uh-huh," she said, sliding up his body.

He chuckled, shifting, so that she wasn't rubbing directly against him. "But even so, there is the old thing of Heaven helping those who help themselves—so I'm not trying to press our luck. Better wait a little bit, make sure things are solid, before, you know . . ."

"Inez is going to go pick up the baby next week with her momma . . . you sure you don't want to make use of this tranquil privacy?" She wiggled her eyebrows and he laughed, then kissed her quickly.

"You know, I can't get used to Yonnie just being able to live here," he said, completely ignoring her offer. "That just shows you, you never know what can happen, boo. I'm focusing on being thankful for a few days, *nothing* else." He closed his eyes but continued to smile at her.

Damali propped herself up on an elbow to stare down at him.

"I'm meditating—leave me alone," he said, laughing.

"I'm not bothering you," she replied, laughing as well. "I was just thinking about things we have to be thankful for . . . like Yonnie got a really sweet deal, even if he's still dead . . . blood hunger, but controllable . . . no pulse, but can do daylight and blueberry pancakes or whatever. I think he kept most of his vamp powers, but has to rest a lot more, if he doesn't have blood in his system—but at least he can't turn people into the walking dead."

"The brother eats more than Mike, girl. The band is gonna have to go back on the road just to feed Yonnie!"

"You know you gotta talk to your boy, right?"

Carlos opened his eyes. "Aw, c'mon, D . . . I was just playing—he don't eat that much."

She playfully swatted his chest. "You know I'm the last one to begrudge anybody food, and Inez would have a coronary if somebody around here went hungry. Be serious, you know what about."

Carlos sighed. "Yeah, I know . . . he can't be messing with a half-angel after getting saved by the Light without marrying the girl." He slung his forearm over his eyes. "See, D, this is why I was just meditating and sometimes don't wanna talk . . . just need a day or two for my mind to get still and empty out, you know?"

"You think Father Pat is up to it, or maybe Yonnie would want the imam . . . ya know, I don't know what Val's affiliation is—nondenominational?"

"Damali, please, baby . . ."

"Know what else I was thinking of," she said, starting to laugh again as he groaned.

"No. But I know you're gonna tell me."

"I was thinking of how thankful I am to have all my family safe and alive . . . and most especially that I have you . . . and whoever we just made."

Her soft voice had lost its playfulness, and, as he looked at her, her smile was so tender that it begged him to take her mouth.

"I'm thankful, so grateful for that, my soul feels like it's gonna bust, girl."

"And I'm thankful that you didn't get so busted up this time," she murmured, touching his bruised ribs and shoulders through his T-shirt, beginning to heal them through his clothes.

"And I'm thankful that you got back up after that blast," he said, touching her face. "You're my angel."

"And I'm thankful that even with the Armageddon going on, seals broken, and the chaos of the world swirling all around, I have an oasis in your eyes." Her breath swept his lips before her kiss.

"I'm thankful that you were never afraid to love me," he said quietly as they broke their kiss. "When you really should have been."

"I was," she murmured. "But I couldn't help it."

"I was, too," he said, his gaze searching her face. "But I damned sure couldn't help it. I was in deep before I could stop myself."

"Then why are you stopping yourself now?"

He stared at her, his irises slowly turning silver. "Because after all the bumps and bruises . . . falls, hitting the water rough-riding, pounding the surf, back-slamming down hard on the beach . . . I ain't trying to tempt fate and be the one to dislodge anything."

"Didn't all the rough-riding, hitting the beach, pounding the surf, blade-pulling, and demon-ass-kicking turn you on?" She smiled a sly smile and stared at him, inches from his face.

"Yeah . . ."

"Then be smooth," she said, teasing him, beginning to kiss down his chest until he shivered. "Take it slow like a pro," she whispered, chuckling against his belly as she pulled up his shirt. "That way you don't have to worry."

"You don't fight fair . . ."

"Nope . . . never do." She lifted her head and beamed at him, wiggling her eyebrows at him again. "But I bet you'll be real thankful for that, too, brother."

There was nothing for him to do but laugh.

Turn the page for a sneak peek at the next Vampire Huntress Legend novel.

THE SHADOWS

COMING IN JULY 2008 FROM ST. MARTIN'S GRIFFIN

In Hell . . . Level Seven

Dead Harpies, messenger demons, and human helper bodies lay strewn across the searing granite floor, victims of the beast's wrath and involuntary black blood donations. The smell of burning, sulfur-ridden flesh smothered the air, and the sound of agonized wails was clotted by the sizzling of meat frying against the dank cavern bottom.

Lilith worked feverishly to staunch the dangerous hemorrhage that gushed from the heir's side while her husband continued to work triage with her, summarily calling for more blood and more bodies for his progeny to consume in order to keep their prized patient hydrated.

Another blast rocked the cavern and Lilith looked up from the task, winded as her patient howled in pain.

"Keep working!" her husband commanded and then looked up. His nostrils flared with blue-black fire and the clatter of his hooves echoed in the chamber as he paced, setting her teeth on edge. "If you lose him on the slab due to your ineptitude, you die!"

Lilith immediately continued, cautiously excavating the eerie, glowing white Light out of the heir's side. The brilliance of the white Light emanating from the Neteru blade bolt was blinding.

There was no way to stare at it directly, and even touching inches near it could injure her limbs permanently. What she could never make her husband understand was that if she placed her mouth over it to tear it out with her fangs, both she and their progeny would die and it would have been all for naught.

This was delicate surgery, but she knew that in his state of mind, the Dark Lord was beyond logic. He couldn't touch the injury; she couldn't touch the injury. Only a black magic blade could be used to make an incision outside the glowing white ember that was spreading on the heir's skin like a rapid cancer. The Light lesion was also imploding, damaging vital organs beneath it, which meant she had to cut wide and deep and quickly. The patient couldn't be anesthetized, for she needed his fury-will to help keep his dark life force going. However, the pain from his injuries, compounded with her ministrations, was sending him into shock.

Frustrated tears stung her eyes. Part of the chrysalis had been damaged. The heir had been born too soon. He was fully formed on the outside, but his internal demon organs had yet to harden. His exoskeleton had only recently been absorbed and covered with his human masking capacity. Even his fangs were new—hadn't hardened—nor had his wing bones turned to steel hardness yet. His spaded tail wasn't even retractable at this point, and it flailed about piteously, trying to push her away as a source of his agony.

Their poor baby was still night blind—his eyes had yet to adapt to complete darkness—and his lungs were not strong enough for the underground sulfur and heat. His heartbeat had yet to die. There was so much that had to be corrected before it had been time. Damn the Neterus!

Vital blood supply veins in the placenta that had been connected to the roof of the birthing cave, which were needed to wash the heir's system clean of the dreaded silver and Light toxin that contaminated him, had been severed. Their patient's breathing labored in the subterranean air. He needed fresh earth-plane oxygen in his fragile, living-species lungs. The chrysalis would have given him that, too.

Ruefully, Lilith looked at their gasping, struggling patient and the partial chrysalis skin that still covered his face. That was the only thing they could quickly improvise while under siege to give him what little air could be siphoned from topside during the onslaught. Beads of black sweat rolled down her face as she leaned over his body. Another blast rocked the cavern, causing stalactites to come crashing down and stalagmites to uproot from the cavern and begin a dangerous subterranean avalanche.

Lilith's and her husband's eyes met as he shielded her and the heir from falling rocks. She was certain that, for the first time in history, probably since the initial battle he had fought in Heaven and was cast down, a lack of surety burned in his bottomless black eyes. He turned away from her, the vulnerability shaking them both. She could feel his power being torn between guarding his future and protecting his current empire from the onslaught of warrior angels ransacking his realms.

"Go, fight," she said as calmly as possible. She stared at him and then down at the patient. "If there is nothing for him to inherit, then he is as good as dead to us, anyway."

"Your life for his," her husband said between his teeth in *Dananu*, beginning to pull away from the table as he smashed another body into the feeding rocks to be sucked dry by the few remaining placenta-attached veins.

"It was going to be that in any regard, so why fear leaving me here to do my very best?" Her gaze narrowed; for once all fear had fled her.

"At this point I trust no one," he said, seething. "As if I ever did. And were it not for your lax security measures, they would have never—"

"Hold it," she said, her voice strong and not wavering. Rare truth burned in her mouth like acid and she spit on the smoldering floor, unafraid. "They followed *your* black energy trail, not mine." When her husband turned away, she pressed on, making the most of the extraordinary moment of having bested the Devil in his own game. "They were able to do that because you underestimated the old priest's power of love." She clucked her tongue, making a tsking sound that caused her husband to whirl on her. "You need me, even if you punish me later for my insolence—so be it. But as the only entity in all of Hell that will tell you the truth, and not just what you want to hear in the midst of a crisis, I implore you to consider me a valuable resource and not waste me in a sudden rage."

When he walked away from her, she knew she had him. Satisfaction spread through her body, filling her with renewed power, even if it was potentially short-lived.

"Can you save him?" he finally asked, his shoulders slumping from fatigue and worry.

"Saving him has always been in my best interest, too, husband, regardless of your opinion of me. However, if you do not prevail then we're *all* dead, even you. So go, fight, and leave me to my work. Preserve what little is left and seal the breaches. There will be time enough to settle the score if I fail. . . . Where on earth shall I run from you, anyway?"

"There will be no shadow dark enough to hide from me, if you fail."

"Failure was *never* my plan. You should know me well enough by now. I *always* play to win." She lifted her chin and stared at him directly. "I told you, Lu, I was in this with you till the very end."

The patient stopped breathing. The two powerful entities stared at each other. Her husband's fangs lengthened to battle length.

"Listen," she hissed.

"He's gone," the beast growled, beginning to circle her.

Lilith pointed up at the network of veins clinging to stalactites that were still pulsing. "Listen," she hissed again. "The shelling by the Light has ceased."

"Just as my heir's breaths have ceased!" A section of cavern wall flew at her and she ducked. Undaunted, she leapt up in a rare show of insubordination. "Stop it! You'll kill him!"

Silence settled between them. Poised for a final black-energy extinction strike, her husband watched as she went to the marble slab and checked vital signs.

"They were linked to *his* dark-energy life pulse." She smiled slowly and closed her eyes, beginning to chuckle. "He's self-aware and finally helping to heal." She glanced up at her husband, who was now towering over her, trying to get a closer look at their patient. "Don't you see . . . he's flatlined to deceive them."

With a wave of the beast's hand, four more bodies were impaled on the stalactites.

"Be proud, Lu . . . he has your cunning and endurance for pain. I must finish my work of excising the wound. You must finish your work of sealing the realms and reinforcing all the gray-zone shadows. Let us not be at odds, but be in collusion toward the same goal." She touched his stonelike chest, glad that he simply closed his eyes for a moment and steadied his breathing rather than ripping the limbs from her body. "I will not fail you."

Slowly he reached out and a length of barbed-wire chain filled his hand. He closed his fist around it as the chain yanked away in a scorching whir through his palm. Attached to the end of the twisted metal was a huge manacle that cuffed three baying hound heads connected to the same dog's body.

The vicious creature's jowls were filled with mangled, acid-dripping fangs, and it scrabbled against the smoldering floor, trying to pull toward the breach in the realms. Thick cords of muscle striated the animal's back legs and barrel chest, its barking now near deafening. It was on the scent of angels. Frustrated at being held back by its master, the creature finally gave in to a mournful howl, red eyes glowing with pure outrage at the assault against the nether region.

Lilith studied her husband's renewed composure as his gaze scanned the vaulted ceiling, deciding where to strike. She watched him slowly wind the chain in his fist, holding the guardian of his primary gate to Hell back, a strategy developing in his mind. That he'd called his favorite pet, Cerberus, to his side meant that he'd refocused himself for war.

"I will not fail you," Lilith repeated.

Her husband simply nodded and looked up again, and then was gone.

Turn the page for a sneak peek at the first book in L. A. Banks's brand-new Crimson Moon series.

BAD BLOOD

A Crimson Moon Novel

COMING IN APRIL 2008 FROM ST. MARTIN'S PAPERBACKS

Familiar scents, hard-driving music, and a blast of heat washed over Sasha as she opened the door to Ronnie's Road Hog Tavern, which everyone also affectionately called the Hawg. It was hard to stay in a bad mood in a joint like this. There was just too much revelry all around.

Ronnie was a local legend in his own right, claiming to have seen Sasquatch up close and personal, and he maintained a neutral position about all things supernatural. In a way, his bar was the preternatural's equivalent of Switzerland, and a comfortable place for her and the guys to hang out. It was haunted, too, they said. Something about a shoot-out and gold miners, but that was ancient history. However, not everything supernatural passed through Ronnie's doors. Vampires seemed to shun the lowbrow life of beef and beer, snobs that they were—and her pack would have to do them, anyway, if they witnessed a civvy being bitten. Regardless, it meant Ronnie's joint was always the place to be, sawdust on the floors notwithstanding.

Werewolves . . . other than the few attempts at black-market experiments, they didn't see much of them anywhere lately, and definitely not here. Besides, the Hawg served the best steak and fries in portions that were ridiculous. The burgers were awesome, too.

As she waded through the crowd toward the bar, an ice-cold beer on her mind, Sasha nodded at the regulars and unzipped her bomber jacket, prepared to stay awhile. The bartender spotted her and held up a Corona, and she smiled, giving him the thumbs-up.

He slid the beer across the wood with deft accuracy and she caught the frosty bottle with a lime wedged in the top with a quick hand and blew him a kiss as a joke. In their ongoing ritual he jerked his head back as though the air-kiss had knocked him out, and then laughed.

"I'll run you a tab, babe."

"Cool, Bruno," she shouted over the din. "Thanks."

Now to find someplace to sit down and eat alone. Everything in the primary bar area was already taken. In the billiards area, tables were temporarily abandoned by players but were already claimed with pitchers of beer and buffalo wings marking territory. Fine. Takeout could work.

She let out a defeated breath but took one last survey of the joint. A couple of guys gave her a bold once-over, but she ignored their silent offers. Bikers and truckers. She wasn't in the mood. If she was going home with anyone tonight, for once she just wished it could be with a guy whom she didn't have to explain things to—things like medications, having to be sure not to get too rough and break his skin, or to worry about a virus ruining his life.

She would admit, though, that the more crowded the establishment was, the lonelier it felt. And who the hell was watching her so hard that it was raising the hair on her arms?

Sasha pushed the lime into her beer with her index finger, lifted the slim bottle to her lips, took a few swallows, and then glanced around.

Moving through the crowd as if she had a specific destination in mind, Sasha enjoyed flowing through the tangle of bodies to the beat of the music. Warmth, sweat, scents, the thrum of pulsing melodies . . . blood, heartbeats all merged as her spine became fluid, her footfalls beyond graceful. Her stomach rumbled as her nose picked up the scent of charbroiled beef wafting from the kitchen. She made a game out of separating scents, sounds, and voices, keying in on bits of conversation as she loped through the large dance floor, headed for the second bar where take-out orders could be placed.

Midstep she stopped, tilted her head, and gazed into the darkened corridor beyond the bar. A cool breeze had brought in a scent from somewhere, a scent she'd never picked up in her life.

Sasha turned her beer up and polished it off, then continued to head toward the second bar, her eyes fastened on the dark corridor. She could smell multiple male scents. The men's room? A back room? An exit? A closed section of the bar? Curiosity stole over her as she clutched the empty bottle tighter. She quickly placed her order, trying to forestall the insanity, but her gaze continually wandered past the server toward the back of the bar.

The scent came to her again, raising her hackles. Suddenly she rounded the bar and stepped into the semidarkness. Fortunately, the server's attention was diverted with the next order. That scent . . . that wonderfully unsettling male scent. All others evaporated, but that one lingered. Dominant. Who the hell was it? Moreover, *what* the hell was it? It wasn't human. At least not wholly so; she could tell. Yet there wasn't the rancid, fecund smell of wet, filthy animal that came with infected werewolves. This was . . . *wonderful*. And all wolf, but somehow different.

Insides on fire, hair bristling, Sasha slipped deeper into the employees-only area undetected and passed through the long corridor scenting locked doors. . . . Faster, moving like a blur, following the scent that led to a cool breeze. Her hand slammed against an exit panic bar, and suddenly she was outside in the back employee parking area clutching an empty beer bottle. Her gaze quickly took in the huge Ford F-150's and Dodge Rams that haphazardly littered the small back lot amid the overflowing Dumpsters.

Still now, she listened to her own breathing, her own heartbeat, keening her hearing to the very slightest movement against the icy ground. There was no sound, but the scent was moving, circling her, producing a delirious combination of adrenaline and something she wasn't prepared to admit.

Moving with the scent, she crouched, lowering her body's center of gravity, arms readied, muscles tensing, turning in a slow circle. A back floodlight instantly blew out, leaving her in total darkness, save the blue-white wash of the moon. She smiled. He had no idea. . . .

He smiled and cocked his head to the side, fascinated that she could not readily detect him. This time she was alone. And this time she was no less exquisite than any other time before. Too bad it was impossible to stay downwind from her this go-round.

Her smoky gray eyes had become almost a translucent crystalline, like that of a husky . . . pupils open so wide they nearly eclipsed her irises. Her stare intense, her honey-kissed skin awash with maddening moonlight, waves of velvet barely skimming her shoulders and yet slowly lengthening as her beast flared right before his eyes. Her beautiful jawline was set hard, her voluptuous curves sculpted beneath a wisp of gray mohair sweater partially hidden by her bomber jacket, her throat so gloriously exposed for a submission bite . . . if she would accept. His gaze raked her lean hips, which tapered into seemingly endless legs all the way down to deep brown hand-tooled leather cowboy boots.

He briefly closed his eyes and inhaled deeply, taking in her scent, wanting her more deeply, needing her more intensely than his pride had allowed until now.

But he had an assassination to pull off. On each previous encounter she'd been with an abomination of their breed. He'd been sickened, scenting the predator on her, especially when his mission was to hunt down the demon-infected werewolves. That was her job, too, but she seemed ignorant of the task. Then again, he hadn't seen the predator in approximately a month. Perhaps she'd done her job and killed him already?

Slightly distracted, he moved again but a footfall broke through the shadows. She immediately spun and lunged at the nothingness, no fear in her eyes, but she missed. He stepped out of the shadows. Her response was a hard snarl as she broke the bottle on the edge of a Dumpster, gripping it like a weapon.

"That's not necessary," he said in a low rumble.

"Fuck that I-come-in-peace line. You were invisible a second ago."

"Yeah, and?"

"I hate you goddamned vampires, ya know." She flung the bottle away. "So what do you want?"

He was so offended that he folded his arms over his chest. "I've been called a lot of things in my time, sis, but a *vampire?* Never."

She cocked her head to the side and sniffed the air, but the confusion was clear on her face. What the hell was he—a new species? Something that moved between shadows and didn't make a sound. Smelled all wolf, all male. The rumble of his voice bottomed out in the pit of her stomach. Still left a flutter in its wake. Accent was strange, had French Canadian and yet West Indian tones embedded in it. His ethnicity was hard to judge. He was a nightmare and a fantasy all rolled into one, wearing a deerskin suede jacket, a charcoal sweater, ripped rough-rider jeans, and well-worn cowboy boots. She rolled her shoulders and began snapping closed the brass buttons on her jacket. "Whatever. You were following me, staring at me while I was trying to get my dinner and mind my business. I didn't appreciate it."

Complete disappointment singed her voice as she yanked the bottom of her jacket down hard and warily turned away to round the building to reenter the bar. The sound of her voice reverberated through him and lingered on the night air with her fabulous feminine trail thickening his groin. Yet he sensed no fraud; she really didn't seem to know what to make of him.

Her piercing gray eyes haunted him as she disappeared around the edge of the huge building. He watched her ass move beneath the leather in an almost soundless stride and decided to follow her back inside.

Sasha boxed the cold away from her arms, realizing that the shiver that had overtaken her wasn't from the frigid temperatures outside. She kept walking toward the back bar, unceremoniously parting the crowd now with sheer shoulder-blocking force and without apologies.

The man was an unbelievable specimen. He was massive. Six-foot-four or five and probably could have ripped her throat out, but didn't. That was some sexy shit, even if he was possibly a vampire messing with her mind. But the scent wasn't of the undead. His sweat held life, vitality, and ungodly testosterone. It was a scent that combined the earth and deep, sensual musk. Geoff had gotten to her with mind games, Shogun she could appreciate visually, but her reaction to this man was different. More . . . real somehow.

She allowed a shudder to pass through her and hailed the bartender. "I'm the monster burger with the works. To go, with a six of Corona," she shouted, determined to shake off the experience.

But as she waited and kept her gaze roving the establishment, she remembered feeling him before, although never seeing him and definitely never scenting him like this. Now she knew his signature and she had an incredibly rugged, too ridiculously handsome face to place with the impressions. His heartbeat was a slow, long thud. Hue—unflawed darkness making his actual age impossible to judge. Skin like rich, dark chocolate that made one's hand ache to touch just to feel the texture. Sasha licked her lips, unwilling to admit that she also wanted to taste it.

Features—strong, nose owned a slight bend in the bridge . . . Native American. Mouth—thick, lush, so sensual a feature that she was mesmerized by it. African. Hair—thick tendrils of dark velvet pulled back into a leather strap with Blackfoot tribal markings on it. Glistening white teeth . . . a warning held in check; a square jaw covered by a dark spread of evening shadow. Eyes—an intense midnight engulfed by shimmering amber. So strange, as though backlit from some inner light.

But the way the guy moved . . . like the night itself, like a thief cloaked within the very folds of every shadow. An assassin's stealth, but owning what had to be anywhere between two hundred to two hundred and twenty pounds of pure sinew. Massive shoulder width, arms and legs lean, muscular, moving as though every joint were a well-greased ball bearing.

How did he do it, though? Not even vampires had been able to catch her unaware: their lack of scent, the very stillness of it as they repressed their lack of life, was always, literally, a dead giveaway, as was the oppressive feel of their power touching the edges of her aura. Ghosts, same thing. The temperature dropped and they moved through the atmosphere like an icy wave or like the clear ripple on a lake's surface before they materialized. Demons made her gag with the foul scent of rotting flesh, and their eyes were red orbs of insanity. Nah. If he wasn't any of the above—then what was he?

Curiosity and a looming presence thickened with a now familiar scent made her jerk her attention toward the entrance. He nodded coolly and parted the crowd with a fluid ease that was unnerving. For a moment, all she could do was watch him walk.

1. What do you think of the implications of the Unnamed One being able to attack Father Patrick in a cathedral?

2. How do you think the dynamics of the Neteru/Guardian compound will change now that Delores, a civilian, and Ayana, a young child, are on the premises?

3. How do you feel about Yonnie's situation and his relationship with Valkyrie?

4. Female Council-level vampires are now part of the equation. Do you think we've heard the last from these women? Do you think the female vamps seem more treacherous than Fallon Nuit and Sebastian?

5. Does the Light seem significantly stronger than the Darkness in this legend, or would you call it a draw?

6. Do you like how the upper realms of the Light are working together? Do you enjoy seeing some of the majesty of Mid-Heaven more or less than of the lower realms?

7. There are senior Guardians who seem to run the team, and there are "lead" Neterus on both the Kings and Queens councils in this legend. Discuss how they come together on behalf of Carlos and Damali?

8. What do you think about the addition of biblical characters, including Abel and Seth, to the battalions of the Light?

9. Do you feel that Carlos and Damali's relationship reaches yet another level during the recovery scene in which they are given a twenty-four-hour hiatus? How do you feel about Damali's need for sedation after all these books and battles?

10. How do you feel about Damali's pregnancy? What dangers, implications, and issues do you foresee? What do you hope she has——a girl or a boy?

St. Martin's
Griffin

CPSIA information can be obtained
at www.ICGtesting.com
Printed in the USA
LVHW091056291019
635575LV00010B/85/P

9 780312 368746